THE
BRONZED
BEASTS

Also by Roshani Chokshi

FOR YOUNG READERS

Aru Shah and the End of Time

Aru Shah and the Song of Death

Aru Shah and the Tree of Wishes

Aru Shah and the City of Gold

FOR OLDER READERS

The Star-Touched Queen

A Crown of Wishes

Star-Touched Stories

The Gilded Wolves

The Silvered Serpents

THE
BRONZED
BEASTS

Roshani Chokshi

WEDNESDAY BOOKS
NEW YORK

First published in the United States by Wednesday Books, an imprint of St. Martin's Publishing Group

www.wednesdaybooks.com

Library of Congress Cataloging-in-Publication Data

Names: Chokshi, Roshani, author.
Title: The bronzed beasts / Roshani Chokshi.
Description: First edition. | New York : Wednesday Books, 2021. | Series: The gilded wolves ; 3 |
Identifiers: LCCN 2021015681 | ISBN 9781250144607 (hardcover) | ISBN 9781250836540 (international, sold outside the U.S., subject to rights availability) | ISBN 9781250144621 (ebook)
Subjects: GSAFD: Fantasy fiction
Classification: LCC PS3603.H655 B76 2021 | DDC 813/.6—dc23
LC record available at https://lccn.loc.gov/2021015681

Our books may be purchased in bulk for promotional, educational, or business use. Please contact your local bookseller or the Macmillan Corporate and Premium Sales Department at 1-800-221-7945, extension 5442, or by email at MacmillanSpecialMarkets@macmillan.com.

First Edition: 2021

10 9 8 7 6 5 4 3 2 1

For my friends, who didn't stop me when I said
I wanted to write something like *National Treasure* meets *Faust*
with a dash of existential crises . . . but make it sexy.
Y'all owe me drinks. And therapy.

Where wast thou when I laid the foundations of the earth?
—BOOK OF JOB

PROLOGUE

Kahina sang to the boy as he slept.

She sat at the edge of his bed, smoothing away the nightmares that crinkled his brow. Séverin sighed a little, turning against her hand, and Kahina felt her heart tighten. It was only here, thieved from the moments when night slowly melted into day and all the world lay sleeping, that she could call him her son.

"*Ya omri*," she said softly.

My life.

"*Habib albi*," she said, a little louder this time.

Love of my heart.

Séverin blinked, then gazed up at her. He smiled sleepily and held out his arms. "*Ummi.*"

Kahina folded him to her, holding still as he fell back asleep. She touched his hair, dark as a crow's wing and curled just at the ends. She smelled the faint menthol on his skin from the branches of eucalyptus she insisted on putting into his evening baths. Sometimes, she hated how little of her showed up on her son's features.

With his eyes closed, he was a miniature of his father, and already Kahina could see how it would mold his future. Her son's smiling mouth would soon hold the shape of a smirk too well. His rosy, full cheeks would sharpen like a blade. Even his demeanor would change. For now, he was shy and observant, but Kahina had noticed him copying his father's elegant cruelty. It frightened her sometimes, but perhaps that was merely her son's instinct for survival. There was power in knowing not just how to move through the world, but how to make the world move around you.

Kahina ran her fingers over his eyelashes, weighing whether she should wake him. It was selfish, she knew, but she could not help herself. Only in her son's eyes did Kahina find the one part of herself that had not been erased. Séverin's eyes were the color of secrets—a shade of dusk shot through with silver. They were the same color as her own eyes, and her mother's eyes, and her grandfather's eyes before them.

It was the eye color of all the Blessed, those marked by the Unworshipped Sisters: Al-Lat, Al-'Uzza, Manat. Ancient goddesses whose broken temples now paved roads of industry. Their myths had been scrubbed clean. Their faces all but lost. Only one commandment had slipped unnoticed through time, held close by the lineage once blessed by the goddesses.

In your hands lies the gate of godhood—let none pass.

As a child, when her mother had told her of their duty to uphold this commandment, Kahina had not believed it. She had laughed, thinking it was nothing more than her mother's fanciful imagination. But on her thirteenth birthday, her mother brought her to an abandoned courtyard in the desert long since left to the goats and vagrants. At the center of the courtyard lay the remains of what looked to be a well, but it held no water. Instead, it overflowed with dusty palm fronds and sand.

"Give it your blood," demanded her mother.

Kahina had refused. This fancy had gone too far. But her mother was determined. She yanked Kahina's arm to her, drawing a sharp stone across the inside of her elbow. Kahina remembered screaming from the hot sear of pain until her blood hit the old stones.

The world trembled. Blue light—like the sky twisted into a single rope—shot from the stones, then split into glowing strands that caged in the old courtyard.

"Look into the well," said her mother.

She no longer sounded like herself. Kahina, overcome, peered over the stone lip. Gone was the sand and the dusty palm fronds, replaced instead with a story that poured through her. Her eyes fluttered shut. Her mouth filled with the weight of a hundred languages, her tongue loosened, her teeth ached in her skull. For a second—no longer than a blink—a different consciousness stretched within her, a consciousness that whispered for roots to uncurl and birds to take wing, a consciousness sharp enough to slice intention out of chaos, carve reason from randomness, set stars spinning through the worlds.

Kahina fell to her knees.

As she fell, she felt her perspective jolt skywards so that the world beneath her seemed like something she might cup in her palms. She saw a mere sliver of that uncanny consciousness burning bright and shattering across a young world. She saw power denting the land, saw clusters of people raise their hands to their eyes, as if new colors had exploded into their vision. She saw these slivers of power folded into the earth, each spot blooming with vines of light, so the world looked scrawled over in a poetic language only angels could pronounce. The earth bloomed above that network of light. Plants sprouted. Animals grazed. Communities—small at first, then, ever growing—began to create. A man waved his hand above the grass, and the blades slowly twisted into a flute. A woman draped in beads pressed her fingers to a child's temples, and the people around her cowered in wonder. Later, Kahina would learn that the Western world called this Forging, both of matter and mind, but the art had more than one name.

Suspended in that eerie consciousness, Kahina felt her perspective shifting again.

In a temple with high walls, threads of the strange light that had spread through the land hovered in the air like hardened sunshine. A group of women gathered the threads. Kahina could see that their eyes had drunk the light and now glowed silver. One by one, the threads were set into an instrument no larger than a child's head. One woman, curious, strummed the instrument. Time shuddered to a halt, and for a terrible moment, the slivers of power within the earth creaked, that calligraphy of light flashing in warning. The woman flattened her hand, killing the sound instantly.

But the damage was done.

Across the world, Kahina saw fires erupting, newborn cities crumbling, people crushed beneath them. Kahina could no longer see her own body, but she felt her soul shuddering in horror. That instrument was not to be played.

In the visions, Time spun forward.

Kahina saw the women's descendants spread across the world. She could always recognize them by the unearthly hue to their eyes, which was just uncanny enough to draw attention, but not enough to arouse suspicion. The strange instrument passed between them, smuggled through portals that pinched time and space, whirling through the ages while empires fought their wars and hungry gods demanded blood and hungrier priests demanded sacrifice, and all the while, the sun fell and the moon rose, and the instrument lay wondrously silent.

Abruptly, the visions released her.

Kahina fell, and it was a fall that seemed to pass through life-times. She felt the scrape of ancient ziggurats against her cheeks, tasted cold coins on her tongue, felt the pelt of extinct animals ripple beneath her feet. Abruptly, she found herself on the ground and staring up at her mother. The vastness that once stretched her soul had fled, and she had never felt so small or cold.

"I know," said her mother, not unkindly.

When Kahina could trust herself to speak—and it took longer than she thought, for it seemed the Arabic she knew kept slipping off her tongue—she croaked: "What was that?"

"A vision granted to the Blessed, so that we might understand our sacred duty," said her mother. "We have other names, I am told, for our family scattered long ago. We are the Lost Muses, the Norns, the Daughters of Bathala, the Silent Apsaras. That instrument you saw holds many names in many tongues, but its function is always the same . . . when played, it disrupts the divine."

"The divine," repeated Kahina.

It felt too small a word given what she had seen.

"My mother spoke of a place built from the ruins of a land whose sacred group misused its power. Played outside the confines of that stained temple, the instrument will unleash a destruction that levels the world," said Kahina's mother. "Played *within* the temple, it is said to join together all those slivers of divinity you glimpsed. Some say that it can be raised into a tower, which one may scale like a building and claim godhood for themselves. It is not for us to know. Our duty is laid out in one command . . ."

Her mother held out her hand, hoisting Kahina to her feet.

"In your hands lie the gates of godhood. Let none pass."

NOW, KAHINA BENT over her son. She turned over his pudgy hand, tracing the delicate blue veins of his wrist. She kissed his knuckles, then kissed each finger and folded it to his palm. She wished she could live in this moment forever—her son, warm and sleeping at her side; the sun glaring elsewhere; the moon keeping watch; this corner of time hemmed in by nothing but the sounds of their breathing.

But that was not how the world worked.

She had seen its fangs and run from its shadow.

Kahina tried to imagine bringing her son to that sacred well, but the image would not hold. It was that fear that had driven her to tell Delphine Desrosiers, matriarch of House Kore, the truth. The other woman would watch over him. She understood what was at stake, and she knew where he must go, should the worst befall them.

Though years had passed, Kahina had not forgotten what she'd glimpsed that day in the broken courtyard. The world beneath her, the lines of power scrawled unintelligibly over jagged mountains and crystalline lakes, vast deserts and steaming jungles.

At one sound of the instrument . . . it could all vanish.

"In your hands lie the gates of godhood," she whispered to her son. "Let none pass."

PART I

I

SÉVERIN

Séverin Montagnet-Alarie stared down at the man kneeling before him.

At his back, a cold wind wrinkled the surface of the dark, lacquered lagoons of Venice, and the prow of a gondola beat mournfully against the shadowy dock. About thirty meters away stood a plain and pale wooden door, its entrance flanked on both sides by a dozen members of the Fallen House. They regarded Séverin in silence, their hands clasped before them, their faces obscured by white *volto* masks that covered everything but their eyes. Over their lips sat Mnemo bugs in the shape of golden honeybees, their metal wings whirring as they documented Séverin's every move.

Ruslan, patriarch of the Fallen House, stood beside the kneeling man. He patted the man's head as if he were a dog, and tugged playfully at the bindings gagging his mouth.

"You"—he said to the man, tapping the side of his head with his golden Midas knife—"are the key to my apotheosis! Well, not the main key, but a necessary step. You see, I can't get my front door open without you . . ." Ruslan stroked the man's hair, the gleaming gold skin of his hand catching in the torchlight. "You should be flattered. How many can say they have paved the way to godhood for others, hmm?"

The kneeling man whimpered. Ruslan's grin widened. Days ago, Séverin would have said the Midas Knife was the most fascinating object he had ever come across. It could rearrange human matter through an alchemy that seemed divine in its making, though—as Ruslan had proved—its use came at the price of sanity. It was rumored that the blade itself had been hewn from the topmost bricks of the Tower of Babel, whose fallen pieces had powered the art of Forging across the world.

But compared to the divine lyre clutched in Séverin's hand, the Midas Knife was nothing.

"What do you think, Monsieur Montagnet-Alarie?" asked Ruslan. "Don't you agree this man should feel nothing but flattered? Awed, even?"

Beside the lined-up members of the Fallen House, Eva Yefremovna, the blood and ice Forging artist, stiffened noticeably. Her wide, green eyes had not lost their feverish sheen in the twelve hours since they had left behind the Sleeping Palace on the frozen waters of Lake Baikal.

You must tread carefully.

Séverin's last conversation with Delphine, the matriarch of House Kore, reared up in his thoughts. They had been crouched in the metal belly of a mechanical leviathan. On the hidden Mnemo panel, Séverin had watched as Ruslan advanced on his friends, slapping Laila across the face, cutting off Enrique's ear. Ruslan was after something only Séverin could give: control over the lyre. Played outside of its sacred temple, the lyre only brought ruin. Played within the sacred grounds . . . the lyre could tap into the powers of godhood.

By then, Séverin knew exactly where he needed to go to play the lyre: Poveglia. Plague Island.

He had heard of the island near Venice years ago. In the fifteenth century, the island had built a hospital for those who fell ill during the plague epidemics, and it was said the ground was more skeleton than soil. Years ago, Séverin had nearly accepted an acquisition project on the island before Enrique had objected.

"The temple's entrance is well hidden beneath Poveglia," the matriarch had said to him the last, and final, time they had been together in the belly of the metal leviathan. "There are other entrances to the temple scattered throughout the world, but their maps have been destroyed. Only this one remains, and Ruslan will know where to look for it."

"My friends—" said Séverin, unable to tear his eyes from the screen.

"I will send them after you," said the matriarch, grabbing his shoulders. "I have been planning for this ever since your mother begged me to protect you. They will have everything they need to come find you."

It had taken Séverin a moment to understand.

"You know," he'd said angrily. "You *know* where the map is to reach the temple beneath Poveglia, and you won't tell me—"

"I can't. It is too dangerous to speak aloud, and I have camouflaged it even from the safe house," said the matriarch. "If the others fail, you must find the answer from Ruslan. And once you do, you must find a way to be rid of him. He will do everything in his power to keep track of you."

"I—"

The matriarch had grabbed his chin, directing his gaze to the screen. Laila had crumpled to her knees, her hair falling across her face. Enrique lay sprawled out, bleeding on the ice. Zofia's hands clutched at her dress, her grip white-knuckled. Even Hypnos, lying unconscious behind Séverin, would be destroyed if Ruslan succeeded. Something cold and inhuman coiled in Séverin's stomach.

"What will you do to protect them?" asked the matriarch.

Séverin stared at his family, lingering a moment longer than he needed to on Laila. Laila and her warm smile, her rose water and sugar-scented hair . . . her body that would cease to house her soul in ten days' time. She'd never told him how little time was left and now—

The matriarch's grip on his chin tightened. "What will you do to *protect* them?"

The question jolted through him.

"Anything," said Séverin.

Now, on the marble threshold outside Ruslan's home, Séverin schooled his expression to blankness and regarded the kneeling man. He forced himself to answer Ruslan's question. He didn't know what the kneeling man had to do with Ruslan's home, or how to enter it, which made his every word hold a strange balance.

"Indeed," he said. "This man should be flattered."

The kneeling man whimpered, and Séverin finally looked at him. On closer inspection, he was not a man at all, but a boy that looked to be in his late teens, perhaps only a few years younger than Séverin. He was pale, with blue eyes and dirty-blond hair. His limbs were skinny as a colt's, and a flower poked out of the top button of his shirt. A lump rose in Séverin's throat. The hair and eyes and flower . . . it was a flimsy echo, but for a moment, it was as if Tristan knelt at his feet.

"My father had a keen sense of understanding about the world," said Ruslan.

The longer Séverin stared at the kneeling boy, the more he began to suspect the uncanny resemblance to Tristan was no mistake. His fingers twitched to reach out to the boy, to untie his hands and throw him into the stinking water so he might escape whatever Ruslan planned.

"Most importantly," said Ruslan. "My father knew that nothing was without sacrifice."

Ruslan's hand blurred forward so quickly that Séverin didn't have time to react. Séverin bit down on his tongue, tasting blood. It was the only thing that kept him from lurching forward to catch the boy and break his fall. The boy's eyes widened for an instant before he slumped forward. Blood pooled from his slashed throat, spreading slowly over the marble threshold. Ruslan stared down at him, the knife in his hand now glossed with crimson. Wordlessly, he handed the blade to one of his followers.

"Sacrifice was built into the very design of our ancestral home," continued Ruslan casually. "Father always knew it was our destiny to become gods . . . and all gods require sacrifice. That is why he named it *Casa D'Oro Rosso.*"

House of Red Gold.

Before, the house had seemed pale and nondescript. But the touch of blood had changed it. What had once been a colorless mosaic floor leading to the pale door, had begun to transform. As the blood seeped into the ground, the translucent stones shifted—a faint hue of crimson deepening to ruby. Cherry-dark garnet flecked the stones, haloed by patterns of pink quartz that formed a decorative geometric design. The color lazily bloomed outward until it hit the door. The white door blushed pink, swirls of dark gold crawling up from the marble and across the Forged wood that smoldered away, revealing the gold and iron scrollwork of a grand entryway. In one smooth motion, the door swung open.

"I believe the inlay stonework is in a style called *cosmatesque*," said Ruslan, gesturing at the threshold. "It's beautiful, is it not?"

Séverin couldn't stop staring at the body sprawled out on the dock, the blood steaming in the cold air. His palms turned damp, remembering the hot slip of Tristan's blood on his skin when he'd held his brother's body to his chest. The matriarch's voice echoed in his head: *He will test you before he trusts you.*

Séverin swallowed hard, forcing his thoughts to Hypnos and Laila, Enrique and Zofia. They were counting on him to find the map to the temple beneath Poveglia. His instructions on the Mnemo bug he had left by an unconscious Laila had been clear: in three days' time, they would meet at the appointed location in Venice. By then, they should have cracked the matriarch's riddles and discovered where the map lay. If not, then it was up to him to find the answer. Once he had the answer, then he needed to figure out a way to be rid of Ruslan.

"It's beautiful, yes," said Séverin, arching an eyebrow. He wrinkled his nose. "But the reek of blood hardly agrees with this stinking Venetian air. Come, let us go, before it puts us off our appetite. One day soon, we shall demand more elegant offerings than blood."

Ruslan smiled, gesturing him inside.

Séverin's hand twitched. He pressed his thumb against the hard, crystalline strings of the divine lyre. He still remembered what it felt like to touch those strings with a bloodied hand . . . as if the pulse of the universe had run through him. In his hand alone lay the gates of godhood.

And in a matter of days, Séverin Montagnet-Alarie would be a god.

2

LAILA

L aila had never felt more alone.

Around her, the grotto burned with cold. Icicles lay shattered on the floor, and in the eerie blue light of the snow-packed walls, the smashed wings of the Mnemo bug bled watery rainbows. A knot rose in her throat, and she squeezed the diamond pendant in her hand, wincing at the sharp pain of its angles.

In the hour since Séverin had left with Ruslan, she hadn't moved. Not once.

She kept staring instead at the bodies of Enrique and Zofia sprawled out on the ice, not three meters from her. She didn't want to leave them, and she didn't want to get closer either. If she touched them . . . if she closed their eyes to make their death appear like sleep . . . it would be like breaking the fragile skin of a dream. One touch, and she would have made this horror *real*. And she couldn't allow that.

She couldn't allow herself to hold the truth wholly in her heart: Séverin had killed them all.

He'd plunged a knife into Enrique and Zofia. Maybe he'd done so to Hypnos too. Poor Hypnos, thought Laila. She hoped he'd at least been stabbed in the back so he'd died without knowing that the person whose love he wanted most had betrayed him.

Séverin had known there was no need to subject Laila to the same fate. There was nothing he could do to her that time wasn't already planning. Laila blinked and saw Séverin's cold, violet eyes staring down at her as he wiped his knife against the front of his jacket and said: "She'll die soon anyway."

Light caught on her garnet ring, the number displayed within the jewel impossible to miss: *Ten*. That was all she had left. Ten days before the Forging mechanisms that held her body together fell apart, and her soul came loose.

Maybe she deserved this.

She'd been too weak, too forgiving. Even after everything, she had let him—no, *wanted* him—to draw her down to him and intersperse their heartbeats with kisses. Maybe it was a blessing that he had not played the divine lyre, for how could she live with herself knowing she had encouraged a monster?

Monster, not Majnun, she told herself.

Yet some selfish part of her broke from knowing how close she had been to life. She'd touched the very strings that could have saved her, but they would not move for her.

Séverin had been cruel enough to want to show her. Why else would he have left the Mnemo bug beside her, and the diamond pendant he had once used to summon her? Laila smashed the Mnemo bug's wings once more, watching whatever memories it held expire with a sigh. Again and again, she knocked it against the ice, gripped by a fierce desire to destroy any sign of Séverin. An odd, choked laugh ripped out of her throat as plumes of colored smoke rose in a thick fog, distorting the grotto around her.

As she stared through the veil of fog . . . a shape on the ice stirred.

Laila reared back, horror filling her. She had to be seeing things. She *had* to.

Séverin must have driven her mad.

Because right before her eyes, Enrique and Zofia stirred to life.

3

⌒⫞⌒

ZOFIA

Zofia woke to a shrill ringing in her head. Her mouth felt dry. Her eyes kept watering. Add to that the sticky raspberry-cherry jam on her shirt—and she did not like raspberry-cherry jam. Slowly, her eyes adjusted to the sights around her. She was still in the ice grotto. Several smashed icicles lay around her. The oval-shaped pool where the leviathan named David had once rested was now empty of the mechanical creature, and the water was very still. A colorful fog rose up in the place where Laila had once stood . . .

Laila.

Panic grabbed hold of Zofia.

What had happened to Laila?

The past hour flew back to her. Ruslan—who had lied to them, pretending to be their friend—shaking Laila, demanding she play the divine lyre, only to find out that Séverin was the one who could. And then Séverin walking toward her holding the knife imbued with Goliath's paralyzing venom. He had grabbed her, whispering:

Trust me, Phoenix. I will fix this.

She barely had time to nod before the world had gone black.

Through the colorful fog, someone ran toward her. The lights of the grotto still stung her eyes, cloaking the figure in darkness. Zofia tried to throw up her hands, but they were bound with rope. Was Enrique still safe? Where had Séverin gone? Had anyone in Paris remembered to feed Goliath?

"You're alive!" shouted the figure.

The person dropped before her: Laila. Her friend grabbed her in a fierce hug, her body shaking with sobs and then, unaccountably, laughter. Zofia did not normally like being hugged, but it seemed that Laila needed this. She held still.

"You're *alive*," said Laila again, smiling through her tears.

". . . Yes?" said Zofia. Her words came out as a croak.

Séverin had told her she would be paralyzed for a few hours, that was all. Such a thing was not deadly.

"I thought Séverin killed you."

"Why would he kill me?"

Zofia searched Laila's face. From the trail of salt down her cheeks, she knew her friend had been crying. Her gaze dropped to the garnet ring on Laila's hand, and Zofia stilled. Séverin had refused to play the divine lyre, which should have saved Laila's life. There was no reason to do that unless the lyre could *not* save Laila's life. But where did that leave their plan to save her? There were still only ten days left before Laila's body failed.

"He said the paralysis was part of the plan."

Laila's expression changed. From relief to hurt and then . . . confusion. A loud groaning sound caught Zofia's attention. It took great effort to turn her head, for her neck ached terribly. To her right, Enrique was pushing himself up. At the sight of him—alive and frowning—warmth surged through Zofia's chest. She studied him. Dried blood was spattered down his neck. One of his ears was missing. She did not remember that happening, although she did remember many loud screams. At the time, she had tried to ignore everything around her. She had been running through the scenarios, trying to find a way to escape.

"What happened to your ear?" she asked.

Enrique clapped one hand to the side of his head, wincing before he glared at her. "I nearly died and your first question is what happened to my ear?"

Laila threw her arms around him, then drew back.

"I don't understand. I thought—"

From the oval pool came a churning sound, and they turned as one to look. The water frothed, steaming as a mechanical pod breached the surface and slid onto the icy floor. Zofia recognized it as an escape pod that had once been inside David the Leviathan, who had held the Fallen House's treasures all these years. The pod, which was fish-shaped and equipped with several windows and a winnowing fan of blades where its tail might be, steamed and hissed as a section of it flapped open.

Hypnos, dressed in his brocade suit from the Midnight Auction last evening, stepped onto the ice and waved happily.

"Hello, friends!" he said, grinning.

But then he paused, his gaze darting to Laila's blank face and the blood on Enrique's neck, to Zofia's bound hands and finally to the colorful fog at the edge of the ice where, for the first time, Zofia noticed the smashed-up mechanism of a Mnemo bug.

The smile slid off Hypnos's face.

FOR THE PAST eighty-seven seconds and counting, Hypnos had not said a word.

Enrique had just finished explaining what happened between them and Séverin, how he'd taken the divine lyre and left with Ruslan before faking their deaths. Hypnos wrapped his arms around himself, staring at the floor for another seven seconds before he finally raised his head, his eyes going straight to Laila.

His voice broke. "You're dying?"

"She will not die," said Zofia sharply. "Death depends on variables that we will change."

Laila smiled at her, before giving a small nod. She had not said much since Hypnos arrived. She'd barely looked at him either. Her eyes kept going to her garnet ring and the smashed Mnemo bug on the ice.

"The lyre doesn't work how we thought it would," said Enrique. "Remember the writing on the grotto wall? *To play at God's instrument will summon the unmaking.* In this case, the unmaking is everything Forged, unless the lyre is played in a specific location, but we don't know *where—*"

Hypnos cut in: "Somewhere beneath Poveglia, one of the islands near Venice—"

"Poveglia?" repeated Enrique, paling.

Zofia frowned. She knew that name. Years ago, Séverin had referred to it as Plague Island. They had almost accepted an acquisition there before deciding against it. Enrique had seemed very relieved they did not go because he found graveyards unsettling. Zofia remembered Tristan playing a joke on Enrique while they'd discussed the matter, sending creeping vines to wrap around his ankles. Enrique had not found it amusing.

"The matriarch told me," said Hypnos quickly. "She said the maps to the locations of other entrances have been lost and this is all that's left. I know the Tezcat routes to Italy. We could be there by tonight. The matriarch even has a safe house waiting for us in

Venice, a place she said will have all the answers we need, but the location is mind Forged."

"Then how will we find it?" asked Enrique.

"She gave me a hint about where we could find the key and its address," said Hypnos. "Once we're settled, we can meet Séverin. He left instructions on the Mnemo bug about how to . . ."

His eyes went to the smashed Mnemo bug on the ice.

". . . find him," he finished, wide-eyed, then looked around them. His gaze fixed on Laila. "I *still* don't understand why you broke it!"

Laila frowned and color rushed to her face. "He took a knife to Zofia and then Enrique, and I thought he . . . he . . ."

Hypnos's eyebrows shot up. "How could you believe Séverin wanted us all dead?"

"*Because he lost his mind and his current plan is to turn into a god?*" said Enrique.

He winced, touching his ear. Earlier, Laila had ripped part of her dress to fashion him a bandage that wrapped around his whole head. The bleeding had stopped, but Zofia noticed that Enrique looked paler. He was in pain. Zofia did not know how to help him, and it made her feel frustrated.

"But if the matriarch mentioned a map, then maybe she'll know where it is," said Enrique.

Hypnos's mouth tugged downwards, and his shoulders fell.

"She went down with . . . with the machine," he said.

Laila gasped, covering her mouth with her hands. Enrique went silent. Zofia bowed her head. She knew she should be thinking of the matriarch—and she did feel sorrow that she had died—but her thoughts flew to Hela. Slowly, Zofia touched her heart where the sharp, jagged point of Hela's unopened letter lay against her skin. She had received the letter a few days ago, but the script was not in

Hela's hand. And if Hela could not pen a letter to her on her own, then that increased the likelihood that her sister was dead. Even the possibility of Hela's death hurt far worse than the matriarch's actual death. Zofia felt that familiar tightening panic in her chest. She reached for the pocket in her dress where she kept her matchbox, but it was gone. She stared around the room, trying to count things and center her thoughts—twelve icicles, six jagged edges in the ice, three shields, four drops of blood on the ground—but Hypnos and Enrique had started raising their voices.

"What are we going to do?" asked Hypnos. "Without the Mnemo bug, we won't know where to find Séverin and then we can't find the map!"

"We don't need Séverin," said Enrique coldly.

Hypnos's head snapped up. "What?"

"You said it yourself . . . the matriarch's safe house will have all the answers we need," said Enrique.

"But the lyre . . ." said Hypnos, looking to Laila.

"Séverin is after godhood," said Enrique. There was a hard set to his mouth. "With or without us, he'll get to Plague Island. That's where we'll find him. There, he can play it and save Laila. That's all we need him for. After that, we never have to lay eyes on him again."

"But what will Séverin think?" asked Hypnos, in a small voice. "Before he left, he told me all he wanted was to protect us . . ."

Zofia watched as a small muscle in Enrique's jaw tightened. He looked to the ice for a moment, and then back to Hypnos. Enrique's brows were pressed down into a flat line, which signified that he was angry.

"The only thing we need protecting from is him," said Enrique.

Protect. Zofia remembered Enrique breaking down the etymology of the word. It came from Latin. *Pro*: "in front." *Tegere*:

"to cover." *Covered in front.* To protect was to cover. To hide. Zofia moved her hand right above her heart, covering the place where the letter not written by Hela lay. When Zofia evaluated the possible outcomes, she knew the letter could only be a formal announcement of her sister's death. Hela had been sick for months. Hela had almost died already. Zofia had failed to protect her sister . . . but she still had a chance with Laila.

Slowly, Zofia forced herself to listen to the others' conversation. There was talk of secret Tezcat routes that would lead them to Venice, and how the members of the Order of Babel were still paralyzed from Eva's blood Forging, which left them only a handful of hours to leave or risk getting caught. Zofia could hardly bring herself to listen.

Instead, she stared at the ring on Laila's hand: ten days.

She had ten days to protect Laila. If Zofia could do that for her friend, then maybe she could make herself open the letter and learn Hela's fate for certain. Until then, she would keep the letter covered. If she did not look, then she did not have to know, and if she did not know then perhaps there was a chance . . . a statistical impossibility, but a weighted number nonetheless, that Hela was not dead. Zofia reached for the safety of those numbers: *ten* days to find a solution for Laila, *ten* days in which she might hope Hela was still alive.

Hope, Zofia realized, was the only protection she had left.

4

LAILA

Laila picked her way through the shadows of a narrow brick alley, pulling tight the cloth that covered her face and hair. Around her, stray cats mewled and hissed, tumbling in the piles of trash. Wherever they were—she had lost track of the Tezcat route after the seventh switch—it was early afternoon, and a wind off the sea carried the stench of dead fish. In front of her, Hypnos laid his hand against a dirtied brick. Zofia stood beside him, holding up a Tezcat pendant she had torn off from her necklace. It was the only tool they had with them. Enrique's research, Zofia's laboratory, Laila's costumes . . . all of it had been left behind in the Sleeping Palace.

The pendant glowed brightly, indicating a hidden entrance.

"This should be the last Tezcat route," said Hypnos, forcing a smile to his face. "The matriarch said from here, the passage would open up right beside the Rialto Bridge. Is that not wonderful?"

"That is not how I would define 'wonderful,'" said Zofia.

Her blond hair had come undone and haloed her whole head,

while her blue gown looked scorched. Next to her, Enrique gingerly touched the bloodstained bandage around his ear, and just then, a fat cockroach scuttled across Laila's mud-crusted slippers. Laila recoiled.

"Wonderful is a hot bath and a foolproof plan waiting for us on the other side," said Enrique. "We don't even know where we're going to find this safehouse."

"We have a hint . . ." said Hypnos before reciting the matriarch's instructions: "*On the island of the dead, lies the god with not one head. Show the sum of what you see, and this will lead you straight to me.*"

"Which means *what*, exactly?" said Enrique.

Hypnos's mouth pressed to a thin line. "That's all I was given, *mon cher*. So we must make do. I'm going to check that this is the correct route. Zofia, will you come with me? I might need that fancy necklace of yours."

Zofia nodded, and Hypnos pressed his hand against a particular brick. His Babel ring—a grinning crescent moon that spanned three knuckles—glowed softly. A moment later, they stepped through the brick and vanished.

Laila stared at the Tezcat door, a desperate laugh clawing up her throat.

When they'd first left the Sleeping Palace, she had almost imagined that things might be salvaged . . . but then Hypnos had revealed the matriarch's "hint," and Laila had known they were well and truly lost. Even if they made it to the island of Poveglia, what then? They had no instruments, no intel, no weapons, no directions . . . and no meeting point either.

Laila squeezed her eyes shut, as if it might conjure whatever she was supposed to have glimpsed in that Mnemo bug. In her mind's eye, she saw Séverin's cool, dusky gaze turning from her. She remembered catching sight of a half print of her rouge just below his collar from when she had kissed him in the night. Laila's eyes flew open, banishing those images.

She hated Séverin. He had overly relied on her belief in him. He had foolishly assumed she would think there was no world in which he would hurt Enrique or Zofia, but he had underestimated how well he'd convinced them of his indifference. Laila could almost imagine him saying: *You know me*. But that was false. She didn't know him at all. And yet the guilt stayed. Every time she blinked, she saw the shattered Mnemo wings, and she didn't know what that moment of fury had cost them in their search.

Laila shoved Séverin out of her thoughts and looked across the alley to where Enrique stood. His arms were crossed, and his gaze looked distant and furious.

"Do you blame me?" she asked.

Enrique's head snapped up. He looked horrified.

"Of course not, Laila," he said, walking over to her. "Why would you think that?"

"If I hadn't smashed the Mnemo bug—"

"I would've done the same," said Enrique, his jaw tight. "Laila, I know how you felt . . . I know what it looked like . . ."

"Even so—"

"Even so, we are not out of options," said Enrique firmly. "I meant what I said . . . we don't need him. We'll find another way."

Enrique reached for her hand, and together, they stared up at the sky. For a moment, Laila forgot about the weight of death on her bones. She tilted her chin up, scanning the high brick walls. They seemed to be part of a spiral of ramparts separating the city from the sea. Overhead, Laila could hear the bustle of a market, and gossip in foreign tongues. The smell of baked bread flecked with honey and spices filled the air, pushing out the rotting stench from the nearby sea.

"Plague Island," said Enrique softly. "Do you remember that prank Tristan pulled on me? We were all talking about whether or not to pursue that acquisition there, and he knew I was a little unsettled by all the talk of bones in the soil—"

"A little unsettled?" teased Laila, a soft smile curving her mouth. "I remember you screamed so loud when Tristan's Forged vines wrapped around your ankles that half the guests in L'Eden thought someone had been murdered in the drawing room."

"It was *terrifying*!" said Enrique, shuddering.

Laila grinned despite herself. She thought the memory of that day would leave a bitter tang, but instead, it brought unexpected sweetness. Thinking of Tristan had begun to feel like an old bruise rather than a fresh wound. With every passing day, his memory became less tender to touch.

"I remember," said Laila softly.

"Burial grounds disturb me," said Enrique, making a quick sign of the cross. "In fact . . ."

He broke off suddenly, his eyes widening. At that moment, Hypnos and Zofia stepped through the Tezcat portal. Behind them, Laila could see a long stone hallway that opened up into a marketplace. There was a white bridge in the distance. Seagulls swooping around the stands of fishmongers.

"Enrique?" prompted Laila. "What is it?"

"I . . . I think I know where we need to look for the safe house key," said Enrique. "*The island of the dead* . . . it must be a reference to Isola di San Michele. Almost a hundred years ago, Napoleon decreed that the island would become a cemetery because of unsanitary burial conditions on the mainland. I remember I'd studied about it in university. You know, there happens to be a particularly unique Renaissance church and monastery on the island that—"

Hypnos clapped his hands. "It's settled! Let us away to the cemetery!"

Enrique scowled.

"What about the rest of the riddle?" asked Zofia.

Laila turned over the words once more: *On the island of the dead . . . lies the god with not one head . . . show the sum of what you see, and this will lead you straight to me . . .*

"I . . . I don't know," admitted Enrique. "Certainly, there are many deities with multiple heads, particularly in the religions of Asia, but 'show the sum of what you see' sounds like we won't know any more until we get there."

Hypnos's smile deflated. "So you aren't certain what it is we're looking for inside the cemetery?"

"Well, no, not exactly," said Enrique.

"Are you certain about Isola di San Michele?"

". . . No."

A quiet fell over them. There used to be a rhythm to determining where to travel. Zofia's calculations, Enrique's knowledge of history, Laila's readings of objects, and then—Séverin. The one who put their findings into context like a lens drawing everything into focus.

We don't need him, Enrique had said.

Did he believe it?

Laila studied her friend: the high color on his cheeks, the wideness of his eyes, the slope of his posture. He'd drawn his shoulders in, as if he suddenly wished to make himself inconspicuous.

"I think it's as good an idea as any."

Enrique looked startled. He smiled at her, but his smile fell the moment his gaze went to her hand and the garnet ring that stared accusingly at them all. Laila knew what it said without looking.

Nine days.

Even so, she would put her trust in those who deserved it. Laila reached out, grabbing Enrique's hand and looking Zofia and Hypnos in the eye.

"Shall we?"

LAILA'S FIRST SIGHT of Venice stole her breath away, and though she had so little of it left, she could not bring herself to mind. Venice seemed like a place half-sculpted from a child's daydream. It was a floating city knitted all over with marble bridges, full of sunken doors wearing the faces of grinning gods. Everywhere she looked, the city appeared enchanted with liveliness. On the merchant tables set up along the banks of the lagoon, Forged lace folded itself into the likeness of a crescent moon and played peekaboo with a grinning child. A string of stained-glass beads floated up from a velvet settee to clasp playfully around the neck of a laughing noblewoman. Elaborate masks covered in gold leaf and decorated in swirling pearls floated regally past them, buoyed into the air by the craftsmen *mascheraris* who worked near the water.

"To get to Isola di San Michele, we're going to need a boat," Enrique said.

Hypnos had turned out his pockets mournfully. "How will we pay?"

"Leave it to me," said Laila.

She walked quickly along the docks. First, she swiped a black shawl left unattended on a stool—a memory of warm, brown hands knitting the shawl pushed through her mind. *Sorry*, she thought. She swept it over her stained and ripped gown. At her throat, her L'Enigme mask lay folded away in a tiny pendant dangling from a green silk ribbon. She tapped it once, and the elaborate peacock mask unraveled and settled around her face. If the other *mascher-ari* hawkers wearing their products noticed something amiss, they said nothing as she passed.

Laila kept an eye on the waters. They had emerged through a passageway of pale, Istrian stone that opened up right beside *Ponte di Rialto*, the huge bridge that looked like a crescent moon had abandoned the sky simply to adorn the city. In the late afternoon, gondolas swiftly cut through the jade water.

The gondoliers paid her no mind as they smoked and played chess by the stone steps. Laila touched the prows of their boats one by one, skimming through their memories—

The first: *A girl with a flower in her hair, her eyes fluttering closed as she leaned in for a kiss . . .*

The second: *A man's frustrated voice: "Mi dispiace . . ."*

The third: *A child holding his grandfather's hand, the smell of cigar smoke surrounding them.*

On and on and on until—

Laila's hands stilled as a static sound filled her thoughts. It was the kind of static that only belonged to a Forged object.

She smiled.

AN HOUR LATER, Laila sat on the prow of the gondola, watching as a frost-colored moon rose over an island in the distance. The cold wind on her face was bracing, and even though she was never rid of the weight of her death on her hand, at least she could have this too.

On the other side of the gondola, Enrique and Zofia seemed lost in their own thoughts. Enrique stared out at the water. Zofia, who had lost her box of matches, had taken to ripping up the scorched ends of her dress. On the cushion beside Laila, Hypnos leaned over and dropped his head against her shoulder. "I fear I am getting ill, *ma chère*."

"And why is that?"

"I am *craving* boredom, as if it is the rarest vintage of wine in all the land," he said. "Such depravity."

Laila nearly laughed. In the past week, she had seen riches that rivaled kingdoms and witnessed the kind of intoxicating power that could unravel the world with a song . . . but nothing compared to the luxury and allure of being able to waste a whole day and think nothing of it. If she could fill a box with impossible treasures, that was what Laila would hide away: luscious, sun-ripened days and cold, star-strewn nights to waste in the company of loved ones.

"I owe you an apology," said Hypnos.

Laila frowned. "Whatever for?"

"I behaved badly when I found out you had broken the Mnemo bug," he said, looking down at his lap. "Though Séverin has my trust, it is obvious he has not earned yours. I don't know what he said to you, but I can assure you he did not mean it. I know it was a ruse to protect you."

That familiar numbness rose up once more in Laila. "I know that now."

"You must know, too, that even though he cares for all of us, it's you that he—"

"Don't," said Laila coldly, before adding, "Please."

Hypnos held up his hands in surrender, leaving Laila to her thoughts. Her gaze dropped to her ring: *9*. Nine days left to breathe this air, stare at this sky. Her mind eagerly lapped up every image as if it were cream—the pale domes of cathedrals, a smudge of thundercloud on the sky. Thinking of Séverin was like dousing all those thoughts in ink. It blotted her mind with dark, and she could hardly see past it. He was not here. Not yet. So she endeavored not to think of him at all.

THE CEMETERY ISLAND of Isola di San Michele was still and quiet, walled in with red and white brick. A domed church wrought of the pale, Venetian stone appeared to float on the dark lagoon. As the gondola pulled toward the dock, a three-meter-tall Forged statue of the archangel Michael spread open its wings and raised a pair of scales in greeting. The bronze scales swung in the frosty February wind, and the seraphim's sightless eyes seemed to fix on them, as if preparing to weigh the good and bad of their lives. Down a white-stoned gravel pathway, stately cypress trees swayed and stood guard over the threshold of the dead.

The moment Laila stepped off the gondola, a strange feeling wisped through her stomach. A *blankness*, there and gone. For a moment, she could not smell the snow on the wind or feel the cold at her neck. Her body felt disjointed and too still, like a thing she must drag with her—

"*Laila!*"

Hypnos caught her around the shoulders.

"What happened?" asked Zofia, rushing to her.

"I-I don't know," said Laila.

Her body felt too still, too quiet. She felt her heart beat slowly, as if fighting through syrupy blood.

"You're hurt," said Zofia.

"No, I'm not, I—"

Hypnos lifted her bejeweled hand. There, Laila saw a slash across her palm. She must have grabbed the wooden spike at the dock too hard.

"Here," said Zofia, tearing off a bit of her scorched hem as a bandage.

Laila took it blankly.

"You've been through a lot," said Hypnos carefully. "Why don't you stay with the boat? We won't be long, will we?"

Enrique stammered. "I can't say for certain, but—" Hypnos must have thrown him a look because Enrique nodded quickly. "Stay and rest, Laila. We'll be fine."

"Are you hurting?" asked Zofia.

"No," said Laila, staring blankly at her hand.

She must have nodded and waved them off, but the whole time her mind screamed with something she could not bring herself to say aloud. She hadn't lied to Zofia. She hadn't felt any hurt.

Laila hadn't felt anything at all.

5

ENRIQUE

Enrique Mercado-Lopez knew many things.

He knew about history and languages, myths and legends. He knew how to kiss well, eat well, and dance well, and though he was uncertain about many situations at the moment, there was one thing he knew without a shadow of a doubt: This was not his place.

And he was not the only one who knew it.

A few paces behind him, Zofia and Hypnos walked in weighted silence. They expected him to know what to do next. They expected him to lead, to give commands, to plan the next steps . . . but that wasn't Enrique.

You wouldn't belong, an old voice whispered in his skull. *Know your place.*

His place.

Enrique could never seem to figure it out. When he was a child, he remembered trying out for the school theatre. All night, he'd practiced the hero's lines. He had propped up his toys on chairs as his future audience. He had bothered his mother until, exasperated, she gave up and helped him practice his lines by reading the script of the female costar. But on the day of the auditions, the nun running the play had stopped him after he said two sentences.

"*Anak.*" She laughed. "*You don't want to be the hero! Far too much work and far too many lines. And the front of the stage? It's a place of terror, trust me . . . you don't belong there. But don't worry, I have a special role for you!*"

The special role ended up being a tree.

His mother had been very proud though, and Enrique had reasoned that trees were symbolically quite important, and so perhaps he could be the hero next time.

But further attempts ended the same way. Enrique entered writing contests, only to find that his opinions had not found an audience. He would try out for debate contests, and if they didn't dismiss his ideas outright, they would take one look at his face, the Spanish features blending with his Visayan heritage, and in the end, all the responses were the same:

You don't belong.

When Enrique had found work as Séverin's historian, it was the first time he had dared to believe otherwise. He thought he'd found his place. Séverin was the first to believe in him, to encourage him . . . to offer friendship. With Séverin, his ideas found root and his scholarship soared to the extent that even the Ilustrados and their nationalist groups whose ideas could one day reshape his country, had let him in, and though he was nothing more than a member on the fringes writing his historical articles, it was more than he had ever been given . . . and it made him hope for more.

A fool's illusion, in the end.

Séverin had taken his dreams, and used them against him. He had promised that Enrique would always be heard, and then silenced him. He had taken their friendship and bent it to his needs until it broke, and Ruslan had picked up the pieces and fashioned it into a weapon.

All of which had left Enrique here: utterly lost in every way, and almost certainly not in the right place.

Enrique reached up, gingerly touching the bandage covering his lost ear. He winced. Since they had left the Sleeping Palace, he had tried not to look at himself, but his reflection in the lagoons of Venice found him anyway. He looked off balance. *Marked*, even. Before, when he was in the wrong place, at least he could hide. But his cut-off ear was a declaration: *I do not belong. See?*

Enrique shoved the thought aside. He couldn't afford to lose himself in pity.

"Come on . . . *think*."

He looked around the cemetery, frowning. The length of the Isola di San Michele cemetery was little more than five hundred meters, and by now they'd circled the perimeter twice. This was the third time they were walking down this path lined with cypress trees. Just ahead, the path would curve into a row of statues of the archangels, who would turn their Forged heads to watch them pass. On the cemetery plots, the granite tombstones stood tall and elaborately curved, many of them crowned with wide crosses draped in Forged roses that would never lose their scent or shine, while the mausoleums bore little decoration on their exterior, hardly anything that would put Enrique in mind of a god with either no head or multiple heads.

"*On the island of the dead, lies the god with not one head,*" recited Enrique, turning the words over in his head, "*. . . show the sum of what you see, and this will lead you straight to me.*"

"Did you say something?" asked Hypnos.

"Me? No," said Enrique quickly. "I'm just, er, reviewing the matriarch's riddle for clues . . . again."

"You still said something," pointed out Zofia.

"Yes, well," said Enrique. He could feel his face start to turn red. "The interpretation affects what it is we're looking for and such. It's quite a vague sentence."

"I thought we are looking for a god with 'not one head,'" said Zofia, raising an eyebrow. "That sounds specific."

"It still leaves a spectrum of depictions!" said Enrique. "For example, there's the Chinese deity Xingtian who kept fighting even though he'd been decapitated. And then the Hindu celestial beings Rahu and Ketu—also decapitated—and then there are the deities who have *more* than one head, so which is it? It seems unlikely that we would find gods of eastern religions on a tombstone in Venice, so there must be something else . . . something hidden, even . . ."

Hypnos cleared his throat. "Let our handsome historian work, Phoenix," he said. "I'm sure he will dazzle us soon with his findings."

The patriarch of House Nyx grinned. For a moment, Enrique was tempted to return it. There was something intoxicating and dreamlike about Hypnos's beauty and verve, the way it lulled one to imagine impossibilities within reach. Only now, Enrique felt the force of it like a dream that had slipped past his fingers.

"Thank you," said Enrique stiffly, turning from them both.

He tried to focus on the riddle, but Hypnos's smile had thrown him off. A mere handful of days had passed since Enrique had confronted him about the imbalance between their affections and the other boy had confessed: *I think, with enough time, I could learn to love you.* The memory was still fresh enough to sting.

Enrique didn't want a forced love. He wanted love like a light, a presence that drove out the shadows and recast the world into something warm. A secret part of him had always suspected he would not find such love with the dazzling patriarch, and maybe that was what hurt him most in the end. Not the loss of love, but the lack of surprise.

Of course, Hypnos wouldn't feel the same way about him. The fact that he was still surprised was either a sign of his optimism or foolishness, and Enrique highly suspected the latter was to blame.

FOR THE NEXT half hour, they paced the cemetery again, until they had once more arrived at the entrance. Some three meters away stood an unfinished grave plot. Of the few tombstones there, only one looked to be completed, though the stone mason had left it carved into irregular ridges. It was the only place they hadn't explored, for it seemed irrelevant. The matriarch's safe house must have existed for years, and as such, there was no reason for it to be on a fresh plot.

"*Mon cher*," said Hypnos, touching his shoulder. "I realize how hard you must be working, but . . . I have to ask . . . are you *quite* certain we are in the right place?"

Enrique felt his face turning hot. "Well, everything in history is conjecture, but this seems to be the only place that would make sense, no?"

Hypnos stared at him blankly, and Enrique almost wished Séverin were there. Séverin had a way of banishing doubt. He connected Enrique's rambling, historical threads into grand narratives of finding treasure that made everyone feel confident.

"I mean, there are lots of 'islands of the dead,' really—Tartarus, Naraka, Nav, etcetera—but they're mythological, whereas this is the only place close to Poveglia and—"

"We have been walking for more than an hour!" cut in Hypnos. "We haven't found anything."

"Soon, we won't be able to see anything either," pointed out Zofia.

Overhead, the light was failing faster and faster. The shadows beneath the statues of angels turned long and bladelike, and the cypresses looked unnaturally still. For a moment, Enrique imagined slender *enkantos* peering out at him from behind the trees, their nocturnal Otherworldly eyes glowing with hunger. His grandmother said they could sniff out dreams and make them real . . . for a price. In that moment, Enrique's wound throbbed. *Have I not already paid it?* He turned from the grove, pushing aside the thought of Otherworld creatures slinking in the shadows.

"We have to keep looking," said Enrique, "keep thinking. If we don't find the safe house key, then we won't have anywhere to go. Zofia needs a place to build her inventions, and I need a library and—"

"Perhaps our time would be better spent finding Séverin," suggested Hypnos tentatively.

Enrique felt stunned. "*Séverin?*"

"We know he's somewhere in Venice," said Hypnos. "We can use what time we have left to try and find him somehow . . . then it won't matter that Laila destroyed the Mnemo bug! I'm certain Séverin will know what to do."

And there it was. *This is not your place.* What was he doing thinking he could lead them or solve a riddle? That was Séverin's role, not his.

"Maybe you can ask him about the 'island of the dead,'" said Hypnos.

Enrique's ear felt hot, and his wound throbbed.

"Oh yes, why don't I do just that," shot back Enrique. He turned to the empty air beside him, then feigned shock. "What's this? Oh yes . . . *he's not here*, and we can't find him without showing our faces and risking the whole thing because the Fallen House thinks we're dead! But I suppose it would be better to risk death than give me a chance."

Hypnos stepped back. "That's not what I said—"

But Enrique had heard enough. He stalked off toward the unfinished tombstones, his heart racing, his breaths coming fast. For
a couple of moments, he stood in the shade of a cypress, watching the shadows swallow up the graves. Maybe they were right.
He should give up and go back, and not waste more of anyone's
time . . . especially Laila's. She barely had any time left to waste.
How would he show his face to her? Footsteps echoed behind him,
and Enrique's hands balled to fists at his side. He didn't want to
apologize to Hypnos.

But it was not Hypnos who appeared beside him. "I don't like
the dark," said Zofia.

She looked small and sylphlike in the dusk. The rising moonlight picked out the silver in her white-blond hair, and her huge
eyes seemed unearthly. Enrique tensed. Was she blaming him
too? But then Zofia reached up to unclasp a pendant from her
necklace.

"I don't have many left," said Zofia. "But it does help with finding
your way through the dark."

The pendant exploded with illumination, like a star caught between Zofia's fingers. Enrique blinked against the sudden brightness,
and when his eyes adjusted, the world seemed a little different. Zofia
did not smile, but held the pendant out expectantly. In that moment,
the light silvered her, so that it seemed as if *she* was what gave off the
light in the dark.

He'd barely had a moment to hold that thought when the light
off the pendant caught on the ridges of a tombstone. The tombstone
stood about a meter high and looked as if it had been fused together from two separate pieces. Lichen splotched the surface, but
as Enrique took a step toward it, he noticed the granite was curiously blank except for a string of numbers etched in relief on the
stone: *1, 2, 3, 4, 5*. The hairs on the back of Enrique's neck prickled

as he got closer and took in the object—the earth around it was slightly sunken, and under the light, he could see that the curious shape of the tombstone was in fact the suggestion of two faces looking in opposite directions.

The god with not one head.

"Look," said Enrique. "I . . . I think we've found something!"

A moment later, Hypnos appeared. He clapped his hands. *"Mon cher!* You did it! I never doubted you."

Enrique glared at him. "Zofia, come look!"

But Zofia stayed some three meters away, holding up the pendant which cast plenty of light. Her hand was placed right above her heart, and she fidgeted where she stood, as if the grave and the falling dark had unsettled her.

"Felicitations etcetera," said Hypnos airily. "Now what am I looking at? Also, it seems prudent to say that in the event I die with you all, which is seeming more likely by the day, *please* get me a far more elegant tombstone than that."

"I thought we were looking for a god," said Zofia.

"It is a god," said Enrique, grinning. "It's Janus, the Roman god of time . . . he looks backwards and forwards. He's the guardian of gates and beginnings, passages and thresholds."

"Janus?" repeated Hypnos. His nose wrinkled. "It also happens to be the name of the *rudest* House in the Italian faction. They're keepers of cartography or some such, and always throw an epic, secret party for Carnevale. Have I been invited to a *single* gathering? No. I am not envious, per se, but I am—"

Enrique placed his palm against the front of the tombstone. He wasn't sure what he thought would happen . . . maybe the lichen would clear, or maybe the faces would spit out a key. But instead, a Forged image contorted the stone revealing a fifteen-centimeter square outlined in light:

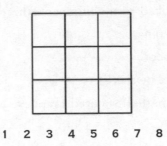

1 2 3 4 5 6 7 8

A few centimeters below the grid, the stone numbers quivered, and the riddle clicked into place.

"*Show the sum of what you see, and this will lead you straight to me,*" recited Enrique. "That seems simple enough . . . maybe even too simple. If it's the key to a safe house, wouldn't the matriarch have protected it more?"

"Sums?" said Hypnos. "Sum of what? The squares?"

"I'm no good at maths, so I'll leave you to—wait," said Hypnos. He glanced down at his feet at the same time that Enrique felt a curious suctioning on the bottom of his boots. The sunken ground of the grave had started to pull them in bit by bit. Hypnos shrieked and tried to lift his leg, but it was stuck fast in the earth. Enrique gripped the tombstone, trying to haul himself out, but that only made the Forging mechanism work faster. Within seconds, he was up to his knees. The light around them leapt wildly, swinging from the grave to the tombstone and the flat eyes of the two-headed god. Enrique wrenched around to see Zofia jumping for a branch in the cypress tree to pull them out, but the branches were too high—

"Hurry!" said Hypnos. "Put in the answer! It's nine, isn't it? Just do it!"

Enrique dragged his fingers across the stone, his heart sinking.

"Nine isn't an option! Maybe it's ten because the whole thing is an additional square?" he said.

But when he looked at the numbers, there was no zero either. Panic laced up his spine.

"*Six?*" tried Hypnos.

"How could there be six?!"

"I'm no good at maths!" shouted Hypnos.

"I couldn't tell!"

The grave dirt made loud squelching sounds, seeping through the buttons of his shirt front and pouring cold across his skin. Enrique tried to kick his feet, only to feel something hard and smooth slide along his calf. On instinct, he recoiled, which only dragged him down farther. Enrique scrambled to hold on to solid earth, but all of it turned soft and sinking to the touch. Hypnos started whimpering, but Zofia shouted out:

"One and four!"

"That makes no sense!" said Hypnos. "Maybe it's only one large square and it's just a terrible joke . . ."

Enrique studied the grid. Nine squares. One big square encompassing it . . . and four squares made up of four blocks within the pattern. *14.*

With shaking hands, he tapped the number *1* and then hit the number *4.* The numbers depressed farther into the rock as the earth pulled him down farther. Cold mud pooled around his shoulders when light abruptly flashed across his eyes.

The sinking stopped.

"Thank gods!" screamed Hypnos, hoisting himself out by his elbows. Enrique grabbed fistfuls of earth, dragging his body halfway out. Hypnos and Zofia reached for his hands, pulling him the rest of the way until he could slump onto the land, breathing hard.

"The—key—" he managed, facing the tombstone.

The Forged stone had contorted once more. Now, an address appeared on it:

Calle Tron, 77

A large key, the kind that might unlock a manor in the countryside, bubbled up out of the stone. Enrique stared at it in wonder. He felt Hypnos clapping his back enthusiastically and heard Zofia demanding that they leave now, and hope swelled in his chest.

The key to the safe house was not the solution to everything. They still needed to find the map to the temple beneath Poveglia. They still needed to play the lyre and save Laila's life. And Enrique still did not know where he belonged . . . but he felt a little surer at the front of the group as he turned to them and said:

"You're welcome."

6

SÉVERIN

All night, Séverin turned the divine lyre in his hands, counting down the moments until dawn. He could hear the Fallen House members standing guard outside his chamber. Carmine and garnets studded the four walls. A Forged chandelier of red Murano glass rotated slowly overhead. There were no windows, but dozens of candles flickering in bronzed sconces conspired to make the red walls look shiny with blood.

In the center of the chamber stood a claw-footed golden bed with a scarlet canopy and matching silks. Every time Séverin looked at it, he remembered a different bed, one carved of ice and draped in frost and gossamer. He remembered Laila astride his lap, looking down at him the way a goddess beholds a supplicant.

On that night, he wondered if his touch was the inverse of alchemy. One touch, and she was no longer as golden and distant as paradise, but human and earthly and entirely within reach. When he touched her, he felt her heartbeat beneath the hot velvet of her skin. When he rose over her, he watched her eyes widen, her teeth catch on her bottom lip, turning it a red so vivid, he had to know what it tasted like. Even now, the flavor haunted him. Rose water and sugar, and the faintest trace of salt from where she'd bitten down on his lip, drawn blood, and apologized with a kiss a moment later.

Séverin knew she must have read the Mnemo bug he had left beside her on the ice by now. He'd had only moments to record it, barely enough time to give her the name of the meeting place in three days' time. But before he had ended the Mnemo recording, he had said one last thing:

Don't forget that I am your majnun. Always.

Even without sleeping, he dreamt of her face and the faces of Tristan, Enrique, Zofia, and Hypnos. By now, they would understand he'd manipulated them. They would be furious at his lies and all his cruelty until that moment . . . but they would forgive him, wouldn't they? They would understand that all he had done, all the ugliness he had committed, it was all for them. Or had he gone too far? He knew he'd made terrible mistakes and broken their trust, but he hoped what they'd seen in the Mnemo bug was enough to earn back a sliver of their belief in him. And once they were together, he would begin to make full amends.

In his hands, the instrument of the divine weighed as much as a bird's nest. For him alone, the ten strings on the lyre glowed like threads of sunlight, like a hope and a promise real enough to touch. With this instrument, the world would never be able to hurt him or his loved ones again. With this, Laila could live and perhaps even love. With this, Tristan could come back to life. Séverin could remake them all with a touch. He could pour sunlight down their veins and fashion them wings if they wished to fly. And he would. All he had to do was get to the temple beneath Poveglia, enter it, play the lyre.

"I will make us all gods," Séverin vowed.

As the candles burned down to their stubs, Séverin weighed his next steps. He needed to get rid of Ruslan, but he couldn't do that until the patriarch of the Fallen House revealed where he could find the map to the temple's entrance hidden beneath Poveglia. In that time, he also needed to establish an excuse to leave Casa d'Oro . . . perhaps Eva could be of use.

Outside his bedroom door, he heard the Fallen House members moving down a hallway. He expected them to follow his every move, and if it looked as if he were cataloguing the home, it would be too suspect.

Ruslan had barely let him glimpse what lay inside Casa d'Oro before he had him escorted to his room. Séverin had walked slowly, feigning exhaustion, but all the while, he noted all that he could. He'd caught the scent of tilled earth and heard the distant flap of wings. A courtyard garden, perhaps? Or a menagerie? Past the entrance, he'd spied a grand, curving staircase disappearing to uppermost balconies, and a door halfway open revealing a kitchen on the main floor. It wasn't enough to make a plan . . . but it was a start.

Though there were no windows in his chamber, Séverin could hear the boats on the water, and, just beyond his wall, the scamper of small feet and fighting orphans. Slowly, a plan began to form.

AT DAWN, SÉVERIN stepped outside the bedroom door. A pair of guards stood, unmoving, not two meters from him. In the dimness, Séverin could just make out the shape of Casa d'Oro. His bedroom branched off from a bloodred hallway with multiple arches. Mirrors lined the walls. Not six meters away, he spied the kitchen entrance. Excellent, he thought. He turned to his guards and smiled.

"Is Patriarch Ruslan awake?" he asked.

The Fallen House member refused to speak. Or perhaps he couldn't. The *volto* mask covered everything but his eyes, and even those had a curious milkiness to them, as if he were blind. Or dead. In place of his lips, a golden Mnemo honeybee whirred. Séverin waved at it.

"Well, if you won't tell me that, will you at least tell me where I might find the kitchen?" he asked.

As if on cue, his stomach growled. The man said nothing, but turned and walked some paces down to the half-opened door Séverin had seen the night before. When he stepped inside, Séverin felt a gnawing absence. He was used to the kitchens of L'Eden, bursting with Laila's latest baking experiments. He imagined Enrique and Tristan fighting over the mixing bowl of cake batter, Zofia licking a spoon of white frosting while Laila hollered at all of them to leave her alone for a moment. He expected sugar on the countertops, a jam bubbling on the stove . . . but the kitchens of Casa d'Oro were entirely empty save for a bowl of red apples on a low-lying table. Séverin took a loud bite of one, then pocketed two more.

"I'll wait to break the rest of my fast with Patriarch Ruslan, but in the meantime, I'd like to watch the sunrise," he said. "If you have no objections, you're welcome to join."

Once more, the man said nothing. Séverin walked to the front door. As he did, four more members of the Fallen House seemed to melt from out of the shadows, falling into step behind him.

"A morning entourage," he said. "I am flattered by the company."

"Stop!" called someone loudly.

Séverin turned to see Eva striding toward him. She wore a yellow-silk morning robe that trailed over the red tiles. Around her neck lay that familiar silver pendant in the shape of a ballerina. Eva was the daughter of Mikhail Vasiliev, a St. Petersburg aristocrat, and a dead prima ballerina. Séverin remembered Laila pleading with her about her father . . .

"We can protect you," she had said. *"You don't have to do this . . . we can bring you back to your father and we promise Ruslan will never be able to hurt him."*

He remembered Eva's hesitation, the way her gaze dropped to the ice as Laila pleaded.

"I know you love him," Laila had said. *"I saw it in your necklace. I know you regret that you left his home . . . we can bring you back to him."*

So that was Ruslan's hold on her. If she didn't follow his commands, her father would pay. Séverin tucked that information aside for later.

"What do you think you're doing?" Eva demanded.

"Going out to appreciate the sunrise," he said. "Would you like to join me?"

Eva's gaze narrowed, before her eyes fell to the divine lyre strapped to his side. "You cannot leave with that."

Séverin shrugged. Biting down on the apple again, he removed the lyre from his person and handed it to Eva. Her eyes widened as she took it gingerly in her arms.

"You may keep it safe, then," he said. He grinned. "Though I expect something more protective than just your arms. I've had them around me before, and I can't say I felt very safe."

Eva glared. Wisps of red hair curled around her face. She looked as if she was going to say something, but then her eyes darted to the five Fallen House members mutely surrounding them.

"I intend to make some excursions, so you will have to construct a box for me. Something that opens with a drop of my blood that

can be kept with Ruslan," said Séverin. "I assume that should pose
no difficulties for an artist of your prowess."

Without waiting for Eva to answer, Séverin walked to the
door. After a moment's hesitation, a Fallen House member jerked
forward and opened it for him, and Séverin walked out onto the
dock.

VENICE WORE THE dawn carelessly. To the floating city, riches
were nothing. Gold slipped off the sky and splashed across the lagoon. Across from him, on the other side of the canal, elaborate
homes carved of pale stone and affixed with the grinning faces of
satyrs and unworshipped gods stared at him. Séverin loudly bit
into the apple. He knew he was being watched in secret, and not
just from the guards. He waited a couple of moments before the shy
rasp of slippers confirmed his suspicions.

Some thirty meters away stood the ruins of a neighboring
house. Once, it must have been a grand address, but now it was
covered in scaffolding. The dock beside it looked half-rotted. From
its stingy shadows, an orphaned boy no more than eight years old
regarded him warily. The boy had greasy black hair and his huge,
green eyes stood out in his pale face. Séverin felt an odd chill run
through him. Laila used to make fun of him for walking in the exact opposite direction of a child.

"They won't bite, you know," she'd said. *"You act as if they're terrifying."*

They were, thought Séverin. It wasn't just their epic tantrums,
one instance of which had nearly convinced him to eject a family
from L'Eden simply because they could not corral their child's crying fit. It was that children had no choice but to need the care of
others, and if someone could dangle your needs before you . . . you

were powerless. To look at a child was to glimpse an ugly mirror of his past, and Séverin had no wish to look.

Carefully, he slipped a hand in his pocket and drew out a second apple, holding it out to the boy.

"It's yours if you'd like," he said.

Behind him, concealed in the awning of Casa d'Oro Rosso, the wings of the Mnemo honeybees whirred faster. Ruslan saw everything. Good, thought Séverin. Watch me.

The skinny little boy took a couple of steps forward, then frowned at Séverin.

"*Prendi il primo morso,*" said the boy in a high voice.

Séverin's knowledge of Italian was scant, but he understood: *Take the first bite.* He almost laughed. This child didn't trust him.

Good for you, he thought.

He took a bite of the apple, and held it out to the boy. The boy waited a beat, then blurred forward on his skinny legs, snatching the apple out of his hand.

"*Ora é mio,*" the boy snarled.

It's mine now.

Séverin held up his hands in mock surrender. Without a backward glance, the boy ran back to the ruined house. Séverin watched him go, feeling a touch confused. The boy hadn't acted the way he'd imagined. For a moment, Séverin wondered how he'd ended up in that derelict house. Was the boy alone? Did he have someone?

"Monsieur Montagnet-Alarie," called Eva loudly. "Patriarch Ruslan desires your presence for breakfast."

Eva stood at the entrance, holding out the lyre to him on a red pillow. Two Fallen House members stood on either side. As he walked back, Séverin noticed the bloodred sheen on the door had begun to dull. The docks looked scrubbed clean of any evidence from last night's murder. Séverin did not want to imagine how many days would pass before the entrance to Casa d'Oro needed replenishing.

If all went to plan, he would be far away from here before then.

EVA SILENTLY LED him through the scarlet-paneled halls of Casa d'Oro. Above the threshold of every passageway loomed a six-pointed star enclosed by a golden circle. It was the symbol of the Fallen House, and every time Séverin saw it, he remembered how many years he'd spent turning over that golden ouroboros, the sigil of House Vanth. For so long, he thought the House was his to inherit, but his true birthright was so much more than he imagined. Séverin ran his thumb down the glimmering strands of the lyre. When he touched it, sometimes he imagined a woman's voice low in his ear . . . murmuring something to him that sounded like a warning and a song.

Eva paused at the threshold of the fourth passageway. Here, that smell of fresh earth he had caught last evening grew stronger, and the sound of wings grew louder.

"What do you think you're doing?" hissed Eva, under her breath.

Séverin raised an eyebrow. "I assume 'watching and waiting with bated breath for my apotheosis' is not the answer you're looking for."

"Your friends," said Eva. "I . . . I don't understand."

"You don't?" said Séverin. "Perhaps we might put the question to Patriarch Ruslan. I'm certain he'd find your interest in my dead friends very intriguing."

For a moment, something pained flashed in Eva's eyes. Her hand flew to her necklace before she dropped it abruptly. Séverin kept his face blank. When he said nothing, Eva stepped away and held back the curtain, her eyes full of anger.

"He will be with you shortly," she said in a flat voice. "I will work on the lockbox for the lyre immediately."

"Good," said Séverin, smiling.

Just before she let the curtain fall, Eva caught his gaze. "Be sure you know how to play."

When she had left, Séverin saw that Eva had left him in a conservatory. Séverin stilled. For a moment, he couldn't breathe. He could not remember the last time he had willingly stepped foot into a greenhouse. Even on L'Eden's grounds, he had ripped out the rose canes Tristan had once tended and salted the earth so they could never grow back. Unbidden came the memory of his brother walking toward him, a flower blooming in his hand, his tarantula, Goliath, perched on his shoulder. Séverin tightened his grip on the divine lyre, letting the metallic wires dig into the skin of his palm. This was the instrument of the divine, and it was *his* . . . his alone to use, his alone to remake the world as he saw fit.

I can fix this, Séverin told himself. *I can fix it all*.

Minutes later, he opened his eyes. Eva's last words echoed in his thoughts. *Be sure you know how to play*. The boy killed in front of him yesterday . . . now the conservatory. Ruslan was deliberately taunting him with echoes of Tristan.

Séverin set his jaw as he stared around the chamber. It was half the size of L'Eden's grand lobby. The walls were draped in ivy, and the vaulted glass ceiling overhead let in the early-morning sunshine. A white-graveled pathway wound its way to a bloodred door on the far side of the room, where Ruslan would no doubt be waiting for him.

There was something odd about the conservatory. He recognized some of the plants from Tristan's gardening . . . milk-white datura and nightshade the color of fresh bruises. A trellis of lavender skullcap flowers bloomed on his left. On his right stood blush-colored foxgloves, and near the entrance of the other room, a stately horse chestnut cast a shade over the chamber. A faint headache brewed at the back of his skull, and Séverin understood what this place was.

A poison garden.

Tristan had kept a miniature version of one years ago, and had only stopped because of edicts from French officials that they could not cultivate fatal flora on the hotel premises. Séverin remembered how furious Tristan had been when he was told he needed to uproot the plants.

"But they're not *deadly*," Tristan had pouted. "Some of these have wonderful medicinal properties! Everyone uses castor oil, and no one seems to mind that it comes from *ricinus communis*, which is highly toxic! *You* have used skullcap and were completely fine."

"At the time, you didn't tell me you'd given me a poisonous flower," Séverin had said.

Tristan had only flashed a sheepish grin.

Séverin looked at the skullcap blooms. Years ago, he had needed to conceal himself in a small cabinet, and to avoid detection from any Forged heartbeat-seeking creature, Tristan had given him a tincture of skullcap.

Be sure you know how to play.

On impulse, Séverin ripped off one of the skullcap blooms and tucked it into his pocket. Ruslan might be insane, but he was still clever, and if he had placed poison outside the room where they would meet, Séverin couldn't fathom what venom waited for him inside.

Just then, the door swung open. Ruslan stepped into the garden. He was dressed in a plain black suit, the sleeves rolled up so as not to hide the molten skin of his left arm.

"Come in, my friend, come in," he said, smiling. "How hungry you must be."

Séverin joined him. Inside, Séverin understood the source of the rustling wings he'd heard the night before. The dining room was filled with Forged animal creations. Glass ravens roosted on the chandelier. Stained-crystal hummingbirds zipped across his line of sight. A marvelous peacock trailed its plumage of garnets and emeralds, the sound of its translucent feathers like chiming bells. The table was smoked glass, and laid out with steaming dishes: eggs baked in roasted tomatoes, frittata flecked with chili, *fette biscottate*, and golden cups filled with dark coffee.

"This was my father's favorite interrogation room," said Ruslan, warmly patting his glass chair. "In here, no one could hide a thing."

"Intriguing," said Séverin, careful to keep his tone bored. "How so?"

He reached for his chair when he felt it . . . a faint electrical current coursing through the glass. When he touched the table, the same feeling followed. The furniture was reading him . . . but for what?

"The room has its ways," said Ruslan, grinning at him.

Séverin remembered the skullcap in his pocket. He had no idea whether the Forged table worked anything like the heartbeat-seeking creatures from his acquisition years ago, but it was all he had. While Ruslan helped himself to coffee and food, Séverin ripped off two petals, feigned a cough, and swallowed them whole.

"I saw you feed a little street urchin today," said Ruslan. "Do you like the boy? We can keep him for you, if you'd like. I've never had a pet, but I imagine it's quite the same . . . He's perhaps a little too stubborn, but we could fix that."

From his sleeve, Ruslan drew out his Midas Knife and tapped the side of his forehead, grinning.

"A superstition, I must confess," said Séverin. "Feed another before yourself and you will never go hungry. Besides, I intend to be a benevolent god."

Ruslan lowered the knife, considering this. "I like this idea . . . *benevolence*. What excellent deities we shall make, eh?"

Ruslan held out his coffee cup, clanging it to Séverin's. Séverin waited a moment before he cleared his throat.

"I find myself eager for my apotheosis, don't you?" said Séverin, reaching for a bit of tart. "We could get the map to Poveglia as soon as you'd like. Tonight, even."

The moment he said it, Séverin knew he had made a mistake. Ruslan paused, regarding him over the rim of his coffee cup. When he lowered it, the grin on his face was uncannily knowing.

"But I'm *happy* here," said Ruslan, with a slight whine. "I don't want to go through any muck just yet . . . we can play and relax and whatnot."

Ruslan speared a piece of egg. A sparrow of black-and-white quartz alighted near his plate, cheeping. Ruslan lowered his fork and held out his hand. The glass bird hopped onto it.

"Let us leave in *ten* days, hmm?" said Ruslan.

A spot of cold opened up in Séverin's heart. Ten days . . . Laila already had only nine left.

"Poor Laila," said Ruslan, crooning to the bird. "She went *on and on* about how she only had ten days left, and now I find the number quite stuck in my thoughts. I assume you have no objections?"

Séverin felt a faint electrical current through his sleeve. Ruslan was seeking something . . . some sign, perhaps, that Séverin cared more than he let on. He took a deep breath, willing his heart to slow. To *calm*.

"None at all," said Séverin. "It will make our apotheosis that much sweeter."

Ruslan stroked the sparrow's glass head with his golden fingers.

"I quite agree. Besides, I know Laila has no way of finding us, but I'd feel better knowing she's well and truly—"

He slammed his hand down. The glass sparrow exploded on the table. A corner of its wing stirred feebly, as if the machine was caught by surprise.

"Dead," said Ruslan, smiling.

7

ZOFIA

Zofia struck the match and watched the little flame seize hungrily upon the wood. The smell of sulfur stinging the air calmed her as she lowered the flame to the candle and surveyed her latest piece of work—a length of metal thinly hammered to the flexibility of a cloth that could ignite on command.

She felt as safe as possible in the matriarch's house, but she knew a time would come when they had to emerge. And when that time came, she'd be ready.

The Fallen House assumed they were dead, but if they found her and her friends, they would turn that assumption into a reality. And they weren't only in danger from the Fallen House. Hypnos's secret contact with House Nyx confirmed that the Order was making inquiries and investigations into the events that had followed the Winter Conclave. If a Sphinx authority got hold of them, they could be arrested, and with only a week left of Laila's life, all their plans would be for nothing.

It had been two days since they had found the address and key to the matriarch's safe house.

"This house better be beautiful because I am not leaving it under *any* circumstances," Hypnos had declared.

When they had pushed open the peeling, wooden door marked 77 on Calle Tron Strada, they found a small, but richly appointed house. Hypnos had explored first, leaving them on the threshold. When he found neither hidden trap nor adversaries lying in wait, he smiled widely, his eyes appearing bright and glossy.

"It's exactly as the matriarch promised," he said.

Inside were several bedchambers, a drawing room with an elegant piano which Hypnos immediately played, a kitchen that Laila instantly perused for ingredients, a vast library littered with strange contraptions along the walls which Enrique had disappeared inside—and, right across from the library, a small room where Zofia might Forge.

It was the smallest suite, with whitewashed walls, a small skylight, and a long, steel workbench. The tools that covered one of the walls were out of date, but serviceable nonetheless. Zofia had immediately run her hands over the glass lathe, the wire cutters, the dusty jars of saltpeter and nitrate, vials of potassium chloride and ammonia, stacks of matchboxes, and the scraps of metal lining the walls. The moment she touched the sheets of iron and aluminum, she could feel the metal within reaching out to read her will . . . Did she want it to bend? To sharpen? To hold fire in its structure?

The touch of the metal eased a tight, coiling sensation that had been building inside her ever since they had left Lake Baikal. All this time, she felt as if she had been walking through the dark, aware that her eyes were wide open, and aware that it made no difference at all. Every step brought her deeper into unknowable territory, so she could not begin to guess or trust what lay ahead.

That was the problem with the dark.

Once, Zofia had accidentally locked herself in her family's cellar. Hela and her parents had gone to the market, and Zofia, frightened, had clutched the first thing she felt: a length of silken fur. It wasn't until Hela had found her and the lantern light spilled over the wooden walls that Zofia saw what she had held so close: a skinless pelt, the creature's head and paws still dangling from what remained of it.

Zofia had thrown it from her immediately, but she would never forget how the dark had tricked her. She hated how it made even the strange turn familiar and the familiar turn strange. As a child, her fear sometimes grew so great that she would crawl into bed beside Hela.

"You are frightened of nothing, Zosia," her sister would mumble sleepily. *"It cannot hurt you."*

Scientifically, Zofia understood this. The dark was nothing more than the absence of light. But these past few weeks, it had also taken on a different absence. The absence of knowing.

It gnawed at her constantly. The only time she did not feel it was when she Forged, and so Zofia threw herself into work. While the others searched for clues regarding the map that would take them to the temple beneath Poveglia, Zofia created invention after invention. She had counted at least a dozen members of the Fallen House at the Sleeping Palace. Each had been equipped with two short-range explosives and two throwing knives. Whether they had other properties, she could not determine, and so she knew her inventions must account for the unknown. For the past day or so, Zofia had built seven miniature explosives, constructed four coiled ropes that could fit in the heel of a shoe, and chewed her way through five matchboxes.

Zofia was putting the finishing touches on the Forged cloth when Laila knocked at the door.

"Phoenix you might be, but you must subsist on something other than flames," said Laila, placing a platter before her.

Zofia scanned its contents: meats and cheeses spaced far apart, and a row of tomatoes neatly dividing the plate. On a separate plate was a dish of olive oil and sliced bread. Her stomach growled loudly, and Zofia reached for the bread—

Laila tutted. "Manners."

Zofia frowned then held out her hand. Laila handed her a napkin. The napkin did nothing to the grease stains on her hands, but Zofia knew Laila liked ceremony.

"You don't have to eat in here," said Laila gently.

"I want to," said Zofia, tearing into the bread. "It maximizes efficiency."

"Would it be so bad to step outside for some sunlight?" asked Laila.

"It would be unnecessary, as I am not a plant and do not need to photosynthesize to sustain myself," said Zofia.

"Well, I may partake in some photosynthesizing this afternoon if you care to join me."

"No," said Zofia, before adding, "thank you."

She cared more about other things, like preparing items for whatever awaited them in Poveglia.

"As you wish," said Laila, smiling.

Zofia noticed her friend's smile did not reach her eyes. Ever since they had arrived here from Isola di San Michele, Laila had grown more silent. When Zofia had gone to bed last night, she saw Laila standing in the drawing room, rubbing her thumb against her palm over and over. In the mornings when they broke their fast, Laila would stare at the ring on her hand. Zofia glanced at it now: *Eight*.

Even though she was sitting, Zofia felt as if she had just tripped.

Eight days left, and far too much left unknown.

"I must work," said Zofia.

She gestured her hands at her workbench, her breaths rising tight and fast inside her.

"Phoenix?" said Laila softly. Zofia looked up and saw her friend's warm, brown gaze assessing her. "Thank you. I appreciate all that you are doing."

Zofia ate hurriedly and returned to her work, but no matter what she did, there was still that stumbling sensation. As if she were blindly finding her way in utter darkness. It was not just Laila's dwindling days that pressed on her thoughts. All the time, she felt Hela's letter against her skin. Seven times a day, Zofia allowed herself to take out the letter and smooth her hands over the creased envelope. It felt worn and soft to the touch, not unlike the grisly pelt in the cellar. The only difference between them was that this time Zofia chose not to know whether it held death.

"Why aren't you scared of the dark?" Zofia had once asked her sister.

Hela turned toward her in the night. Even though she could not see Hela's gray eyes, Zofia knew they were open.

"Because I know I just have to wait a little while, and then the light will come back," said Hela, reaching out to stroke her hair. "It always comes back."

"What if you get lost in the dark?" Zofia had asked, curling closer to her.

She did not like to be touched, but Hela was soft and warm and knew not to hold her too closely.

"I would do the same thing, sister . . . I would wait for the light to show me the paths before me. And then I would not be so lost."

Alone, Zofia pressed her hands to her heart, thinking of Hela and Laila. Whatever lay inside the envelope held a variable that could not be changed. But Laila's fate was dependent upon elements Zofia could still control. It was not unlike being lost in the dark. All she had to do was work and wait, and eventually, when the light came . . . she would be able to see the path before her.

"PHOENIX."

Bleary-eyed, Zofia looked up from her workbench to see Enrique standing in the archway. A low thrum of heat coursed through her belly at the sight of him. He had lost an ear, but his effect on her when she was unguarded remained the same. Zofia studied him, annoyed. Was it the curious sheen of iridescence to his black hair? The inky depth of his eyes or the prominence of his cheekbones?

For the past two days, she had caught glimpses of Enrique working in the library. Enrique was never still. He hummed. He tapped his foot. He thrummed his fingers along the spines of books.

All of this should have annoyed her, but instead, it made her feel less lonely.

"Phoenix . . . did I disturb you?" asked Enrique, stepping inside. He surveyed her workbench, his eyes widening. "You have enough for a small army."

Zofia regarded her inventions. "I have enough for, perhaps, fifteen people."

"You do realize we are a company of five individuals."

Zofia frowned. "We do not know what waits for us in Poveglia."

Enrique smiled. "Precisely what I wished to talk to you about.

Would you mind waiting in the library? I'll fetch Laila and join you in a moment."

Zofia nodded, pushing her chair. Her back ached, and her eyes burned as she stepped from the dimly lit laboratory and walked across the hall to the library. Hypnos met her by promptly bursting into song.

"Ah, my fair and feral muse!" he sang, before speaking: "How goes your cultivation of destruction?"

Zofia remembered Enrique's wide eyes.

"Productive," she said. "Potentially excessive."

She found herself smiling as she took a seat on a high stool beside him. Hypnos always seemed able to make people smile. Although, lately, Enrique did not seem to smile at him. It was different from how they had been at the Sleeping Palace, which only added to the confusing darkness of her thoughts. She remembered watching them kiss, and the way they had melted against each other. There were moments when she imagined herself in Hypnos's place. But simply because they were no longer attached did not mean that Enrique would ever want to do that with her. Ideas had no physical mass, but Zofia felt the thought like a stone thudding in her stomach.

"You and Enrique have been so preoccupied," said Hypnos. "Meanwhile, I've tuned a piano and sang bawdy songs to the shadows. They are a very cold sort of audience. No applause whatsoever."

Zofia looked around the library. It was a small room with low ceilings, four chairs for sitting, and two long tables. The only illumination came from eight rose-shaped sconces in the joints where the ceiling met the wall. All across the walls stood shelves crowded with books or paintings, statue busts, and maps. On one wall stood a large, gilded mirror. Zofia glanced down at her necklace, but her two remaining Tezcat pendants did not light up, which meant it was probably nothing more than a mirror. On one of the tables stood a teetering stack of papers that could only belong to Enrique. A still-dripping quill lay balanced across an unstoppered jar of ink. Beside it stood a small, ivory bust of a god with two heads, one facing in either direction. Zofia remembered the deity from the graveyard. Janus, he was called. The god of time.

"Good," said Enrique, walking into the room with Laila on his arm. "We're all here."

Laila was oddly still as she settled into a nearby chair. Her brows were pulled down, her mouth looked thin. Zofia recognized that she was concerned.

"What's the good news, *mon cher*?" asked Hypnos.

Zofia noticed his voice was a little more high-pitched. He sat up straight, flashing a wide smile at Enrique. Enrique did not acknowledge or return the smile.

"Good . . . and bad," said Enrique, strolling forward. He walked to the middle of the room and faced them. "I believe I know where the map to the temple in Poveglia is being kept."

Laila's eyes widened. "Where?"

"For a while, I thought it would be here . . . somewhere . . . tucked in all these books and research," said Enrique, gesturing to the library. "It is sensitive information, and so the matriarch might have concealed its whereabouts somewhere on these premises. But now I believe the map is in the possession of House Janus."

"House Janus?" asked Laila, frowning. "I am not familiar with them."

"*I* am," grumbled Hypnos. He crossed his arms. "Like I said before—if anyone *bothered* to listen—they are a faction of the Italian Order who throw an *exceptional* party for Carnevale and have never once invited me—"

"They are renowned," said Enrique loudly, "for their collection of Forged cartographical and nautical objects, which, according to the documents in this library, take most unusual shapes. For example, many of them are priceless and mind Forged."

"A mind Forged *map*?" repeated Laila.

Zofia was familiar with the idea of the art form, but it was a very temporary and dangerous art. The idea that an object could retain the implanted memory of its artist over centuries was a degree of skill that had long been considered lost.

"I don't know the specifics of its location," said Enrique. "But I believe that's where we'll find it."

"How?" asked Hypnos. "The location of House Janus supposedly changes each year. The only time anybody ever sees that reclusive House is during a secret Carnevale. Otherwise, they consider themselves guardians of their treasure and never bother to auction it off or interact with the other Houses."

"Carnevale is two days from now."

"What is Carnevale?" asked Zofia.

"It's a celebration," said Enrique.

"I wouldn't know," said Hypnos bitterly.

Enrique cleared his throat. "It all started in the twelfth century."

"Here we go," muttered Hypnos.

Zofia knew that others found Enrique long-winded, but she liked listening to him. Enrique saw the world differently, and sometimes when he taught her something new, it was as if the world had changed ever so slightly.

"It's thought to have originated as a celebration over Venice's enemy, the Aquileia," said Enrique. "People used to gather in the streets wearing elaborate masks designed to disguise an individual's class and rank, so that all might join in the revelries. Eventually it became part of the celebrations for Lent, but it was outlawed about a hundred years ago by the Holy Roman Emperor, and so it can only be celebrated off-season and in secret, and the place to go is—"

"House Janus," said Hypnos. "Though you need a special—"

"Mask," finished Enrique.

He reached for the papers on the long table, holding up two illustrations of a Venetian mask. It had an odd design, the nose long and curved like a bird's beak. The eyeholes were circular. The other sketch showed a checkered black-and-white mask outlined in glitter that would be held up by two long, black ribbons.

"*This* is how we find an invitation to House Janus's Carnevale," said Enrique. "Hypnos? Care to explain?"

"Supposedly, there is a place where one receives such invitation," said Hypnos, picking at an invisible speck on his pants. "A *mascherari* salon, I'm told. Inside, one may pick their specific mask, and when it is held to one's face, it reveals the party's location through mind Forging, and then you must go to said location in all your finery and drink and dance the night away etcetera etcetera."

Zofia frowned. "That is too many instructions to attend a party."

"I know," sighed Hypnos. "It's all so dreadfully enigmatic, I can't help but be lured. Its exclusivity taunts me."

"But you said Carnevale is two days from now," said Laila, slowly turning the ring on her hand. "And we have no idea where to begin with finding this *mascherari* salon."

"No," said Enrique, before he looked around the room. "But I think the information is hidden here. The matriarch told Hypnos that the safe house would have everything we need to find the map."

"What about Séverin?" asked Hypnos.

Enrique's mouth pinched. "What about him?"

"We were supposed to meet and figure out what to do next.

How will he know what we're doing if we don't even know where to meet him?"

"Séverin needs to find the map for himself," said Enrique, scowling. "He'll do that with or without us, and our paths will either cross at Carnevale or in Poveglia. Trust me. He won't miss the opportunity for a power grab."

Hypnos frowned, but he stayed quiet. Zofia looked at Laila. Her friend seemed distant as she cradled her jeweled hand against her. The longer Zofia looked at her, the more she realized that she was not the only one stuck in the dark. Laila, for all her smiles, walked through it too. Séverin, wherever he was, had no idea that they had lost the meeting point. Hypnos's expressions suggested confusion, and even Enrique's plans carried much unknown.

In that second, Zofia remembered her mother sitting beside the fire. She had tilted up Zofia's chin, her watery blue eyes shining. *Be a light in this world, my Zosia, for it can be very dark.* Zofia had not forgotten her mother's words, and she was determined to embody them.

"We will find the map," said Zofia. "Solving a problem requires a piece-by-piece approach, and that is what we are doing."

Laila looked up at her, a soft smile curving her lips. Hypnos nodded. Even Enrique flashed a small smile. A rare feeling of calm centered Zofia. For her friends . . . for herself . . . Zofia would find a way out of the dark.

8

SÉVERIN

At dawn, Séverin stood by the docks and turned an apple over in his hand. In the astrology room at L'Eden, he had kept a bowl of apples on the low table. Once, early on, when Enrique had demanded food during the discussion of a new acquisition, Séverin gestured at the bowl of apples and said, "Help yourself."

Enrique had looked appalled. "Apples are hopelessly boring, either too sweet or too sour."

"It will satisfy your appetite for a time."

"*Or* it shall tempt me to abandon this intellectual endeavor entirely in pursuit of *real* food," said Enrique. "It is the fruit of temptation, after all. Eve tempting Adam into sin and such."

As if to demonstrate, Enrique had placed a red apple in his mouth and raised his eyebrows suggestively at Laila, Zofia, Tristan, and Séverin, who were seated across from him. Tristan grimaced. Laila bit back a laugh, and Zofia tilted her head to the side. "I saw a similar pose last night on the banquet table."

Enrique spat out the apple. "That was a roasted pig!"

Zofia shrugged. "The pose is identical."

"*Focus*," Séverin had said. "We need to think about this next acquisition—"

"Thinking requires better incentive than an apple."

"Like cake?" suggested Laila.

Séverin remembered how she had reclined on her favorite green settee. She'd plucked an apple from the bowl and stroked its shiny peel, and his mouth had gone oddly dry at the sight.

"Definitely cake," said Enrique.

"And cookies," added Zofia.

Séverin had given up. He shook his head, and such began the tradition of Laila baking, pushing in a cart piled high with sugary treats every time they started to plan a project.

Now, Séverin stared at the apple, bemused. He wanted to annoy Enrique with the fruit. He wanted to hold it up to Laila's lips and compare their colors. Temptation, indeed, he thought, lowering the apple. When Tristan had died, Séverin had tried to isolate himself from his friends, and he thought he'd succeeded.

But he was wrong.

Even if he was cruel, even if he was cold . . . at least they had been near. At least he could catch the ghost of Laila's perfume in the hallways, hear the clanging of Zofia's Forging, smell the ink from Enrique's endless letters to the Ilustrados, stare out at the gardens where Tristan had once walked.

One more day, thought Séverin.

One more day until he could see them . . . and tell them what?

He had made a mistake with Ruslan, and now he was bleeding time . . . time that Laila couldn't afford to lose. Séverin felt the loss of every hour as if it had been forcibly ripped from him.

Without the Forged map, they could wander Poveglia for years and never find the hidden entrance to the temple. And even if there was some other way to discover it, Séverin had not found a way to be rid of him. The patriarch of the Fallen House was never alone. No food passed his lips without a Fallen House member confirming its safety. Daily draws from Eva rendered him immune from blood Forging.

Séverin was turning over those thoughts when he heard the shuffle of small feet some distance away. The orphaned boy from yesterday stepped out of the shadows. Behind him stood a smaller, even more ragged child. His hair was dirty blond, and his hazel eyes looked like dimmed lanterns in his face. The first boy held out his arm, as if shielding the other one.

"*Un altro,*" said the first boy, sticking out his hand.

Another one.

Séverin grinned. He tossed an apple to the child, who caught it one-handed, then he removed another from his pocket and tossed it over too. The first boy immediately bit into it, before offering the second to his companion. After a moment of glaring at Séverin from the shadows, he muttered a quick "*grazi*" and fled.

Séverin watched them go, before stepping back into Casa d'Oro.

Inside, Eva waited beside the door in a high-necked scarlet gown the color of blood. The silver ballerina pendant was tucked away. Around her waist she kept a jeweled knife. Three members of the Fallen House in their *volto* masks stood against the walls, their Mnemo honeybees whirring and watching.

"Here," said Eva, thrusting out a box. "But before it can be used, it is missing something."

"Which is?" asked Séverin.

Eva reached for his hand. Her taloned pinky ring winked in the light before she slashed it down the top of his hand. Séverin sucked in his breath, glaring at her, but Eva didn't seem to notice. She traced a complicated sigil in blood over the box, whispering something.

At first glance, the box seemed delicate, like something from a children's book. Forged of ice roses and twisting vines. A thorn jutted out from its clasp. A faint blush tinge rose from its base.

"Now it will know you by your blood," said Eva. "Try it."

Séverin took the box. He pulled at the edges, but it wouldn't budge. Atop the clasp was a little thorn. When he dragged his thumb across it, he felt a sharp sting as the metal broke skin and drew blood. One drop was all it took. The thorn accepted it readily, and that faint blush spread across the box as it sprang open to reveal the divine lyre nesting on a blue velvet pillow.

Séverin removed the lyre gently. The plan he had been turning over in his head all night slowly took shape. He met Eva's eyes. "You look very beautiful today."

Eva startled. Behind her, the Mnemo honeybees on the masks whirred louder. Good. He had caught Ruslan's attention. Eva's face was shrouded from view, but Séverin was fully visible.

He looked at Eva's green eyes, imagining a pair of cygnet-black eyes in their place. When her lips flattened, Séverin conjured a different image—a lush mouth shaped to drive poets to distraction. Eva tugged at her red hair, and Séverin pretended it was a fall of ink flecked with sugar.

He reached out, his knuckles brushing against her jawline. "Very beautiful indeed."

BEFORE SÉVERIN ENTERED the formal dining hall, he nibbled on the edge of the skullcap bloom he had stolen from the poison garden. After yesterday's breakfast, Ruslan had avoided him completely. Séverin knew why. His own eagerness had betrayed him. Ruslan might be unhinged, but he was no fool, and perhaps he suspected that even now, Séverin was only acting in the interests of his friends. He must be careful. He needed to hide his intentions and change Ruslan's ridiculous timeline to act in ten days . . . otherwise Laila would be dead.

Séverin took a deep breath, then walked through the Tezcat door camouflaged as a painting of an old god with a melting face. On the other side, the formal dining room looked like a vision of blood and honey. A long, black marble table rose like a solid block from the middle of the room. The walls were a lattice of interlocking golden stars against red velvet fabric. Candles shaped like long-stemmed, black roses burned and melted on the table. At the center, a carafe of red wine stood beside a plate of cut fruits and thin slices of marbled meat. Usually, the golden plates were already heaped with food, but this time they were empty. At the center of the table he noticed a slender, glass vial no taller than his pinky. Séverin picked it up. A smokey, clouded substance moved freely within the glass.

"An added sensory experience for our dining," said Ruslan, stepping into the room. He wore a dark suit that only made the golden skin of his arm gleam brighter. "*Do* try it."

Séverin hesitated. It was obviously mind Forged, but to what purpose? Conjure nightmares to force out the truth or—

"Oh, come now!" Ruslan pouted. "We are friends. And friendship requires trust. Surely you trust me?"

Séverin forced a smile and then unstoppered the glass. Wisps of smoke emptied out of the bottle, dissolving into the air. Séverin braced himself, but even then, he was unprepared for what awaited him. It was an art form of mind Forging, the likes of which he had never known. He was familiar with exquisite illusions, but this place was *real*. And *old*. Séverin was dimly aware that he was standing in a dining room in Venice . . .

But his senses claimed otherwise.

Before him, he saw the lush foliage of an ancient jungle. The ground beneath his feet squelched. All around him, the jungle boasted exotic blooms the color of melted jewels. Moths the size of dinner plates with dappled wings flitted around him. That sharp smell of grass filled his lungs, and the lullabies of jewel-bright birds engulfed him. Séverin reached out to touch a flower. He could see the dew beading on the leaf. He could almost feel the satiny petal against his skin when the vision vanished—

When he blinked, it was not a petal he had nearly touched, but Ruslan's face, now centimeters from his own.

"Boo." He grinned.

Séverin stumbled backwards.

"Ah, my friend, the wonder transfixing your eyes!" said Ruslan, clapping his hands. "You looked like a hero from a poem. All dashing and mournful and whatnot . . ."

"What was that?" asked Séverin. His voice came out harsher than he'd planned.

"Mind Forging, as well you know," said Ruslan, taking his seat.

"That is unlike any mind Forging I have ever come across," said Séverin.

Even the most beautiful mind Forging illusions always had a tell . . . a flimsiness to their edges or a fragrance that did not fit. This, however, had been as seamless as knowledge. In fact, Séverin had the uncanny realization that if he were to cross the ocean by several hundred miles, he would know exactly where he would find such a paradise.

"It is a real place," said Ruslan, taking a long sip of his wine. "And you have now witnessed its exquisite map."

Séverin's mind snagged on that word: *Map*. It was a hint, he was sure of it. Was it possible that the map to the temple beneath Poveglia could appear in such a form? Was it a sign that Ruslan was finally ready to tell him where to go? Or was it just another game?

Séverin sank into his dining chair, reaching for his wine, when Ruslan snatched his hand and turned it over.

"You know . . . when I impersonated the patriarch of House Dazbog, I cut off his arm and it worked perfectly," said Ruslan, thoughtful. "Perhaps I could do the same with you, and then the divine lyre would answer to me? I only need your hand. I have no use for the rest of you."

Séverin kept his hand still. Ruslan's mind did not function like others. What did he want? Séverin's mind turned back to all the times Ruslan had shown him a new Forging tool or tried to get his attention. *He wants to play*, he realized. Séverin grinned, then wiggled his fingers. "Shall we try it?"

Ruslan picked up his Midas Knife, tapping the point on Séverin's palm. "We could."

"It would be a boring indulgence, though," said Séverin. He was careful not to betray a tremble in his fingers.

"Boring?" repeated Ruslan.

"You already remarked at the wonder in my face," said Séverin. "Wouldn't you like to see it again when I behold you in all your divine raiments and glory? Wouldn't you rather *we* converse than the dull members of your House, who are far more like chattel than companions? If not, then you are not as interesting as I'd hoped. How disappointing. If so, take my arm, cut my throat, and spare me the boredom."

"That was rude of you, Séverin," complained Ruslan, withdrawing the knife. "My feelings are wounded."

Séverin slowly withdrew his hand, watching the patriarch.

Upon being called boring, Ruslan's countenance had changed. He speared a piece of cheese and angrily shoved it in his mouth.

"Forgive my little joke," said Séverin. "Your conversation is endlessly amusing, as always. I am, however, finding the days a bit tedious . . . would it not be—"

Ruslan turned his head slowly. He smiled, but it was a closed-mouth grin, like a child on the verge of denying he'd stuffed his face with forbidden sweets. A flash of acidic panic seized Séverin.

"Ten days," said Ruslan primly. "And don't forget, Monsier Montagnet-Alarie . . . I get bored too, and perhaps you will not always like what I find diverting."

Séverin feigned indifference. Just then, a door near the back of the room opened. Eva entered, holding a vial of blood Forging liquid. Ruslan clapped his hands eagerly.

"Mine, mine, mine," he sang, then licked his lips. "Juicy, sweet protection, though I do detest the regularity of it all. Once a day keeps the liars away . . ."

Ruslan held out his wrist. A faint sneer curled on Eva's lips as she flicked her taloned ring across his skin. Blood beaded at the wound, and she collected it in her vial. She held it tight for a few moments. The blood darkened by a few degrees. When Eva emptied out the vial, the molecules rose into the air, twisting like an image of spilling ink centimeters away from Ruslan's nose. Ruslan cocked his head, and then he leaned forward, snapping at the Forged blood like a creature eating something out of the air.

Blood spatter flecked his mouth.

He grinned, tonguing the corners of his mouth and cheeks. "It won't be necessary when we're gods, will it? No need for protections from deception . . . I'll make sure of it." Ruslan grinned up at Eva. "Though I don't know what I'll do with you. Maybe I'll eat you."

Eva's face paled as she set the vial back on its tray. It trembled in her grip. Séverin waited until she was nearly at the door before he spoke.

"Ruslan, I hope you do not take offense when I tell you that I am lately deprived of beauty."

Ruslan moaned and tapped his bald pate. "I have no delusions regarding my looks, sadly."

"I fancied I might take the lovely Eva on a gondola ride this evening."

Eva stilled, looking between Ruslan and Séverin. Ruslan chewed thoughtfully on a piece of fruit before shrugging.

"I have no objections," said Ruslan.

"*I do*," said Eva loudly. "I don't want to go anywhere with him—"

Ruslan laughed. "Silly Eva. You know how I find your outbursts charming, but if you do it again, I will bring your father and kill him in front of you." His voice was calm. Warm, even, in a way that brought goose bumps to Séverin's skin. "And after that, I'll fill your mouth with burning embers to scald all those *fiery* outbursts away."

Eva paled. She turned to Séverin. "I would be honored to accompany you this evening."

Séverin felt a little ill watching the exchange. Eva had betrayed them, yes, but she was trapped too.

Are you any different? a voice inside him hissed. *The things you've done to the people you claimed to love . . .*

Séverin pushed aside the voice, summoning a grin. "Excellent."

AN HOUR LATER, Séverin sat in the gondola of the Fallen House, a Forged black-lacquered boat that required no gondolier. The sigil

of the Fallen House appeared on the side. On the prow, a honeybee clicked its metal wings. It could watch them, but it could not
hear them. Even so, Séverin kept his back to it. From the docks, a
member of the Fallen House watched him silently. Clutched in his
hands lay the lyre within its blood Forged box.

"I thought we could see the famous *Ponte dei Sospiri*," said Séverin
as the boat glided into the water.

Eva said nothing. She stroked the scabbard that held her jeweled knife. "I promised you company, but—"

"Company is all I expect," said Séverin. "Conversation is op-
tional."

They passed the next half hour in silence. The watery thorough-
fares of Venice were alive tonight. Lovers cozied up, lost in one another. When they kissed, their Forged boats—carved in the shapes
of floating roses or cleverly sculpted hands—closed up around
them, hiding them completely from sight.

Up ahead, an intricate bridge arched over the waters of the Rio
di Palazzo. The white stonework was a marvel in itself—spirals
crested along the top of the fully enclosed bridge like sea waves,
and along the bottom arch appeared ten faces wearing expressions
of horror and fear. Only one face smiled. Two small windows, both
netted over in marble, regarded them solemnly as they passed beneath it.

"It's aptly named, is it not?" asked Séverin, gesturing to the
bridge and the palatial buildings that it connected.

Eva looked unimpressed. "I do not speak Italian."

"*Ponte dei Sospiri* means the Bridge of Sighs," said Séverin. "It
connects the new prison on our left and the interrogation rooms of
the Doge's Palace on our right. For a doomed man walking across
the bridge to the prison, those windows held his last sight. And

what a sight it must have been . . . certainly worthy of a sigh or two."

"What do you want?" asked Eva sharply.

Séverin reached for her hand. Behind him, that was all the Mnemo bug would see: two young people with their heads bent together and their hands clasped.

"I can help you," he whispered.

Eva's green eyes blazed. "I will not be dragged from one man's mercy to another. Least of all *you*. Do you expect me to trust you after you killed them? They were . . . *good* . . . people."

Séverin held Eva's gaze. "And if I told you they were safe?"

Eva paused. "How?"

"Does it matter so long as it is true?"

Eva released his hand. "Only if you can prove it."

"Tomorrow," said Séverin. "One, or all of them, I don't know, will meet me at the Bridge of Sighs at midnight. It's all planned. We can get you out."

Eva's mouth twisted. "And how do you know they will come for you, Monsieur? You may not have killed them, but even I could see that how you treated them was a death of its own."

Séverin sat back, the words buzzing in his skull. Eva was wrong. They would understand . . . they would give him one more chance. Wouldn't they?

As the gondola slipped through the water, Séverin regarded the inky lagoon beneath them. It seemed alive. A hungry thing that swallowed the reflections of cathedrals and *palazzos*, lapped up stone archways and chewed off the faces of angels carved into the frames.

The water fed upon the city.

Séverin leaned away from his reflection in the black surface.

For a moment, the canal seemed to mock him, whispering to him in the dark.

My belly holds the bones of empires. I've eaten sighs, and I've eaten angels, and one day I'll eat you too.

9

ENRIQUE

Enrique touched his bandage gingerly. In the three days since he'd lost his ear, the pain had subsided to a low ache. He traced the strange new flatness against his skull, the little nub of scabbing skin where his ear had once been attached. As a child, he had been willing to give up his ear. Eager, even. For he thought it meant that his dreams would come true. When he was nine years old, he'd even gone so far as taking a knife to his earlobe before his mother caught him and started shrieking.

"Why would you do such a thing?" she had demanded.

"For the trade!" Enrique had replied. "For the *enkantos*!"

His mother had not been impressed, and she had promptly complained to his grandmother, who only laughed. After that, his mother forbid his *lola* from telling him more tales, but the very next day, Enrique crept to her side and sat by her feet and tugged at her long, white *baro*.

"Tell me a story," he begged.

And she did. His *lola* used to tell him tales of the *enkantos* in the banana groves, their long fingers parting the shining leaves and their wide eyes aglow in the dusk. Even though she wore a cross around her neck and never missed mass on Sundays, his grandmother never forgot the *enkantos* outside. Each week, she left a bowl of rice and salt outside the door. When they went on walks and passed beneath the trees, she would bow her head and whisper, "*tabi tabi po.*"

"Why do you do that?" Enrique asked. "Why do you say 'excuse me' when there's no one here?"

"How do you know, *anak*?" his grandmother would say, with a twinkle in her eye. "*They* have been here long before us, and it is only polite to ask that they allow us to cross their territory. The *enkantos* and *diwatas* are a proud folk, and you would not wish to offend them, would you?"

Enrique shook his head. He did not want to be rude. And besides, he would love to see the creatures from his grandmother's tales. Maybe if he was very polite, they would come out and say hello to him. He even tried to see them. Once, he had stayed up all night watching the hallway outside his bedroom, convinced that if he simply waited long enough, a dwarf would appear in the shadows and ask him what he wanted. Enrique planned to give the dwarf a gift of rice cakes that he'd stolen from the family breakfast table, and then he'd ask to be taken to the grove where the *enkantos* lived. There, he would make a trade.

"The *enkantos* love a good bargain, *anak*," his grandmother used to say, lowering her voice as if she were letting him in on a secret. "For your most precious memory, they might give you a bag of gold. For the length of a young bride's hair, they will give her immortal beauty for a year."

Enrique had sat by her feet, enchanted. He remembered her reaching down, tugging gently at his ear.

"I once heard of a farmer who gave an *enkanto* his ear, and in return, he could see the future."

Enrique brightened. "If I give the *enkanto* my ear, will I see the future too?"

"Why would you wish to see the future, *anak*?" His *lola* laughed. "What a terrible burden that would be."

Enrique disagreed. If he could see the future, he would know when his elder brother Marcos was planning to tease him. He would know when his mother planned to bring home *puto bumbong* before anyone else, and he could help himself to the best pieces. And most importantly, he would know who he would be. Perhaps a sea-faring pirate with a deadly crocodile pet who adored him and ate all his enemies . . .

Enrique's future would be clear, and all he had to give up was a little part of himself.

But now, Enrique had made that sacrifice. Or rather, someone had made it for him. He stared at the gilt mirror on the far side of the library wall, turning his head one way and another before looking around at his scattered notes and research. He had given up his ear, but his future was no clearer.

History was all around him, and yet he had no idea where he belonged within it. He was lost. For all that he had dreamed of leaving a mark on the world, the world had marked him and kept moving.

A sound by the doorway startled him. Enrique looked up to see Zofia in her black apron. Soot had gotten smudged on her pale cheeks, but for some reason, it only drew attention to the vivid blue of her eyes and the Christmas red of her cheeks. Her candlelight hair had slipped out of its braid, and for a moment, he had the bizarre urge to feel it between his fingers . . . to wonder if it would feel, somehow, like light on his skin.

He stood suddenly, nearly scattering some of the documents on the table beside him.

"Phoenix," he said. "What are you doing here?"

"I'm finished with my work," she said.

"Oh . . . well done?"

She looked around the room. "You have not found what you are looking for yet."

Enrique deflated a bit. Ever since their meeting the night before, he had been searching for clues in the matriarch's safe house about the location of House Janus and the Carnevale gathering. But so far, he had found nothing. In the other room, Laila was busy reading all the objects she could, searching for a hint. An incognito Hypnos had gone to make secret inquiries in Venice about the *mascherari* bar that created the invitations. So far, all Enrique had managed to do was pull every book and framed picture off the library wall.

"You need help," said Zofia.

Enrique was a bit stung, but he had grown used to the way Zofia processed the world around her. She never meant it as an insult, merely as an observation.

"I do," he said, sighing.

There were only three days before Carnevale. Hypnos had made it clear that he thought if they could not find a hint about House Janus or the *mascherari* salon soon, then finding Séverin was their best chance of getting to the temple beneath Poveglia.

"We must face it, *mon cher*," said Hypnos, right before he'd left the house. "He always knows what to do and where to look."

Perhaps in the past that had been true, but now? Enrique had no trust in this new Séverin and the things he wanted. A vicious part of him imagined Séverin waiting for them at the meeting place, only for them not to show. Would he feel abandoned? Would he look at all the things he had done and hate himself? Would he be shocked? Enrique hoped so. Then, maybe, Séverin would know how they'd felt.

"What should I do?" asked Zofia.

"I . . . I have no idea," said Enrique, gesturing to the two tables piled high with papers and objects. "I arranged most of the items on the tables. I figured it would be useful to look through them. House Janus is named for the Roman god of transitions and change, and is generally depicted with two heads. He's often associated with doors, so perhaps look for a key? Or something that changes shape?"

Zofia nodded, walking to the first table. Enrique was too ashamed to tell her that he had already examined all the objects in the safe house. And he was far too ashamed to admit to himself that the person whose perspective he wanted most was the same person he would be happy never to see again.

Enrique could almost imagine Séverin as he had once been . . . wearing something immaculately tailored and chewing on a clove as he surveyed a room. He had an uncanny ability to know where treasure liked to hide. It was something Enrique had grudgingly admired, how Séverin could contextualize an object and weave a story around it.

"Treasure is like a beautiful woman," Séverin had once said. "It wants to know that you have taken the time to understand it before it reveals itself."

Enrique had feigned gagging. "If I were treasure, and I heard you utter that, I would sink to the bottom of the ocean where you would never find me."

He then proceeded to parrot the line for six months straight.

Séverin had not been amused.

When Enrique thought of it now, he almost smiled, but the

movement disturbed the wound where his ear had been. His smile dropped.

"What's this?" asked Zofia.

He turned to see Zofia holding up a small metal frame. Inside were five clay fragments, their surfaces covered in a wedge-like script. Before, he would have held it closely—almost reverently—to his heart. He would have traced the air above the wedges, imagining the blunt reed that had taken an idea and pinned it to this shape. Now he glanced away.

"Assyrian cuneiform, I believe," said Enrique. When Zofia looked at him expectantly, Enrique took it as an invitation to explain. Zofia did not always want to listen to him. On more than one occasion, she had simply walked off when he was in the middle of a lecture, and so he had learned to wait and let her decide. "About ten years ago, the Society of Biblical Archaeology wished to corroborate events in the Bible with historical events, particularly the deluge."

"Deluge?" asked Zofia.

"Also known as the great flood," said Enrique. "Noah and the ark."

Zofia nodded in understanding.

"There was an article published in 1872 that talked about the discovery of cuneiform tablets in the Library of Ashurbanipal near Nineveh . . ." said Enrique, glancing at the frame. "When they translated the tablets, they found another mention of the deluge. It was the first time people realized there were various instances of a 'great flood' occurring across the world . . . across different cultures, different traditions. As if this one great event didn't belong to a single people. It's groundbreaking, really, though the Order of Babel has tried to block further research and translation of the tablets ever since."

"So they no longer wish it to be proven?" asked Zofia, frowning.

"The higher the frequency of a recorded event, the higher the likelihood that it actually happened."

"Not if it contradicts their view of themselves, I suppose," said Enrique.

He couldn't hide the bitterness that snuck into his tone. In the past, he would have been livid. He remembered an essay he had written at university arguing that such practices were an effort to take a paintbrush and pair of scissors to history, an act that no human had a right to commit. At the time, anger shook through him, turning his handwriting scratchy and feverish.

But now, he felt curiously flat. What was the point of his frustration? Of his essay writing and plans for great speeches? Would it even make a difference in the world, or did the right to make a difference only lie in the hands of the privileged few?

The Order of Babel riffled through history as if it were a drawer. To them, culture was little more than an appealing ribbon or glittering ornament. Then there were those like Séverin and Ruslan . . . people who could flip the world order, but only if their wants were at the center of it all. And then there was Enrique, suspended between it all like a useless jewel left to hang between them—wanted merely for appearance's sake.

"Their view of themselves," said Zofia slowly. "Perhaps they do not know how to see."

"Perhaps," said Enrique.

His gaze went to the mirror on the far side of the wall. He didn't understand why the matriarch had placed it there. It did not fit amongst the books and objects. It didn't even seem to face the rest of the room. From this angle, it was unevenly skewed to show the library's entrance. Perhaps it was to keep track of strangers entering the room? At first they had suspected it might be a Tezcat door, but Zofia told them it was not.

How does a treasure wish to make itself known? Séverin used to say when it came to finding something. *What does it want you to see?*

Enrique shoved the words out of his head. The last thing he wanted to do was think of Séverin.

"I have not found anything," Zofia announced. "No key. No object that changes."

Enrique blew out a breath. "I figured as much."

"On Isola di San Michele, you said Janus was a god of time."

"And?"

"And time does not share the same traits as a key," said Zofia.

"The key was more of a manifestation of the setting he rules over," said Enrique, waving his hand. "Art is very self-referential and such . . ."

He sank into the nearest chair, letting his head fall into his palms. Hypnos would be back within the hour, and he would have to admit that he'd been wrong. There was no hint about House Janus here. He would have to watch Hypnos's smile turn smug and sympathetic, hear him fawn over how *Séverin* would have known what to do—

"Tell me more about the setting he rules over," said Zofia loudly.

Enrique looked up, torn between annoyance and the faint flicker of joy at the thought of explaining anything about myths and symbols. None of the others had asked about Janus's particular role in the Roman pantheon. Leave it to Zofia to question him when he had no wish to discuss further.

"He is said to guard passages of all kinds," said Enrique. "He was a god of dualities and transitions . . . oftentimes worshipped in the same breath as Zeus, who they called Iupiter. Janus also went by Ianus, which lent its name to Ianuarius and, thus, the month of January. As the first month of the year, it's the moment where we may look backwards and forwards at once. It's why Janus is often depicted presiding over doorways and doorframes. Why, even the Latin word for door is *ianus*—"

Enrique paused. A faint tingling sensation traveled down his spine. He stood slowly, then turned to face the mirror. He saw his stained bandage and the slight bulge where his ear had once been before Ruslan sliced it off. But beyond that—beyond the way the world had marked him—he saw the threshold of the library.

He had never noticed it before, the wood carved into elaborate shapes and set with gold trimming. It had seemed like another beautiful, decorative thing in a house full of beautiful, decorative ornaments. But now his gaze snagged on a faint, glowing spot set into the wood. At first glance, it seemed like a trick of the light . . . the flame of a candle or sconce bouncing off the silver mirror. It was situated up high, almost near the joint where the mantel and the frame met. A place no one would have cause to examine too closely.

"Zofia," said Enrique. "I'm beginning to think you really are a genius."

"You sound surprised," said Zofia. "Why?"

Enrique grinned as he walked past her, his hand outstretched to the door . . . the traditional haunt of the two-faced god.

"Is there a stool?" he asked, casting about.

Zofia picked one up, bringing it to him. Enrique clambered onto it, kneeling. He touched the glimmer set into the wood. It poked out like an innocent splinter.

Enrique pinched it and slowly *pulled*.

The wood around the glowing splinter yielded with a sound that reminded him of someone riffling through the pages in a book. Enrique held his breath. Whatever he had grabbed hold of gave way with little resistance. Light burst across his vision, and something fell, the sound was like a dish clattering to the ground.

"What is that?" asked Zofia, moving closer.

It was a silver demi-mask. Perhaps there had once been ribbons affixed to the side, but they had long since disintegrated. The mask itself looked plain and unfinished, the metallic paint chipped in some places. And yet, the moment Enrique touched it, he felt a presence invading his thoughts . . . a glimpse of the inside of a salon, masks dangling from the ceiling, the soft glow of chandeliers. There was only one place it could be, the *mascherari* salon that hid the location to House Janus.

Maybe it was nothing more than fanciful imagination, but in that moment, Enrique wondered if something of that old Roman god had moved through the room. After all, Janus was the god of change and beginnings. And in that second, Enrique could almost taste the change in the air. It tasted of silver and ghosts, like the resurrection of an abandoned hope that was stirring, once more, to life.

10

LAILA

Laila watched the wedding party approach the bridge. Behind them, a moon as pale as the bride's neck rose over the cathedral's sloped roofs. Bleary-eyed stars winked in the sky and bore witness to the lovers. Laila's throat felt tight as she watched them. She told herself not to look, but she couldn't help it. Her eyes hungrily roved over every detail of the bride and groom.

They moved in tandem, as if to a song sung only for their ears. The bride's frost-colored gown trailed over the cloud-white steps of the Bridge of Sighs. She had light brown hair, neatly pinned beneath a capped veil, and pearls wrapped around her forehead. Her groom, a weak-chinned man with wide eyes who became nearly handsome when he smiled, stared at her as if he had never beheld color until this moment. Behind the bride and groom, their friends and family cheered and laughed, throwing rice and petals in the air.

Laila moved back against the railing as they passed. She hadn't meant to end up at the Bridge of Sighs, but her walking path away from the Piazza San Marco and past the Doge's Palace had led to her being caught in the rain, and this was the fastest way back to the safe house. Beneath her, the white stones were still rain slick. The bride, unheeding in her joy, tripped and would have sprawled onto the stone if her husband hadn't caught her. As her bouquet of snowdrops tumbled from her hand, Laila, unthinking, reached out and caught hold of the blue ribbon that held the flowers in place. The wedding party cheered, and she blushed without knowing why.

"You dropped this," she said, trying to hand it to the bride.

But the girl shook her head, grinning. "*No, sua buona fortuna per te.*"

Laila had very little grasp of Italian, but she understood *buona fortuna*. The bride was saying it was good luck for her. Laughing, the bride folded Laila's hands over the bouquet.

"*E tuo,*" she said.

It's yours.

The bouquet's memories knifed through Laila. She saw the snow-drops bound by a blue ribbon that had once adorned the bride's blanket as a child. She saw the bride's mother weeping softly into the flowers, whispering prayers into the petals. She heard the bride laughing as she took it from her sister—

Laila yanked her consciousness back. When she glanced down, her garnet ring looked like a fat bead of blood. *Five.* Five days were all she had left.

She stared at the snowdrops in her hand.

Laila tried to imagine a future where she was a bride. She tried to picture her mother, still living and weaving jasmine through her hair. She imagined aunts she had never known sliding gold bangles onto her wrists. She conjured the scent of *henna*, like rain-sweet hay, adorning her hands and feet, her bridegroom's name hidden in the design as a secret invitation to touch her skin for the first time. Laila imagined the *antarpat* curtain that separated them slowly falling, her bridegroom's face concealed behind a *sehra* of pearls. In her daydream, a pair of violet eyes met hers, and in his gaze, Laila felt that she was all the wonder and color in the world.

Laila nearly dropped the flowers.

"Foolish," she told herself.

She would never be a bride. With every hour that passed, Laila realized the garnet ring would be the only ring she ever wore. Laila clung to her hope, but every day she felt it collapsing a little more. Every minute, she felt the space between her consciousness and the dark waters of oblivion vanishing. Sometimes, it was as if those dark waters were whispering to her, taunting her that it would be so much easier to let go. To drown.

Somewhere, a bell tolled, startling her from her thoughts. It was nearly midnight, and the others would be wondering where she had gone. There was work to be done. Objects that needed reading, plans that required finalizing.

But for that moment, Laila wished she could unfasten herself. She wanted to let in the moon and the clouds, the roofs of the cathedral and dim stars, and let it all burn and scrape inside her.

Around her, the sky deepened to shadows and velvet. Her mother used to tell her the oncoming night was the god Krishna wrapping them up in his arms, for his skin was the color of midnight. Laila used to love hearing tales of Krishna, the god of preservation reborn as a mischievous, human child.

One day Krishna's human mother suspected he had eaten something he should not, and told the boy to open his mouth. Eventually, she convinced him. Behind Krishna's teeth—in the lightless dark of his throat—burned suns and moons, dying stars and ice-rimed planets. His mother did not ask him to open his mouth again.

Laila knew some people could carry such things inside them.

Some people could walk with galaxies tilting at their heart, planets grinding against their ribs, whole worlds dragging in their wake and never stealing their balance.

Her mother used to say Laila was one of those people. She was born to carry more than herself. She could hold up, and cherish, the weight of others—their worries, their mistakes, their hopes of who they might be.

All this time, she had tried not to think of Séverin, but that foolish daydream had summoned his face to her thoughts. Now she knew for certain that he was the one person she could never hold.

She didn't doubt that he cared for his friends in his own way. She didn't even doubt that he felt deeply for her, or that it must have hurt him to forsake her and pretend to kill the others just to keep them safe.

But they would forever want different futures, and she could not hide that from herself anymore.

Laila wanted safety. A home. A dining table groaning with food, always set for friends and family.

And Séverin? Séverin wanted godhood. Holding on to him would be like trying to wrestle down the moon. Already, Laila's death was a needy, cloying thing, so heavy it felt as if she were carrying the night and all its stars. Already, a nonexistence—that blankness she'd felt on Isola di San Michele—mushroomed through her body.

She had no room left for Séverin.

Not anymore.

In the distance, a sleek gondola cut through the onyx water, as if heading straight to the Bridge of Sighs. Laila took one last look at the bouquet of snowdrops, then dropped the bouquet. The ribbon broke, the bells tolled midnight. The white petals scattering into the lagoon looked like a broken star.

II

SÉVERIN

Séverin had once imagined that gods had no weaknesses, but now he knew he was wrong.

Even gods had a secret, soft throat. To wound them, you must not want them. You must turn your face and laugh at their riches. Rejection was a mortal blade that would always find purchase.

From his vantage point on the gondola, the stark face of the nearby clock tower announcing that it was half past midnight confirmed what he already knew: They weren't coming.

At first, he told himself that something had gone wrong. But that was impossible—he had left the Mnemo bug beside Laila. There was no way it could have been misplaced. Then he wondered if some ill had befallen them, if the Order had somehow found them . . . but surely Ruslan would have crowed about such a finding. For nearly twenty minutes, Séverin had stood in the gondola and stared up at the Bridge of Sighs. He kept imagining them in every stray laugh or distant sound of feet. When he had first neared the meeting point, he even convinced himself that he'd seen a slender figure stealing into the shadows.

They did not want him.

They had chosen *not* to come.

Dimly, he knew he had to go back.

If he stayed away any longer, Ruslan would punish him for it.

Séverin felt as though he couldn't breathe. He sank into the gondola cushioning, an unfamiliar tightness constricting his chest as Eva's words floated back to him.

How do you know they will come for you, Monsieur? You may not have killed them, but even I could see that how you treated them was a death of its own.

Séverin felt ill. He gripped the edge of the gondola, nausea roiling through him. He had done this to himself. He leaned over the boat, on the verge of vomiting, and it was then that he saw the white petals float past him.

For the first time in years, he heard his mother's voice. He had blocked out the smokey sound for so long, but now it had found him. He remembered one of the last times he saw her: He had cried out for her after a nightmare, and his father had allowed Kahina to sleep beside him, though he grumbled that Séverin would become soft from such coddling.

"Listen, *habibi*, and I will tell you the tale of the rich king and the most beautiful flower in the world," Kahina had said, smoothing his hair away from his forehead.

"How beautiful was the flower?" asked Séverin, for it had seemed very important, if the bloom was worthy of a king.

Kahina smiled. "The flower's petals were white as milk, and its fragrance like something stolen out of paradise. The king asked the flower if he might take it to his kingdom, and the bloom agreed, but only if the king promised to care for it."

Séverin had frowned at this. None of the flowers on his father's estate had ever spoken to him. Perhaps they did not imagine him a king. He would have to wear his best clothes tomorrow and inform them otherwise.

"The flower asked for sunshine, and the king declared that he had something better than sunlight—he offered the flower golden coins rinsed in milk and honey. The flower cried out, for the hard, gold coins bruised its petals. The flower then asked for water, and the king declared that he had something better than water, and he poured upon the flower all the rarest wines from the corners of his kingdom," said Kahina. "The flower cried out, for the wine was sour and its roots shriveled at its touch. Slowly, it began to die. The king was furious, and he demanded an explanation. 'I have given you all the best things in the world,' he said. 'You *must* flourish!' But the flower declared, 'That was never what I needed,' and then defied the king by dying."

Séverin did not like the story. Couldn't the silly king see that all the flower wanted was water and sun?

"Why didn't he listen?" Séverin had asked.

Kahina was quiet. Her hands stilled on his forehead. "Sometimes those with too much power think they know best . . . they forget how to listen. But you will not be like that will you, *habibi*?"

Séverin shook his head.

"Good," said his mother. She lifted his hands and kissed his knuckles one by one. "Because you are far more powerful than any king."

Now, Séverin watched the white petals float past him.

Look at what you've done. You hurt them. You did not listen. And now you are alone.

He was a fool. All his powers, all his wealth . . . it meant nothing.

Séverin sat back in the gondola, something crystallizing in his thoughts.

Laila, Enrique, Hypnos, and Zofia didn't need him to get to Poveglia, but they would need him to play the lyre. If he got to them fast enough, then maybe he could apologize. He could beg them for another chance . . .

All this time, he had been stepping daintily around Ruslan's whims. But there was nothing left the patriarch of the Fallen House could take from him. He had lost all that mattered, and in that way, he was finally as powerful as he could be. Only by having nothing to lose could he finally force the patriarch's hand. They would not be waiting ten days to reach Poveglia. They would be leaving immediately.

SÉVERIN THREW OPEN the doors of Casa d'Oro, walking past the dozen members of the Fallen House.

The moment he entered, their Mnemo honeybees whirred loudly.

"Where is my lyre?" he asked quietly.

A guard stepped out of his room, holding the ice and glass box. In the shadows of the hallway, Séverin caught sight of Eva's red hair. She must have been waiting for him, expecting confirmation that the others were alive. But he had no proof, which meant she was no help to him any longer. Séverin pressed his thumb to the thorn, taking out the lyre.

"Bring your master," he said to the guards. "*Now.*"

"Monsieur Montagnet-Alarie—" started Eva, moving toward him.

He strode toward her. Her green eyes went wide in panic, and she moved to run, but he was too fast. He caught her around the waist, dragging her back to his chest. She thrashed, clawing at him, but he didn't care. He was only after one thing. A moment later, and he had removed the jeweled knife Eva kept around her waist. She sprang away from him, breathing hard.

"*Where is Ruslan?*" he yelled.

Eva cowered against the wall. "What are you doing?" Her voice dropped to a whisper. "What happened to them? You promised me—"

"Get the hell away from me," he snarled. "This is no longer about you."

Eva blanched. Fury stole into her face, and her hand reached for the pendant around her throat before she fled into the hall.

The Fallen House members stepped toward him. They were less than three meters away from him now. As one, they drew out pairs of knives from inside their black sleeves. Séverin laughed. He felt wondrously drunk on this new power.

He raised the jeweled knife to his throat, smiling lazily at all of them. "Ruslan has bored me. I no longer wish to find godhood with him."

He watched the words sink into the atmosphere.

"In fact, I would rather be dead," said Séverin. He pressed the knife harder against his skin. "He is welcome to the use of my limbs afterwards. I care not—"

Someone had begun to clap. Séverin looked up to see Ruslan stepping out of the red-brocade wall that had been nothing more than a Tezcat portal in disguise. A wide smile spread across his face.

"I *knew* it!" said Ruslan. "I knew you would not be so dull!"

Séverin jerked his head to where the patriarch stood. The movement made the blade sting on his skin.

"Oh no no no," pleaded Ruslan. "Stop that, my friend, you have made your point."

"And what point is that?" asked Séverin coldly.

"That I have been a poor host," said Ruslan. "Forgive me . . . I wanted to see who you were if I were to peel back that placid veneer of yours. I wanted to see how sharp your teeth could be. And oh . . . you did not disappoint."

Séverin did not move his hand.

"Come, my friend," said Ruslan, stepping toward him. "It is time to prepare for a Carnevale celebration."

"I have no desire for parties," said Séverin.

"The celebration is held in a place that contains the map to the temple beneath Poveglia," said Ruslan, speaking quickly.

Slowly, Séverin lowered the knife. He felt the hot slide of blood down his throat. In his other hand, the lyre seemed to hum.

Ruslan smiled. His golden hand caught the light. "We must celebrate, for one last night, what it means to be mortal. It will be a little souvenir we can take with us when we become gods."

PART II

12

SÉVERIN

When Séverin touched the lyre, he heard impossible things. He heard his soul stirring sleepily under his bones. He heard stars creaking overhead.

But he could not hear *her*, the voice of the woman he had not been allowed to call "mother." *Her* voice alone meant all hope was not lost.

He stared at his hands. They looked raw and chafed from hours spent gliding his fingers over the instrument, careful to press hard enough that he could hear the dim pulse of the universe in his skull, but not so hard that he bled.

"Where are you?" he asked. "Speak to me."

He had been begging the lyre for a sign for two days straight. Ever since he had returned from the Bridge of Sighs, and Ruslan had finally begun preparations for Poveglia: explosives and goggles, scraps of research and plans to fetch a mind Forged mask. Séverin should have been pleased with the progress, but instead, his thoughts kept returning to the empty Bridge of Sighs.

They had left him. He had fallen too far in their eyes.

He did not blame them.

Enrique, Hypnos, Zofia . . . Laila. He was broken. In the new cracks of himself, he thought he could hear the lyre whispering to him. Sometimes, the voice was dark and sensuous. Other times, it was a voice of caution. He felt split and ragged, and he wondered if this was how Tristan had felt all those years. As if he were just pushing back the tide of something far worse that always lurked within him. Maybe Séverin was the same. Maybe there was some inexorable *wrongness* about him that drove away all the people he loved, no matter what he did.

His friends had offered grace and kindness, and he had repaid them with cruelty and sabotage. He told himself that what he was pursuing would excuse any pain, but that was false. He had pursued his plans without once letting in his friends, and in the end, he would have the power he sought. But at what cost?

Séverin thought of the myth of King Midas, whose wish for gold had given him a godlike touch. His food turned to gold. Then his drink. Eventually, his daughter. In the end, when he had washed his curse into a stream and sprouted the ears of a donkey, his reflection revealed what he really was: an unequivocal jackass.

Séverin knew how the old king must have felt. All that power, and still—he'd ended up alone.

Outside Séverin's chamber door came the shuffle of boots and muffled voices. Though there were no windows in his room, he knew the hour had grown late. Soon, Eva would fetch him.

He couldn't make himself move. For a moment, he toyed with smashing the lyre against the wall, but his hands stilled. Was the instrument even a gift of the gods . . . or was it a Midas curse, doomed to destroy him?

"I am begging you," he whispered to the instrument. "Give me a sign. Show me this power is real. Show me I'm on the right path . . . speak to me."

For the hundredth time that day, Séverin dragged his thumb down the shining string. He winced.

One last time, he told himself.

At the back of his skull came the dim, warning pulse of the universe. *Stop now*, it said. *Stop*. Séverin pushed harder. In the Sleeping Palace, he had merely cut his hand and smeared the blood on the strings. That mere vibration of the strings had been enough to feel the divine wisp through him.

Now . . .

Now it was something else.

He felt the string cutting into his flesh. His skull throbbed. The music of the lyre built inside him, hungry for release. It was not a music of this world. It was the moan of falling stars and the sonorous yearning of tree roots, the exhale of the sea before it rose up to swallow a village whole—

Séverin.

His thumb stilled on the lyre. Its frantic music went silent. It was as if he had reached the threshold of something, because here, finally, he heard the voice he craved.

He had first heard his mother's voice after he confronted Ruslan and clutched the lyre to him in the night. She had said something to him, something that conjured light in his thoughts, something that gave him hope. He had been starting to think he had imagined it.

Habibi . . . listen . . . listen to me.

Kahina's voice was a thousand candles springing to life in the dark, and Séverin felt every luminous halo as if it were a step leading him out of chaos.

"I'm listening, *ummi*," he said, shaking. "I hear you."

Time contracted around him. For a moment, he was a boy once

more curled up in his small bed. He remembered Kahina folding his pudgy hands into fists and kissing them twice.

"In your hands lie the gates of godhood," she whispered. "Let none pass."

A loud knock at the door jolted him. Séverin's eyes flew open. He was breathing fast. His hands shook, and sweat beaded down his back.

"Are you nearly ready, Monsieur Montagnet-Alarie?" asked Eva sharply.

Ready?

The world slowly came into focus. Séverin blinked, staring around him: red room, red bed. The past two days rushed back into his thoughts: the empty Bridge of Sighs, the knife to his throat, Ruslan's plans for tonight.

"Hello?" asked Eva again.

"Yes," said Séverin, swallowing hard. "I . . . I'm nearly ready."

He could hear Eva lingering at the door, but then she turned and left. Slowly, Séverin eased his thumb off the string, careful that it should not tremble. His thumb looked purple. He brought the divine lyre to his forehead as if it were the cold hand of a priest.

"Thank you," he said fiercely. "*Thank you.*"

This was the sign he had begged for. This was the proof he needed that he was no cosmic joke. There was a reason for it all, and his mother's voice proved it:

In your hands lie the gates of godhood . . .

He had failed his friends miserably, but not all was lost, for he was on a greater path. He may have been an unequivocal ass in the way he'd pursed his dreams, but he would not end up like King Midas. His riches were meant to be shared.

Séverin closed his eyes, picturing the moment he would see Enrique, Hypnos, Zofia, and Laila again. A sharp ache ran through his chest. They were, justifiably, furious with him. But he would prove that he was worthy of them. He would make amends. He would never leave them in the dark again.

And surely, once they saw the lyre's power . . . once they saw that he had always intended to share its gift . . . they would forgive him. For a moment, he pictured Tristan's gray eyes shining once more. He saw Tante Feefee, the matriarch of House Kore, resting her warm palm on his cheek. He would tell her he had found a way to make his love more beautiful. She would be proud of him, he thought.

When Séverin stood, he smiled.

His mother's voice moved through him like an unfurling dawn. This was the kind of light that remade the world, and Séverin felt its warmth on his skin like a promise.

"YOU SEEM MUCH changed, Monsieur Montagnet-Alaric," said Ruslan.

"How so?" asked Séverin, straightening his plum and silver–brocade jacket as he stepped outside his rooms. He was immediately met with two members of the Fallen House. Séverin heard the familiar creak of the hinge on the glass and ice box, still opened from when he had last removed the lyre. A beat passed. If he was going to get rid of the patriarch and leave with his lyre, the blood Forged box posed a problem. Eva might have been the solution, but one glance at the stoney-eyed girl standing next to Ruslan did not fill him with confidence.

"You seem . . . newly invigorated," said Ruslan, tilting his head to the side. "Whatever were you doing all alone in your rooms? Scheming, perhaps, for tomorrow's acquisition of the map to Poveglia?"

Eva moved closer, laying a hand on Séverin's arm. It might have looked like a gesture of confidence or intimacy, but she was wearing a new, onyx ring on her hand. And when it touched his skin, Séverin felt an unfamiliar presence against his pulse that was not unlike the interrogation table in Ruslan's dining room.

It was testing to see if he would tell the truth.

Séverin raised an eyebrow, then dropped the lyre into the box. "If you must know, I was preoccupied with stroking my instrument."

The presence on his skin stilled.

A speaking look passed between Eva and Ruslan. Ruslan threw his head back and laughed.

"Oh, how I like you!" said Ruslan, reaching out and tousling his hair. "Now, you shall be quick, Eva, will you not?"

Eva nodded, removing her hand from Séverin's arm. Tonight, she wore a peach-colored gown with a high collar at her throat. The bejeweled knife from around her waist was gone.

Ruslan snapped his fingers.

A member of the Fallen House stepped forward, a length of black cloth dangling from his hand. Séverin frowned.

"What is this?"

"For you, my friend," said Ruslan. "To keep where you are going a wondrous surprise!"

Séverin stilled. Ruslan knew something and didn't trust him. What had he found out?

"Very well," Séverin said, careful to keep his voice neutral.

The black cloth settled over his eyes. It was Forged, of course, and the moment he blinked, he was in utter darkness. His senses felt heightened. He could smell the rot on the lagoons even from here.

"You will select two masks from the *mascherari* salon," said Ruslan. "Once you possess them, you will know where to find House Janus's Carnevale party."

House Janus. Up until now, Ruslan had shared only vague details of his plans. Séverin had known that the location of the Carnevale party held the secret map to Poveglia's temple, but the information about House Janus was new. Séverin knew little of the small Italian faction, but he remembered they specialized in treasures of cartography and considered themselves guardians of their acquisitions, which remained untouched.

"Two masks?" asked Séverin. "You will not be joining us?"

"I am officially a persona non grata at such events," said Ruslan, sniffing disdainfully. "The Order thinks I'm somewhere in Denmark and is currently hunting for me there. I cannot risk showing my face, not after the reported discrepancies."

Séverin felt his heartbeat notching higher. "Discrepancies?"

"The body count after we left the Sleeping Palace is not what it should be," said Ruslan. "According to my contacts, the Order of Babel cannot locate the remains of the patriarch of House Nyx. They did, however, find the matriarch of House Kore at the bottom of the lake."

A twist of heartache ran through Séverin. He remembered Delphine Desrosier's fierce, blue gaze, the way she'd set her jaw when she told him that she would sacrifice herself.

"A pity," said Séverin, forcing the emotion out of his voice.

"They cannot find the bodies of Monsieur Mercado-Lopez, Mademoiselle Boguska, or Mademoiselle Laila either."

The moment of silence stretched out. Even in the dark, Séverin could sense Eva tensing beside him.

"Laila loved them very much," he said calmly. "She might have buried them herself, or else is keeping vigil over their bodies while she waits to die. She's . . . pathetic like that."

"Perhaps," said Ruslan quietly.

Séverin bit back a shudder as Ruslan's cold, golden hand trailed down his cheeks. "But what if they are alive? What if they seek to deprive you of all that you so richly deserve? We can't have that."

"That would be quite the spectacle considering you saw me kill them."

"The world is full of marvels both wondrous and terrible, Monsieur," said Ruslan. His lips were next to his ear. "I am merely keeping my perspective open."

"HE WILL KILL you if you try to betray him, you know," said Eva.

Séverin turned his head to the sound of her voice. Despite the gondola rocking beneath him, the blindfold had not budged. For all he knew, anyone could be recording him . . . documenting his movements, noting the inflection of his voice.

"Why would I betray him?"

Eva was silent a moment, then her voice dropped to a whisper. "He said there were discrepancies . . . and yet the proof of life you promised me never manifested. How am I supposed to trust you?"

Séverin was quiet. How am I supposed to trust *you*? he wondered.

Some twenty minutes passed before the Forged gondola stopped. Séverin heard the rustle of silk as Eva stepped out. He could hardly make out which of the neighborhood *sestieri* she had brought them to, but he could hear the hiss of cats in an alley and far away, the mournful note of a lone violin.

The black cloth fell away from his eyes, revealing a dimly lit street on the water's edge. It looked abandoned. Nothing moved except an unpainted porcelain *colombina* mask. On a person, the half mask would have left the wearer's face only partially concealed. But the mask was not for people. It dangled from a lonely iron hook in the wall beneath which lay a dingy window lit only by a stub of a candle. The candlelight shone through the eyeholes of the mask, and on the opposite plaster wall, the shape of a grinning face flickered in and out of the light not high above the cobblestone streets. There, just beneath the mismatched shadows . . . the faint outline of a door beckoning them to the *mascherari* salon within.

Inside stretched a chamber the size of a generous ballroom. Dozens of patrons wearing masks carved in the shapes of grinning tigers or human expressions of rigid joy and terror danced around the room. Forged platters bearing *amaro* in crystal cups next to bowls of ice floated through the crowd, perfuming the room with bitter aniseed and myrtle. Around Séverin, the voice of an unseen opera singer could just barely be heard over the rustling silks and muffled laughter of patrons in the corners. At the threshold of the salon, a person wearing a mask that was nothing but a large, black oval and a painted, toothy grin bowed low to Séverin and Eva at the entrance.

"Here, we remove the faces we show the world and submit to something greater," said the individual. "Welcome, friends . . . may you find that which you seek. May you leave our sanctuary able to face the world anew."

It was a strange sanctuary, thought Séverin as he studied the room. Far above him, dozens of metal beams rotated slowly in the air. Draped over the beams lay a constellation of silken threads, from which swung hundreds of sculpted faces. Some were unfinished, nothing more than a voluptuous mouth painted on plaster. Some were lifelike—the Forged plaster capable of grins and long lashes blinking back to reveal hollows for eyes. The traditional masks of Venice appeared amongst them: The *bauta*, with its protruding chin, the hollows of its eyes adorned with gilded diagonals. The *colombina* half mask, crushed pearls baked into its edges. In the recessed balconies of the chamber, the *mascheraris* worked furiously. On their

faces, they wore clever shields that looked like liquid mirrors clinging to their features so that any who tried to guess at their identity
would only see themselves reflected.

Something on the back wall caught Séverin's eye. At first
glance, it looked like nothing more than a heavy, emerald-colored
curtain that hung from the ceiling to the floor. But a second glance
revealed at least a dozen hands poking through the drapes.

Some patrons ignored the hands as they walked past. Others
dropped coins and letters and ribbons. One partygoer wearing a fe-
line mask lightly touched an extended hand. An invitation, it seemed,
and one that, a moment later, was accepted as the feline-masked person was pulled, laughing, through the curtains.

Séverin was still staring at the curtain when Eva touched his
arm. "Wait here. I'm going to get the masks myself."

Séverin protested, but Eva held up her hand. "Ruslan might
have sent us both here, but the Order will be looking for you. They
may even have one of the *mascherari* workers reporting to them in
disguise. You're . . . you're safer here."

Eva was right, though why she would protect him when she had
said she didn't trust him was strange. Perhaps she was like him . . .
hoping that she had placed her faith in the right person.

"Thank you," said Séverin.

"I'll find you soon," said Eva. "It should not take me longer than
half an hour."

With that, she disappeared into the crowd. Séverin watched her
go. The scraps of a plan itched at the back of his skull, but there
was nothing for it to tether itself to. And there was still the problem of the lyre. Ruslan was not coming with them, which meant he
would expect the lyre to stay by his side. Perhaps Séverin could
switch the instrument with an object of identical weight, but how
could he do that without Eva's help—

"Do you wish to sample a different fate, *signore*?" interrupted a voice at his side.

Séverin turned to see a short, pale-skinned man speaking to him from behind a large mask carved to the likeness of a frog with bulging, glassy eyes.

"Here you can be anyone you wish," said the man, gesturing to the back wall and the curtain of disembodied hands. "You merely have to pluck a face from the air itself . . . or perhaps you might wish to open your hands to fate, and see what love and fortune befalls you . . ."

Séverin was on the verge of dismissing the man entirely when a slender figure caught his attention. A woman. She was too far away for him to see her features, but there was something in the way she moved. She moved the way he imagined a star-touched goddess would step through the night sky, aware that the brush of her ankle or tilt of her hip might knock a man's destiny askew.

"*Signore*?" asked the short man again.

"Yes," said Séverin, distracted. "Let me open my hands to fate."

He felt a low buzz ringing in his ears as the man led him to the samite curtains. The woman had disappeared on the other side, guided through some Tezcat portal hidden in the mirrored wall. Séverin felt the loss of her presence like a physical ache. Before him, masked patrons flitted past the curtain of hands. He watched a person pause before an open hand, dropping a kiss at the center of a palm before walking away. The hand curled around the kiss, then withdrew completely.

Séverin walked down the row of outstretched hands. At least a dozen or so stretched before him, but only one called to him like a siren.

Near the end of the row, he paused before a woman's bronze wrist. His breath caught when he saw her index finger. There, a familiar welt that had healed to a pale scar caught his eye. He knew that mark. He was there when it happened, standing beside her in the kitchens of L'Eden, furious that a pot had dared to burn her hand.

I cannot stand to see you hurt.

Unthinking, Séverin caught hold of the woman's wrist. He felt her pulse, frantic as his. And maybe it was that—that barest hint that perhaps she felt as much apprehension as he did—that possessed him to do what he did next. Séverin raised her hand to his lips, pressing his mouth to the place where her pulse fluttered like a trapped bird.

An internal mechanism within the floorboards reeled him in through the Tezcat curtains until he found himself in a small silk-lined room. Forged, floating candles dripped pools of golden light.

Laila stood before him, her eyes wide with shock.

Just days ago, he had memorized the poetry of her features. To be faced with them so unexpectedly struck him like bottled lightning let loose behind his ribs. He knew she'd had every right to leave him standing beneath that Bridge of Sighs. He knew that he should fall to his knees and start groveling the moment he laid eyes on her, but for this second, he could not help himself. Joy transfixed him.

Séverin smiled.

Which was precisely when Laila slapped him across the face.

13

LAILA

It was not the first time that evening Laila had left a man heartbroken.

An hour ago, Hypnos had thrown quite the fit before she'd left the matriarch's safe house.

"I said I'm sorry," said Laila, her hand on the doorknob. "You know if the circumstances were different, I would have no issue with you going in my stead."

Hypnos lay facedown on the ground of the matriarch's safe house. He had refused to move for the past two minutes and counting. Enrique sighed and crossed his arms. Zofia chewed on a matchstick, staring down at Hypnos curiously.

"So, the weight of his sorrow brought him to the ground?" she asked.

"The weight of *unfairness*," groaned Hypnos into the carpet. "I have been *waiting* to go to the *mascherari* salon for nearly five years, and now, all because of the Order lurking about, I cannot. Everyone is out to harm me, and I don't know why."

"Yes, completely unjustified paranoia on the Order's part," said Enrique. "There's nothing alarming about going to a Winter Conclave, then finding yourself paralyzed for several hours and an exiled house resurrected and run by a psychopath who will take one look at you, know the rest of us are alive and probably kill us all—"

"*Oh very well, I understand,*" said Hypnos, rolling onto his back. "But I can't move from the sheer injustice of it all."

Zofia toed experimentally at his arm, which moved a couple centimeters. "Look!"

"I am cured," said Hypnos flatly.

Laila bit back a laugh. "And *I* must go."

From her hand, a silver demi-mask caught the fading light. The first time she had put it on, she had felt the force of mind Forging as if someone had punched through her thoughts. It wasn't just the location of the salon, but an instruction: Show the silver mask to the artisans, and each mask they made would function as a ticket.

Hypnos made a loud *harrumphing* sound. Laila offered her hand, and after one more aggrieved sigh, Hypnos took her wrist and hoisted himself up.

"Please pick out a mask for me that brings out my best attributes," he said.

"What attributes?" asked Zofia. "Your face will be covered."

Hypnos's grin turned sly. "Ah, *ma chère*, I am flattered, but one might argue that my best attribute is actually—"

"Please don't pick out anything yellow," said Enrique loudly over Hypnos. "Makes me look sick."

Hypnos looked affronted. Laila raised an eyebrow, then looked to Zofia. "Any aesthetic requests?"

"Aesthetics don't matter," said Zofia.

Behind her, Enrique and Hypnos looked deeply insulted.

"The utility is most important," said Zofia. "We need something that can hide tools."

"What kinds of tools?" asked Enrique suspiciously.

"Useful tools."

"Phoenix . . ."

"Hmm?"

"You are not actually thinking of hiding a large explosive near our faces, are you?" asked Enrique.

"No," said Zofia.

"Good—"

"It's a very tiny explosive. Hardly larger than six centimeters."

"*No*," said Hypnos and Enrique at the same time.

Laila took this as her cue to leave.

NEARLY AN HOUR later, she had finally made her decision.

Around her, the *mascherari* salon thrummed with life, and Laila felt a sharp ache for the Palais des Rêves. She missed the smell of the wax on the dance floor, the way the dust motes caught in a beam of chandelier light, the crisp snap of a strand of pearls breaking under her heel. Weeks ago, she had promised her stage manager that L'Enigme would return "in time for the new year." Clearly, she had not. Laila wondered what they thought had happened to her. Did they think she was dead? Or that she'd merely disappeared? The other dancers had always teased that she was bound to run off with a Russian prince on her travels.

She hoped they believed that was her fate.

"*Signora*?" asked the Forged artisan.

Laila turned to face the *mascherari* work table, which was situated to the far right of what looked like a grand ballroom that was curtained off in sections. This side of the chamber carried a distinctly eerie demeanor. Here, it was quiet and hushed thanks to a Forged veil which locked out sound.

"The four masks you requested," said the Forged artisan.

Laila found it hard to look at the man. He wore a mask like a melted mirror, which adhered to every feature—even his eyes— and rendered him strangely reflective.

"*Grazi,*" she said, leaning over the table.

In the end, she had chosen the same for all four of them.

"*Il medico della peste,*" said the artisan, a hint of unease tinging his voice.

The plague doctor's mask.

Each of the four masks covered the whole of the face. The closely set round eyeholes were covered with shimmering glass, and instead of a hole for the nose and mouth, the mask cinched and elongated into a hooked beak. All four were painted a shade of eggshell white and plastered with sheet music.

"*È perfetto,*" said Laila graciously.

And it was, in its own way, perfect. Zofia had requested a mask that might hide tools and this was large enough to do so. And the mask held an echo of their final location, Plague Island.

The Forged artisan smiled. Even his teeth were silver. In four deft movements, he folded the masks until they were as thin as handkerchiefs and could fit easily inside the reticule at her wrist.

Laila had just turned to leave when she felt it.

The blankness.

It doused her like sudden rainfall. One moment, her nostrils burned from the cigarette smoke, her ears rang with the throaty purr of a woman's laughter, and her fingertips skimmed over the rough-hewn pearls of her beaded purse.

The next moment, Laila felt like a grasping shade. Textures vanished. Sounds collapsed. Colors muted.

No, she begged. *Not now . . . not yet.*

The blankness hadn't stolen through her since the Isola di San Michele visit. She had almost convinced herself that it was a waking nightmare until this moment. Laila looked down.

Four.

Four days left to live.

Laila tried to pull air into her lungs. She couldn't feel her ribs expanding or the perfumed air irritating her nose. She must have succeeded else she would have passed out by now . . . but perhaps that was not how she was made.

The idea sickened her.

She looked up, staring at the revolving sculpted faces. For a moment, she remembered her village in Pondicherry, India. Was this what the *jaadugar* had done for her parents? Had he merely skimmed his wizened hand across a ceiling of ribbons before he found the face she would wear for the next nineteen years?

"*Signora*, you look as though you wish to start over."

Laila turned, as if in slow motion, to the woman speaking to her. She was tall and dark-skinned, her golden eyes just barely visible behind an all-velvet *moretto* mask. The woman gestured to a section of the room Laila had barely paid attention to when she had first entered. Hands stretched through curtains, patrons walking past dropping anything from coins to sweets into waiting palms.

"Let fate give you guidance," said the woman. "Take some sweetness into the world and start anew . . ."

"I—" Laila tried to speak, but her tongue felt thick.

"Come, come," said the woman. "It is a beloved custom for those who visit our sanctuary. For only here can you divest yourself of the face you put on for the world. Only here might you tempt love in a new form or summon a new fate entirely."

A new fate.

Slowly, she followed after the woman. The numbness hadn't retreated. If anything, it had intensified. The world had taken on a blurry sheen. Her pulse was thready, sluggish.

"In here, *signora*," said the woman warmly. "Merely ask for what you wish, and see what fortune provides."

With that, the woman drew the curtains shut. Laila stood still, the world swaying around her. Before her, the silken fall looked like the veil to a different world. Laila stuck her hand through the fabric. She didn't feel the weight or scratchiness of the raw silk on her wrist. That blankness engulfed her. Laila felt unmoored from the world, no more than a flimsy wisp of consciousness on the verge of being folded back into that darkness.

Laila cleared her throat, whispering, "I wish for life."

She waited a few moments. She was on the verge of withdrawing her hand when she felt the slightest touch on her wrist. She froze.

On the other side, someone lifted her hand. Dimly, she felt the scratchy weight of the curtain, caught the ghost of cigar smoke clinging to the drapes. The stranger brought their lips to her wrist, and Laila felt the heat of their kiss like an unfurling bloom. The colors of the room sharpened. The background noise she had taken for granted earlier rushed in to shatter the silence. If her soul had felt flimsy before, now it seemed to tether itself back to her bones.

Around her, the world spoke its eloquence in perfumes and chandelier light, the velveteen nap of parting curtains, the gnarled nubs of wood poking through her slippers. Laila felt intoxicated by it all. And yet, there had only ever been one person who made her feel the vividness of the world like this, and, as if summoned by the thought, the room yanked the stranger inside—

For a moment, Laila lost track of where she was. The small, silk-lined room full of Forged candles melted away when she saw him. She'd always considered Séverin a warning . . . the wolf in bed. The apple in a witch's palm.

But he was so much more dangerous than something from the pages of a fairy tale.

He was someone who believed them.

Someone who thought magic and wonder had made an exception for him.

Séverin glanced at her wrist, then her face, and then . . . he smiled. It was a glib grin of delight, as if he knew that he was the one who had made her feel alive again . . . as if it meant he had a right to her.

She hated him for it. In that second, her hand moved of its own accord.

Séverin winced at the slap, his hand moving to the reddening mark on his cheekbone.

"Undoubtedly, I deserved that," he said, looking up at her.

For the first time in what felt like years, Laila studied him. The past few days had changed him. There was a new sharpness to his features. He seemed like a well-constructed sword, the line between danger and beauty too blurred to distinguish. There was something feverish to his handsome features that seemed to singe the very air around them. His black hair—now a touch too long—fell across his brow, drawing attention to those strange eyes that were the precise color of sleep.

"Laila . . ." he said. His eyes looked wide. Frantic. "I know I have made mistakes. I know I said unforgivable things, and grief was no excuse. I know I will regret those moments for the rest of my life, but

I can make it up to all of you. I swear it. Are they here?" He looked around the room, a hopeful smile touching his face. "Are they well? Can I see them?"

Laila managed to shake her head.

"Please, Laila, I can take care of everything—"

Finally the words snapped out of her.

"But you didn't," she said coldly.

Séverin stilled. "I know my actions in Lake Baikal looked unimaginably cruel—"

"Actually, they didn't," said Laila. Her throat felt raw. The words she had longed to say rushed out: "I wish I could say I was surprised, and yet, I wasn't. You had already changed so much. Everything . . . every person . . . was disposable to you." She advanced on him, her hands trembling. "All this time, you thought you could get away with devastation so long as it justifies some irrational calculus in your head. And now you apologize for appearing 'unimaginably cruel'?" Laila laughed. "What you did was so in line with who you are that when I became conscious, I wanted nothing to do with you. I *smashed* that Mnemo butterfly because I knew there was nothing you could show me that I wanted to see. Nothing you could leave me that I wanted to chase."

Séverin's smile finally fell. "You broke it?"

She nodded. She watched his eyebrows twitch upwards. It might have looked like surprise, but she knew that look. Not surprise, but caution.

"What can I do, Laila?" he asked finally. "You can hate me until the day you die . . . but let me make that day your choice. Let me use the lyre to help you . . . to help all of us."

Laila felt rooted to the spot. Séverin took a step closer to her. He lowered his mouth to her ear. "Name any penance, and I will pay it kneeling."

This close, she caught the mint and smoke scent that clung to him. Before, she used to imagine that Séverin burned a new path wherever he went, and that the smoky smell of fire shadowed his steps. But she was wiser now, and her mind recognized what her body did not. She remembered the scent of mint and smoke from the funerary fires burning along the banks of the river of her childhood. Even the fragrance that clung to him was fatal.

"And how do you plan to do that?" she asked. "By turning yourself into some kind of god?"

His eyes flashed. "If that's what it takes," he said.

But there was a caged quality to his voice, and when Laila searched his eyes again, she found the words for what she could not decipher before:

He *wanted* godhood.

More than that, he believed he would get it. She could see it in his eyes. That ice in his gaze had melted to something shining and zealous.

"You are out of your mind, Séverin."

"I've seen and felt something you wouldn't understand," he said fiercely. "And I know there's power at the end of it. Enough to extend your life. To fix the things I've ruined. Maybe even to bring back what was lost. But I will never leave you in the dark again. I want us to go into the light *together*."

Laila stared at him. "How can you believe such things?"

His eyes seemed to take on an otherworldly sheen beneath the candlelight. "Laila, there has to be a reason for it all . . . a reason why I have this ability, why our lives crossed, even how we ended up here. How else do you explain it? How else do you explain how I would be on the other side of that curtain? How I would have known you anywhere even from something as small as your hand—"

"*Stop*," she said loudly.

Séverin froze. Whatever light had shone in his eyes retreated, and when he spoke, there was a clipped mechanical quality to it: "You know as well as I do that our best chances to get to Poveglia lie with each other. I assume you will be at Carnevale tomorrow. Let us meet there, find the map, and leave for Poveglia together. Then . . . then I can show you that I am not some fool . . . that I am speaking the truth."

Laila narrowed her gaze. "And Ruslan?"

A muscle in his jaw ticked, as if he were chewing on something invisible. Laila had the bizarre urge to press a tin of cloves into his hands.

"At sunrise tomorrow, I will send word to the piazza with a plan," he said.

Laila nodded. She was familiar with the famous piazza of Venice. "And tomorrow?"

"I'll be there at midnight."

"How will you find us?"

A sad smile touched his mouth. "I would find you anywhere."

The words moved through Laila. He could be so caring when he wished to. Unbidden came the memory of the time she'd burned her hand on a hot pan, and he had been so panicked that she was in pain that it had taken her nearly twenty minutes to convince him that she did not need a physician. Laila moved away, but he caught her wrist.

"You know we can't leave like this," said Séverin, his voice low in her ear. "We've been here . . . in this spot for lovers' trysts or fate's machinations, whatever you wish to call it, for nearly half an hour. If we leave as we entered, surely that will draw suspicion."

"How thoughtless of me," she said.

Laila pressed her palm deeply against her lips. Then, rather un-gently, she swiped her hand across his mouth. Rouge blurred at the edges of his lips and chin. She tugged at the opening of his shirt, relishing the sound of scattered buttons hitting the floor. Her ring had twisted toward her palm, and when she dragged her hand down his chest, she felt him wince at the jewel's edge scraping down his skin, leaving a red mark.

Last, she tugged at his hair. There was a cruel familiarity to her gestures. It had only been a handful of days since that night in the ice palace when their hearts had beat in sync, and everything seemed awash with hope. But when she pulled back her hand, she saw the dwindled days left to her. That fullness against her ribs ached and said: *No more. I can hold no more.*

"Is this how you want me, Laila?" Séverin asked. There was no jest in his voice, but a wounded hopefulness. "Bloodied up by your hand?"

"No," she said, reaching for the curtains. "I don't want you at all."

14

ENRIQUE

At dawn, Enrique scrutinized his appearance in the long mirror in the library. He wore a black suit. A white cravat. He had changed his bandage so that it was soot dark and almost—*almost*—blended into his hair. His scab throbbed a bit as he lowered a black hat over his head and arranged the brim over the nubbed wound. He glanced at himself in the mirror. The hat's brim was tugged so low, one could no longer see his left eye.

He looked like the incompetent villain in a pantomime.

"Ugh," said Enrique, dragging the hat down lower.

Ever since Laila had come home last night with the news that Séverin would be joining them at Carnevale and would send word at sunrise to the Piazza San Marco, Enrique could not stop thinking about what he should wear. Though it had only been days, he was not the same Enrique that Séverin had appeared to leave for dead. He wanted Séverin to see that at first glance. He wanted him to be struck by his patina of . . . manliness? No. *Independence*. Independence haloing him like an aura. Pigeons flying out from behind him in a maelstrom of feathers.

Perhaps that would be too much.

Besides, no amount of mind Forging had been able to corral the pigeons of Venice.

All night, Enrique couldn't sleep. He polished his shoes. He washed his hair and neatly set it with wax. He plucked at every stray bit of dust on his suit. He wanted to press the words *I don't need you* into every stitched line of his jackets and pants.

At first, Enrique had balked at being given the task to meet with him alone tomorrow.

"Why do I have to see him?" he had asked. "He'll find us at Carnevale anyway."

Laila hesitated. Her gaze flicked—there and away—to his wounded ear.

"It's Ruslan," she said. "We can't leave for Poveglia with the Fallen House on our trail. They must be dealt with, and Séverin said he would come up with a plan. So. Who will go to the piazza tomorrow?"

"Me!" said Hypnos, raising his hand.

"And risk a Sphinx authority catching sight of the patriarch of House Nyx?" asked Laila.

Hypnos lowered his hand slowly. ". . . Not me."

"I have work," said Zofia, eyeing the folded up Forged masks that Laila had brought back.

"I already dealt with him last night after I got our masks," said Laila stiffly. She turned the ring on her hand.

Enrique felt a shudder run down his back when he thought of the four, cruel-looking, mind Forged masks. When Laila had returned and brought them out, he was curious. Each mask looked like a monstrous skull. When he placed it over his face, he wasn't prepared for the force of its power. It was like his consciousness had been yanked out of him, images flashing of paths through alleyways and past waterfronts, familiar to him as a memory . . . and yet not a memory he had ever made. The mind Forged visions ended before a mosaic-patterned wall in an alley, which he supposed would be the entrance to Carnevale tomorrow.

"And I still have things I need to read around the safe house," said Laila. "I want to make sure we don't miss anything."

Which left Enrique.

When they had all agreed, Enrique looked to Laila, who hung back while the others exited the room.

"What is it?" she asked.

"You never said what he was like when you saw him. Should we truly trust him?"

Laila lifted her chin. An imperial indifference settled over her features.

"He was . . . contrite," she said. "And I *do* believe he means to help us, but he seems possessed by his idea. Like a man half-maddened. And yet underneath there *were* glimpses of . . ."

Laila broke off, shaking her head. Enrique knew what she had been about to say.

Glimpses of who he had once been.

But they both knew those were dangerous grounds for hope. And even if Séverin had found his way back to who he had been, Enrique refused to be the person *he* had once been, the foolish, wide-eyed historian whose trust was easily bought simply by indulging him. He wouldn't be that fool. And he didn't want to look like it either.

In a few minutes, he would have to leave for the piazza. Enrique studied his appearance one more time, turning his chin this way and that.

"You know," said a voice at the entrance. "You are perhaps the only person I know who could look ravishing with one less ear."

Enrique felt a dull pang of warmth as Hypnos—beautiful and immaculately dressed as always—stepped into the room. For the past few days, they had circled each other cautiously. Even on the evenings when Hypnos tried to enliven the group with some music, Enrique would not let a smile cross his lips.

"One, don't toy with me," said Enrique. "Two . . . since when are you awake before dawn?"

Hypnos didn't answer him. Instead, he walked toward him slowly. The closer he got, the more Enrique felt as though he were testing a bruise. Did this hurt? What about now? A part of him winced at the other boy's closeness, but it was no longer a jagged wound.

The truth was that Hypnos had always been honest with him. It was Enrique who hadn't been honest with himself. Which made it all the more confusing when Hypnos reached out to cup his face, his fingers circling the outer edge of his bandages.

Enrique went still. ". . . What are you doing?"

"I'm not sure yet," said Hypnos thoughtfully. "I believe it's called 'comforting,' though such emotional exertion seems exhausting. If you require a distraction instead, you know I enjoy distracting you."

A long dead flicker of *something* stirred weakly in Enrique's heart. He pushed away Hypnos's hand. That wasn't what he wanted from him.

"I know I behaved badly," said Hypnos.

Around them, the house was quiet. The candles in their sconces flickered. It felt like time could not touch them here, and perhaps that was what moved him to speak the truth.

"And I know I saw what I wanted to," said Enrique.

Hypnos looked up at him. His frost-colored eyes looked unexpectedly warm. "When I said that I could learn to love you . . . I meant that . . . that someone like me needs time."

Enrique stared at him. When Hypnos had spoken those words to him a few days ago, that was not how he had interpreted them. The words had hit him like a rejection, as if he were someone difficult to love. Now, a confused warmth spread through his chest.

"I—"

Hypnos shook his head. "I know now is not the time, *mon cher*. I merely wanted you to understand what I meant . . ." The other boy reached out, gently brushing the back of his hand against his bandage. "I am not here to hurt you. I am not here to tell you what a future such as ours might look like. I merely wanted you to know that at the very least, I can be your friend. I can hold your secrets, if you'd let me."

A sigh loosed from Enrique. He did not move away when Hypnos stroked his face. An ache he did not realize he'd carried eased off of him.

"Thank you," he said.

"Does that mean we are friends at least?" asked Hypnos hopefully.

At least. His mind would have to untangle that . . . later. Perhaps days later.

Enrique sighed. "I suppose."

"Excellent," said Hypnos. "Now. As your friend, it is my duty to tell you that your outfit is abominable, and as I fully expected this, I have another one already steamed, pressed, and ready for you to wear."

TEN MINUTES AND some cursing later, Enrique—in a completely different set of clothes—waited in the Piazza San Marco.

Normally the piazza was crammed with people, but the day was cold, and the sunrise was little more than a wisp of gold on the lagoons. And so, for the past twenty minutes, he shared the view with no one but the pigeons. Eventually, the pigeons realized he had no food and abandoned him with a coo and a huff, fleeing for the gilded eaves of St. Mark's Basilica which crowned the public square.

For a long while, Enrique could do nothing but stare at the piazza. This early, the square was alive with magic. The pale basilica seemed carved of antique moonlight and old snow. Its half-moon archways bore scenes of St. Mark's bones arriving in Venice. Atop the precious porphyry marble columns, the four bronze horses stolen from the thirteenth century sack of Constantinople looked ready to burst from the church's facade and take flight. Enrique had been to the piazza before, but he had never experienced it like this . . . as if history had pinned him to one place.

On one side of the basilica stood the Doge's Palace—with its hundreds of columns and arches like frozen lace—and the rust-colored bell tower on the other. Around him, the square seemed to whisper in a thousand languages and traditions. Domed Islamic lanterns and jewel-encrusted North African *alfiz* arches stood side by side with the grand basilica. Inside it, the bright Byzantine gilding tempted one to imagine that the church had sliced out squares of sunshine and fixed the pieces one by one to form the cupolas' gleaming bellies. Here, time had softened the lines of history and alchemized them into a collective story of humanity.

In that second, Enrique felt as though the buildings were watching him.

"*Tabi tabi po,*" he whispered.

Please excuse me.

He hoped his lola's words worked, that the spirits in the buildings regarded him not as a trespasser but a humble visitor. Or perhaps a pilgrim. Someone looking for their place in the world.

His ear throbbed in the winter air, and Enrique touched it gingerly.

"Could you give me a sign?" he asked the silent buildings. "Please?"

Enrique closed his eyes. He felt the wind on his face. The stark February sun folding away the mist—

Something tugged at his jacket. Enrique's eyes flew open. For a second, he almost imagined an *enkanto* peering up at him . . . its long fingers holding out a prize. *We accept the trade*, it would say, eyeing his lost ear.

But it was not an *enkanto* that stared up at him, it was a child. A boy no older than eight, wearing dirtied pants. His unruly hair was shoved under his cap.

"*Per te*," said the child, dropping a red apple in his hand.

Enrique frowned, trying to hand the child back the apple. "*No, grazie—*"

The boy stepped back, scowling. "*L'uomo ha detto che questo è per te.*"

Without a second glance, the boy fled the square, leaving Enrique with the apple. Enrique's Italian was fairly decent, but it took him a moment to parse the words:

The man said this is for you.

All this time he'd been expecting Séverin, but he hadn't shown. On the one hand, it would've been too difficult otherwise. And yet, Enrique felt a little foolish staring down at his carefully chosen clothes and polished shoes . . . on some level, all of his armor had been for nothing. And yet, when he stared up at the buildings, he felt oddly watched. As if he had caught the attention of something greater than himself, and so perhaps his finery was not a waste.

Enrique turned the apple in his palm. In its rind, he noticed the tiniest slit. He pressed his thumbs around the crack, and the fruit broke open, revealing a folded-up note:

Harbor #7
The Phoenix's fire must hold through midnight.
Be there in three hours.

15

ZOFIA

In the early-morning hours, Zofia held two halves of a broken heart, each made of glass and about the width and length of her smallest finger.

The pieces had come from the crystal stag in the Sleeping Palace. She knew it was not alive, but she had grown fond of the intricate machine whose Forging artistry was unlike anything she had encountered thanks to the Fallen House. The ice creatures could communicate—in the most basic of senses—with one another. They could detect light, and pursue it; sense weight, and bear it; and, depending on the tampering of its settings . . . sense an intruder and attack them.

Before they had left the Sleeping Palace, she had removed this heart from the stag and taken it with her, thinking she might study it a little further. Now, with some added metallurgical Forging of her own, she had created a bonded pair of explosives capable of communicating with each other. When one detonated, so would the other.

Zofia was not sure if it would be useful, but at least it addressed an unknown. Looking around her laboratory, Zofia wondered whether she had done enough. She had Forged miniature explosive devices, tools capable of muffling sound, lengths of rope and retractable blades. And that was not including the tools now concealed in the long robes for tonight's Carnevale.

One unknown at a time, Zofia told herself.

There were three days left until the number on Laila's garnet ring read zero. Three days to find the light that would lead Laila out of the dark. Three days until Zofia would face the unknown contents of Hela's letter. Even now, she could feel the softened edges of her sister's envelope against her skin. Twice today, she had removed the letter and smoothed it onto her worktable. But she could not open it, not until there were less unknowns ahead of her. It was just as Hela had told her all those years ago:

I would wait for the light to show me the paths before me . . . and then I would not be so lost.

Every day, Zofia felt as though she were working toward more light.

She was on the verge of lowering the two halves of the stag's heart into a fireproof box when Enrique burst through the doors of her laboratory. He was breathing fast. High color touched his cheeks, and his hair looked mussed.

"Drop what you're doing!" he cried.

Zofia frowned. "Is that wise? This is a bomb."

Enrique's eyes went wide and he waved his hand. "Never mind, do *not* drop that."

In the other room, Hypnos had been singing loudly and playing the piano, but now the music stopped abruptly. "Isn't it too early in the day to toy with explosives?" he called.

Zofia considered her worktable. "Not for me."

"How was Séverin?" asked Hypnos, appearing in the doorway.

"He wasn't there," said Enrique, holding up an apple. "But a boy gave me this."

Zofia remembered Enrique complaining about the apples in L'Eden years ago. "I thought you don't like apples."

"I don't, but—"

"You don't like apples?" asked Hypnos. "But *tarte tatin* is a gift from the gods!"

"*Tarte tatin* is different—"

"But it's made from apples—"

"Enough about apples!" said Enrique, waving his hand. "It's a message from Séverin."

Zofia gently set the halved explosives into their box and stood.

"*Harbor number seven . . . the Phoenix's fire must hold through midnight,*" read Hypnos aloud. "What's that supposed to mean?"

"Harbor number seven must be where they keep the Fallen House's gondolas. Séverin needed a plan for us to get rid of Ruslan, so this must be it." Enrique glanced at Zofia and smiled. "The reference to Phoenix's fire is an obvious nod to her gift."

"Gift?" said Hypnos, peering at Zofia. "I wasn't aware of any gifts other than the ability to deliver morbid statements with an exceptionally flat affect. Oh, and wonderful hair."

He was grinning, so Zofia knew this was a joke and smiled back.

A small smile touched Enrique's lips and his gaze flew to hers. It was the way he had once looked at Séverin at the successful end of an acquisition. It was . . . pride, Zofia realized.

Enrique was proud of her.

The thought made her face feel strangely warm.

"Ruslan might be a demon, but blowing up his gondola seems . . . grisly," said Hypnos.

Enrique scowled, touching his ear. "If the tables were turned, I doubt he would feel the same hesitation."

Zofia agreed with Enrique.

"What about the rest of the instructions?" asked Hypnos, before reciting: "*Fire must hold through midnight.* What does that mean?"

"He used that code in the past," said Zofia. Hypnos's eyebrows scrunched together, which meant he did not know what she meant, so Zofia explained. "Séverin used it as code for an explosion that must not be detonated until an appointed time."

Enrique sighed, tugging at his hair. "So we need to get close enough to the Fallen House gondola to put an explosive on it, and then figure out a way to detonate it from a distance?"

"What can explode something at a distance?" asked Hypnos, frowning.

Zofia glanced at her worktable and the bonded explosive pair.

"A broken heart," said Zofia.

AN HOUR LATER, Zofia, Enrique, and Hypnos watched the gondolas cross the Grand Canal from beneath the shadows of an archway on the Rialto Bridge. Zofia had not left the safe house since they had arrived, and it struck her suddenly that she was in Venice. She was so far away from Paris and Poland, so far from all the things that had always been so familiar, and yet even here, the sun rose and the sky looked blue. When they were children, Hela said the dawn was secretly a broken egg, its yolk dribbling slowly across the sky. Hela said that if they were only tall enough, they might scoop up the sticky sunshine in their palms, slurp it down, and turn into angels.

It did not sound particularly appealing to Zofia.

She did not like the smell of raw eggs. And she did not like the sliminess of egg yolks. What she did like was her sister's voice whispering stories to her in the dark. And it was this thought that warmed Zofia despite the February air that turned her every exhale into lace.

Beside her, Enrique lowered his binoculars. "We have a problem."

"Just the one?" asked Hypnos.

Enrique glared at him. "See that?" He pointed to the wooden spikes that the gondolas were tethered to. "They have Mnemo bugs on them. If we try to access the gondola from the street, they'll know and find us."

"Then it's a good thing I'm here," said Hypnos.

"Somehow I don't imagine the Fallen House realizing that you're alive and here is good for anything," said Enrique. "Besides, Laila will be furious when she finds out you left the safe house."

Laila had left soon after Enrique to explore the grounds around House Janus. She was certain she would find something that would give them a hint about where to find the map to Poveglia's temple.

"I am taking every precaution," said Hypnos. "I'm even in this hideous disguise."

Zofia did not think he was in disguise; he was merely wearing ordinary clothes for the first time. That said, his Babel ring, a crescent moon that stretched across three knuckles, was hidden beneath a pair of thick gloves.

"If we can't get to the gondola through the street, then we'll go through the water," said Hypnos.

"How?" asked Enrique. "If we get into a gondola, they'll recognize us immediately."

Hypnos pointed to the canal. Even this early, the river was alive with traffic. Zofia watched as three boats holding cargos of winter fruit pushed past the slower, Forged gondolas that were heavily decorated and advertising plays and restaurants. Around the bend, a different boat drew into focus. This one was wider and shorter than a gondola, and sat only three people. Its wooden wings dragged across the surface of the lagoon. The boat's prow curved like a swan bowing its head. Inside the boat, sat a man and a woman, their hands interlinked. They were staring at each other and smiling. A third person sat at the front, pumping their legs to cycle the boat forward. They skirted past the boats by less than thirty centimeters.

"Your solution is a bird boat?" asked Enrique.

He did not sound impressed.

"*Non*, watch, *mon cher*," said Hypnos. "They are bound to do it soon."

"Do what?" asked Enrique.

"Shhh."

In the swan boat, the man and woman leaned forward and their mouths touched. Zofia's face warmed at the sight, and she would have turned her head had not the boat suddenly transformed at their kiss. The white, swan wings folded up, swallowing them completely from sight.

Zofia started to count the seconds . . . fourteen, thirty-seven, seventy-two, one hundred and twenty. Abruptly, the wings flapped down and the couple appeared once more. Their faces looked red and their hair looked more mussed than before. They shared a small smile with each other.

"Keeps you on the other side of the watching Mnemo bugs, gets you close to the gondola," said Hypnos. "And awfully cheap too at this time of day. Trust me, I've utilized many a Love Boat on my trips to Venice."

Enrique's face turned red. "I . . . um . . ."

"That is not a bad idea," said Zofia.

"See?" said Hypnos. "I'm more than a pretty face."

"Of course you are," said Zofia.

Hypnos clapped his hands to his heart. "Ah, *ma chère*, so kind—"

"You have shoulders and feet, and a neck . . . though I do not know whether those would be considered pretty."

Hypnos scowled.

"But who will be the couple?" asked Enrique. "And who will pedal the boat?"

Zofia looked at the two of them. She had seen them kiss more than once, and they seemed to enjoy it, so she didn't understand Enrique's hesitation.

"Oh," said Enrique, turning even redder. "We aren't—" He paused, gesturing between Hypnos and himself.

"We're currently friends," said Hypnos, not looking at Enrique.

"You don't know how long you will be friends?" asked Zofia.

"Oh, we will *always* be friends, but whether there will be something more, who can say?" said Hypnos lightly. "So it will have to be you and one of us, Zofia. Which will it be? I vote me." He bowed low. "First, I'm exceptionally handsome. Second, I'm certainly more handsome than our historian—"

Enrique frowned. "What does that have to do with—"

"And *third*," said Hypnos, talking loudly over Enrique. "I am a wonderful kisser."

He winked, which made Zofia laugh because it indicated that it was friendly and joking, but at the same time, Hypnos's mention of a kiss summoned a strange gap in her plan that she had not considered.

With Séverin's acquisitions in the past, acting was sometimes necessary. That did not bother Zofia. She liked being given rules of how to comport herself and what to say or do. It eased her mind to know all the rules in advance. But she had never acted romantically. She had never even been kissed. It was something Hela had teased her about before she left for Paris.

"Going all the way to Paris, and yet to kiss a boy! Don't you want to kiss someone, Zosia?"

In truth, there were very few boys Zofia *wanted* to kiss. She knew how *want* felt . . . a low pulse in her belly, her heartbeat rising faster . . . normally, the thought of putting her mouth on someone else's struck her as awkward and faintly off-putting, but the idea of touching mouths with certain people made her feel caught somehow. As if she had been running to a place, and had been stopped against her will, and now all she wished was to get there. It had first happened around a young professor who was very kind and had light brown hair, but Zofia could not bring herself to speak to him. Now, she had those same sensations around Enrique, but they were more intense. Around him, she felt unsettling warmth and twinges, odd skips in her pulse that left her pleasantly light-headed when he looked at her for too long. She liked being around him. And when he left, sometimes she felt sad. This was attraction, but what was its fulfillment? What happened after? What if those sensations became so heightened she fainted? What if she wanted more than a kiss? Then what?

"It should be me," said Enrique.

He spoke quietly, but there was a force to it that made Zofia feel unbalanced, but not unpleasantly so.

Enrique cleared his throat. "I meant, I can help if there's anything that needs deciphering . . . besides, Hypnos shouldn't be seen. This way, he won't draw any attention to himself. He can keep his head down and pedal the boat."

Hypnos groaned. "I hate when you combat joy with reason."

Enrique ignored him. "If we move fast, we shouldn't have a problem."

THERE WAS A problem.

In harbor number seven rocked not one boat . . . but two. Within minutes, both would be within Zofia's reach. She wrinkled her nose as they moved closer. Hypnos pedaled fast, spraying water on the swan's wooden wings.

The gondolas looked nearly identical: black lacquer, an ornamental scorpion tail *risso*, precise purple velvet cushions. On the back of the first boat, Zofia expected and recognized the sigil of the Fallen House: a hexagram, or six-pointed silver star. What she hadn't expected was that the second boat would bear the same sigil, except in gold.

"Which one do we attach the device to?" asked Hypnos. "I can slow down, but we can't linger in front of the boat, it will draw too much attention."

"I . . . um," said Enrique, tugging at his hair. "There has to be a difference in the symbols. Or the color, perhaps, but what?"

"*You're* the historian!" said Hypnos, slowing down his pedaling. "How should I know?"

Zofia leaned forward, getting her device ready. In the pocket of her jacket, she felt Hela's letter inching forward. Her nose wrinkled from the nearness of the sewage water.

"It's an old symbol, but more recently seems to be linked to Jewish identity," said Enrique.

"We call it Magen David," said Zofia.

The Star of David, though her sister told her it was not an actual star, but was also a symbol on an ancient king's shield.

Beside her, Enrique fidgeted with his hair, murmuring to

himself. "What's the symbol saying?" he asked, rocking back and forth as he rattled out the history of the symbol, half mumbling to himself. "Encircled, the hexagram represents Solomon's Seal, which has Jewish and Islamic roots. Hindus called it *shatkona*, but that's a representation of the masculine and feminine sides of the divine, not connected at all to what we know about the Fallen House. Maybe if we knew their real name, we'd have a clue, but all we know is that they like gold, but that could be a trap and—"

"Oh gods," breathed Hypnos.

Zofia looked up and heard Enrique suck in his breath. Ruslan appeared on a bridge not fifteen meters away, his back to them and the lagoon. A pair of hooded guards stood on either side. A hint of gold glinted beneath the cuff of his coat, and Zofia felt a chill remembering that golden hand clenching her arm.

"We have to go!" hissed Hypnos, pedaling forward.

"Not before we figure out the gondola situation!" said Enrique.

The swan boat whirled in a circle, narrowly avoiding colliding with a different gondola.

Zofia flung out her hand for balance, her hand skimming the outside of the Fallen House gondola decorated with the silver star. The moment she touched it, she heard a whisper of metal deep in the boat . . . *gold. I can bend at your will.*

"Stop!" she cried out.

"Zofia, what are you doing?" demanded Enrique.

She crouched forward, bracing both hands against the different gondolas. She strained her senses and felt the shiver of metal through her skin. Within seconds, she knew. The gondola with the silver star was actually made of gold that had been Forged to distribute weight differently, while the one on the right with the golden star was solid wood.

"It's this one," she said, pointing to the silver.

"He could turn any second," said Hypnos. "We have to leave *now.*"

Zofia fumbled with the device, leaning farther out of the gondola. The ends of her coat brushed the lagoon water, and she forced herself not to gag. Zofia shoved her will into the invention: *You want to be here; you want to be part of this object.* Over and over, she chanted it through her mind until—

The detonating device melted seamlessly into the boat.

"Now get away from it!" said Hypnos. "We're drawing attention!"

Zofia tried to move back—her hand was stuck.

She moved again, but it was like the metal wanted to pull her into itself. *Not me, you don't want me*, she told the metal. It loosened, but she wasn't strong enough to pull away.

"Start pedaling," she said, gritting her teeth as she tugged at her right arm with her left hand.

Slowly, it unclasped, and Zofia winced as the skin of her palm scraped.

"I've got you, Phoenix," said Enrique. He wrapped his arms around her waist, tugging hard. Zofia fell back against Enrique, and the movement rocked the boat, nearly crashing them into another gondola—

"Attento!" shouted the gondolier.

Zofia sat up, her hand burning. The canal had grown more crowded. The gondolier had started shouting at them, which made the other boats slow down to watch. Zofia looked up at the bridge. She saw, as if time had slowed down, awareness prickling through the line of Ruslan's shoulders. He started to turn.

Zofia whirled to face Enrique. "Kiss me."

His eyes went wide. "Now? Should I—"

Zofia grabbed Enrique's face and brought it to hers. Instantly, the wings of the swan shivered around them, hiding them from sight. Venice vanished around them. The shouting went mute. All she could feel was the sudden tug of the boat through the water as Hypnos spirited them away from Ruslan's notice. Zofia was so caught up in the kiss as a distraction that she almost forgot it was a kiss—

Until she didn't.

It was dark and warm inside the closing of the swan's wings. Enrique's lips felt wind-roughened and dry. Zofia broke the kiss. It had all been rather anticlimactic, though she was not sure what she had expected.

"That was not awful," she offered.

Enrique paused, and she felt her face flaming, something inside her shrinking fast in embarrassment.

"But it could be so much better," he said.

"How?"

She wanted to know. The next instant, she felt his warm hands sliding up her cheek. Zofia's eyes were wide open in the dark, not that it let her see any clearer, but it felt important that, for what happened next, her eyes should stay open. She felt the space shift in front of her, the softest gust of warm air against her lips, and then—

Zofia was kissed.

Zofia understood the concept of heat. She knew that it was the result of atoms and molecules colliding, the motion of which generated energy. Warmth—not like a flare, but a slow, rising wave—swept up from her toes to her heart. And yes, there was energy in this . . . in being kissed and kissing *back*. She was a participant in the unseen particles spinning in an invisible choreography. Like a dance inside her bones. She leaned forward eagerly into the unexpected warmth of Enrique as her mind registered new sensations: the scratch of his unshaven cheek, his teeth on her lower lip, the wet heat as his mouth opened hers. It was not unpleasant. It was the very opposite, in fact. Enrique held her close, close enough that she could feel her heartbeat on his. And that was when she noticed it—or rather, the *absence* of it.

Hela's letter was gone.

16

SÉVERIN

On the night of Carnevale, Séverin stroked the bruised violet bloom of a poisonous larkspur flower and waited.

Almost three years ago, Laila had made a feast of flowers as a special dessert for some prominent guests staying at L'Eden. It was late spring, and the city of Paris seemed like an irritable bride on her wedding day—sulky and sweating at a perceived lack of attention while blooming flowers shone like jewels on the city's limbs.

Tristan had cleared a space in the gardens, and a Forging artist who specialized in textiles had constructed a silk tent that would keep in the cool air and later stir around the guests as if moved by a mild breeze. On a banquet table absent of any silverware, Laila was nearly finished arranging piles of golden dahlias, crimson roses, cloud-blue hydrangeas, and wreaths of honeysuckles. They looked eerily lifelike. On the rim of a cowslip, a single drop of dew seemed ready to slide down the petal.

And yet, even from where he stood at the head of the banquet table, Séverin could smell the marzipan and vanilla, cocoa and citrus beneath the artfully sculpted flowers. One bloom did not look as though it belonged. It was a long, blue larkspur, each violet petal streaked blue like the sky at twilight.

"You snuck a poisonous flower into the arrangement?" asked Séverin, pointing at it. "I doubt our guests will be brave enough to try it."

"And what if I told them that it was the sweetest out of all these blooms . . . that underneath those deadly petals is a thick almond cream with a ripple of spiced plum down the middle?" said Laila, her eyes sparkling with slyness. "Surely such a taste is worth a brush with death, wouldn't you say? Unless you are not quite as brave as I imagined."

"Well, now you're appealing to my vanity *and* my curiosity," said Séverin. "Which means, of course, that I can't help but be tempted."

"So it's working, then?" said Laila, grinning.

"Of course it's working," said Séverin. He reached out, snapped off a bit of the larkspur's sugar leaf, and ate it. The taste of vanilla and cardamom rolled over his tongue. He held out a bit to Laila, who immediately popped it into her mouth. She raised her eyebrows at the taste, clearly pleased with her work.

"What do you think?" she asked, looking up at him.

She was so close, he had to look down at her. It was before he had ever touched her, ever kissed her lips or the scar down her spine. She was a wonder to him, a sunlit crystal that could peel back the light to reveal its secret, multihued veins.

"I think it's fair to say that you have witchcraft in your lips, and hands, and there is as much eloquence in a sugar touch of them as there is in any of your desserts."

He had meant the words to sound sophisticated . . . distant, even. After all, they were not his words, but a line stolen from Shakespeare's *Henry V*. But when he uttered them, the words turned like a spell. Maybe it was the soft lights of the tent or the painted sugar petals. Whatever it was, his elegantly meant words came out earnestly, and though they were obviously borrowed lines, his tongue did not know the difference. They felt true.

"Fine words," said Laila, color deepening in her cheeks. "But words without action are hardly convincing."

"What do you I propose I do to be convincing?"

"Surely you can think of something," Laila had said, smiling.

He was too stunned by what he'd said and that she hadn't laughed at him outright that it didn't occur to him until the next morning that she might have *actually* welcomed his attention. He should have kissed her hand. He should have told her that her smile was a snare from which he never wished to escape.

I should have, I should have, I should have . . .

There was no poison more potent than the shadow cast by those words, and they haunted him with renewed fervency ever since he had left the *mascherari* bar.

Séverin was still thinking of this when he heard footsteps behind him in the poison garden. He did not turn. His hands were behind his back, clasping a pair of garden pliers.

"Did you find something?" asked Eva. She touched his back. The gesture was soft, but her voice was harsh.

"In my hand," he said.

He had found the pliers this morning when he was searching for an object of comparable weight to the divine lyre. He would need it if he was going to fool Ruslan.

Eva took the pliers, and he heard the rustle of silk as she tucked it into her sleeves. She angled her body as if she were embracing him fondly, wrapping her arms around his waist. In his ear, she hissed: "If I catch even a whiff that you are trying to deceive me, I will kill you. I could make your blood *literally* boil."

"If I thought any different, I would not have trusted you at all," said Séverin mildly.

Eva was still. He could hear her breathing hard. Last night, she had confronted him after they had left the *mascherari* bar.

"I saw her," Eva had said, furious. "I recognized her as she left the salon. Did you really think you could hide her from me?"

"No—" Séverin started.

"All that nonsense about meeting at the Bridge of Sighs," Eva had snarled. "Was it a trick? Did you decide not to help me after all? Because I know what I saw, and I will go to Ruslan and—"

"Spare me the threats, and tell me what you want," said Séverin harshly. "I had no intention to leave you in the dark, but I doubt you'll believe me even if I did tell you the truth. All that matters is that we both need to be rid of Ruslan, and now I am certain we can come to an arrangement."

And so they had.

Séverin turned slowly, ignoring the Mnemo beetles on the wall. For all they perceived, he had been admiring the flowers and she had moved closer. He bent around Eva, and her arms went about his neck.

If they were lovers, it was natural that they should embrace, that she should tuck her head into the curve of his neck and press a kiss beneath his earlobe. Eva rose up on her tiptoes, her lips at his ear, her hand tucking something into his pocket. He could feel the roughness of the leather straps.

"He knows something is wrong."

SÉVERIN'S PULSE SPIKED as he adjusted the leather-strapped wristlet Eva had smuggled to him against his arm. With his costume sleeves, the wristlet would be undetectable beneath his robes.

Soon.

He would see them soon. The knowledge moved inside him, desperate as a prayer. How were they? Was Enrique in pain after losing his ear? Would Hypnos clasp him as he would an old friend? Was Zofia well?

Would Laila ever look at him the way she once had?

It was a selfish cycle of questions, all of it centering around his own wants. He couldn't help himself. Hope was an exercise in delusion. He could only hope for such things if he secretly believed he was deserving of them, and though he knew he had disappointed them beyond belief, he was still holding an instrument of the divine. And with the lyre in his hands, he could believe anything.

"Monsieur Montagnet-Alarie. Are you ready?"

Eva stood in the doorway, holding out the ice-and-blood Forged box. Beside her stood a masked member of the Fallen House. Séverin moved toward them, catching sight of his reflection on the shining red walls as he passed. For his costume, Eva had selected a red-lacquered *medico della peste* mask, which now hung off the back of his billowing, crimson robes. From here, it looked as if he was sprouting horned ridges along his back, like a chimera not yet formed.

Séverin held Eva's gaze as he pressed his thumb to the thorny lock of the box. Blood welled on his skin. The box swung open.

"How stiffly you greet me, my love," he said, forcing a grin to his face. "Have I displeased you?"

"I found your behavior quite cold earlier," said Eva, turning her head.

"I was distracted," he said, holding out his hand. "Will you forgive me?"

Eva smiled, then sighed. She moved the ice box to the crook of her left arm, then reached for him. But as she reached out, she stumbled. Séverin caught her, his hand sliding up her wrist, his fingers finding the garden pliers strapped to her arm beneath the heavy, green folds of her robes. He slid it out, and Eva adjusted, the case tumbling to the floor some distance away.

"The box!" she cried.

Beside Eva, the Mnemo honeybee on the mouth of the Fallen House member fluttered. Watching. Séverin knew what it saw. An empty box, and a girl who fell.

"Allow me," said Séverin.

He moved back a step, bending over the box. In full view of the Mnemo bug, he drew out the lyre from the folds of his billowing sleeves, taking care to make sure it was seen disappearing behind the lid of the box. He pretended to fuss over the instrument as he quietly swapped it with the garden pliers. A few moments later, he shut the lid. He picked up the case one-handed, holding it to him protectively.

"Is this really necessary?" he asked Eva. "Perhaps we can ask Patriarch Ruslan if he'd at least bring it onto the gondola with him? If we have all our supplies ready, we could leave for Poveglia immediately after Carnevale."

Eva frowned. "I'm not certain—"

But then Ruslan stepped into the shadows behind Eva. "I think that's a *wondrous* idea."

Séverin nearly succeeded in hiding the sudden tremor that ran through him as Ruslan came into view. His grip on the box tightened. The divine lyre pressed against his skin, held snug by the Forged wristlet straps which had immediately wrapped around the instrument.

"You do?" asked Séverin.

"Why, of course! Why would I delay godhood? I already know

the first thing I'm going to do"—Ruslan rubbed his bald head—"grant myself perfectly flowing locks." He closed his eyes and smiled, as if imagining it. "But I doubt we will all be able to leave at once. It would draw too much attention. It might be best if the three of us left for Poveglia from the House Janus location, and I send for the rest of my House after."

"An excellent plan," said Séverin.

And it would be. There was something strange about the Fallen House members. Their limbs moved with an inhuman stiffness. When he looked at their eyes beneath their masks, they looked clouded and gray. They did not blink. Even without Ruslan, they seemed incapable of any agency. Eva had said that without Ruslan, they might as well be powerless.

"May I?" asked Ruslan, holding out his hands to the box.

Séverin's heart rate kicked higher. May he what? Open it? Hold it?

Séverin held out the box. As Ruslan took it, the garden pliers slid and knocked into the inner wall of the box. Séverin stilled, wondering if Ruslan would notice. But the patriarch merely turned on his heel.

"Come," he said. "Our gondola awaits."

AS EVA DIRECTED them toward the drop-off location for House Janus's Carnevale, Séverin noticed that the patriarch never took his eyes off him. Séverin held his gaze.

"You've told us precious little about where to find the map to Poveglia's temple," said Séverin, with feigned boredom. "I assume it is something mind Forged, like the vial you showed me during supper some time ago."

Ruslan ignored the query. Instead, he glanced at his Midas Knife, turning it in his hands. "I've never told you my House's true name, have I?"

Up ahead, the lantern light of elaborate *palazzos* spilled across the lagoon. Judging by Eva's gestures, they would dock any moment now. Séverin forced himself to be patient.

"No," he said. "I have not had the pleasure of that information."

"Hmm," said Ruslan. He tapped his teeth with the point of his Midas Knife. "It is a teasing name. My father told us we had the greatest treasures out of all the Houses . . . and yet such priceless objects were mere nail clippings of the *real* source."

He knew Ruslan meant the Tower of Babel, the biblical construction that had nearly touched the belly of heaven. Western theory held that it was the scattering of such a building—brought about by a confusion of languages that halted its construction—that ushered Forging to the world. Where the pieces fell, Forging bloomed.

But that was only one view, as Enrique would say. And it was a dominant view simply because it belonged to those who had dominated.

Ruslan turned the knife in his hand. "I thought I could change myself, you know . . . I thought I could make myself fit in the world, or make the world fit me." He started to laugh. "Now I am walking alchemy! I am the transmutation of flesh to gold! I am . . . so *hungry*. Truth, godhood . . . they will fill me up and I shall never be hungry again. That is all I want, my friend. An end to emptiness."

Séverin held himself still. Usually, Ruslan would pose a question, would try to play. But there was nothing in the other man's face but a naked hope. An unwelcome pity streaked through him. Ambition had made Ruslan toy with an object that gave him power, but that power came with madness. In some ways, it was not Ruslan's fault. But that was not Séverin's responsibility.

"We shall have it soon," Séverin made himself say.

"Promise?" asked Ruslan. He was staring into his lap, running his thumb along the golden blade. He whispered under his breath: "I'd do anything."

Séverin felt as though he were looking at a corrupted mirror. He knew that pose, that focus, that endless repetition of touching an object that had brought both hope and sorrow. His mother's voice moved through him:

In your hands lie the gates of godhood . . .

He was different. He was not giving chase to something, he was already chosen. His hope was merely unrealized, not impossible.

He was not Ruslan.

Séverin reached up for his hood, pulling the mask over his face as the gondola came to a stop at a silent archway attached to a drab gray building.

"If you want godhood so badly, then why not give me more than a hint to the map that will take us to the temple?" asked Séverin.

Ruslan pouted. "Because I want you to be *worthy* of it, my friend. And I want to be worthy of it by having chosen you as my co-deity, you see?"

Séverin set his jaw. "You realize that by testing me, you might be denying yourself."

Ruslan bowed his head. "In that case, I will consider myself judged by the universe to be undeserving of such a gift." Then he looked up and laughed. "Everything in life requires *faith*, Monsieur Montagnet-Alarie. I have faith in you! Besides, you've already had a whiff of such a map, my friend, as you so cleverly surmised." He gestured to a Fallen House member who brought a small box, no larger than a jewelry case. "Store it in this to preserve its knowledge."

Eva moved closer to Séverin. Her *colombina* mask of silver and sapphire winked in the light.

"Oh, and Monsieur Montagnet-Alarie," said Ruslan, leaning forward. "Watch out for dragons."

THROUGH THE ARCHWAY, they stepped onto a short landing. From there, a dimly lit staircase spiraled into the dark. Séverin had taken a couple of steps when he realized Eva had not moved.

"Are you not coming?"

"And be killed on sight by the others?" said Eva. "No, thank you. I'll wait for you here. But . . . will you tell them that I . . . I—"

"I will tell them," said Séverin.

Eva swallowed hard, then nodded. "Go."

The long staircase led to a courtyard roughly the size of a dining room. On the stone walls, watery light waved and spangled. Above, a Forged ceiling of glass revealed that he was underwater. The shadows in the water looked like plumes of ink. Just then, the long, dark belly of a gondola slid across the ceiling and vanished out of sight.

Set into the wall niches were statues of angels with their hands pressed together, their heads bent in prayer. Three statues of animals, all three meters in height, adorned the middle of the room. Their backs were stretched and hollowed out, forming something of a bench within each. One was a great wolf, its jaws cracked, tongue lolling, carved fur standing on end. Another was a winged lion mid-roar. Séverin recognized it as the emblem of Venice, the sigil of St. Mark, patron saint of the city. The third was a creature Séverin only recognized from Enrique's lectures in the past: a lamassu.

An Assyrian protective deity with the head of a man, body of a lion and bird wings folded around its rib cage.

Séverin studied the room, a familiar prickle of awareness sweeping through him. This used to be his favorite part of acquisitions, the quiet way in which a room revealed its secrets. There was no obvious door, and thus the statues must operate as both exit and entrance. He turned, as if to tell someone beside him.

But Enrique, Zofia, Hypnos, Tristan, and Laila were not here.

There was no one to feed him history, summon more light in the room, jest about the smell, conjure strange flora, or tease out the secrets of an object.

There was only him. But he would find them. He would make amends.

Séverin looked up. There, shimmering as if suspended in the water, glowing writing appeared:

TO ENTER ANY UNKNOWN, WE WALK THE PATH OF THOSE WHO CAME HERE FIRST.

He smiled in understanding.

Arrogance might lead someone to pick the winged lion. It was the mark of Venice after all. But where did attributes such as wings come from? The present was a palimpsest, built upon the layers of that which had been sacred or profane from years past. The lion was meant to protect . . . but before the lion was an older version, an older symbol of protection.

This was House Janus's test of humility.

They considered themselves the guardians of cartographical treasures after all, and perhaps knowing where one stood in the world was a treasure in and of itself.

Séverin walked to the lamassu, resting his hand on the rough stone of its body. They had nearly acquired such a piece from the kingdom of Prussia. Enrique had said the lamassus would have once been more than four meters tall, part of a pair flanking either side of the lapis-lazuli entrance to a palace.

"The king was considered semi-divine, and as such, he would be guarded like the location of heaven itself," Enrique had said.

Séverin slid into the bench embedded in the back of the lamassu. Immediately, the wings lifted off the statue's body. It rose unsteadily. Tiny rocks dislodged, hitting the ground. Where the wall had once been solid, now it thinned to translucence. Beyond it, Séverin could make out the distant glimmer of chandeliers, the blurry color of rich costumes. The lamassu lurched forward, preparing to take him through the wall.

Séverin felt his heartbeat rise steadily. With each step of the lamassu, the lyre rubbed against his skin. Its steady, uncanny hum wound through him, as if it had woven itself into his very heartbeat. He imagined Laila, Hypnos, Enrique, and Zofia standing before him, and hope glowed in his chest.

Behind him, the writing on the wall slowly vanished. Séverin kept his gaze forward, his senses alert. Even so, he felt a little smug.

It was natural that he would walk the path of the ancients.

He thought of his mother's voice, the power in his veins.

He was meant for this.

17

ENRIQUE

Alone in the library, Enrique quietly breathed into his palm and sniffed.

It wasn't bad.

Maybe there was a whiff of the coffee he'd drank from earlier, but nothing so repulsive that it explained why Zofia had yanked back in shock, clutching her heart as if he'd mortally wounded her with a kiss. When she'd pulled back, a wash of nerves fizzed through him.

"I'm so sorry," he'd said, panicking. "Did I . . . did I misunderstand?"

"No," she said, breathing fast.

"Are you upset?"

"Yes."

But Zofia would not say more than that. The moment they had returned to the safe house, she'd fled to her laboratory to finish what inventions were needed before they left for Carnevale within the hour. Laila was not back yet. In the music room, Hypnos played the piano and sang a love song, pulling Enrique's thoughts back into that kiss.

He'd thought it was rather suave of him, the whole "it could be so much better" line. He'd meant it too. The moment Zofia's lips touched his, it was like answering a want he hadn't been able to articulate. He'd wanted this. Wanted *her*.

When he kissed her again, a slim beam of light knifed through the swan wing enclosures of the boat. He'd glimpsed the bright blue shine of her eyes, the fey-like sharpness to her chin and the lit-candle gold of her hair. For whatever blunt words she spoke, Zofia's lips were soft as snowfall, and the kiss blanketed his thoughts. For a while now, Zofia had unquieted something in him. They understood each other in a way he hadn't experienced, in a way that made him feel safe and heard. But maybe it had always been a one-sided emotion.

It wouldn't be the first time.

"Daydreaming?"

Hypnos leaned against the doorframe.

"You have been quite distracted since we returned," said Hypnos. Something knowing gleamed in his eyes. Enrique's face flamed.

"Well, yes, I mean, there's the fact that we have no clues for what awaits us in Carnevale, and I'm still gathering my notes on Poveglia and—"

"And you kissed Zofia."

"Please leave."

"Nonsense," sang Hypnos loudly. He cleared his throat and continued speaking. "Don't worry, I'm not envious. I have a big, generous heart and a big generous—"

"Hypnos."

"I was going to say 'sense of humor.'"

"Lies."

Hypnos grinned, then clapped his hands. "Well? How was it?"

Enrique glared at him.

"Oh, come now, *mon cher*," said Hypnos. "Friends tell friends secrets!"

"We have been friends for less than a day."

"Hmpf," said Hypnos before turning around and exclaiming in delight. "Little Phoenix! You join us once more!"

Enrique stood straighter as Zofia entered the room. He was nervous about making eye contact with her, but it was impossible to see her over the pile of robes and masks in her arms. She lowered them slowly onto the wooden table in the library before turning to face them. She regarded Enrique mildly. It was as if nothing had ever happened between them, and he wasn't sure if that left him grateful or gutted.

"Where's Laila?" she asked.

"Here."

Laila stepped inside, wearing a white dress. The color, he thought, looked funereal on her. Though she was no less kind, a distance had crept into her gaze since last night. Oftentimes, her fingers went to her wrist, as if she were checking her pulse.

"We're supposed to meet Séverin at midnight," she said.

Enrique's jaw clenched. "How will he find us?"

Laila looked as if she was about to say something else and then thought better of it. "I'm sure it won't pose a problem to him."

"But where do we go when we get there?" asked Hypnos. "I *imagine* if one is throwing a party, the setting will be magnificent, possibly labyrinthine—"

"Leave that to me," said Laila, wiggling her fingers. "Servants always see something. It's easy to brush against their sleeves or touch what they're holding and look into the rest of the room. Zofia, what have you brought us?"

Zofia touched the robes on the table. "Six explosives, a silencing board, one spherical detection device, five filtration devices for smoke, and smoking light deflection."

Hypnos blinked. "That's . . . that's rather thorough."

"Not to mention what's sewn into this," said Laila, patting the corsetry of her dress.

"Three daggers, four meters of steel rope, and phosphorous lenses in case our light source fails," rattled off Zofia.

Now Hypnos looked a little nervous. "This seems like an awful lot of dangerous objects required just to find a map . . ."

Zofia shrugged, chewing on a match. Hypnos looked to Laila, but she had gone distant once more. She twisted her ring, and Enrique's heart broke a little. The number of days left was weighing on her. And why shouldn't they? How could anyone breathe around that terror? But they were so close to finding an answer. So close to something that could change their lives.

Enrique reached out, holding her hand. He smiled. "We've got hope, a flimsy plan, and a great deal of explosives. We've gotten by on less. Let's go."

THE MIND FORGED masks told them where to go for the Carnevale, but not how to enter.

Half an hour before midnight, Enrique, Hypnos, Zofia, and Laila stood before a black-and-white wall of mosaic tiles at the entrance of a concealed alley that was empty and lined with refuse. Before them, the mosaics stretched about seven meters high, and three meters wide. Despite the arrangement of the tiles, it didn't resemble anything. On the bare wall beside it was a small square full of colored Forged lights—red, blue, yellow, and orange—each no larger than a coin. At its center was a blank, circular depression. The colorful lights would easily fit within it like a key, but why was such a thing necessary?

Enrique pushed back his mask. The cold, February air kissed his face. A passing breeze stung at his bandage, and he bit back a wince.

"Why does this feel like it's going to be another riddle?" asked Hypnos. "I already hate it."

One by one, they pushed their masks over their heads. Enrique touched the Forged lights, frowning as they wiggled beneath his fingertips. He'd seen this kind of decoration before in L'Eden. Depending on its arrangement in a wall sconce, the colorful lights could recast the hue of an entire room.

"Found something," said Laila.

He turned to see Laila walking toward a lone shoe at the end of the alley. When she touched it, she startled and glanced back at the mosaic.

"It's not supposed to look like that."

"What do you mean?" asked Enrique.

Laila frowned. "It *looks* like we're in the same place, but what I saw showed that this wall isn't supposed to be black and white tiles. It's supposed to be colorful . . . like an actual painting of something, but I couldn't see too clearly, the details were muddled."

Zofia reached beneath the neckline of her robes, tugging out her necklace. One of her pendants glowed.

"It's a Tezcat entrance," she said, before placing her hand against the tiles. "But it's locked somehow. Like it requires a key or a password."

At her touch, words swirled across the mosaic tiles.

Hypnos groaned. *"Again?"*

DEAR GUEST,
MAY OUR JOYS BE VERDANT.

Oh, thought Enrique, glancing at the bright lights. It was a color puzzle.

He waited for someone to speak first, but the others were silent. When he looked at them, he realized they were looking at *him*. It was a look of trust and expectation, an expression that Enrique had never felt the full weight of.

"What do we do?" asked Hypnos.

Enrique felt as if his rib cage were expanding as he gestured to the square of lights. "It's simple really . . . the hint is even in the line. 'Verdant' comes from the Latin '*viridis*,' which means . . . green. So we must make green on the color wall."

"There is no green light," said Zofia.

"Right—we must make it."

He reached for the blue light. It peeled easily off the wall. He slid it into the depression of the square, filling half of its depth. Then he reached for the yellow tile, placing it on top. Green light radiated outwards, first soft and then building in intensity. The green hue melted outwards, spreading across the black and white mosaic tiles like pooling ink. An image took shape as the wall soaked in light and color. A blue tinge spread up from the bottom half of the wall, narrowing into a glassy stream. The dappled emerald of stately cypress trees leapt up on either side. At the center, a pinprick of light grew and grew, and the wall of tiles shimmered with translucence until it melted away entirely to reveal a grand hallway.

Enrique's eyes widened as he took in the entrance to House Janus's Carnevale party. The festivities were spread across three levels. From here, the design of the main floor was like a sun with radiating beams. Or, Enrique realized as he tilted his head . . . a compass rose, which seemed fitting given House Janus's cartographical treasures.

At the center of the room revolved a golden, circular platform roughly the size of L'Eden's grand ballroom where dancers laughed and spun around, sometimes teetering on the very edge, centimeters away from the surrounding pool. Others splashed in the water, thin gowns clinging to their wet skin. Above the partygoers rotated a stained-glass and crystal candelabra, from which masked musicians performed.

If the center was the sun, then each of its beams led to a different entrance. On their left, a group of women wearing velvet *moretto* masks and bloodred gowns appeared to ride past a dark archway on the back of a massive, winged horse carved of stone. To Enrique's right, a pale-skinned woman wearing a *colombina* mask that appeared to be made of solid gold walked through a wall of roses.

"It's a whole network of Tezcat doors," said Zofia.

For the first time that evening, she seemed mildly interested.

Hypnos clapped his hands. "Come, let's go! The drinks await!"

Laila coughed lightly.

"Allow me to amend that. Our mission . . . and drinks . . . await?"

Laila rolled her eyes.

Some paces from the mosaic entrance rocked a Forged barge in an inky stream. Twin rows of potted cypresses, like an extension of the mosaic mural, arched over the water.

Enrique pulled his mask down over his head, feeling its weight press against his temples, his scalp, the tenderness of his wound. Through the eyeholes, the world seemed focused, the Carnevale party less like a fantastic Otherworld and more like a secret half-revealed. It stoked a familiar hunger inside him. The simple desire to *know* . . .

Enrique hadn't felt that twinge of curiosity in what felt like months. Lately, all his research had an undercurrent of panic and urgency. It still did, but now there was a new facet to it . . . he was learning not just for the sake of others, but for himself too. Slowly, Enrique felt as if the pieces of himself were falling back into an order he recognized. And when his friends moved around him, he was less like a piece buoyed along by momentum, and more like an anchor, certain and secure. Around him, the world seemed to reveal more and more of itself, and with every revelation, Enrique felt certain he would discover his place within it.

Beneath the mask, he smiled.

IT TOOK LAILA no more than ten minutes to determine where House Janus kept their treasures. As they moved through the party, Laila brushed her fingers against platters held by servants, towels slung over arms, the occasional lantern hanging on a pillar.

"This way," she said.

Laila led them past the throng of partygoers, and down one of the many hallways radiating off the main platform until they arrived before a short, empty hallway. At the far end, a sprawling silk tapestry covered one wall.

Enrique studied the tapestry. Embroidered across it was another compass rose, the diamond-shaped points reflecting the territories that fell north, south, east, and west of them. In the north, glaciers sewn together with silver thread. In the south, thready, golden sands. In the east, mountains of green knots, and in the west, woven blue waters.

"From the objects I read, I got the impression that the entrance to the treasure is connected to the tapestry," said Laila.

"Then let's go—" said Hypnos.

He took a step past the entrance, but Laila caught his arm.

"Zofia?" said Laila.

Zofia reached into her sleeves and rolled a spherical detection light across the stone. All along the sides of the hallway, coin-sized red lights sprang up next to the lit torches. Enrique's stomach sank.

"What are those?" asked Zofia.

"Shape-detecting Mnemo devices," said Hypnos, annoyed. "We employ the same ones at House Nyx. They raise alarms if they detect a moving shape in the background. Usually to get past, one must have a deflecting device that disrupts the machine's sensors."

"Then how will we get past?" asked Enrique.

"Simple." Zofia tapped the end of her mask's beak. "We remove detection of all shapes."

In a deft motion, Zofia pinched the long, hooked end of her beak. Puffs of steam uncurled from the nostrils in the bone-white mask, obscuring the blue of her eyes. In her long, navy robes with her face and hair hidden, Zofia reminded him of a psychopomp from a myth . . . a figure tasked with ferrying souls away from mortal realms.

Laila copied the motion, and Hypnos did the same. Enrique reached for his mask, feeling the slight groove of a depression in its design. A second later, steam poured out.

Zofia must have added a barrier within the mask because he could neither smell nor feel the steam, though he did see it gusting outwards and momentarily clouding his sight. As it cleared, he saw the Forged fog climb up the hallway, blanketing it in a thick, impenetrable mist.

"I counted ten paces to the wall," said Zofia. "Go."

Enrique walked through the blankness, his heartbeat thudding loudly in his ribs. He wondered how they might have looked in that second to anyone who might glimpse them . . . like envoys from hell, cursed angels with plague curling out from their nostrils.

He stretched out his hand, feeling the rough texture of the tapestry under his palm. The hallway seemed to exhale like a long-held sigh. The blankness of the fog gave way to a different hallway as they crossed through the Forged tapestry.

Enrique thought they would be met with silence, but a figure waited for them not two meters away from where they emerged.

A figure dressed in red, head bowed, with a lacquered mask the color of a slit throat.

Slowly, they raised their head. Gloved hands slid up, shoving back the hood, and Enrique sucked in his breath.

A slew of emotions ran through him. Joy, then anger . . . the bizarre desire to laugh punctured by the sudden throbbing of his wound.

Séverin's hair was mussed from the mask, but he stood tall and regal in his red robes. He arched an eyebrow, his mouth curving into a grin.

"I told you I'd find you."

18

LAILA

The moment she saw Séverin, Laila felt the ground melting beneath her, and her belly swooped with sudden weightlessness. It was not desire or even surprise. It was a moment when the present thinned, and the bones of the past showed through.

Laila saw the past.

She saw Séverin reaching for his tin of cloves and an extra packet of matches for Zofia. She saw his mouth curving into a grin as he listened to Enrique's newest historical finding. She saw his eyes lift to hers before he winked as if they were in on a secret.

The present was a different beast.

None of them had removed their masks. Séverin's smile fell. For a brief moment, he looked like a pilgrim: worn and penitent. On a mirror behind him in the hall, Laila saw what he must see before him. Robed figures with cruel masks, judges from another world sent to weigh his sins.

Hypnos was the first to throw back his mask.

"You found us!" said Hypnos, grinning. "I knew you would!"

Séverin returned his smile with genuine warmth . . . and relief.

Against her will, Laila remembered how the blankness had stolen through her last night at the *mascherari* salon . . . how texture turned slippery, sound faded, colors bled to white . . . until he touched her. She remembered how beautiful he looked in the dark room. How wounded.

I would find you anywhere.

"Oh, come now, we can't stay in those stuffy monstrosities," said Hypnos, gesturing at his face.

Enrique grumbled as he removed his mask. Séverin looked at him eagerly, but Enrique didn't make eye contact. Next went Zofia. Her expression jolted Laila.

When Zofia had returned from the gondola trip, she'd told Laila how she had lost Hela's letter. Laila knew that for someone like Zofia, the panic of the unknown was far worse than whatever news lay inside the envelope. She'd tried comforting her friend, promising they could send word once all this was over, that surely her family must have contacted L'Eden, and as soon as it was safe, they would get in touch with their Parisian staff. But Zofia had remained stiff-faced, terrified and silent. Until now.

When Séverin appeared, something in Zofia shifted. Her shoulders dropped. The tightness around her mouth relaxed. It hit Laila all over again that no matter what he'd done to them, some part of them trusted that Séverin could fix anything.

Her jaw tightened.

The same could not be said for her.

She could feel Séverin's gaze on her face. His lips tightened . . . as if in sympathy. Did he think she hid her face because her emotions were so vivid, she could not control herself? Did he think he was being merciful by indulging the privacy of her mask?

Séverin stepped forward, eyeing them hopefully. *Warily.*

"I . . . I know that what I did was . . ."

"Irrelevant right now?" said Laila. She tossed back her mask, her eyes blazing. "You found us. Good. For now, I'd rather focus our attentions on the map to Poveglia. I've done as much intel as I could. What do you have for us, Séverin?"

"Other than remorse in your heart?" said Hypnos. "A sufficient amount of guilt, perhaps, that we might all *move on*?"

"Technically, he cannot have remorse in his heart," said Zofia.

"I second that," said Enrique.

"He has blood, ventricles—"

Enrique sighed. Hypnos shook his head and seemed about to speak when a low laugh threaded through it all. Séverin. Laughing. Laila had forgotten the sound of it, deep and full-bellied.

"I've missed you all terribly," he said. "In fact, I—"

"How much more of my time do you wish to waste?" asked Laila coldly, facing them. She raised her hand, the number *three* plain in her garnet ring. "I expected better of my friends."

Hypnos reeled back as if slapped. Enrique's eyes went wide with hurt, and Zofia's gaze dropped to the ground. Laila didn't want to look at Séverin, but when he spoke, his voice was urgent.

"That will change, Laila," he said. "I swear it."

He drew back the sleeve of his robes, revealing the divine lyre strapped to his arm. Laila stared at the instrument. She hadn't forgotten how it had felt when his bloodied fingers touched a single string. As if her soul threatened to unhinge and slip past the loose cage of her bones. A shiver ran down her spine.

Séverin yanked down his sleeve, a determined expression on his face.

"I believe the map to Poveglia will be a mind Forged object," said Séverin. "A vial, perhaps. Not a traditional map at all. Ruslan gave me one hint before I left."

"Which was?" asked Enrique, crossing his arms.

Séverin's smile was mirthless. "Watch out for dragons."

ON THE OTHER side of the Tezcat tapestry, Laila discovered they had emerged in the railed-off upper galleries of House Janus's headquarters, looking down over the revelries. Along the curved walls hung dozens of ancient maps, each of them stretched, pinned, and framed by shining curlicues of gilt brass. A domed skylight above let in the moonlight, and when Laila peered over the edge of the railings, the nautilus of staircases revealed the revelers like a sea of undulating gold far beneath them. She dragged her fingers along the frames, the walls, the joints of paintings . . . but the objects were silent.

At first, Séverin walked ahead of the group, and it was as if a spell from the past fell over their feet. It was natural to fall into step behind Séverin. Easy, even. Too easy. Laila hung back, feeling a touch spiteful. Enrique, on the other hand, shook himself and practically stomped ahead.

At the end of the hall, Séverin paused in front of the final map, a circular silk screen printing of a clay tablet about a meter in diameter. Laila didn't recognize the script. It looked like a collection of sharp angles.

"Well, Enrique?" she asked.

Séverin, who had opened his mouth, quickly closed it. Enrique looked rather smug as he turned to face them. Was it her imagination or did Séverin step to the side, as if moving out of someone else's spotlight?

"This is *Imago Mundi*," said Enrique. "Otherwise known as the Babylonian Map of the World. It's a replica of the original clay tablet, of course—the original dates back to the early Achaemenid period. Babylonians certainly had dragon-like deities, such as Tiamat, a primordial goddess of the sea, so this *could* be part of the hint—"

Séverin studied the framing, stepping back. "I don't think so."

Laila imagined the room growing a touch colder.

"Excuse me?" asked Enrique.

"I doubt House Janus would want their entrance to treasure to be based on something that isn't an original. It would feel . . . insulting. As for the dragon link, I imagine it would not be so tenuous."

"So you think we need to look for an *actual* dragon?" asked Enrique.

"Maybe not quite so literal, but something more rooted to the word perhaps."

There was a certain logic to it. Again, the past intruded. Laila remembered how joyously Séverin used to read rooms of treasure, as if he understood, on some fundamental level, how precious things liked to hide. Once, it had made her feel special . . . how he, alone, had found her all those years ago, unearthed her skills, kept her safe. Treasured her. Laila pushed it from her mind.

"Fine," said Enrique tightly. "We can try it."

For the next ten minutes, the group split up to comb through the halls' maps and statues once more.

"I imagined this would be far more exciting," said Hypnos, bored. "Considering the dragons."

"What about this?" called Zofia.

The four of them turned to face her. She stood near the end of the corridor before a small map that was hardly fifteen centimeters long. Zofia had snapped off one of the pendants from her strange necklace, holding it up like a light and pointing at something written off to the side.

When they reached her, Laila didn't see anything at first except yellowing paper, sepia ink outlining and shading stretches of mountains, rolling waves and hillsides, flat plains. Long ago, the map had been Forged, and though time had weakened the Forging bond, a wisp of will gusted across the page. An invisible wind ruffled stalks of wheat. The depiction of waves rolled gently and disappeared into the frame. Enrique leaned forward, following Zofia's finger to an expanse of blank page broken only by the appearance of a dorsal fin knifing in and out of the water. And beside it, in slanting font so small that Laila would've missed it completely, a phrase in Latin:

HIC SUNT DRACONES

Dracones.
Dragons.
Laila stared at the word, hope needling painfully in her chest.
"It's a reference that means territory unknown," said Enrique excitedly. "Ancient cartographers believed that the land they could not see must necessarily be populated by ancient beasts, monsters, etcetera, although the most common Latin phrase mapmakers used was '*terra ignota*' first seen in Ptolemy's *Geographia* in the year 150. This particular phrase hasn't been seen except on the sixteenth-century Hunt-Lenox globe."

Territory unknown. Laila smiled. She liked that idea. That in the vast places where the world became unfamiliar, there might be something as beautiful and remarkable as dragons lying in wait.

Out the corner of her eye, Laila saw Séverin smiling at Enrique. Enrique didn't look at him, but his jaw clenched as he said: "Zofia, I believe you know what to—"

Zofia didn't wait for him to finish before she snapped off another pendant, shoving it behind the framing.

"Is that going to destroy the map?" asked Enrique, alarmed.

She reached for a small, square of metal in her sleeves. Laila recognized it as a Forged muffler, designed to soak up sound. Zofia pulled out seven of them, lining them along the wall. They were surprisingly effective objects, considering their size—powerful enough to disguise both the clanging kitchens of L'Eden and an orchestral performance in the grand ballroom so that the guests who retired early for the night on the same floor heard nothing at all.

"Stand back," said Zofia.

Everyone stepped aside except Enrique.

"Could we *try* not to destroy—"

Hypnos yanked him backward at the last moment. A flash of heat and a loud banging sound rattled the wall. Seconds later, the now-smoking framed map hung off two hinges, revealing a candlelit passageway.

"—things," finished Enrique weakly.

Laila waved away the smoke.

"Check for Mnemo devices," said Séverin.

Zofia reached for a spherical contraption hidden in the folds of her blue skirt, then rolled it down the hallway.

"Clear," she said.

Séverin nodded, then clicked his heels together. Two slim blades jutted out. He extracted them, holding out one to Hypnos and keeping the other for himself. He hit his arm against the wall, and the interlocked garnets and rubies on his suit lit up. He grinned at them before walking into the passageway.

For the second time in the past hour, Laila swayed a little on the spot.

All of it—Séverin's calm, Zofia's fire, Enrique's lecture—felt too familiar. Part of her wanted to lean into the easy rhythm of it, but beneath that temptation lay the truth. She could not afford to be lured by easy smiles. She turned the ring on her hand toward her palm, the number *three* flashing on the jewel and inside her heart.

She didn't have the time.

THE PASSAGEWAY STRETCHED out at least ninety meters before them. The black stone walls gleamed wetly. In the recessed niches lit with candles, Laila saw exquisite Murano glasswork Forged to the likeness of delicate *ciocche*—bouquets of glass flowers that gave off the scent of neroli—or *ovi odoriferi*, broken ostrich eggs brimming with rose water. Fragrances teemed through the hallway. Perfumes of peppercorn and ambergris, violets and woodsmoke stung the inside of her nose.

"Too many smells," choked out Zofia.

"Who perfumes their treasury?" groaned Enrique.

Séverin stopped walking. "Cover your noses. Now."

"We'll be fine—" started Hypnos.

"It's a trap," said Séverin. "If they're confusing your sense of smell, it's because that sense must be a key."

Zofia reached for the hem of her robes, hoisting them up. Enrique looked about the room, alarmed and turning red. "Um, is undressing truly necessary—"

"Yes," said Zofia curtly.

Within seconds, Zofia had ripped strips off the petticoat beneath her robes. She tossed a shorn piece to Laila who caught it one-handed. The material was perforated silk, and the dull thrum of its material told Laila it was Forged.

"A filter," Zofia explained, throwing the last piece to Enrique who, up until a few moments ago, was staring at the floor as if it were the most fascinating thing in the world. "It was intended for smoke, but it will work for scents too."

Laila knotted the silk around her nose and mouth, and the others did the same. Enrique, she noticed, dithered a little, his face bright red.

"Oh, *mon cher*, must you be so innocent," said Hypnos, grabbing his piece of cloth and knotting it around Enrique's face.

Any sound of protest was quickly muffled.

Six meters from them, the treasure room glowed dimly. Laila felt her pulse ratcheting higher. Her body felt almost feverish. They were so close. They had the lyre. They had the location for the temple where it could be played.

All that was missing was the map to reach it.

Some distance away, they arrived at the landing of a short, glass staircase that descended into a rather spacious chamber the size of L'Eden's grand lobby. The marble floor had been Forged with phosphorescent threads, casting a warm glow throughout the room. A domed skylight stretched about eighteen meters above them, shedding moonlight on the treasures below.

Only, they didn't seem like treasures at all.

There were twelve chest-high black pedestals, six on each side of the room. At the base of each pedestal was a little metal sphere, no larger than her palm. Atop each pedestal stood an exquisite glass perfume bottle. Each one looked fluted, the glass teased into shapes of unfurling violets or tight-budded roses, the warm glow cast from the floor tangled in the glossy crystal.

"Where are the maps?" asked Hypnos.

"Those *are* the maps," said Séverin. "A rare, mind Forged substance that will drop knowledge of a place inside one's head."

Across the back wall stretched a large, square panel roughly the size of two large dining tables and filled with thick coils of blown glass. The pigment within them swirled with vibrant shades—mint green and persimmon orange, dusky rose and garnet red, a teeming riot of color. It undulated until the colors wavered like a hypnotic warning.

Laila touched the covering on her nose and mouth. Through the Forged silk filter, she caught a whiff of something else. Something scorched and fetid.

"No one wants their treasures out in the open," said Séverin. "We have to engage all our senses. Enrique, is there anything worth noticing here? Any pattern of historical significance?"

Enrique startled at the sound of his name. He eyed the room and then Séverin, who was staring hopefully at him. Enrique cleared his throat.

"The bottles look like Murano glass, and perfume was a powerful tool to the ancients, which strengthens the conclusion that these might be maps to temples."

Séverin grinned. "I knew you'd see something." Enrique ignored him.

Hypnos shuffled, tugging at the neckline of his robes. "Does anyone else find the room far too hot?"

Now that he mentioned it, the room *did* feel uncomfortably warm, but perhaps that was due to insulation. Laila pushed her damp, curling hair away from her forehead as Séverin eyed the room warily.

"Something about the room prefers this temperature," he said.

"You make it sound like the room is alive," said Hypnos, uncomfortable.

"Perhaps it is," said Séverin. He eyed the staircase, then the panel of glass coils before stepping onto the first landing. "I'm going down."

"Very well," said Laila, following after him.

Séverin blocked her way. "We don't know what we're dealing with yet, let me—"

"Let you what?" demanded Laila. "Martyr yourself? *Again?* If you die, this whole thing fails anyway because we can't use the lyre. So either you stay back and watch us go, or suffer the fact that we're going in with you."

Behind her, Enrique, Zofia, and Hypnos looked a little shocked. Hypnos raised his hand.

"I . . . don't have to go?" he said.

Laila glared at him.

Séverin sighed, then moved back. "You are right. I am yours to command."

"If only," muttered Laila, walking down the staircase.

The moment she stepped onto the top step, she reached inside her sleeves, touching the corsetry around her waist that Zofia had outfitted with her Forged creations. Laila drew out one of the portable lights, flashing it onto the perfume bottle on the first pedestal. Something flashed inside.

"Keep an eye on the back wall," said Séverin.

Zofia nodded, positioning herself at the front of the room.

Inside the first perfume bottle was a small, golden key. Here, the smell of rotting meat was even stronger.

"It's definitely holding a key," she said, covering her nose.

"May I?" asked Séverin.

Laila tossed him a portable light. He shone it across the bottles.

"They all have keys," he said.

"How do we know what they unlock?" asked Enrique. "It could be *any* of these."

"There's only one way to find out where the maps lead," said Séverin, eyeing the bottles. "Split up. Unstopper them as little as possible . . . mind Forged maps are intense and very powerful, so be prepared."

"We're looking for signs of the temple beneath Poveglia . . . think craggy land, caves, that kind of setting," added Enrique.

Laila braced herself as she reached for the cold, smooth glass of the bottle. She glanced at the back wall, alight with coiling glass. It looked unchanged.

Laila slowly unstoppered the bottle. A tiny wisp of mind Forged perfume wafted into the air. The moment she breathed in, it was as if her consciousness had been yanked elsewhere. When she blinked, she saw a ruined cliffside deep in a jungle where coffins dangled from the canopies of trees and a pit of bones glinted with gold. She blinked again, and the vision faded.

Laila replaced the stopper, her hands shaking as she turned to the others.

"A jungle somewhere," she said. "Not Poveglia."

"Ugh, this one's a grave pit," said Hypnos, stoppering a bottle.

Enrique set down a different bottle, shaking his head. "This one leads to a castle."

"A glass door in a tundra," said Zofia, moving to a different pedestal.

Laila removed another two stoppers, her vision clouding with images of snowy temples with curved peaks and secret alleys hiding in plain sight of bustling cities. But nothing she reached for held any resemblance to Venice's Plague Island, which made her wonder if it was even here . . .

Or if—

"Found it."

Laila turned to see Séverin clutching a perfume stopper. For a moment, his pupils looked blown out with fear. He shook his head, his expression returning to normal, but Laila could tell he'd seen something disturbing.

"You're certain?" asked Enrique.

Séverin looked away from them, managing a tight nod.

"So do we just take the bottle and go?" asked Hypnos.

Laila studied the room. It hadn't changed. It was still stiflingly hot. The lights on the floor hadn't altered, and even when they'd opened and checked every mind Forged perfume bottle, not even the coiled glass at the back wall shifted. Above them, the cold winter moon stared down through the domed sky glass.

Séverin eyed the podium.

"We don't know what will happen when I remove the bottle, so we must be prepared for the worst-case scenario," he said. "Zofia. What do we have?"

"Fourteen explosives, six close-range blades, steel rope, and Forged muffling cloth," said Zofia, before pointing at her robes. "And *these* are fire-repellent."

"Wonderful, deadly items which, I'm certain, will not be necessary . . . yes?" said Hypnos, looking at them. "*Yes?*"

Séverin grabbed the perfume bottle from the podium, stashing it in the box Ruslan had given him. All remained still and quiet.

"See?" said Hypnos. "Nothing."

Laila felt a change in the room. There was a slight shimmer to the air, the room crimped with a dredging of heat. A dribbling sound caught her attention. She turned just in time to see the glassy staircase entrance fusing into a wall, eliminating their exit. On the back wall, the undulating coils of glass twisted together, and Laila felt her heart slam into her throat.

They had never been coils.

They were scales.

19

⌇⌁⌇

ZOFIA

Z ofia did not have room for fear.

Her mind grasped at the scene, breaking it down into parts. The liquid glass oozed from the panel, falling to the floor and gaining shape. Within seconds, the glass fused into a long snout, sharp claws, a thick tail, and a body that towered nearly fifteen meters high. The glass creature swung its head to face them.

"Remember how I asked for a dragon?" said Hypnos. "I take it back."

Zofia noted the hot fan of its translucent wings, the stripe of scarlet up its belly, the clear teeth the size of her hand, and the lashing tail twisted with blue pigment. She smelled and tasted the molten metal in the air, coppery like blood. She heard the smash of its huge tail against the floor, like the sound of a shattering chandelier.

"Watch out!" shouted Laila.

She grabbed Zofia's arm, yanking her to the floor just as the glass dragon's tail whipped out, slamming against the wall. Normally, the force should have shattered the vials, but they stood perfectly intact. At the base of each pedestal, Zofia noticed a dimly glowing metal sphere. She recognized the structures immediately: Gaia Dots. Lightweight, but designed to absorb shock. That was what had to be holding the vials in place.

Just then, the dragon roared, the sound like the bellows of a furnace. Zofia forced her heartbeat to remain steady. Distantly, she registered that they were in trouble, but she knew she was no use to her friends if she could not think.

Her gaze flew to the creature's taloned feet. They seemed to melt into the marble, allowing it slow but labored movement across the floor. It was not built for speed, but—Zofia glanced at the fused door and the skylight thirty meters above them—it did not need to work quickly.

Meltingly slow, it slid forward, its tail whipping out, its jaws snapping.

"I don't know how to defeat a dragon!" said Hypnos.

"It isn't a dragon," said Zofia. "It's glass."

The glass dragon slid one step closer. Its tail spun out, but Zofia noticed that it never arced upwards; its Forging mechanism was careful not to disturb the skylight. The room's cloying heat pressed against her robes. Séverin had called the heat intentional . . . a *preference*. An idea snapped through her thoughts.

"We need to stress the dragon," she said.

Hypnos frowned. "I'm not sure now is the time to tell it about my existential woes—"

"Glass experiences thermal shock when the temperature rapidly changes between two surfaces," said Zofia.

"Hot glass doesn't like cold air," said Séverin. "We need to introduce some cold into the room."

"But the door is melted shut!" said Enrique.

Zofia glanced up. "The skylight isn't."

"We can't reach that!" said Hypnos.

"Yes, we can," said Laila. She ripped open her robes, reaching for the Forged steel Zofia had concealed in her bodice.

"The skylight will need significant mass to break," she said, casting about the room for something to attach to the rope.

There was nothing around them but delicate perfume bottles.

The dragon moved closer, molten heat rippling from its body. The flowing glass surrounded four pedestals, two on each side.

"We need to move!" said Enrique, standing.

Séverin stayed where he was, pointing above them. "This is the best place to access the skylight—"

"Séverin," said Laila, her voice full of warning.

"Buy me some time," said Séverin.

"Take your robes off," said Zofia, ripping off the heavy cloth.

"Normally I love that suggestion," said Hypnos. "But—"

Zofia reached forward, grabbing at his sleeves and tearing. "The robes are Forged to inhibit heat. We can use it as a barrier against the hot glass."

Hypnos shrugged out of his robes, tossing it to Zofia. The liquid glass pooled around the edges of the cloak. It wouldn't last more than three minutes, but it was something.

"We need something to throw against the skylight!" said Séverin, casting about.

Zofia pointed at the metal spheres at the base of the pedestals. Séverin followed the line of her finger and grinned.

"Gaia Dots," he said. "Phoenix, that's brilliant! They should've absorbed plenty of shock by now—"

The glass dragon roared, its wings flapping, waves of heat fanning against Zofia's cheeks.

"What are you waiting for?" shouted Enrique.

Séverin swiped one of the Gaia Dots off the ground, wincing a little as he tethered the sphere to the rope. He lassoed the whole contraption around his head, flinging the bottle up where it shattered against the skylight.

The glass fractured, but it didn't break.

"Again!" yelled Enrique, tossing him another Gaia Dot.

Séverin swung the rope. The window fractured a little more, but still it did not break.

"The cloak—" said Hypnos, pointing at the mess of Enrique's flame-retardant cloth.

Liquid glass seeped over it, hardening over the golden cloak in the disturbing way of insects trapped in amber. The glass dragon closed in on them. In the glossy sheen of its belly, Zofia could see her reflection stretched and twisted. The heat closed around them. Sweat ran down her back, and her clothing gummed to her skin. She hated the sensation.

Think, Zosia. Think.

She touched the pendants of her necklace. One of them was an explosive, but would it be enough to break the glass? Laila choked on the air, her hand flying to her mouth, and Zofia's decision crystallized on the spot.

She tore the pendant, flinging it toward Séverin—

"Try this!" she yelled.

He caught it one-handed. At the same time, Zofia felt a *whumph!* of concentrated air—

At the periphery of her vision, an enormous glass wing shot through with green and gold paint knifed toward her head. One moment, Zofia had only just registered it. The next she found herself slammed to the ground, her skull thudding on the marble. She blinked to see Enrique braced above her, the dragon's glass wing missing his head by mere centimeters.

"I, um—" started Enrique, rolling away from her.

"Cover your heads!" called Séverin.

A huge shattering sound echoed far above them. The dragon screeched.

Zofia shielded her head as shards of glass rained down above them. The glass dragon howled. The temperature in the room dropped, the heat ebbing away—

The panic she had fought down for so long now asserted itself. Heat on her face, a hollow in her heart left behind from losing Hela's letter, worry for Laila, Enrique, Séverin, and Hypnos.

Count, she told herself. *13, 26, 39, 52, 65, 78, 91 . . .*

The seconds melted together. The weight squeezing her chest slowly lifted until she could concentrate once more on her surroundings. She lowered her arms, lifting her head. It was silent. The glass liquid had stopped a meter away from them and begun to harden. Zofia looked up to see the enormous glass dragon frozen right above them—its wings outstretched and gleaming, jaws flung wide and talons extended.

Séverin flopped back onto the marble, resting his head against one of the podiums. He kicked out his legs, smoothed back his hair, and flashed a smile.

"Good work, Phoenix."

Séverin used to say that with frequency back in Paris. The words felt comforting. The longer she looked at him, the more she recognized his smile. Laila had once called it his "sated wolf" grin.

She had not seen it since Tristan died, but she remembered it. It was the smile before an acquisition fell into his hands; the smile when the plan performed to standards; and it was as familiar to Zofia as the glass alembics and measuring devices that had once lined the shelves of her L'Eden laboratory.

Lately, she had not allowed herself to think of what she had left behind in L'Eden because it seemed statistically unlikely that she would ever see it again. But if Séverin's smile could return, perhaps other things could return as well.

"I know," she said.

Séverin laughed.

AFTER AN HOUR and two stumbling routes through the hidden passageways of House Janus's headquarters, they were finally outside. The cold air burned in Zofia's lungs as she, Hypnos, Enrique, Laila, and Séverin wound their way through the low-ceilinged passageways that threaded the streets of Venice. Zofia's ears were still ringing from the explosion, and she had begun to count the lanterns tucked into the eaves of the street. She told herself that every light she crossed was one step out of the dark.

The unknown terrified her. It settled inside her like an itch that scratched through her thoughts. It was only the reminder that Laila depended on her that forced distance between herself and her panic, but she hadn't stopped thinking about Hela, and all the sounds and chaos from the Carnevale acquisition only served to remind her that there was far too much she did not know. She was so focused on counting the lights that she almost missed the conversation around her until Séverin said her name.

"What?" she asked loudly as they came to a stop before a curved archway.

In the distance, she could see the black, shimmering water before the Rialto Bridge. The market kiosks were closed by now, and nothing but the occasional stray cat crossed their paths.

"The explosion," said Séverin. "I assume there were no problems attaching it to Ruslan's gondola."

Problems? No, thought Zofia, her mind momentarily returning

to the kiss she had shared with Enrique. That aspect had been pleasant . . . happy, even, in a way that reminded Zofia of winter fires in her parents' sitting rooms, the feeling of utter safety. But then she remembered Hela's lost letter, and her face crumpled.

"There was no problem attaching the detonation device," said Zofia. She reached into her sleeve, where the other half of the bonded bomb pair lay against her forearm. She pulled it out. In the moonlight, it looked as if it was carved of ice. "When this is triggered, the other half will explode."

"Good," said Séverin. He shifted a little on his feet, not looking up at them. "We need to deal with Ruslan before we go, and we cannot afford the risk that he will jump off the gondola to safety. He doesn't trust me."

Laila's eyes narrowed, her shoulders lifted. Zofia recognized that posture. It was as if Laila were bracing herself for something.

"Meaning?" asked Enrique.

"Meaning . . . we will have some help," said Séverin.

"From *who*?" said Enrique.

Séverin said quietly, "You can come out now."

A figure stepped into their line of sight, Zofia recognized the person immediately: long, red hair, a talon ring on the pinky. Eva Yefremovna.

When Zofia had seen the blood Forging artist in the past, Eva had not been expressive. Her mouth was usually in a flat line, which suggested anger. And she had not been kind to Laila, but there was a reason for that unkindness. Zofia remembered Laila pleading with her to help them in the Sleeping Palace, promising Eva that she no longer had to follow Ruslan's bidding, that they would be able to protect her and her father, whose life Ruslan threatened. Eva's gaze darted to Séverin's. Her eyes were wide, which led Zofia to conclude that she was worried.

"I . . . I'm here to help," said Eva.

"I've seen what your help looks like," shot back Enrique. His hand flew to his ear.

"Can we really trust her?" asked Hypnos.

Eva opened her mouth to speak, but it was Laila who answered. "Yes," she said.

"After what she did?" said Enrique.

"You cannot corner a wild animal and scold it for snapping at you," said Laila. Her voice was even and unwavering. Zofia could not tell if she was angry. "I know what I read in Eva's objects."

Eva's eyes widened, her lips parting slightly. That meant she was shocked by Laila's response. Zofia was not shocked. Laila was the kindest person she knew.

"All I want is a new start," said Eva. "I want . . . I want to be free." Eva raised her chin, looking them each in the eye. "I can make sure Ruslan is temporarily paralyzed and cannot leave the boat."

"And in return," said Séverin, his gaze sweeping over them, "I have promised Eva living quarters in L'Eden, future protection both for herself and her father from the Order of Babel—"

Hypnos grumbled. "Yes, fine."

"And potential employment," said Séverin.

Laila stiffened a little. Zofia noticed that it was Laila he looked to last. It was a familiar pattern. In L'Eden, whenever Séverin made plans, he always looked at Laila. To see him do it again made Zofia think of all their former patterns. It was like physics, the study of working mechanisms and the interplay of light. Laila was a fulcrum, the point around which all things in their group seemed to pivot. Séverin was mass, the weight that changed their direction. Enrique gave them depth. Zofia hoped she offered light. She was not sure what Hypnos contributed to the group, but she could not imagine it without him. Perhaps that made him perspective.

"Then it's settled," said Séverin.

Zofia looked up. She had not been listening.

"We must work quickly," said Eva, looking at the lagoon. "He's coming."

ZOFIA AND ENRIQUE huddled together in one of the two gondolas Eva had rented and carefully positioned in the lagoon. Hypnos was waiting for them on the shore, to buy time for them before anyone came to investigate the inevitable explosion. The boat rocked slowly in the water. A small telescopic device that had once been part of Laila's bodice now poked out from the top of the gondola. Through it, Zofia could see Ruslan's gondola about six meters away. Séverin stood on a paddleboat, slowly pushing his way toward the patriarch of the Fallen House. Once Eva made the signal, she would detonate the explosives.

"And now we wait," said Enrique.

The crystal detonator lay on the bottom of the boat in front of Zofia. At Eva's signal, she would trigger it, the gondola would explode, and they would be free to sail to Poveglia by morning. Perhaps by this time tomorrow . . . Laila would be safe. The thought warmed Zofia.

"Zofia . . . I'm sorry about, um, earlier," said Enrique.

Zofia startled from her thoughts. She turned to look at him and frowned. What was he talking about?

"I feel like I wasn't a good friend to you."

That did not seem true to Zofia, but before she could say anything, Enrique spoke faster.

"Good friends put aside their ego and ask about each other," he said. "And I didn't ask how you were after our kiss because I thought it had bothered you. Now I think it's something else. But if it is about the kiss, I'm sorry about that too."

"I'm not sorry that we kissed," said Zofia.

"You're not?"

"It was without compare—"

Enrique beamed.

"I've never kissed anyone, so I have nothing to compare it to."

Now he frowned.

After a moment, Zofia added: "I liked it."

It was the truth, but it made Zofia ache a little. She knew he had kissed her so that the swan wings would fold up and hide them from Ruslan. Whereas she would have kissed him without the motive of camouflage. She had *wanted* to kiss him. If she were not waiting on Séverin's signal . . . if there were less unknowns in the world . . . she would have liked to kiss him again.

Enrique's expression changed. "Zofia, I—"

Out the corner of her eye, Zofia caught sight of Eva's signal, which meant her rented gondola was in line with Ruslan's. Through her viewpoint, Zofia could see that Ruslan was frozen, his arms caught mid-movement, his jaw dropped. His eyes looked wide and furious.

Now.

Zofia slammed her palm onto the detonator, and light exploded around them.

20

LAILA

Five minutes before the explosion, Laila held her breath, her hands splayed against the bottom of the gondola. She could feel the boat's memories brushing lightly against her thoughts. It wanted to tell her about the toddler who had tried to dip his hand in the dirty water, to the horror of his parents. It wanted to tell her about the smell of early spring, the violets garlanding the bridges to ward off the sewage stench. Laila pushed the boat's secrets away from her and kept her gaze on the dark floor. The water carried the sound of conversation, and in every beat of silence, she felt as if her fate was being woven before her.

"How was your last human fête, Monsieur Montagnet-Alarie?" Ruslan.

Laila could hear the smile in his voice. Warm and generous, soft and curious. That was the same voice he had used before he raised his golden hand and slapped her so hard her teeth ached. A shudder ran down her spine.

"Exceptional. I now have everything I need."

This time, Séverin's voice.

A beat passed. Laila could hear the soft knocking of the nearby gondola hitting the wooden pier. Inside, Enrique and Zofia waited on Eva's signal.

"*Everything?*" repeated Ruslan.

"Almost everything."

Another twinge of silence. Laila's pulse was made of fire.

"Give me the lyre box."

This was it.

The signal.

Laila heard the rustling of heavy cloaks, and then—

Slam.

Laila couldn't see, but she could hear the plan unfolding. Ruslan's hand flipped over, the metal talon slicing down his wrist and Eva's blood Forging artistry taking root. Every day, the patriarch of the Fallen House took a tonic to ward off manipulation.

Today, his dose had been altered.

Ruslan's voice turned high-pitched, panicked. "Séverin, what are you—"

"Apotheosis draws nearer, but I am afraid that heaven is crowded . . . and I am told there is only room for one god."

The gondola went still. Ruslan was choked into silence.

"By the way, Eva hopes you rot and that even the lagoon water finds your soul so dirty it expels it straight to hell. Oh, and also? The *real* Monsieur Montagnet-Alarie sends his regards."

Beside her, Laila heard a soft laugh. "An excellent flourish. *Bon chance*, Eva."

Laila turned to her right. There, the real Séverin stretched out beside her, his eyes near-black in the moonlight. For Eva's ruse, he had given her a drop of his blood to Forge so that she might wear his face and speak in his voice. She wore his outfit too, with added explosive protection from Zofia's Forged robes, which left him wearing a thin, ivory-colored shirt that stretched across his shoulders and opened at the throat. He seemed unbothered by the cold.

The whole time they had waited together, Laila had done her best not to look at him.

I have no time to deal with this, she told herself.

But when she looked at him in that second, she felt an unwelcome tug of familiarity.

And then the world exploded.

The force of Zofia's explosion knocked Laila's gondola back against the pier. Something crashed into the side, wood splintering like cracking bones. The world felt too bright, too loud. Her ears rang.

"Laila!"

Laila felt her body being gathered, thrown down. What an odd feeling of déjà vu. They had done this before in the Palais des Rêves. She remembered the scorched note in Séverin's voice, his body flung over hers. Séverin's arms were caged around her. He was breathing fast.

"Are you hurt?" he asked.

Laila heard the next explosion before she saw it. The rented boat she was hiding in slammed backwards. A jagged piece of wood flew out, catching Séverin in the stomach. He looked stunned for a moment and then slumped forward.

On the paved walkway lining the lagoon, Laila heard loud footsteps.

"We must go!" yelled Hypnos.

Laila's mind was screaming. Faces flashed through her thoughts: Ruslan's stretched grin, Eva's sorrowful eyes. But all of it constricted to one image before her: Séverin. He lay prone on the gondola, a slow pool of blood gathering around him. Laila could hardly breathe. Her fingers shook as she reached for him.

No . . .

No no no.

"Laila!" called Hypnos, more insistently this time.

Laila touched Séverin, moving the hair out from his forehead, as if he were merely sleeping. He had protected her . . . as he had always promised to do, and like always, even his protection managed to cut her to the quick.

"If you die, *Majnun,* then I cannot stay mad at you, and you at least owe me my anger. Let me keep that," she said, her voice breaking. "Do you hear me? You have to live."

Laila was convinced that his eyes would flutter open at the sound of her old name for him. She stared at him, willing him to stir.

But he didn't move.

PART III

21

SÉVERIN

Séverin's first father was Sloth.

Out of all the sins who fed him, clothed him, berated and cajoled him, it was Lucien Montagnet-Alaric's oily mark he most wished to erase from his person. Lucien was lazy in the way of a venomous snake sunning its cold blood and colder skin on a rock. Deadliness was merely how he rewarded interruptions to his schedule of revelries and rest, fine food and finer women.

Lucien gave his son no more than what was expected of him: the family name, the sharp line of his jaw, and the pale hue of his skin. The last was an unexpected "gift," for it let Séverin pass through the society of France as if he were fully one of them.

As a child, Séverin had been fascinated by his father, who seemed so powerful that the world anticipated his whims and supplied them without him ever asking. At the time, Séverin was too young to spot the difference between power and its pinch-mouthed cousin, privilege. He was especially entranced by the sigil of House

Vanth his father wore on the lapel of his jacket: the golden snake swallowing down its own tail.

"What does it mean?" Séverin had asked one day.

Lucien was attending to his correspondence in the main study, and he startled when Séverin spoke. He regarded his son like a dish he had not remembered ordering at a restaurant, with a mixture of faint curiosity and wariness of what might next be expected of him.

"The snake," Séverin had said.

"Oh," Lucien said, glancing down at the symbol. He tapped it once. "Infinity, I suppose. Or perhaps, entrapment of humanity. We can never escape ourselves, my boy. We are our own end and beginning, at the mercy of a past which cannot help but repeat itself. Which is why"—he paused to stroke the nose of an elephant statue recently acquired by House Vanth—"we must take what we can before the world has its way with us."

Lucien had smiled. He looked young. And yet, some of his teeth were black, and loose skin gathered beneath his chin. It unsettled him.

"I don't like that," Séverin had said, staring at the ouroboros. Outside, he could hear the footsteps of someone coming to fetch him away.

"Nothing is new, child," said Lucien. "Everything repeats. The sooner you know that, the happier you'll be."

Séverin had disliked his father's summary. It felt weak and powerless. Surely, those were words of defeat. Surely, if he made a mistake he regretted and learned from . . . then history would not repeat itself.

And yet it had.

The moment the explosion ripped through Ruslan's gondola . . .

the moment a chunk of wood splintered the boat where he and Laila crouched and waited . . . it was like muscle memory. To go to her. To shield her body with his.

To protect her above all else.

In those seconds before he lost consciousness, Séverin felt a line drawn between this moment and the one in the Palais des Rêves, the moment where he'd flung himself over Laila and left Tristan's throat at the mercy of a blade-brimmed hat.

That moment had been the floor on which his life pivoted sharply from what he had imagined. That moment had neatly sheared away all the things he thought he'd wanted, scraped clean the dreams he'd once held, and left room for something beyond imagination.

Perhaps his father was right in one way.

History had repeated itself, but it was a matter of perspective. The ouroboros was merely a serpent biting its own tail. Held far enough away, it became a lens through which to focus the world beyond it.

And that was how the world felt as Séverin regained consciousness—newly refocused.

Dimly, he felt a hard, satin couch beneath him, a pillow propped under his head. As his eyes adjusted to the light he saw that some- one had left him a glass of water. There was a musky odor here, a closeness to the Grand Canal that seeped through the floorboards of wherever he was. A dull ache hit his ribs. He drew back his jacket and then stopped, the cold weight of panic slamming through his body.

The divine lyre.

It was gone.

He patted his chest again, then jerked to a stand, frantically feeling around the surfaces of the settee—

"It's in another room," said a familiar voice. "Guarded by Hypnos and Zofia. They have the Poveglia map with them too. We were just waiting on you to wake up."

He heard the flare of a match, and then the room slowly brightened as dozens of interlocked Forged lanterns blazed to life. Séverin held his breath as Laila came into view. If this were a fantasy, he wanted to remain utterly still, to keep this phantasm of her in place.

"You were bleeding earlier," said Laila haltingly.

Séverin looked down at his torso, only now realizing that he wasn't wearing anything besides his formal coat and trousers, and that he was swaddled in linen from his bare chest to his navel. Laila averted her eyes.

"Given what happened last time your blood hit the instrument, we thought it was best to keep it away from you," she said.

The rational corner of his mind agreed with that, but the other half—the animal half that recognized only danger in the dark— froze over. Anything could have happened to him after Ruslan's gondola attack. But he was safe. They were furious with him, but they had taken him back to their hideout, cleaned his wounds, bandaged him up, left him in the dark to rest, and guarded over him as he slept.

"What is it?" asked Laila.

Séverin winced as he pushed himself up and flashed a weak smile.

"I haven't felt like this in a long time."

"I hardly believe that," said Laila tightly. "How many near-death traps have you escaped? You should be accustomed to the feeling by now."

"That's not what I'm feeling."

"Then what?"

She had not moved from her spot by the door, and though it

hurt that she was instantly prepared to bolt, he knew he deserved it. He touched the bandage at his side, breathing deeply.

"Taken care of," he said.

"No one's ever cared for you?" she asked mockingly. "Are you saying that all the times I've tried to pull you back from grief, or Hypnos tried to be there for you, or Enrique and Zofia—"

"This is different," said Séverin.

As the room brightened, he recognized the furious color in her cheeks and the hard set to her mouth. Séverin felt something un-hinge inside him, a door swinging open that he'd long kept shut. The things he had no desire to say spun out of him.

"All those things you have done for me, which I so ungrate-fully cast aside, shame me. And yes, those were acts of compas-sion. But this is different. I was bleeding in the dark, and you brought me somewhere safe. When I could not think for myself or act for myself"—he looked into her swan-dark eyes—"you pro-tected me."

The fury abated in her eyes, but the hard set to her mouth re-mained.

"I didn't come here to fight," she said. "We've been taking turns checking your bandages. I thought you would be unconscious. If you'd prefer someone else—"

"Why would I prefer someone else's touch to yours?"

Her eyes widened. Color flooded her cheeks, and his panic ebbed away. Something else seeped in.

Laila had changed out of her costume from the Carnevale, and into a blue dressing gown embroidered with a hundred sequins at the hem so that it looked like she was a woman of the waters, crafted from moonlight hitting the sea. Belatedly, he realized he was staring.

Laila scowled, looked down at her dress and sighed. "We trusted

Hypnos with procuring garments and food. I told him to buy something 'subtle.'"

"You look beautiful," said Séverin.

"Don't," said Laila tiredly.

She sat beside him, and the faint scent of sugar and rose water drifted through his senses. He lifted his arms. Laila did not look at him as she worked with cold efficiency, making quick work of his bandages and drawing out a clean set. Every brush of her fingers felt like fire inside him, and perhaps that was what woke up some corner of his memory. He remembered the sudden, crushing pressure against his skull . . . the stench of the lagoon water sloshing up the sides of the gondola, dampening his pant leg. The world dissolving to black until he heard her voice.

"If you die, I can't stay mad at you, Majnun, and if I can't at least be angry with you, I'll break."

She'd called him *Majnun.*

Perhaps it had been nothing but days since she'd uttered that name, but Séverin felt their absence inside him like years grown old and mossy.

"I heard you," he said.

"What?"

"I heard you call me *Majnun.*"

Laila's hands on him stilled. He felt the slightest tremor of her fingers on his skin. Foolish or no, he couldn't lose the chance to speak plainly to her.

"I am yours, Laila . . . and you can fight it or hide it as much as you want, but I think part of you belongs to me too."

She looked up at him, and there was such grief in her eyes that he almost felt ashamed for speaking.

"Perhaps," she admitted.

His heart leapt at the words.

"But that small part is all I can spare," said Laila. "I have so little of myself left. I cannot give any more to you."

He reached for her hands. "Laila, I have been a fool. I don't know why it's taken me so long to see this, or say this, but I love—"

"No. Please, don't," she said, pushing his hands aside. "Don't put that burden on me, Séverin. I cannot hold it."

A terrible weight settled in his chest.

"Would it truly be that?" he asked. "A burden?"

"Yes!" said Laila fiercely. "What I feel for you is a burden. It has *always* been a burden. I move closer, you step back; you move closer, I step back. I don't have the time to play this with you! We may have gotten this far, but what about everything else? Plague Island and the lyre and *everything*. You're still convinced that somehow you'll get these powers of divinity, and what if it doesn't work? Do you really want me to divide my attention between keeping myself and my friends alive and loving you based on whatever whim guides you for the day? Because I can't."

"Laila—"

But she wasn't done.

"You once offered me impossible things, Séverin. A dress made of moonlight, glass slippers—"

"And I'd make that happen!" said Séverin. "Laila, you don't understand the power I felt when I touched that instrument. Anything you ask, I could give you—"

Laila wrapped her arms around herself, shaking. "Can you give me safety, Séverin? Can you give me time? Can you carry my trust?" She paused, taking a deep breath. "Are you even capable of ordinary love?"

He felt slapped. "What do you mean?"

"I mean that when I go to sleep, I dream of someone who knows which side of the bed I favor, who sits across from me in happy silence, who argues over which dishes belong in which cabinet," said Laila quietly. "Someone whose love feels like home . . . not some insurmountable quest ripped from a myth. Someone whose love is safe . . . Do you understand that?"

He did.

Because that was how she made him feel.

Safe.

He wanted to make her feel safe.

"I can be that person."

Laila laughed, but it was a hollow sound. Séverin felt a chasm opening up inside him. He stared at the inside of his wrists where his veins stood out, full of the only bloodline that the divine lyre answered to. For all his power, he was powerless to stop her grief.

He watched her, his eyes drawn to the garnet ring on her hand where the number *three* stared accusingly at him. Shame snapped through him. All she had was two days, and he was forcing her to spend even a minute justifying why she wouldn't be with him? What was wrong with him?

"Gather the others," he said, forcing himself up on his elbows. "I won't waste any more of your time by telling you how I feel."

Laila looked away. "Séverin—"

"I am your *majnun*, am I not? My hopes may make me foolish, but it is something I cannot help." He reached for her chin, turning her face to his. Her eyes were wide, full of hope and wariness all at once. "My hope is this . . . that I may show you that I can be the person you deserve."

WITHIN TWENTY MINUTES, Enrique, Hypnos, Zofia, and Laila gathered in the library. Séverin felt a familiar pang of recognition at

Enrique's research documents—paintings, maps, statues—strewn across the long table. He could almost see the historian hunched over them, delicately turning the frail pages of an ancient scroll of paper. At the end of the table was the small, golden box holding the map to Poveglia. Beside it, the lyre. The moment he saw it, a pressure inside his chest unknotted.

Séverin glanced at his crew. He had longed for this for days, and now he had it. And yet the image seemed knocked askew from his wishes. They did not smile. They did not recline on the chairs, balancing sweets on their laps, and joking.

Enrique's face was stony. He looked caught between wanting to scream and wishing to stay silent. Zofia looked wary. Laila refused to look at anything except the ring on her finger, and Hypnos kept grinning at him, then grinning back at the others—to no avail.

"Ruslan's gondola exploded," said Zofia suddenly.

Séverin felt a little stunned. It was as they'd planned, was it not? And yet, out of nowhere, came the last memory he had with Ruslan . . . of the patriarch staring up at him, wild-eyed with hope.

"Yes," said Séverin.

"He did not survive it," said Zofia.

"No," said Séverin slowly. "He did not . . . but Eva—"

"Eva got out," said Laila, still not looking at him. "She took a third of Hypnos's funds—"

"*Emergency* funds, I might add," sniffed Hypnos.

"And she said that when the time came, she would call on you."

Séverin nodded, and they stood in silence for a minute.

"He was not a good man," said Zofia quietly.

The unsaid part of her sentence hung in the air: *And yet . . .*

And yet they had killed him.

It left Séverin with a cold sense of awareness. But not guilt. He did not regret what he had done to keep them safe, but he mourned the man Ruslan might have been had power not corrupted him.

"We did what had to be done," Séverin said. "We'll carry the weight of that always, but we didn't have a choice. We *need* to get to the temple beneath Poveglia, and now we can. But . . . before we make any more plans, I owe all of you an apology."

"And an ear," snapped Enrique. He touched his bandages. "What gave you the *right* to do what you did? We trusted you, and you threw it all in our faces. You manipulated me. You might've killed Laila. You blackmailed Zofia into staying with you when her sister was sick—"

Séverin frowned. "I thought Hela was healed?"

"I don't know," said Zofia, her face bleak. "I lost the letter."

Séverin frowned. He had no idea what she was talking about.

"Though it's been days, you might as well have missed years," snapped Enrique.

Séverin held himself still. He forced himself to look each of them in the eye.

"I had no right to act as I did," he said. "I thought I was protecting you, but I went about it the wrong way. Forgive me. When I lost Tristan—"

"You weren't the only one who lost him," said Enrique coldly.

Laila lifted an eyebrow. "We *all* lost him."

"And we all grieve differently," said Hypnos, turning to Enrique and fixing him with a look. "Don't we, *mon cher*?"

"I can make amends," said Séverin quietly. "These past few months, I wasn't myself. I saw something, and I lost sight of all else . . . but I have found clarity and—"

"Do you still want to be a god?" asked Enrique.

The question warped the atmosphere of the room. Séverin almost expected tendrils of frost to unfurl across the wooden parquet floor. How could he answer this in a way that proved he hadn't lost his mind, but rather found a dream worthy of attaining? His fingers twitched to reach for the lyre, to feel the purr of its power against his skin.

Enrique threw up his hands, turning to the others. "You *see*? He's not the same! Who—"

"Let me be clear . . . I do not expect that at the end of all this, puny mortals will erect a temple to us," said Séverin.

Hypnos sighed. "Well, there goes my motivation."

"I believe in the lyre's power," continued Séverin. "You don't understand what it felt like to play the instrument. You saw what it could do at its worst . . . imagine what it can do at its best. Call it fate or destiny or whatever you have to, but I *believe* in it. I believe we can harness what it has to offer. I believe we can save Laila. I believe I was meant for this . . . Why else would I be able to play an instrument no one else can?"

Hypnos flinched away from his gaze, as if embarrassed for him. Laila was tight-lipped, her eyes unfocused as if she was trying her best not to look at him. Zofia's brows were drawn in disbelief. Enrique's fury had melted into something far worse.

Pity.

"Do you remember the story of Icarus?" asked Enrique.

Séverin knew the myth well. Icarus, along with his father, Daedalus, the famous inventor, escaped imprisonment on a pair of wax wings. Daedalus warned the boy not to fly too close to the sun, but Icarus did not heed his father's warning. The sun melted his feathers, and Icarus fell to his death.

"I remember it," said Séverin.

"Then perhaps you would do well to remember the tragedy of flying too high."

"Is Icarus the tragedy?" asked Séverin. "Or is it Daedalus? Someone who had the power to do impossible things and still could not manage to protect the people he loved most?"

Enrique fell silent at that.

"If you can try, why not do so?" asked Séverin. "If you could give yourself the power to change the course of history, wouldn't you?"

Enrique turned his face away, but Séverin caught a flash in his eyes.

"If you could save the ones you love, wouldn't you?"

At this, he looked at Laila and Zofia, both of whom met his eyes steadily. He turned to Hypnos.

"And if you—"

Hypnos perked up. "*Oui?*"

"I actually have no idea what you want, my friend."

Hypnos grinned and clapped his hands, staring around at everyone. "I already have what I want. But I would not say no to a temple, harems, etcetera."

"All I am asking is one last chance to discover what we can do," Séverin said.

For a moment, he imagined they were back inside L'Eden, standing beneath the glass dome, where the sky looked more like a bowl of stars that had been upturned over their heads. He thought of the beginning of every acquisition—the cushy armchair Enrique favored, the velvet green settee Laila lounged on, Zofia's high stool with a plate of sugar cookies balancing on her lap, Tristan seated between them hiding Goliath in his jacket. And himself, standing before them.

"If you think what we're doing is impossible, then let us rewrite what possibility means . . . *together.*"

He looked up just in time to see Enrique shake his head, his hands clenched at his side as he stormed from the room.

"Enrique—" said Laila, starting after him.

"Sorry, *mon cher*," said Hypnos apologetically, before he darted after Enrique and Laila.

Only Zofia was left. His engineer regarded him warily, twirling an unlit matchstick in her hand.

"Phoenix?" he said softly.

"I do not like what you did."

Something inside Séverin shrank.

Zofia's burning blue eyes lifted to his. "But I understand why you did it."

"Do I have your forgiveness?"

Zofia considered this. "You have . . . more time."

"I'll take whatever you will give me," he said, and smiled.

22

ENRIQUE

Enrique set off down the hallway, his ears—or rather his one ear and what was left of the other—burning.

"Enrique!" called Hypnos behind him.

Enrique whipped around, snarling. "Am I not allowed a single moment to myself?"

Hypnos looked stunned. His outstretched hand snapped back to his chest. Beside him, Laila rested a hand on his shoulder, a parental gesture that said "let him go," which only made Enrique more furious as he stomped off.

Initially, it had felt so *good* to stomp out of the room—as if he was doing something productive, as if he really could just unfasten himself from all the chaos around him. But it was a false relief that faded almost immediately into cold and sticky shame.

What the hell was he doing?

He couldn't walk away, and he didn't want to. Every hour they lost put Laila's life in danger. Still, he needed a moment to himself if he was going to function.

Enrique slammed the door of the music room behind him. He rarely came in here. It was, more or less, Hypnos's domain. It was here that the patriarch of House Nyx released his beautiful, singing voice and perhaps something of that beauty clung to the walls because, finally, Enrique could breathe easier. Now what? he thought. Unbidden, his mother's voice called him.

"One way or another, you'll have to face the *tsinela*," she'd say.

Enrique shuddered. A *tsinela* was technically nothing more than a sandal, but in the hands of a Filipino mother, it gained an aura of inevitable horror.

Cirila Mercado-Lopez looked like a doll of a woman. Small-boned and spare, with bird-black eyes and fine, dark hair swept into a neat black bun, Enrique's mother hardly looked like the kind of woman who could drive her three, tall sons into deadly stampedes trying to get out of the house.

But her anger was legendary.

It could be because one of them—usually Enrique or Francisco—had found the desserts earlier and gotten a head start before dinner. Or a prank on the neighborhood had been traced back to them—generally Enrique or Juan. Or one of the brothers—almost always Enrique—tried to skip church on the pretense of illness, only to be found swimming in the ocean. Sometimes, they'd get away with it. Other times, the house would be silent and then . . . *thud*. The moment the brothers heard the sound of their mother's wooden *tsinelas* sliding off her feet and hitting the floor, the three of them would prepare to bolt.

"*Buwisit!* Go ahead and run!" Their mother would laugh. She'd pick up her sandal and smack the stair bannister lightly. "The *tsinela* will be here when you come back."

Enrique almost missed his mother's punishments. He would've much rather faced a wooden sandal than Séverin.

Part of him felt furious that Séverin would throw off the course of their plans by even asking for forgiveness, and the other part felt relieved that he wanted it in the first place. The moment he'd returned to them at Carnevale, Enrique felt dislocated. Every stilted interaction reminded him of how they used to be. But then he remembered the months of cold silence. He recalled, all over again, that weightless rush he'd experienced in the Sleeping Palace.

Séverin had known his dreams and used them against him. Séverin had let him imagine that he was unwanted, his scholarly work unneeded. For all that he'd once promised to lift him up, he had kept him small. Intentionally malleable.

It made Enrique nauseous all over again.

And yet . . . he knew Séverin had been *off*. That sheen of desperation still clung to him. Enrique knew he wasn't perfect. He too had moments of deliberate unkindness.

Once, an old, white curator had come to visit the galleries of L'Eden and see the works Enrique had acquired for the hotel. In the past, the man had been a rather harsh critic of museums, but when Enrique and Séverin met with him, he was a shriveled thing, his clothes hanging off him, his glasses askew. He got historical dates wrong, mispronounced the names of kings. Enrique had savored correcting him as pompously as possible until the old man was reduced to stammers and tears. Later, Laila had admonished him. The curator had a neurological condition that had impaired his memory. He had come to L'Eden not to write an article of critique, but to try and familiarize himself with the activities he'd once loved in the company of another renowned historian.

Ashamed, Enrique had slunk into Séverin's office. "I was intolerably cruel."

Séverin, who had been in the middle of reviewing some papers or another, barely looked up. "What do you want me to do about it?"

"Do you have a *tsinela*?"

"What?"

"Never mind," said Enrique. "I was mean and thoughtless and awful—"

"And not yourself," finished Séverin. "So you had a dark moment. It happens. Do you know what makes a star appear so bright?"

"That sounds more like a question for Zofia."

"The darkness around them," said Séverin, closing the book before him and giving Enrique his full attention. "Growth and remorse are rather like stars: the surrounding dark makes them vivid enough to notice. Invite the old curator once more and apologize. Tell yourself that next time you'll do better."

Enrique frowned. "I know you did not devise such wisdom on your own."

"Quite right. I stole it from Laila. Now please leave my office."

In the music room, Enrique almost laughed.

He stood there, thinking about the darkness between stars. He had no doubt that Séverin had fought through darkness. Who was Enrique to deny anyone the chance for light? And would he also deny that light to himself?

Just because the threat of the Fallen House was gone, that didn't mean there wasn't still plenty left of the world that demanded changing. He'd seen that much even inside the matriarch's safe house.

Yesterday, when he had been researching in the library, he had stumbled on a slim, pale volume hiding amongst the matriarch's belongings: *The White Man and the Man of Color*. Enrique knew the title well. It had been written nearly twenty years ago by the

Italian physician Cesare Lombroso. His university classmates had argued loudly about its merits, but he'd never bothered to open it until now. Curious, he flipped to a bookmarked page.

"Only we whites have achieved the most perfect symmetry in the forms of the body . . ."

Something cold wound its way up his ribs. The words rooted him to the spot. Enrique put the book down when Lombroso blamed criminal tendencies on the residual "blackness" of white communities.

Now, Séverin's words flitted through his head.

If you could change the course of history and lift up those who had been downtrodden in its path . . . wouldn't you?

That had always been Enrique's dream.

He wanted to be like his heroes, to light a path to revolution, to carve out a space for himself in a world where people told him he was not wanted. He yearned to do grand things—brandish a sword (though preferably not a heavy one) and sweep someone off their feet, to utter deadly one-liners and swish a cape behind him. More than anything . . . Enrique wanted to *believe* in something better. And he wanted to believe that he could be part of bringing that vision to life. That he could stand at the front instead of in the shadows.

In that second, he made a decision.

He would not merely want . . . he would *do*. Even if it meant opening himself up to hurt once more.

On the other side of the door, someone rapped lightly. "Enrique?"

Zofia.

When Enrique opened the door, he found himself face-to-face with Hypnos and Zofia. Of course, he'd spoken to and seen both of them earlier, but it only dawned on him at this second that he was staring at the two people he'd most enjoyed kissing in the entirety of his existence. And he had never noticed until now how similar and yet different their eyes were. Two shades of blue: one like the heart of a candle flame, the other the hue of winter.

"Are you . . . done?" asked Zofia.

The blunt question knocked the whimsy out of him. He sighed, nodding. "I'm ready."

"Thank every pantheon," said Hypnos. "This much responsibility ages me."

WHEN THEY ENTERED the salon, Séverin practically leapt out of his chair. Enrique's old hurts roared back at him, but he couldn't ignore the painful hope in the other boy's eyes.

"Growth and remorse are rather like stars . . . the surrounding dark makes them vivid enough to notice," said Enrique, before arching an eyebrow. "Which is to say that I expect a damn constellation out of you in the future, Séverin."

Séverin's eyes widened. A fragile smile lifted the corner of his mouth, and although it felt like an unsteady step in the dark to Enrique, it was a step forward all the same.

"And you will have it," said Séverin quietly.

"Where did Laila go?" asked Hypnos.

"She said she needed to get something, and that we should feel free to start examining the map without her," said Zofia.

Enrique looked to the long, wooden table strewn with his research. The world cinched around the lyre and the small, gold-filigreed box beside it which held the mind Forged map. Enrique didn't blame Laila for not wanting to be here. He couldn't imagine staring so closely at his last hope.

Across the room, Séverin met his gaze and lifted one eyebrow.

Oh, thought Enrique, turning to face the room. In the past,

Hypnos and Zofia would look only to Séverin. But now, their gazes were divided between them. Enrique felt as if some hidden light shone more closely on him.

"The matriarch of House Kore left plenty of documents containing rumors of what we might find. I've compiled my own research, but I think it's most useful to compare it to what we can gather from the map," said Enrique. When Séverin nodded at him, Enrique gestured to the box. "Shall we?"

As Séverin reached to unstopper the mind Forged perfume, a shudder ran down Enrique's spine. The others might laugh at his fear, but Plague Island unsettled him. He couldn't help but imagine the soft ash of human remains coating the ground. It seemed an unlikely place for a temple capable of tapping into such divine power . . . but what did he know of the preferences of gods?

"These sensations can get overwhelming," said Séverin. "Remember . . . what you see is real but not presently before you. Nothing inside it can hurt you."

"Yet," muttered Hypnos.

Séverin twisted the top of the perfume bottle, and air hissed from the sudden opening. Enrique dug his fingers into the frayed silk of the armchair, bracing himself as fat ribbons of smoke rose, spreading across the ceiling. Then, it slowly dissolved . . . disintegrating into something like rain. The moment the droplets hit his skin, gray slivers of awareness wrapped around his senses.

Dimly he heard Séverin call out:

"Reattaching stopper *now*—"

But the sound of rushing water and bird calls lapped over Séverin's voice until it seemed like an uncanny twist of the wind. Enrique blinked. He no longer felt the scratched-up satin of the armchair beneath his arms or the notebook in his lap or the smooth metal of the pen clutched in his hand, even as a corner of his mind whispered that he was still sitting in the *palazzo*'s salon. He was standing on an unkempt sidewalk, thorns and nettle jutting out from a tangle of wild grass. The pointed scaffolding of roofs thrust into the skyline. Villagers moved in the early light, their garments little more than animal skins and crude cloth.

The mind Forged visions around him sped up, winding his consciousness along the canals before they were ever canals, past hastily constructed temples and down a passageway until he stood before a statue bust of a woman. Her lips were pressed tight, her blank eyes opened wide in fury. He could just discern the carved feathers sprouting from her cheekbones when her jaw suddenly unhinged. The dais on which the bust stood lurched. Down, down, down he went, plummeting at least thirty meters or more into an underground tunnel. Here, the smell of unstirred, still water hit Enrique's nose. His vision adjusted to the dimness of a vast cave. Pale stalactites studded its rooty ceiling, as sharp and numerous as teeth. Ankle-high brackish water stretched out nearly half a kilometer before him.

His consciousness was tugged down to something at his feet, and horror slowly crawled up his throat.

A trail of light blinked through the water, as if something were slowly waking. A humming sound rang through the cave, shaking droplets of water from the stalactites, so the cave felt like a thing that had begun to salivate in hunger. Now, he could see clearly through the illuminated water—the domed curve of a skull, a gnawed tibia, a slim bridge made of hooked jawbones. And at his feet, one skeletal arm was outflung—

The remains of a woman.

Enrique's gaze snapped over the details. The shroud clinging to her sunken chest. The wisps of blond hair on her skull from which boney protrusions curled back from her forehead. Someone had gilded her bones, so they shone even in the dark. In her cracked open jaw, a sign etched into a paper-thin slab of marble:

Με συγχωρείτε.

Forgive me.

ENRIQUE SNAPPED BACK into himself at the sound of shattering glass. He blinked, looking around. He was no longer in his armchair, but crouched on the floor, his notebook and pen scattered around him. The shattering glass sound had come from Hypnos who had dropped his wineglass. Beside him, Zofia was breathing hard, the grip on her chair white-knuckled. Séverin looked faintly nauseous, but there was an unmistakable gleam of curiosity to his eyes.

He looked up at them.

"What did you see? Let's start with the entrance."

"The people were . . . not of this time," said Zofia.

Séverin nodded. "Makes sense, the temple would be far older than Poveglia. What year would you place this at, Enrique?"

Enrique envied his calm. When he first tried to speak, his voice seemed stuck in his throat. He tried again:

"Sixth century, I believe . . . the people were most likely refugees from Padua during the early barbarian invasions," he managed. "The statue of the woman . . . might be older."

"Woman?" said Hypnos. "She was mostly feathers!"

"Depictions of ancient deities often straddle the wild and mortal worlds," said Enrique.

"Did you notice her lips?" mused Séverin. "They were pursed so tightly, like someone trying not to speak."

Enrique turned the image over in his mind. By now, his thoughts had adjusted to the weight of what he'd seen and allowed him some distance from the vividness of it all.

"Or sing . . ." he said slowly.

Enrique pinched the bridge of his nose, the iconography falling into place, although he didn't see how it fit with what they'd seen in the caves.

"Perhaps the statue represented a siren," he said. "The Roman poet Virgil makes some mention of them being worshipped in parts of the empire."

Séverin tapped his fingers on the table. "But why a siren song? What's the point of it?"

Enrique frowned. "I don't know . . . their song is considered deadly. Mythologically speaking, the only person who was able to hear their song without drowning himself was Odysseus, and that was only because he was tied to the mast of his ship while his crew plugged their ears with beeswax."

Séverin fell silent for a moment, tipping the liquid map backwards and forwards, the replenished remnants of smoke swirling inside the glass.

"A siren's song is something that lures us . . . something beautiful that promises to end only in death," he said slowly. "What does it have to do with the temple beneath Poveglia? Does it require music or some kind of harmony to unlock the entrance?"

Enrique stared at him. For all of Séverin's perceptiveness, he seemed to be forgetting the one explanation that stared him in the face.

That the bust of a siren's head could be nothing more than a warning.

"What if it means the temple itself is the siren's song," said Enrique. "In which case it would be the last, beautiful thing we'd see before death."

Hypnos and Zofia fell quiet. Enrique had thought Séverin would be angry with that line of reasoning, but instead, he grinned.

"Maybe it's a matter of perspective," he said. "I seem to remember you showing me a piece of Slavic art that also depicted a being with the head of a woman and the body of a bird. Not unlike the deadly siren."

"A Gamayun," said Enrique.

He remembered the piece. It was the size of his thumb and crafted entirely of gold. It was Forged to speak in the voice of the artisan's dead mother. A curious, haunting thing. He had declined to acquire it for L'Eden's collection. It seemed wrong to hold a dead voice hostage in the halls.

"What's a Gamayun?" asked Hypnos.

"A bird of prophecy . . . said to guard the way to paradise," said Enrique. "Presumably, she knows all secrets of creation."

"Siren, gamayun . . . death or paradise," said Séverin. "Perhaps what waits for us in Poveglia might have traits of both depending on what we do."

"Perhaps," Enrique allowed.

He felt a little foolish for his dramatic conclusion, but he wasn't entirely convinced that he was wrong . . .

That cavern did not seem like a place that knew paradise.

"And what do we make of the skeleton at the cave's entrance?" asked Séverin.

Séverin paced the room. Enrique watched as his hand went to the front of his jacket, the place where he used to reach for his tin of cloves to help him think. Séverin frowned as his hand came away empty.

"The Greek translates to 'Forgive me,'" said Enrique.

"So . . . they must have done something wrong?" asked Hypnos.

Enrique remembered the ice grotto inside the Sleeping Palace, the message carved into the rock and left for them to find. But before he could say it, Zofia spoke:

"*To play at God's instrument will summon the unmaking,*" she said.

"You think the apology is for playing the instrument?" asked Hypnos.

Zofia shrugged. "It makes sense."

"Or it could be something else," said Séverin. "A ritual, perhaps, a sacrifice made before an act was committed."

"What's the difference?" asked Hypnos. "There's still someone dead, a dark lake with God knows what inside of it, and a very eerie cave which is putting me off any appetite for godhood."

"The difference suggests what we'll find," said Séverin. "If it's an act of ritual, that would suggest that what lies inside that cave is a real place of worship, a place where playing the divine lyre would *work*. If it's an apology, then—"

"Then maybe playing the instrument would be a cataclysmic mistake," said Enrique. "And that's their way of telling us."

"Who are *they*?" asked Zofia.

"Whoever came before," said Enrique. "The fabric on the skeleton is far too decomposed to date. They might even be one of the Lost Muses who once protected the divine lyre."

"Any other observations?" asked Séverin.

"A thin foil of metal had been applied to the skeleton's bones," said Zofia.

"An interesting decorative choice, but still not indicative of the skeleton's purpose," said Séverin.

"It had horns," said Enrique, remembering the protrusions from its forehead.

Séverin paused. "Horns?"

He reached up, touching his forehead. Enrique remembered that strange hour in the catacombs more than a year ago . . . the gold ichor that dripped across Séverin's mouth before giving him wings that shot out from his back and a pair of horns that curled from his temples before vanishing moments later.

"Bull horns, I think," said Enrique, remembering himself. "Which to me suggests ancient Greece, or the Minoan civilization."

"Like an animal, sacrificed . . ." said Séverin. His face lit up. "Like a scapegoat."

"Scapegoat?" asked Hypnos.

"An animal ritually burdened with a community's sins, then driven away. People did it to avoid catastrophes. They'd sacrifice an animal to avoid plague or a terrible storm," explained Enrique. "It's an ancient practice that's mentioned in Leviticus, but they used goats, not people, hence the origins of the word 'scapegoat.'"

"She wasn't an animal," said Zofia, almost angrily.

"Of course not!" said Enrique hurriedly. "But the process was similar. Some communities did use people. In ancient Greek, the scapegoating ritual of a person exiled from the community was called *pharmakos*."

Hypnos reached for a new wineglass. "So you think this woman could have been exiled from a place and burdened with its sins?"

"I think that depends on what else we find inside that cave," said Séverin.

As Séverin reached once more for the mind Forged map, Enrique found himself thinking about power. He didn't know if he fully bought Séverin's optimism that the lyre would grant them godlike power, but he was confident of one thing. When Enrique closed his eyes and thought of the mind Forged illusion, it wasn't the golden bones or the siren's stone lips that rose to the top of his thoughts . . . but the stench.

The cave brimmed with the stinking breath of something ancient and hungry. It was like standing before a creature who opened its jaws, the better for one to glimpse the cracked limbs still caught between its yellow teeth.

23

LAILA

Laila brought the blade to her palm and pressed down. She winced, but only out of habit . . . not pain. In those seconds, Laila felt nothing. Not even the pressure of the knife.

The blankness that had stolen through her the moment she and Hypnos had gone after Enrique came on fast and blinding. She could barely tell Zofia to begin without her before she stole into the kitchens and locked the doors behind her. Alone, she tried to breathe, but she could not feel air stirring in her lungs. The world around her dulled and dimmed.

The last time this had happened, Séverin's touch had revived her senses, but Laila refused to go to him. To lose any more power over herself would be its own death.

Feel something, she urged her body, staring at the cut. *Anything*.

One second, then two . . . then five. Something thick and tarry glugged from the wound. For years, Laila had avoided looking too closely at what was inside her. All her life, her father's words chased her.

You are a girl made of grave dirt.

Now, Laila felt no horror. If anything, it was pride that moved through her. By all accounts, she should not be alive.

"And yet," said Laila fiercely. "Here I am."

Another second ticked before she finally felt it: a dull throb. Laila snatched greedily at the pain.

When she was young, she had imagined different miracles. Like reaching into a tree and finding a mango made of solid gold. Or a prince who might find her washing clothes in the river and be so taken by the sight of her that he would whisk her away to a palace of moonstone and jasper. But now, Laila was old enough to recognize pain for the miracle it was. Pain was a loud, angry line between the living and the dead.

Days ago, Laila had kneeled on a floor of ice . . . her pain so great, she could not breathe through it. She imagined she would never see Hypnos wave around another glass of wine, Enrique open a book, Zofia reach for a match, or Séverin *smile*. For every piece lost to her—seconds and heartbeats and texture—each hope regained was a torch flaring to life, and it would hold back the dark.

This blankness might be death's shadow, but it was not yet the end.

PERHAPS THE UNIVERSE was delighted with her foolish optimism because it soon revealed even more wonders. At the back of the pantry, Laila found a jar of, if not newly baked, then at least baked within a reasonable amount of time, sugar cookies. It didn't take her long to find caster sugar which she turned into a pale royal icing to frost the cookies just how Zofia liked them. There was bitter cocoa in the cabinets, which became hot chocolate for Enrique and Hypnos, and when she searched for cinnamon to add to the concoction, her fingers closed around smooth, metal edges, and she drew out a tin of cloves.

When she saw it, she laughed.

"Very well," she said aloud.

Laila balanced the tray full of food and drinks in her hands as she made her way to the salon. She'd made a similar walk dozens of times in the past, but this one had an air of ritual about it. As if she were making an offering to something greater than herself, and all she could do was hope that it was enough. The door was slightly ajar, and as she opened it, she felt a strange warp in the air.

"Laila, wait!" someone called. "We opened the map again—"

But it was too late.

The door had opened. The moment she stepped inside, a wet droplet splashed onto her wrist. It felt like rain, but it was colder, and *alive* with a Forged awareness that snuck through her skin, entering her bloodstream and filling her head with visions. When she looked out, the salon room was gone, replaced with something she'd never seen before.

She was standing ankle-deep in a dark lake. Above her, glittering stalactite studded the vaulted ceiling of a cave, surrounded by glossy chunks of obsidian and jet so that it seemed as if someone had taken a hammer to the night sky and arranged its fragments into a cavern. Her consciousness felt pulled forward, skimming over the lake. Only now did she realize the lake was strewn with human bones. The water stretched out many hundreds of meters ahead, ending before a huge wall of carved, semitranslucent amber. The wall seemed backlit by distant fires, shadows licking across the surface and blurring the details of what lay behind it. There, huge and impossible, stood the unmistakable silhouette of giants flanking a squat, jagged structure.

Laila stretched out, as if she could reach past the amber wall . . .

"Not the cookies!"

She blinked, and the salon came into view once more. Enrique stood in front of her, one hand steadying the tray of treats. A bit of hot chocolate had sloshed down the sides of one of the mugs, and the rich scent of cocoa returned her to her senses.

"What was that?" asked Laila.

Séverin's dark eyes found hers immediately. "Hope."

ENRIQUE SLURPED DOWN the rest of his cocoa, frantically compiling the notes he'd taken on everything they'd witnessed through the mind Forged map. Beside him, Zofia happily munched on a cookie.

"Possible siren statue, lake full of bones, shiny skeleton—"

Hypnos raised his cup. "Can't forget the shiny skeleton."

"*Massive* structures!" said Enrique excitedly. "The kind that, I can't believe I am saying this, but it could . . . I mean . . . *could* it be the Tower of Babel? I'm certain it is not the exact one that the Western world credits for the origins of Forging. For all we know, there could be multiple sources, but the tower—"

"It was not a tower," said Zofia, frowning. "It was far too wide."

"Which proves my point, actually," said Enrique, setting down his mug.

He walked to his research table, rummaging around before he paused to pull out a faded, yellow illustration. It was a low-slung, jagged, rectangular brick structure with carved steps surrounding it from every angle. It looked about the size of a town square, and its flat top reminded Laila of a massive platform.

"This is an illustration of the Ziggurat of Ur, first excavated about thirty years ago in what we now know is the ancient Sumerian city of Uruk," said Enrique. "The Tower of Babel was most likely not a narrow construction like we might imagine in Western architecture, but an ancient stepped pyramid like the temples of Babylon and Sumeria." Enrique tapped the top of the illustration.

Séverin studied the image. "If we were to come to such a temple, then the lyre would be played . . . where, exactly?"

"Probably in the innermost shrine at the top of the temple," said Enrique, tapping the paper. "It was thought that only priests and kings were allowed to enter this area as it was considered the point at which heaven and earth met. All kinds of sacred rituals might have taken place there, including *heiros gamos*."

"Which is?" asked Hypnos.

Laila noticed that Enrique's cheeks pinked.

"Er, a sacred marriage," said Enrique. "Sometimes, a king and a chosen priestess would, um, assume the form of a god and goddess and renew spring throughout the land by . . . having relations."

Hypnos frowned. "On a stone floor?"

Enrique looked even more pink. "No, I believe there was a sacred bed and such."

"I wonder how they got it up all those steps," said Hypnos.

"What about those gigantic . . . figures beside it?" asked Laila.

Enrique looked relieved at the change of topic. "Ah! That was my next point! I came across these the other day and was wondering why the matriarch would have them in her possession." He went to one of the shelves, drawing out a bronze figurine on a little platform. "These were popular in ancient Greece. Many of them were water-powered for parades, but not this kind."

When he touched it, the bronze figurine gave a loud creak as its jointed limbs moved up and down.

"It's an automaton," said Zofia.

"Exactly!" said Enrique.

"Roullet & Decamps make dozens of automata," said Hypnos. "It's not exactly rare."

"But it *is* ancient," said Enrique. "Hephaestus, god of smithing, made the bronze Talos, a giant automaton designed to protect the island of Crete. King Ajatasatru of eastern India supposedly had—" He paused to consult his notes. "*Boo-tah va* . . . Laila, help."

He sighed, holding up the page to Laila who read it aloud:

"*Bhuta vahana yanta* . . . 'spirit movement machines,'" she translated. "They're said to guard the relics of Buddha."

Enrique nodded. "To me, all the iconography is in line with what we'd expect for, well . . ."

"For someone safeguarding the power of God," said Laila.

A hush fell over the room. Laila felt a strange prickling anticipation rippling through her.

"What about the wall?" asked Zofia.

Laila saw the semitranslucent amber wall in her head and ached to touch it.

"Now *that*," said Enrique, slumping into his chair. "I have no idea."

"It didn't appear in our first experience of the map," said Séverin slowly. "Perhaps it operates as one giant Tezcat?"

"Maybe the name of the temple would provide us with a hint of how to access it," suggested Hypnos.

"A good thought," said Séverin. "But to my knowledge, this temple is nameless."

"Why?" asked Enrique.

"Too powerful, perhaps," mused Séverin. "A name is dangerous. It can pin something into place, tie it to a country, a religion. Perhaps the temple remained anonymous so that no one could be blamed for even knowing of a place where the lyre could be played and the Babel Fragments could be linked together."

"Maybe . . ." said Enrique, but he sounded unsure.

"I need to think on it more." Séverin's brows pressed together. His hand moved to the front of his jacket. An old gesture, one that Laila had nearly forgotten since Tristan had died.

"Here," she said, reaching for the tin of cloves on the tray. "This might be useful."

She tossed it in the air, and Séverin caught it one-handed. He stared at it in disbelief. Her face turned hot.

"It's to help you think," explained Laila.

"Thank you."

"You're welcome."

She could hear the mechanical tonelessness in her voice, and she sensed everyone—except Zofia, who was preoccupied with her third cookie—shifting uncomfortably. Let them, she thought. She had told Séverin the truth. Yes, he had a corner of her heart. But he had no claim to her dwindling time, and if these ended up becoming her last days, then she would spend them the way anyone should spend their life: giving herself what she deserved.

"What happened to your hand?" asked Séverin, his voice darkening.

Laila stared down at the bandage. By now, a black spot of blood had stained the wrapping. It ached a little, but not nearly as much as it should have.

"Nothing." She glanced once at Séverin and knew immediately he was not convinced. "How soon can we leave for Poveglia?"

"We just need a couple more supplies from a night market and we can leave within hours," said Enrique.

"Transport?"

"Already arranged," said Hypnos.

Séverin nodded, not taking his eyes off Laila. "Then we leave before dawn."

24

SÉVERIN

In the early hours of dawn, *La Rialto Mercato* seemed like a place that should only be visited by denizens of the Otherworld. As Séverin walked around, he imagined bright-eyed fae creatures with spindly fingers hawking a necklace of dreams for the price of a kiss or rattling jars full of scales plucked from a fish that could speak prophecy. Around them, the predawn air whispered frost over the empress plums and dusky figs. Piles of currants in the fruit stands gleamed like cut rubies. Miniature Venetian masks chimed together, and women with hunched backs and blue-veined hands draped delicate lace beside carved brass keys. The glass artists had only just begun to set out their wares, and Séverin watched in wonder as Murano glass ornaments blown into stained-glass swans flew from one stall to the next while delicate bouquets of crystal flowers wilted and bloomed by the hour.

Séverin, Hypnos, and Enrique walked to the *pescheria*, where Hypnos had made arrangements for a local fisherman to take them to Poveglia. Back at the matriarch's *palazzo*, Laila and Zofia were finishing up final preparations. All the while, Séverin found himself turning to Enrique, wholly expecting the historian to wax poetic about the Gothic architecture and the Byzantine cathedral or go into extraordinary detail about an algae-covered statue until he was forcibly dragged away from the spot. But every time Séverin worked up the courage to speak to him, Enrique would turn his head, and the sight of that bandaged wound would hit him like a physical blow.

Séverin had let that happen to his friend.

Worse, he'd let Enrique believe he was unwanted . . . when he was anything but.

While he was still trying to work out what to say and how to say it, Enrique fell into step beside him. He looked tense . . . hesitant.

"It's beautiful here, isn't it?" he asked suddenly. "Reminds me of something you'd commission in L'Eden."

On Séverin's other side, Hypnos grumbled, pulling his ermine furs more tightly around his neck. "It's *cold* is what it is."

"Perhaps something for a spring commission," he found himself saying. "It could be an interesting installation in the lobby. A magical Night Bazaar perhaps."

Enrique's eyebrows shot up his forehead. A wary grin touched the historian's mouth and he nodded. "Perhaps."

Before, Séverin's hopes had felt massive and vague . . . but this was small. This was a hope that could fit inside a room. That at the end of all this winter there would be a spring and something beautiful to mark the occasion.

Smiling to himself, he reached into his breast pocket, past the divine lyre sewn into his jacket by Zofia's Forged steel threads, and grabbed his tin of cloves. He popped one of them into his mouth, its powerful, burning flavor flooding his senses immediately.

Enrique wrinkled his nose. "I hate that smell."

"Laila doesn't mind," said Hypnos with a knowing grin at Séverin.

In the past, Séverin would have brushed them off and gone silent . . . but had he not promised them transparency in all things? And were not issues such as this supposed to be discussed among friends? He turned the clove over, letting the bitterness flood his tongue before he said, "Laila minds quite a lot of other things. Including, but not limited to, the reckless disregard of her feelings, faithlessness to our friends, and—her opinion, not mine—an egocentric and zealous pursuit to right my wrongs and protect my loved ones. I doubt she has the space to mind my clove habits."

Enrique winced, and Hypnos sighed and shook his head.

"And you've apologized . . . ?" asked Hypnos.

"Obviously."

"And reminded her about the, um—" Hypnos wiggled his ring finger.

"Interestingly enough, reminding the woman I love that she's been carrying around a death sentence didn't factor into my romantic agenda," said Séverin coldly.

Enrique smacked Hypnos on the back of his head.

"Ow!" said Hypnos. "It was just a thought! Near-fatal situations make me, ah, *comment dire*, very amorous, *non*? Hungry for life! All the more so when you know your situation will soon be remedied."

"I doubt she would feel similarly," said Séverin.

Hypnos frowned then snapped his fingers triumphantly. "I know! You should try showing up naked in her bedroom. I call it, *La Méthode de L'Homme Nu.*"

Séverin and Enrique stopped walking and stared at him.

"*The Naked Man Method?*" asked Enrique. "Are you serious?"

"I'd rather be naked." Hypnos crossed his arms. "Trust me, it works. If the lady or gentleman is not intrigued, then they leave the room."

"And probably burn their bedsheets for good measure," muttered Enrique.

"And if they consent, well, then you have made the process of intimacy that much easier. You should try it."

"*No*," said Séverin and Enrique at the same time.

Hypnos huffed. "Enjoy your utter lack of inspiration."

By then, the lovely mercato had changed. The baking smells and perfume of sliced fruit soured as they approached the *pescheria*. Housed beneath lichen-splattered vaulted Gothic arches on the banks of the Grand Canal, the fish market was a smelly landmark of the city and, for better or for worse, the meeting place for their transport. Even from a distance, Séverin could see the pale, writhing piles of freshwater eels. Water Forging artists walked among the fish stalls, levitating blocks of ice into the stalls to keep the catch fresh.

"There he is," said Hypnos, pointing his chin at a grizzled man leaning against one of the pillars. The fisherman nodded in acknowledgment.

"I'll finalize payment, and then we'll be off," said Hypnos, walking toward the fish market.

Séverin couldn't remember the last time he'd been alone with Enrique. Before, they used to have an easy camaraderie . . . but now, every sentence felt like a heavy step on thin ice. Enrique didn't look at him. He had turned his attention back to the stretch of market kiosks before the street turned into fish stalls.

"She likes flowers," said Enrique quietly. "You could start with that?"

Séverin followed Enrique's gaze to a little market stall operated by an old woman who was already dozing even though the market had just opened. On the table before her was spread out a handful of delicate, glass artwork: chrysanthemums with milky quartz petals, roses carved from thin slices of carnelian stone. Séverin's eyes fell on a glass lily, its artistry so vivid that each petal looked snipped from a flame

Enrique nudged him. "Go on."

Séverin hesitated. "You don't think it's a lost cause?"

"If I believed in lost causes, you would be at the bottom of the lagoon," said Enrique primly.

"Fair enough. And what about yourself? You don't want to get her flowers?"

"Who? Oh . . ." Enrique glanced away. "Is it that obvious?"

"Only when you stare, *unblinking*, at her."

"I think she'd be more interested in the mathematical ratios of the petals than the flower itself. I have to find something that would be like a flower to her." Enrique frowned. "Something flammable, I'm afraid."

"I'd be afraid too."

"You are not helping."

A FEW HOURS later, Séverin made an uncomfortable discovery: the divine lyre had a heartbeat. It was as if the instrument was slowly coming alive the closer they got to Poveglia. Séverin could feel it against his own pulse, a persistent *thump, thump, thump*.

If hope had a sound, this would be it.

His friends looked cold and miserable in the dingy boat. At the helm, the fisherman did not spare them a glance and had been adamant about his responsibility to them.

"I will get there as fast as I can, and I will not wait for you. How you make your way back is on your head, God help you."

As the wind whipped around them, Séverin imagined his mother's voice carried along its path. *In your hands lie the gates of godhood. Let none pass.*

He was *meant* to play the lyre.

He was *meant* to save Laila.

He was *meant* to protect his friends.

Séverin risked a glance at Laila. She managed to look regal even in this dingy boat. Her back was ramrod straight, the fur of her jacket ruffling around her neck as she twisted her garnet ring. She had pulled her hair back in a braid, but strands of black silk twisted free to frame her face. Her full mouth was pursed tight, and he noticed the rich brown of her skin had lost its sheen overnight.

When he looked at her, all that power he'd felt tipped uneasily inside him.

He had failed her a thousand times, but in this, he would succeed.

The islands of Lido and Poveglia ahead of them turned sharper, larger. Silver brume clouded the water, swallowing the silhouettes of cathedrals and docks, so that it looked like a residence for ghosts.

"I don't understand why this place has to be on a *plague* island," grumbled Hypnos.

Enrique, who had grabbed a rather crusty-looking blanket, now peered at them from underneath it. "Did you know—"

Hypnos groaned. "Here we go."

From under a waterproof rubber tarp, Zofia poked her head out curiously to listen to Enrique.

"The word 'quarantine' comes from the Italian '*quaranta giorni*' for 'forty days,' which was the number of days that a ship must stay away from Venice if it was suspected of harboring plague. Islands like Poveglia were one of the first *lazaret*, or quarantine colonies. Isn't that fascinating?"

Even in the rainy, frigid gloom, Enrique beamed expectantly at everyone.

Séverin sat up a little straighter. Enrique had doubted his support. He would do better this time.

"Fascinating!" he said loudly, clapping his hands.

Everyone stared at him.

Too late, he suspected his actions lacked a certain subtlety.

He looked at Enrique. For the first time, the historian looked as if he were holding back not a scold . . . but a laugh.

"How . . . enlightening?" tried Laila.

"Why the number forty?" asked Zofia.

"That I don't know," said Enrique.

Zofia frowned, disappearing under the tarp once more.

"I feel like I'm going to get the plague the longer I stay on this godforsaken boat," muttered Hypnos.

Eventually, the boat came to a stop, docking beside a curious statue of an angel with her wings hunched and folded around her head. The moment the fisherman threw down the anchor, the statue drew back its wings and raised one stony arm that pointed back to Venice. The message was clear:

Leave.

At first glance, Poveglia didn't strike Séverin as a place for ghosts. There was dirt on the ground, not soft ash. The gossipy caw of ravens rasped through walled-up grottoes, and above the line of trees, the old bell tower kept a watchful eye on the island.

But that was only at first glance.

The longer Séverin stared at the island, the more he felt it: a worn-out numbness. The kind of cold vacuum that fills the body when it has been emptied of all its tears and prayers and pleading.

The hairs on the back of his neck lifted.

He scanned the island, listening closely.

In his pack, he felt the torches and supplies they'd gathered along with the jagged point of the gilded box that held the bottle of the mind Forged map to Poveglia. Its contents were gone, distributed amongst the five of them, already tugging their consciousness down an overgrown path of weeds to where the scaffolding skeleton of a former quarantine station beckoned. And yet, no one moved.

Everyone turned to Laila, a silent understanding moving through them. For all that Séverin may have boasted about his dreams for all of them, when he tried to picture what would happen when he finally played the divine lyre in the temple shrine, it wasn't his face he saw transfixed by celestial light.

It was hers.

Her smile, unburdened by the weight of death . . . her laughter turned reckless, knowing this was merely the first in an infinite string of joys. Séverin wanted to see that so badly, he would've rushed down the path this instant, but he would not step ahead of her.

This was her journey too.

And though Séverin knew power sang through his veins, he also knew that it was only for her sake that the others had even entertained giving him another chance . . . and so he waited. Beside him, Enrique bowed his head, as if praying. Zofia stood with her hands clasped, and even Hypnos's usually irreverent grin had been smoothed into a thoughtful expression.

Séverin watched as Laila looked up at the sky. She turned her palms up and closed her eyes. Slowly, she bent and touched the ground, then touched her forehead.

On occasion, Séverin had seen her practice *bharatnatyam* in L'Eden. She liked practicing in the early mornings best, and often used the spare suites that adjoined his office. Sometimes, he'd stop working just to listen to the chime of her anklets. Whenever he caught her before she began, he noticed that she brushed her fingers against the floor and pressed her hands together in prayer.

Once, Séverin had leaned against the doorframe, watching her. "Why do you do that?" He vaguely imitated her motions, and Laila raised an eyebrow.

"You mean *Namaskaram*," she said. "We do this as an offer of prayer, and to ask the permission of the goddess of the earth to dance on her."

He'd frowned. "It's only dancing. It's beautiful, but surely not so dangerous that a goddess needs to give her permission."

Séverin would never forget how she smiled at him. Serene and somehow terrifying too. He remembered how the sunlight through the stained glass backlit her silhouette and turned her loveliness inhuman.

"Do you know how the world ends?" she asked softly.

"Fire and brimstone, I imagine?"

"No," she said, smiling. "It ends in terrible beauty. Our Lord of Destruction is also called Nataraja, the Lord of Dance. In his movements, the universe will dissolve and start anew. So yes, we must request permission for beautiful things, for they have hidden hearts of danger."

Slowly, Laila walked toward him. Her anklets chimed softly. Her hair, long and unbound, curled around her waist.

"Can't you feel that danger, Séverin?"

He had.

But it was not destruction of the world he'd feared when Laila turned sharply from him and began to practice.

Watching her now, Séverin wondered at her movements. Was

she requesting the earth's permission for beauty . . . or its forgiveness for destruction? He didn't know how to ask her.

When Laila was finished, he turned to the others.

"We know the landscape has changed considerably, so we must pay special attention to any ruins," he said. "We may need to explore more shadows than not."

Zofia raised her hand. "I can light the way."

"I'll go with her," said Enrique.

"She has all the explosives, yes?" said Hypnos. "I'm going with her too."

Séverin rolled his eyes. "Then I'll guard the back. The siren bust should be no more than a half kilometer away according to our map."

He thought Laila would walk to the front, but she didn't. She remained a couple of paces ahead of him, just out of reach. Every now and then, she'd pause and stare around at the dull greenery. She must have been feeling restless. Worried. He wished he could comfort her, but what if everything he said came across as an unwanted demand of her time? She would think him insensitive or worse, unchanged and selfish.

As he moved, he felt the edges of the glass Forged fire lily in his front pocket. He should never have gotten it. How would he give it to her anyway? *Here, take this extremely fragile thing and please do not perceive it as a metaphor for our relations.*

He should smash it on the ground.

He was turning the idea over in his head when Laila suddenly spoke. "I wish it were spring," she said.

Séverin's head snapped up. Cautiously, he took a few strides faster until he fell into step beside her.

"Why?" he asked.

"For wildflowers," said Laila, laughing a little. "I should've looked more closely at them last spring."

She wanted flowers. How strange that of all the things he couldn't give her, he could at least do that. Slowly, he reached into his jacket, pulling out the lily. He held it out to her.

Laila stopped in her tracks, staring between him and the glass flower in his hand.

"I picked it up earlier. In the markets. I thought—well, hoped really—that you would like it."

Laila raised an eyebrow. Slowly, she took the lily. She twirled it between her fingers. The sunshine flowed through the crystal, painting the ground scarlet and orange.

"Do you like it?" he asked, before quickly adding: "It is perfectly acceptable if you don't, of course. I merely thought it was . . . nice. I suppose. And a far better alternative than—"

He stopped himself right before he referenced Hypnos's Naked Man Method. A look of disbelief crossed over Laila's face.

"Séverin. Are you . . . nervous?"

"I—" He paused, gathering himself. "What answer would please you best?"

Laila didn't respond. But for a moment she looked—or perhaps he was deluding himself—as if she were on the verge of laughter. With a small smile, she tucked the flower into her sleeve and kept moving forward.

THE MIND FORGED map led them to the outskirts of an abandoned quarantine station. Some distance away stood the ruins of a church. Behind it, a lonely belfry tower with bricks the color of old blood loomed against the winter clouds. The air tasted of salt and rust.

On the ground, Séverin saw nothing but piles of bricks, rags trampled into the ground, and the eerie remains of hastily thrown down shovels. He did not wish to think how many souls were buried beneath the ground he stood on.

"Where's the siren statue?" asked Enrique, turning around. "It . . . it should be here."

Laila drew her shawl tighter. "What was this place?"

Séverin glanced down. They were standing in the remains of a former room. Or perhaps a courtyard, judging by the bleached rubble of a fountain. Thin, metal beds lay in various stages of ruin. Along the broken semicircle of the wall, black ivy clambered around the stone, slowly choking the pillars that might have once adorned the circumference.

"I think it was a convalescence room . . ." said Séverin, toeing a piece of broken glass. It was uncommonly large, more like a panel that would have belonged in a skylight rather than a window. "Whoever hid the entrance in ancient times would not have used something that could be easily removed . . . so what happened when it was found again once people started building stations here? Did they find the statue bust and try to hide it? Or celebrate it?"

Séverin picked his way toward the wall. The more he spoke, the more he imagined the room as it had once been. The early sunlight streaming through the glass, the gurgling fountain, and the rasping breaths of a patient fighting to see the light.

He stretched out his hand, his fingers sinking into the wall of ivy. He kept his eyes on the ground. He remembered a detail about the statue . . . something about the shape of the pillar's base.

"Perhaps the builder would've found it strange that he could not move the statue," said Séverin. "Maybe he even tried to cover it up with plaster or paint that has worn away by now."

As he walked, he brushed back the dirt with his shoes until an odd shape caught his eye: a pair of clawed talons.

At the same time, his fingers hit something cold and rough.

"Zofia?" he said quietly.

Zofia appeared at his side. She snapped a small pendant off her necklace and held it to the leaves. Tendrils of smoke curled into the air as the ivy smoldered and fell to the ground. As the blackened leaves cleared, a scorched face appeared in the leaves. The siren.

Séverin felt Hypnos, Laila, and Enrique drawing closer. Enrique sucked in his breath.

"You found it," he said softly. "But how do we get it open?"

Séverin frowned, staring at the statue. "In the image, the siren's mouth dropped open . . . triggering the entrance."

He reached out, tracing the exquisitely carved feathers that sprouted along the siren's cheekbones and melted into her hair. Her mouth had been shaped into a pursed, angry line. Her eyes were closed shut.

Séverin paused. Lightly, he touched the statue's eyelids.

"A siren sings to lure in sailors . . . but to do that . . . they must spot you in the water," he said.

"So?" asked Enrique.

"This statue's eyes are closed . . . which means she cannot see us," said Séverin. "Not yet."

He pressed his fingers into the statue's eyelids. The stone gave way, a lost mechanism creaking loudly as the rocky eyelids pulled back.

"What is that?" asked Hypnos, stumbling backwards.

Beneath them, the ground quivered. Séverin flung out his arms, steadying himself. Laila stumbled, and he caught her around the waist, clasping her to him just as milky, quartz stones rolled into the siren's eye hollows.

"Everyone hold tight to one another—" Séverin started to say, but his words were drowned out as the siren's jaw unhinged with a sound like growling thunder. The earth around them lurched and fell away, and Séverin barely had time to reach for Enrique's hand before a clammy darkness swallowed them whole.

25

ZOFIA

Zofia could not comprehend the space around her all at once. Instead, it came in blips of awareness:

The descent—so long she had counted all the way up to seventeen—and the *thud*. In the end, she did not fall, but stumble, as if she had missed the last step on a staircase.

Something cold touched her toe. Her shoes squelched. A sharp rock had torn a hole through the leather. Beneath her boots, Zofia could faintly make out the damp silt ground, the kind that belonged to the shores of a lake.

Her ears buzzed. She blinked and blinked, but she could not see anything beyond a circle of light, the circumference of which was hardly more than three meters. Its source came from hundreds of meters above them, which Zofia recognized as the opening from which they had fallen. To cross that much space and feel it as nothing more than a stumble indicated they had fallen through several Tezcats to arrive here.

But what was *here*?

Zofia could hear her friends calling and shuffling around her, but she tuned them out. *One thing at a time*, she told herself. She had to parse this sense by sense . . . starting with sight.

Cloying darkness pressed all around them. Zofia felt the hairs on the back of her neck prickle. Dimly, she heard her mother's voice.

Be a light, Zosia.

With trembling hands, Zofia tore off one of her pendants and reached for a match. Even before she could see what lay before her, she did not like what she smelled. The cave was earthen and sweet, but musty. Like summer ponds full of sickly green water and buzzing flies. A faint, coppery note lingered beneath it all. It reminded her of blood. A damp chill settled into her clothes.

Zofia struck the match, raising it to the pendant. Light flared around her, and with it came a new calm. Her breaths loosened. Séverin appeared at her side. He smiled. "Mind sharing the light, Phoenix?"

She nodded, holding out the pendant. One by one, Séverin lit their torches and handed them off to Enrique, Hypnos, and Laila.

"No one move," said Séverin, holding up his torch. "We need to compare what's before us to the mind Forged map. Beyond what research we've gathered, we don't know anything about how the cave will react to our presence, so stay alert and stay close."

Huge stalagmites—Zofia counted fifteen—jutted up at the edges of the cave, and dozens of mushrooms bloomed in the crevices. Not three meters away, a dark lake stretched out at least half a kilometer long. It was silent except for the occasional plink of water droplets beading off the cave ceiling and hitting the lake. The water lapped against a wall of shining black rock on the far end. She remembered from the mind Forged map that there was something behind the wall . . . a gleaming, amber light and autom-atons the size of buildings.

"We need to move closer to the lake," said Enrique. "I thought the gilded skeleton would be here, but I don't see it . . ."

They each took one step forward. At the front, Séverin held out his torch. The light traveled over the uneven ground before catch-ing on a mottled piece of marble poking out of the silt about two meters away. Zofia recognized it as the paper-thin marble sign that had once been in the jaws of the skeleton.

But the skeleton was gone.

"That can't be right," said Enrique.

He moved to take a step forward when Séverin caught his hand. "Careful."

Slowly, Enrique crouched on the ground. He pulled out a pair of gloves from his pocket and drew out the plaque before walking back to them.

"It still reads *Forgive me*," he said, tilting his head and examining the marble. He turned around. "But how could the skeleton have vanished already? There's no signs of rockfall that would have dis-turbed its place. And the lake must have been covered up until now."

"Something could have taken it deeper into the lake," said Séverin, eyeing the water.

"What, like a . . . creature?" asked Hypnos.

Beside him, Laila looked uneasy. Her gaze darted around the cave.

"We can't be sure, but we *can* try to run some experiments from here, without disturbing anything else. It could be that parts of the chamber require activation before they reveal themselves to us," Séverin said. "The best thing we can do is unload our belongings, evaluate our surroundings, and perhaps test the lake for reactions?"

Zofia nodded alongside Laila, Hypnos, and Enrique. Séverin dropped his rucksack and began rummaging through its contents.

"Secure the surroundings and check for any sign of recording activity. We can't afford to rush anything at this stage, so move as slowly as you have to," said Séverin. "Hypnos and Enrique, examine the shoreline. Laila, see if you can't source anything un-Forged that can tell us more about what to expect. Zofia, use your nautical devices and measure the depths of the lake. Also, Enrique—"

Séverin paused, looking up.

"Enrique, what are you doing?"

Enrique was poking something into his uninjured ear. "Giving myself some added protection in case there are any sirens."

Zofia frowned. "Sirens are not real."

"But they could be a symbolic stand-in for something," said Enrique. "Sonic blasts or earsplitting Forging devices, or what have you."

"How does disturbing your earwax assist in that endeavor?" asked Hypnos.

"BEESWAX IS WHAT WORKED FOR ODYSSEUS WHEN HE FACED THE SIRENS," said Enrique, far louder than he needed to.

Laila winced. "We heard you."

"WHAT?"

"We heard—" started Laila, then she shook her head. "Forget it!"

"*WHAT?*"

Séverin motioned for him to take out the beeswax, which Enrique did before looking curiously at everyone.

"I brought enough for everyone?" he said.

"How are you going to hear us if you've got that in your ear?"

"Just wave your hands and I'll see it. I can hear a little through my bandages, but not much," said Enrique, shoving the wax back in.

"Say nothing if you agree that I am the most handsome man alive," said Hypnos quietly.

Enrique, who was preoccupied with his research notes, said nothing.

"Hurrah!" said Hypnos.

Zofia was about to say that was not a real victory when Laila called, "Come see!" She gestured to one of the dark boulders separating the shore from the water. "I almost didn't notice it. It's definitely Forged."

Zofia followed her. Near the water's edge stood a large gray boulder with a hollow, conical protrusion. Zofia touched it lightly. It had been bronze once, but was now mottled green and gray. The metal whispered the will that had long ago been Forged into its structure:

Hear and repeat and resound.

"It's . . . it's like a sound amplifier," Zofia said, confused.

Why would the device need to amplify sound if the cave was silent?

"Let's measure the lake and go back to the others," said Laila. "I think Séverin will want to see this."

Zofia dropped her satchels onto the ground, drawing out her measuring devices and a length of steel rope, Forged to retain a calibrated tensile strength at all times. She would need to lower the device into the water without losing it. As she assembled her instruments, she counted the things around her, steadying herself—seven rocks, four square-shaped, three roughly rounded; four stalactites directly above her; three rock shelves jutting from the cave wall on the right; zero rock shelves jutting from the cave wall on the left; three used matches lying beside her boot.

Zofia returned to her reading instruments, frowning as she translated the measurements. The lake was deep, but there appeared to be an obstruction running down the middle. Zofia was about to call out to the others when her torchlight roved over something pale and moving in the shallows of the lake: a skull, toppled onto its side.

Zofia yelped, skittering backwards.

"Zofia!" called Laila, rushing to her side. "Are you all right?"

Zofia stared into the water, goose bumps erupting over her skin. Skeletons didn't normally frighten her. To her, they were like machines devoid of use, their anima flown out of them and moved onto something else in the unseen equation and balancing of the world.

But the way it had seemed to rear up out of the dark had thrown her. There was something in the way it turned and listed to one side . . . Hela's head had turned in an identical fashion on one of the evenings when her fever raged at its worst. Beneath her sister's blond hair and gray eyes was a skull. It might already *be* only a skull.

Zofia had been able to push the unknown from her mind until now, but seeing that skull summoned her fear up close in her thoughts. She felt frozen by all the things she did not know, all the things that threatened to undo her calm. Was Hela safe? Would Laila live? What would happen to them?

"Zofia . . ." said Laila. "What's wrong?"

Zofia pointed wordlessly at the skull.

"Oh," said Laila. "Don't be frightened . . . it's nothing. We knew there were dead down here, remember? They can't hurt us . . . and . . . and I'm sure they are not hurting either. They're dead, after all."

Zofia looked up at Laila. Her friend looked different. Zofia regarded her features: paler skin, sunken eyes. Laila smiled, which should mean that she was fine, but Zofia recognized that smile. It was forced and stretched, which meant it was a smile performed for her benefit.

Hela had worn the same smile many times.

Zofia's gaze dropped to Laila's hand on her arm. Blood ran down Laila's arm from a gash just below her elbow.

"You're bleeding," said Zofia.

"What?"

Laila looked down at her arm, her brows pressed down, eyes widened. It was a look of horror, Zofia realized. Laila touched the cut on her arm, her fingers coming away black as machine oil and not the dark red of blood. Blood smelled like old coins and salt. Laila's blood did not. It smelled like metal and sugar, and reminded Zofia of the charnel houses in Glowno.

"I didn't realize," said Laila. She looked up at Zofia, her eyes huge in her face. "I . . . I didn't even feel it."

Zofia knew that was not common, and she knew that Laila's uncommon moments made Laila feel sad and too different from other people. She didn't want her friend to be sad, not when they were so close to a solution.

"I'm not feeling a lot of things lately," said Laila quietly.

Zofia drew herself up. Her worries had no place right now.

"We will change that," said Zofia. "It is why we are here."

Laila nodded, wiping the blood off her arm.

"This"—Zofia pointed to the gash on Laila's arm—"is a symptom of a mechanical failure. That's all. We are all machines, and you are no different. We have parts that break and need fixing, and they perform different functions and have different utilities. We will find that break and fix it."

A slow smile curved Laila's lips. "Then I'm lucky you're my engineer."

"Luck is—"

"Zofia," said Laila, leaning forward. "I am glad you're my friend."

Warmth zipped through Zofia, and she was quiet until she remembered that when someone says something kind, it is expected to be returned, even if she considered the information repetitive or obvious. A sharp whistling sound interrupted her train of thought.

Zofia and Laila turned to see Séverin waving his torch roughly fifteen meters away from them. They got up, making their way to him. Séverin stood above where Enrique had pulled the *Forgive me* marble plaque out of the dirt. When they arrived, he shone his light on the damp ground.

"See this?"

Hypnos arched an eyebrow. "Dirt mixed with . . . dirt?"

"Drag marks," said Séverin.

The longer Zofia stared at the ground, the more she saw it—disturbed earth forming neat tracks, the narrow distance between the thin trenches reminiscent of—

"THOSE LOOK LIKE CLAW MARKS," said Enrique loudly.

"We heard you," said Séverin, frowning. "Take out the beeswax!"

"WHAT?"

"Are you telling me that this skeleton thing just up and clawed through the water?" asked Hypnos.

"Something might have dragged it from inside the lake," said Séverin, but he did not look convinced. "How deep is the water, Zofia?"

"I measured at least twenty-five meters deep. I also picked up signs of an obstruction that stretches through the middle of the lake, perhaps a makeshift bridge?"

"CLAW MARKS!" said Enrique again. "It's a *skeleton*. They're not supposed to move!"

"Maybe there's something Laila can read in the stones?" suggested Hypnos. "Laila?"

Zofia turned, expecting to see her friend behind her, but Laila was still by the water's edge, one hand on the boulder with the sound amplifiers.

"I will get her," said Zofia. "We found something too. Sound amplifiers, I think."

"Amplifiers?" asked Séverin.

"DID SHE SAY AMPLIFIERS?" asked Enrique loudly.

Zofia winced. He was standing very close. Zofia pointed at the conical protrusions on the boulder, tapped her ear, and then gestured widely with her hands. Séverin glanced at the amplifiers, then back at the dark lake. His eyes narrowed.

"If possible, bring one back," said Séverin. "Cut it off as carefully as you can. If there's amplifiers hidden around the lake, then perhaps there's a trigger we don't know yet, some sort of mechanism that's key to accessing the far wall."

Zofia nodded, then headed toward Laila. Her boots splashed in the puddles dotting the shoreline. As she walked, a tendril of cold touched her toe. A shiver ran up her leg. For a moment, she imagined that a freezing finger stroked the inside of her skull.

Zofia paused, looking down. The hole in her boot was larger than she thought, and a fine grit of mud squished under her toes. She did not like the texture of this sensation. In her rucksack, she had packed extra chardonnet silk. Perhaps she could pack the shoe and stop it from dampening her socks or—

"*Zosia . . .*"

The hair on the back of Zofia's neck stood up. Someone was calling to her. And the voice did not belong to Laila.

When Zofia looked up from her boots, she saw something that

should not have been possible, and yet every one of her senses confirmed that it was true. A figure stepped out of the lake, and Zofia recognized her sister immediately.

Hela stood before her, her pale hand stretched out. She wore the same thin shift she'd worn on her sick bed. Water dripped off her sleeves. Her gray eyes looked bruised with sleeplessness, and her hair looked sweat-dampened, clinging to her neck.

"I called to you for help, but you didn't come. Do you not love me? Did you not get my letter?"

Guilt closed around Zofia's throat like a cold hand.

"I lost it," she found herself saying.

"How could you?" sobbed Hela.

No. Wrong. This is wrong, whispered something in Zofia's mind. She forced herself to look up, prepared to count the stalactites on the cave ceiling. Instead, she saw the white paint of her uncle's townhome in Glowno, the fracture left in the corner by the window from heavy rain that summer. Zofia spun around, expecting to see her friends and the shore, but they were gone, and all she saw was the wall with framed portraits and pictures of her uncle's family.

"Zosia?" called Hela. "I will forgive you if you hug me."

Zofia turned back around.

Wrong. Wrong. Wrong.

She looked down at her feet, part of her mind expecting to see dark water lapping at her boots. But she saw only the frayed carpet that once led to Hela's sick bed, and when she looked up, she saw her sister coughing softly into her handkerchief, her pale hand outstretched.

She must go to her.

Zofia took one step forward, then flinched from a sudden cold.

Had she left one of the windows open in Hela's room? Hela did not like the cold. The window, however, was closed tightly, and yet for some reason Zofia imagined she could hear Laila's voice carried to her on an invisible wind, her voice raw as if she were screaming, and yet Zofia only felt it as a whisper:

"There's something in the water."

PART IV

26

ENRIQUE

One moment Enrique was crouched on the ground, tracing the drag marks. How was it possible? Even if natural
changes in the ecosystem had shifted the skeleton, it should not
have left marks like this. As he bent down to study it, a fine spray
of water soaked his jacket, hitting his neck.

Enrique shivered, annoyed. Séverin needed to move more carefully in the lake shallows. He turned once more to the ground
when he saw something strange . . . bits of gravel bounced on the
silt. A low vibration sang through the bottoms of his shoes. It was
as if the earth were bristling.

Séverin grabbed his shoulders, hauling him to his feet. The
Forged beeswax blocked out sound in Enrique's left ear, while
the right was so heavily bandaged that even a scream registered
as a low muffle.

Séverin's scream was no different.

Enrique strained to hear through the bandage, but the words

slipped past him. He held up his torch, the better to read Séverin's lips.

A mistake.

Beyond Séverin, the black water of the lake writhed and boiled. Stalactites trembled on the ceiling like loose teeth, crashing into the surface. The moment they hit the water, rings of light bloomed across the inky water.

A second later, the lake ripped in half, rising up into watery sheets that stretched toward the ceiling. An unearthly, green glow pulsed in the depths as skeletal hands broke through the sheets of water and grinning skulls shoved their heads through the waves, sightless eyes snapping toward the shore. Tatters of silk and broken strands of jewels circled their wrist bones and snapped necks as they walked disjointedly toward them.

Around him, Enrique felt the vibrating thrum of music the way one can perceive light behind closed eyes. He was right. The siren had been a warning.

Séverin kicked at him, his eyes wild and his hands clamped over his ears. His lips moved so quickly that Enrique caught only a handful of words:

TRAP . . . DON'T LISTEN . . . AMPLIFIERS.

A flash of movement caught Enrique's gaze. Zofia stood in the water, her hands grasping at the air. Thirty meters away, the skeletons slouched toward her.

Laila yanked on Zofia's hand, her mouth opened in silent yelling. "Zofia!" called Enrique.

But she didn't turn her head. She was shaking, sobbing, her hand stretched out. Laila kept tugging on her, but Zofia didn't move.

The siren's song is the last beautiful thing you see before death.

Too late, Enrique realized what was happening. It made sense that Laila, mostly Forged herself, would not be affected by a mind Forged manipulation running through the cave. But Hypnos? Séverin? Zofia? They were all at risk.

Images of Zofia pulled beneath the black waves shot through Enrique's head. Nausea gripped his gut. He almost ran to her right then before Séverin elbowed him out of the way. He jerked his head behind Enrique, his words unintelligible except for one thing:

AMPLIFIERS.

"Why would I do that?" asked Enrique. "What if it just amplifies their song and makes the illusion more powerful?"

But if Séverin heard him, he did not answer. Instead, he ran after Zofia and Laila. Enrique spun around to see Hypnos stumbling toward him, a wild look in his eyes. His hands were clamped over his ears.

Ears.

That was it! If he could get out more beeswax, than the mind Forged song wouldn't affect any of them. Enrique fumbled for the rucksack slung around his hip. He tore it open, his hands trembling as he brought out the pale box. Surely there would be enough for all of them. He had just counted out a fifth piece when a violent tremor slammed through the ground.

Enrique stumbled backwards, the wax pieces falling from his hands and sinking into the water. Lightning spangled across the cavern. In the slim space where the lake water split into two, a glowing structure creakily jutted out of the silt. It was a bridge, made of interlocked bone. It stretched from one end of the lake to the other, and the moment it broke free of the dirt, the black rock wall on the other side of the cave glowed brightly. A flash of amber scuttled across its surface, rendering it translucent. For a split second,

Enrique glimpsed the temple that lay on the other side: huge and jagged, flanked by silent automaton guardians.

Even the mere silhouette of it stole his breath. It was tauntingly close, and now they might never reach it.

The skeletons moved closer. Now they were less than fifteen meters from Laila, Séverin, and Zofia. A cold panic shot up Enrique's spine as he watched Séverin's expression suddenly go slack.

One moment, he was helping Laila drag Zofia back to shore.

The next, his hands dropped to his side. His eyes went wide, and he smiled.

Images flickered before Enrique, as if the mind Forged artistry was just barely seeping through his bandages. It was as if there was a ghostly overlay of people atop the skeletons.

Six meters away from Séverin, a ghostly Tristan opened his arms. Beside the illusion of Tristan stood a girl who looked a few years older than Zofia. She wore a pale nightgown and reached out her hand. Laila screamed, tugging on both of their arms. Brackish water splashed onto her clothes as she dug her heels in the shallow banks.

Enrique froze. He couldn't look away from Tristan—his shy smile and tousled blond hair. All he was missing was his tarantula perched on his shoulder. A wild hope seized Enrique. What if it wasn't an illusion? What if it was a reward for getting this far, and Tristan really was back?

But then the light shifted. Beneath the thin-skinned illusions moved stained bones, and though he could not hear it, Enrique imagined their brittle jaws clacking loudly. He stumbled back, his heart racing.

Hypnos stepped in front of him, his mouth moving and his hands clapped over his ears:

"WHAT DO WE DO?"

Enrique racked his brains. The wax was gone. As far as he knew, blocking out the sound of the sirens was the only way to avoid their call. Enrique stared around the cave before his gaze fell to the boulder.

The sound amplifiers.

They weren't for amplifying the sound of the temptation . . . but for drowning it out completely.

"SING!" said Enrique.

Hypnos looked confused. Enrique ran toward the boulders. He grabbed at one of the conical protrusions. Years ago, it must have been lightly attached, but time and humidity had practically welded the brass to the stone. It was stuck fast. Enrique tugged harder. Bits of metal came off on his hand.

Ahead, the skeletons drifted ever closer. Behind them, dozens more skeletons slipped out of the water, their jaws hanging open, necks distended. A frantic rhythm churned through the water. Enrique could feel its hungry pulse climbing through his skin. Enrique closed his eyes, focusing on the protrusions. With a last burst of strength, he tore it off the rock.

He tossed it to Hypnos, shouting: *"Sing!"*

Hypnos shot him a panicked look and then opened his mouth. Enrique could hear nothing, but he felt the slightest change in the air, as if a gentle breeze had broken through the fog. The once-frantic rhythm spidering through the ground stumbled. The skeletons staggered back.

Enrique grabbed Hypnos's arm, dragging him forward as they marched toward Séverin, Zofia, and Laila. The noise must have grown louder because now the illusions of Tristan and the other girl snarled. Their nostrils flared. A flat, inhuman look crept into their eyes, turning them completely black. The Tristan illusion reached out his hand, but Séverin jerked back, shaking his head. The skeleton crumpled to the ground and the illusion vanished.

Enrique pointed at the bridge. "Go!" he yelled to Séverin. "RUN!"

Laila looked to Zofia.

"I've got her!" said Enrique.

Laila gave a sharp nod. She and Séverin ran, water splashing around their legs as they reached for the bridge of bones. The moment Laila touched it, the bridge glowed brighter.

"Zofia!" called Enrique.

But Zofia did not move. Even with Hypnos's song hopefully drowning out the siren's song, it was as if Zofia were choosing the siren. She shook her head. The illusion of the girl grew stronger, the bones of the skeleton were hardly visible. She looked at Enrique, smiling widely.

Her grin was clear: *I win.*

"NO!" screamed Enrique. "Zofia, come on!"

He reached out to grab her hand when the skeleton-illusion swiped out a bony claw. It snagged on his bandages, loosening them. For the first time, sound rushed in. Hypnos's song broke off, and he gasped for air.

In those few seconds, an unearthly music filled Enrique's senses. It was unlike anything he had ever heard—like the sound of honey-eyed light and the throaty laugh of daydreams. The song diffused through him like sugar in hot milk, and he might have stayed in that moment for eternity if Hypnos hadn't jabbed him sharply and, once more, began to sing.

Enrique shook himself.

Water sloshed around her ankles as Zofia walked, hand in hand with the skeleton, into the lake.

"No!" he cried out. "Wait!"

For the first time, Zofia paused. She looked over her shoulder. Enrique lunged forward to snatch her arm and drag her away when the skeleton snapped her teeth. Enrique heard its voice in his head: bitter and sly.

Play fair, trespasser . . . your temptation versus mine . . . grab her, and I will show her an illusion so sweet, you will watch her drown before your eyes. The temple will gain another guardian.

Enrique's throat tightened. "Zofia . . . please. Come back with us. Look. The bridge isn't far . . ."

It was true. The bridge was hardly three meters away. Already, Laila and Séverin were halfway to the other side. The moment they were on it, they would be safe.

"Why should I listen to you?" asked Zofia.

The waves rose higher, teetering, threatening to crash.

"Because we can't do this without you, Zofia! Laila needs you!"

Don't listen to him, Zosia. I am the one who needs you. I am your sister. He is no one.

The illusion's voice changed to dulcet tones. Dimly, Enrique realized he was staring at an illusion of Hela, Zofia's older sister.

This is the boy who couldn't be bothered to kiss you unless it was tied to a mission. He does not want you. And Laila is safe and well! She is waiting for us inside the guest rooms. You shall see if you follow—

Enrique tried to touch her hand, but Zofia yanked it back as if stung.

"She's lying, Zofia—"

"She is right," said Zofia dully. "We are friends."

"Yes. But"—Enrique felt as though he were lifting up a veil to reveal some secret corner of himself—"but I like you far more than a friend probably should. I . . . I *liked* our kiss. If things were different, I'd probably be trying to figure out how to do it again—"

Zofia turned her head a little. "Is that true?"

He lies, sister! Come away, come away—

"How do you know you like me as more than a friend would?" she asked.

Around them, the waves slowly curled over. The skeletons loomed six meters away. Now five. Hypnos's voice turned scratchy and thin. Even with the amplifier, his song would give out soon.

Enrique wished he could show Zofia the strange equation that rebalanced the room whenever she entered it. He wanted to show her the sum frequency with which her candle-blue eyes and candy-red lips cropped up in his thoughts. But she knew him well enough to know that he did not process the world as such, and so he could only give her the answer that was honest.

"How do I know I like you?" repeated Enrique. He forced a grin to his face. "I don't know. It comes from some other place inside me. The place that believes in superstitions . . . stories. It feels like . . . like belonging."

Zofia whirled to face him. Her eyes adjusted, widened. With a sharp gasp, she let go of the skeleton's hand. She staggered toward Enrique, and he caught her shivering, sobbing body in his arms.

"Hush, Phoenix, it's all right, I'm here," he murmured into her hair.

YOU CANNOT TAKE THAT WHICH BELONGS TO THE TEMPLE. SHE IS OURS NOW—

At that exact second, Hypnos's song gave out. The siren song built into a crescendo, but it was ruined by the sound of water threatening to crash down over their heads.

"Now!" yelled Hypnos.

He grabbed Enrique's hand, and the three of them ran to the bridge. The water arced over their heads, threatening to drown them. Dozens of pale, skeletal hands stretched out, spindly fingers cutting through his bandages, catching on his sleeves. The bridge of bone loomed larger. Water swirled around Enrique's ankles and he slipped. For a moment, the world seemed to slow. He could feel every passing second as if it were a needle trailing along his skin.

As he fell, he pushed Hypnos and Zofia onto the bridge. Water closed up around his waist. A skeletal leg folded around his hip, the movement a corruption of intimacy.

He blinked wildly as water sprayed in his face. The emerald glow of the lake haloed Hypnos's and Zofia's bodies, gilding them like saints. If they were his last sight, he would have been happy—

Zofia flung something into the water. Fire caught on one of the skeletal heads, and the thing roared. The mind Forged creatures scuttled back, their hold on him loosening. The water slammed over their heads, but instead of sweeping them into the lake, it flowed over a hidden Forged obstruction. Enrique stared up at the glassy tube encircling the bridge of bone. Brackish water flowed around them, and the only sound came from the ugly thud of skeletal bodies crashing into one another. The moment Enrique clambered onto the bridge, Zofia and Hypnos grabbed his hands, and together they ran to the sudden glowing light on the far end of the wall.

27

LAILA

Laila could not feel anything.

Not even horror.

She remembered running across the bridge of bone, toward the illuminated far wall . . . but now that lightness had vanished. And with it, her feeling of sensations. She could not feel the hard, wet pebbles that should have been biting into her legs. The blankness had stolen through her the moment they'd crossed the bridge of bone. Her vision kept flickering to black. Her lungs should have ached. Her nose should have filled with the stale scent of the lake. Séverin turned and spat out water, gasping for air.

Moments later, Hypnos, Enrique, and Zofia fell onto the shore alongside them. Laila could hear them coughing and spitting. She could hear Séverin speaking in hushed, worried tones.

But it was as if she were listening to them from under water.

She should have been ecstatic. She should have been weeping that they had made it to the other side. But the blankness that snuck through her was a subtle devourer. It sipped on her joy, nibbled on her panic, and left her with nothing but a crust of herself.

Laila told herself this was normal. She had felt this before, and sensation always came back. But another part of her hissed and whispered: *It is taking longer and longer to feel human isn't it, little broken doll?*

Laila forced her attention away, turning instead to the others. When she focused on them, their voices seemed louder. Clearer. Moments passed, and their faces and expressions gained clarity. But beyond them, the cave was a blur of shadows and emptiness.

Hypnos rolled over onto his side, heaving. Enrique lay on his back, his chest moving up and down. Beside him, Zofia drew herself up, clutching her knees to her chest and shaking.

"Enrique?" said Séverin, shaking him. "Are you hurt? What's happened? Say something, please, I beg you."

Enrique opened his mouth, whispering something.

"What's wrong with him?" asked Hypnos, his voice prickling. "Is he all right?"

"I—" rasped Enrique. He raised his hand, brushing something at his temples. "Told—you—so."

And then he flung the beeswax at Séverin's forehead. Séverin looked unfazed.

"Do you feel better now?"

Enrique snuck a glance at Zofia and then Hypnos. "A little."

"Do you wish to get off the ground? Or is the weight of sanctimony too great?"

Enrique grinned. He held out his hand, Séverin took it and hoisted the both of them to their feet.

More than anything, Laila wanted to smile. But her face felt frozen.

"Laila?" asked Zofia, looking up at her. "Are you injured?"

Maybe, thought Laila. But she couldn't feel, so she didn't know. At first, the words glommed in her throat.

"I'm not in pain," she said slowly.

She could hear the dull, flatness of her words. Séverin turned toward her. Once, she would have been able to feel the force of that gaze. Now, it did not signify. She forced herself to stand. Every movement was like the indifferent jerk of a puppet string.

"Laila," said Enrique. "You were the only one who wasn't affected by the mind Forged siren music," he said.

He made it sound as if it was a good thing.

"Because she's a goddess, naturally," said Hypnos.

"It's because I'm Forged," said Laila. "Manipulation by mind Forging only affects normal humans, it seems."

She tried to make it sound light, but her voice came out flat. The smile dropped from Hypnos's face.

"You're more than human," said Enrique, reaching out and taking her hand. "And if you weren't, we'd all be strangled to death by those skeletons."

Hypnos shuddered. "At least we got to the other side of the lake."

Zofia frowned. "Our supplies did not."

"So then what are we going to do about . . . *this*?" asked Hypnos, unhooking his Forged lantern from around his waist and shining it on the cave wall.

The crudely hewn obsidian towered dozens of meters above them, and appeared to stretch at least thirty meters in either direction from where they stood. Ragged boulders jointed over the seams where the obsidian wall met the craggy walls of the cave. The wall was definitely a Tezcat of some kind, judging by the glow of Zofia's necklace, which meant it needed a trigger to open fully to the temple they believed was concealed behind the rock. It would have been a difficult task even with their tools . . . but now?

Laila was almost grateful she could not feel her own panic. It could not reach her when she was like this.

"What do we have on hand?" cut in Séverin loudly.

The five of them proceeded to rummage through their pockets and pat down their garments for Zofia's hidden inventions. Minutes later, a not insignificantly sized pile lay in front of them. There were three pieces of rope which could be tied together, two broken lanterns, one stick of dynamite, three knives, four packs of matches, the gilded box holding the empty mind Forged bottle that had led them to Poveglia, and a lace fan.

Enrique turned to Hypnos. "*Why* did you bring a fan?"

"I get hot easily," said Hypnos defensively.

"It's February," said Enrique.

"I remain hot year round, *mon cher.*"

Séverin stared at the pile and then at the wall of rock. He walked to it, running his hands over the shining jet. "Can you tell if it's Forged?"

Belatedly, Laila realized Séverin's question was directed to her.

The others stepped aside, clearing a path from her to the wall. Laila opened her mouth, closed it. Horror used to be a slow creep of cold up her spine. Humiliation used to scorch her face. Now, there was nothing but the dull thud of knowledge that her own emotions felt submerged and distant.

"Laila?" asked Séverin, taking a step to her.

But she was spared answering by Zofia. "The wall is Forged," she said. "I can read and hear metal inside it."

Laila gave silent thanks for her friend.

"I cannot determine which metal runs through this wall, though—it's a combination of alloys I'm unfamiliar with . . ." said Zofia, splaying her hands across the rock. "And it's fire resistant."

"So even if we could blow it up, it wouldn't open?" asked Enrique.

Zofia shook her head.

"The wall reacted to something earlier. There was a moment when it went translucent," said Séverin. "What was it? What happened?"

Zofia: "Water?"

Enrique: "Singing?"

Hypnos: "Hopefully not the wave of the undead?"

"Many Forged objects come with a release mechanism, some sort of hint between artist and audience—" said Séverin, reaching for one of the matches and the lantern.

"Those are the rules set forth by the Order of Babel," said Hypnos. "This place . . . it feels different. Even that mind Forging song of the sirens was unlike anything I've ever heard. It was . . . alive?"

Enrique shuddered. "It's almost as if this place has a consciousness of its own."

Séverin rapped his knuckles on the wall. "The intensity might be due to its proximity to the source of all Forging . . . and if the place has a consciousness of its own, then that's good."

"How?" demanded Hypnos. "This cave could just as easily decide that it's done watching us dither about, and have the lake swallow us whole!"

"It's good because . . . like any living thing, it possesses a desire for self-preservation," said Séverin. He raised his torch light to the craggy walls of the obsidian cave. "I imagine that if any part of it were truly threatened, there would be hints to free whatever lay inside or access it so that the knowledge would not be lost forever."

The wall of rock stretched out like a shorn mirror. Laila's face reflected back a thousand times, and she sucked in her breath as she stared at her bruised cheek, the cut along her lip, her sunken eyes, and her lank hair.

Broken doll, broken doll, chanted a cruel part of her mind. Dimly, Laila remembered every evening she'd spent dancing in the Palais des Rêves, her face made up to perfection, her reflection glowing in the champagne room lined with mirrors and chandeliers. But beneath all the shining smiles and pearls stood the real L'Enigme: bruised and too sharp, death on her hand and mysteries in her blood. The cave was not showing her anything she did not already know about herself, and Laila refused to be cowed.

For the first time in the past hour, feeling flared into the tips of her fingers. She curled her hand, feeling the pinching stiffness of cold. She smiled and then reached forward. The moment her skin touched stone, an alien awareness shoved against her hand.

Laila recoiled instantly.

"What was that?" she said loudly.

Séverin frowned. "What was . . . what?"

Laila's glance slid to the wall.

"The wall . . . it has *emotion* to it. It's like Enrique said. There's a consciousness at work here."

Hypnos whimpered. "I hate this place."

"What emotion are you reading?" asked Séverin.

Hesitantly, Laila placed her hand back against the rock. She expected that rush of alien awareness to be annoyed . . . *hostile,* even. But it was warm. Yielding.

"It's . . . it's worried," she said, turning to the others. "About us."

Hypnos blinked, then threw up his hands. "Am I flattered? Disturbed? Both?"

Slowly, light gleamed across the rocky surface. It was nothing at all like the suffusion of translucence and amber they had glimpsed while they ran from the false sirens of the lake, but more like a vein of unexpected gold shimmering roughly six meters up from the ground.

The light zigged and zagged across the rock, illuminating a string of letters.

Δώρο των θεών

"*To dóro ton theón*," translated Enrique aloud. "The . . . gift . . . of gods?"

"The gods gifted us a rock wall?" asked Hypnos.

Séverin ignored him. "What *did* the gods gift humans? Earth, perhaps?"

Enrique knelt, scooping some of the silt into his hands. He flung it onto the rock. Nothing changed.

"Fire?" said Hypnos. "That was Prometheus's gift to humans, was it not?"

"The wall is fire resistant," said Zofia. "I'm sure about that."

"Maybe there's another clue along the wall?" asked Enrique.

"We can split up and look," said Séverin. "Our torches don't carry very far. If you see something, call out. I'll stay here and see if anything else appears beside the writing."

Laila nodded. "I'll take the left side."

Enrique and Zofia set off to explore the wall on the right, and Hypnos jogged after them, a bright bouncing beam in the dark.

Laila had barely moved six meters when a painful twinge in her ankle made her slip. She flung out her hand, catching herself on one of the jagged rocks and wincing. An ache flared behind her ribs, and Laila dimly recalled Séverin elbowing her out of the way of a grasping, skeletal hand as they fled to the bridge. She hadn't felt it then, but she did now.

More aches dribbled slowly through her senses, setting her teeth on edge. She took a few more steps before pain shot through her ankle once more. This time when she slipped, it was not the rocks that caught her, but Séverin.

"What aren't you telling me?" asked Séverin, his voice low and dark.

"God!" yelped Laila in alarm, spinning out of his grip.

Her lantern light caught his smirk. "Not yet."

"How very charming and blasphemous, now excuse me—"

"What are you hiding from me?"

"It's nothing—"

Séverin blocked her. "Haven't we played that game enough times?"

Laila bit her lip, hard. Too hard. At once, the feeling of numbness eased away. Once more, her eyes could pick out the plum and scarlet colors in the dark stones of the cave wall. She could smell the lake water, the cloying earth, taste the metal sweetness of her own blood on her tongue. Slicing through all of it, Séverin's presence. He smelled of smoke and cloves, and he stood before her, half-haloed in the light, expectant and victorious as a king. It was no different from that night in the *mascherari*, when his touch had returned her to herself and his smile had been so smug. As if he already knew that only he could have this effect.

"Why must you do that to me?" she asked.

Séverin looked away, shame flashing in his eyes. "The only thing I am doing is checking that you are well, since you looked as though you'd hurt yourself. I only wished to help you. I . . . I am not here to corner you with my feelings, Laila. I realize how selfish you think me, but give me this benefit, at least."

Laila almost laughed. How could she tell him that it had nothing to do with that?

"I am merely acting as a friend would," said Séverin.

"Does that make us friends, then?"

Séverin arched an eyebrow. "I think we're past that."

Laila looked up at him and then quickly wished she hadn't. The slanting light drew out the regal angles of his face and the wolfish set of his mouth. He looked far too comfortable in the dark, and yet he wondered why she didn't consider him safe.

"Tell me what's wrong, Laila," he said softly. "Tell me, so I may fix it."

Laila hesitated a moment, and then the words she'd been fighting down burst from her. "Your presence . . . your touch, rather, does more than enough."

He frowned. "I don't understand."

Laila flashed a weary smile. "I'm dying, Séverin. And my body, I suppose, is preparing itself. When I'm injured, pain takes hours to find me. My blood no longer looks red. Sometimes I cannot hear. Or see."

Horror crept into his eyes. A muscle in his jaw clenched.

"Do not worry too much on my account," said Laila. "Perhaps it will please you to know that the blank sensations tend to dissipate faster when you . . ." Her glibness faltered. "When you touch me. And before you think it is your doing alone, know that eventually it *does* come back to me, but you . . . I suppose you amplify it in a way. I don't know how. There. Are you pleased with yourself and your divine abilities? Will you crow about it to everyone?"

Séverin's voice was soft. "Laila—"

"Shall I beg for you to make me feel alive?" she asked, a harsh laugh leaving her throat.

Her laugh made the lantern light gutter, then go out. An abrupt darkness fell over them. Séverin was quiet for a moment, and then his voice found her in the shadows. He had moved closer. "There's no need to beg for something I'd give without question. Is that what you want from me, Laila?"

Laila might not have heard the siren song in the cave, but her blood answered to a different call. The thrum of memory filled her—his mouth on her skin, her name on his lips.

The world told her she was a thousand things—a girl sculpted from grave dirt, a snow maiden flirting with spring's thaw, an exotic phantasm for men to pin their lusts upon just to keep her in place.

But with Séverin, she was always Laila.

The wet ground squelched underfoot. He had stepped toward her, closing the distance between them even more. Even in the dark, she could tell Séverin was standing utterly still.

For once, he was the one waiting, and Laila savored it for only a breath before she reached out, touching his face. Séverin groaned, whatever stillness he had mastered vanishing the second she touched him. The lantern crashed to the ground, and he crushed her to him in a kiss.

Laila thought often of what it meant to be lost in a kiss. The sensation so heady and drowning that the world beyond it ceased to exist. But in this kiss, Laila was not lost, but found. Her senses turned diamond-sharp, her body felt like a column of flame greedily devouring every scent, texture, taste it could find as he pushed her up against the wall.

"Are you all right?" shouted Enrique. "What was that sound?"

Laila wrenched away. There was a pause, a soft sigh, and then—

"We're fine," called Séverin, out of breath. "I dropped the lantern."

There was a familiar *rip* of the match as Séverin relit the dead wick. Light flared between them, and with it, the too-bright knowledge of what a selfish mistake she'd committed. She looked up at Séverin, ready to apologize, but the sight of him stopped her short.

Séverin's violet eyes might have been the precise color of sleep, but his gaze was restless and alive, fever-bright with longing. For her.

It was too much. All the bruises he'd left on her heart made it too tender to hold that gaze, and so she said the first thing that came to her mind.

"Thank you."

Séverin closed his eyes, and immediately Laila knew she'd said the wrong thing. "Please don't thank me for something I already wanted to give."

"I . . . I have nothing else to offer."

"So you've said." He turned away from her, his hand on the wall, his head bowed as if he wished to rest his forehead on the rock. "Did I at least make you feel alive, Laila?"

Laila nodded, then realized he couldn't see her. "Yes."

But he made her feel other things too, and the sensation on her heart felt like air blown across a new wound. The only thing that would heal it was time, a commodity she barely had left.

"Then for that I'm glad," he said.

He took a deep breath, sighing. The moment he pushed himself off the rock, amber light flared over the stone. The sudden light was like a window abruptly revealed by the parting of drapes.

Laila gasped, and Séverin raised his head just in time to see the flash of sudden radiance. It bloomed right where his hand touched the wall, expanding to the size of a large dinner platter.

A second later, Séverin's hand melted through the rock. Jeweled light limned his submerged wrist just long enough for Laila to glimpse a corner of what lay inside—

Carved walls, hundreds of stone steps disappearing out of sight, massive bronze hands. A floor that looked like the vaulted skies of heaven, and a ceiling rich and green as Eden.

But no sooner had she glimpsed it than the image faded.

Translucence there and gone.

Not far off, Laila heard the others call out, racing back as the amber light dwindled and began to fall in on itself. Séverin snatched his hand away just in time for the rough obsidian wall to close up, fast as a blink.

Enrique, Hypnos, and Zofia arrived, breathless, at their side.

"How did you do that?" asked Enrique.

Séverin's eyes found Laila's in the gloaming. "I have no idea."

28

SÉVERIN

Séverin touched the obsidian wall, dragging his hands over the jutting hanks of glossy rock.

Where had the light gone?

The radiance had been a sudden thing. Almost violent. Against his skin, Séverin had felt the lyre's pulse turn frantic, the strings burning hot. A moment later, all of it had crumpled to darkness. Even the lyre's heartbeat slowed.

When he blinked, he saw the ghostly imprint of light. It was like Laila's kiss all over again. One moment, she was in his arms, burning hot like a star, and then, just as quickly, out of his embrace. The jolt from one state to another was what forced him to turn to the rock wall.

He was powerless. He was losing her—not her love, not her attraction to him—but *her*. If Laila needed to kiss him until his heart broke to feel alive, he would offer it up on the spot; if she needed his hope for kindling to feel warmth, he would watch himself go up in flames.

But he couldn't fix her.

He couldn't open the damned wall.

And then—

Light.

There and gone, leaving him not with despair, but with anger. Heaven would not dare to shut him out, not now. Séverin would have what he'd fought so hard for . . . one way or another, he would sink his teeth into that amber light and grab power by its soft, furred throat until he owned it.

"I don't get it," said Enrique. "The writing on the wall was clear: *to δóro ton theón,* 'the gift of the gods.' This was the spot where the translucence appeared, wasn't it?"

Séverin nodded.

"Did your lantern touch this spot?" asked Zofia, tapping the rock with her match.

"No," said Séverin.

"But that would mean it isn't fire, even though everything points to that element and Zofia has already said that it's fireproof!" said Enrique. "We already tried earth. Was it something about the waves? Not that I think we should go anywhere *near* that lake—"

Séverin ignored him. Before anyone could stop him, he took a couple of steps toward the lake, scooped water into his palm, and flung it onto the wall.

The water slid down the rock.

"You just!" Enrique spluttered. "Why!"

Séverin dried his hands on his jacket. "Now we know it's not the water."

"Not light, not water," grumbled Enrique. "What else would have been a gift from the gods? Free will?"

Hypnos cleared his throat. "I *will* you to open up!"

The rock wall remained indifferent.

Séverin canted his head to one side, thinking of past acquisi-tions. *Don't follow the clues, follow the room.* The story of the room was a treasure of its own. Séverin imagined that he was the maker of this place, the master of a shining cavern full of terrors torn out of myths.

"I could try the explosives," said Zofia thoughtfully.

Enrique crossed his arms. "I realize fire is your element, but—"

At Enrique's words, something nudged at Séverin's thoughts.

"What did you just say?"

Enrique lifted an eyebrow. "I was telling Zofia that explosives are hardly the answer."

"What did you tell her *exactly*?"

". . . I realize fire is your element?"

"Yes," said Séverin slowly. "We have the wrong element."

"How?" asked Laila. "Fire and earth don't work. Water had no effect, and air is all around us."

Séverin took a step toward the wall. His shoes slipped and squished. The earth did not feel as it had on the other side of the lake. And it was not simply because of the damp.

"What is this?" he asked, lifting his leg and examining the bot-tom of his shoe.

Zofia knelt, touching the ground, reading the elements within. "Clay."

"*Clay?*" echoed Enrique. "Was the other shore made of clay?"

Zofia shook her head.

A slow smile curved Séverin's lips. "I see it now."

He took a handful of clay, squeezing it, the lantern forgotten by his feet and casting an unearthly illumination on his hands. "What was god's gift to man after we were molded from something as base as clay?"

"Life?" said Hypnos.

"No," said Laila, smiling. "*Breath*. That's the name for Forging in India . . . the *chota sans*."

Séverin recognized that phrase: *the little breath*. The rest of the world had a hundred names and explanations for the art the Western world called "Forging." But its artistry worked the same no matter what name it carried.

Séverin placed his hand against the rock wall.

Before, he had turned from Laila, sighing—exhaling—and hating how powerless he was. Now, when he breathed out, it was full of hope. It was cold in the cave, and his breath plumed before him, holding shape in the air for an instant before unraveling on the rock—

Light bloomed.

The light was no larger than the span of his hand, but it was a window nonetheless . . . an aperture through which a corner of the temple was revealed. Through the shining pane of amber, Séverin glimpsed jagged steps. His mother's voice rang clear as a bell in his head:

In your hands lie the gates of godhood.

A weightless sense of giddiness swept through him. The pulse of the divine lyre, like a heartbeat laid atop his own, paused . . . then synced. As if they were one. Even when the light faded, Séverin felt as though it had moved inside him as he turned to the others.

Enrique looked awed. Zofia's eyes were huge in her face. Laila bit her lip, her chest rising and falling as if she could not gulp down enough air in that moment. Even Hypnos, serene and smirking as always, shook his head, trying to dispel what he'd seen.

"Before we do this . . . I want to apologize in advance for all the garlic I consumed in Italy," said Hypnos.

"Breathing on it is not required," said Zofia. "It requires a gust of air. That was why the crashing waves revealed its translucency to us earlier."

"How are we going to do something like that?" asked Laila, casting about for something on the shore.

Hypnos reached into his pocket and whipped out his fan. "You. Are. Welcome."

Séverin grinned, but Enrique asked, "Will it really work?"

"Only one way to find out I suppose," said Séverin. He nodded at Hypnos. "Shall we?"

Hypnos spun the fan between his fingers, then deftly flicked it open. When he turned to face the wall, Séverin noticed that the smirk on his face faded. His throat bobbed. A rare expression stole onto his face . . . one of true nerves. Hypnos glanced at Laila, who smiled at him. Séverin reached forward, clasping his shoulder for a moment.

Hypnos rolled his shoulders back and began to fan. Dust blew off the jagged stone. Seams of light wove their way up from the roots of the rock wall. As the light grew brighter, Séverin wondered what the cave would say if it could speak. Laila had said there was an alien consciousness and feeling flowing through the stone. What would it make of them now?

A tall archway shaped like a tear formed in the rock. Its edges glowed.

No one spoke as they stepped across the threshold.

Though it was the place that might have inspired a confusion of tongues and the beginning of language, words failed Séverin as he beheld what lay before them.

On the other side of the threshold was an island wrapped in mist. It did not belong to any country. Perhaps it did not even belong to this world.

Silver fog wreathed the boundaries of the temple, so it looked as if it were cast in moonlight. A melted image of the night sky adorned a wide glass floor that formed close to the edge of his boots. The artistry was so vivid that Séverin's stomach swooped, imagining he might fall through the darkness between the stars.

Thirty meters away appeared the first steps of the ziggurat. Séverin tilted his chin up . . . and *up* . . . and still he could not see where the ziggurat ended. He imagined a temple like that would scratch the sky, but instead, it seemed to disappear into a lush hanging garden. Like Eden itself tipped upside down. The silvery fog picked out flowers the color of pearls, and thick, reaching vines like the grasping hands of a new lover. The lush forestry curled down, resting on the shoulders of two massive automatons flanking either side of the ziggurat. In the dimness, they looked sculpted out of shadows. Their faces were serene and inscrutable. Atop their heads, they wore crowns of intricately carved stone.

When Séverin breathed deep, he caught the lingering whisper of incense on the air. And when he closed his eyes, he could hear an impossible wind rustling through the branches.

He did not touch anything.

Instead, the temple reached out to touch him.

29

ZOFIA

Zofia did not consider herself particularly religious.

She had grown up going to synagogue and hearing of God's works, but she had struggled to understand divine rationale behind the actions. Why did he punish? Why did he hurt? Why did he deliver? What were the constants behind his choices?

When she asked, no one could give her an answer. After all, God was not a being whose expressions she could study and put into context.

Only her father had understood her frustration.

"I like to think of the divine in terms of an unknown factor," he said. "Think of the universe as an infinite equation, Zosia. Perhaps the things which are added and taken away . . . new siblings or lost homes and countries . . . perhaps they are simply part of the balance of that equation . . . the sum of which we cannot see."

"But then we'll never understand it," said Zofia, frowning.

"Ah, Zosia," her father had said, smiling widely. "Who said we were meant to understand?"

When he smiled widely, that meant there was nothing to worry about, and Zofia had felt a knot loosening inside her.

"I believe we are meant for more wonderful things, yes?" said her father. "We are meant to live as best as we can with what we have been given. Time is the common denominator for us all, and it is not infinite."

Zofia had liked that explanation, even if it frustrated her at times. Over the years, she clung to her father's words. She thought of that grand, unknowable equation when her parents died, when she was expelled from school, when Hela fell sick.

It was not a cruelty, but a balancing.

That was all.

She did not have to see or understand the equation to trust that it was there.

But now, standing at the strange threshold between the cave and the temple, Zofia *felt* that equation.

She never liked the sensation of mind Forging. It was the intrusion of an alien image and feeling. What she saw and felt in that second was something entirely different.

It was as if the temple was telling her the story of itself. Behind her eyes, Zofia glimpsed what should have been impossible. She felt the knowledge that hundreds of hands had patted down straw and mud, had fed the fires of a thousand brick kilns. She heard dozens of languages whose names she did not know, and yet she understood what was being said:

Keep safe. Keep hidden. Don't look.

Deep in her chest, Zofia felt seized by a vast weightlessness . . . as if she had peeked over the brink of a cliff above a lightless chasm.

The sensations disappeared instantly.

Zofia's eyes flew open. Her hand was on her mouth. She did not remember bringing it there. Her fingers brushed over the indent above her top lip.

"*Right there,*" Hela had once told her in the dark. "*That's where the angel pressed their thumb down and locked up all the secrets of the world right before we were born.*"

Zofia had liked the tale even if she found the logic faulty and implausible. Now, she breathed deep, feeling calmer than she'd felt in ages.

That presence of a vast equation was brief, no more than a match struck and quickly blown out. But the feeling remained . . . the sense that, for a moment, some part of the universe had been unlocked for her.

30

ENRIQUE

Enrique stumbled forward as the temple released his mind.

He stared at the glassy, night floor . . . the huge ziggurat that disappeared into a forested ceiling. He could still smell the sun-baked bricks. His ears held the trilling echo of a thousand vanishing prayers. And at the end of it all, he was left with awe.

Enrique had hunted for proof of his research in the corners of ripped, ancient maps and in the verdigris patina on old bronze artifacts . . . he had never dreamt to see it so fully.

In his mind's eye, he could picture those ancient peoples stringing together the divine lyre. That label the Western world had given them was too small. They were not just the Lost Muses. They held other titles from other nations . . . they had been priestesses of un-worshipped goddesses . . . and even though moments ago Enrique had known those other names, they now dissolved to obscurities on his tongue.

It was strange, he thought, with a sudden laugh. As a historian, he regarded the world in hindsight, but history was never dead. It was furiously alive even if it was lost, even if it existed only as phantoms haunting conquerors or woven into bedtime stories whispered to children. All his life, Enrique had traced the edge of truth in those tales and fiercely *believed*, but now he *knew*. The difference was more than night and day . . . it was like standing before the very first dawn and watching the world draw into focus.

"I . . . I can't believe it," he said, trying to speak around what he'd witnessed.

Beside him, Laila was quietly shaking. Enrique's heart lurched, thinking that she was weeping . . . but no. She was laughing. He hadn't seen her smile like that in more than a year. A loud exhale caught his attention. Hypnos knelt on the ground, his lips parted and eyes wide. Even Zofia seemed stunned.

Finally, his gaze went to Séverin, and for a moment it was as if nothing had ever soured between them.

Séverin smiled, and Enrique recognized that old grin. It was the sly and yet giddy look of disbelief that used to follow a successful acquisition. And this time, Enrique shared it with him.

Silently, they turned back to the temple. The wonder of the place had not faded, but now his eyes had adjusted to the brightness. Little by little, he was able to pick apart the details . . . to *notice* the way the room came together.

There was something about the giant automatons that caught his attention. He had assumed they were automatons, but they did not move.

Enrique didn't even notice he'd taken a step forward until Séverin raised his arm, blocking him right before his boot touched the glassy floor, the circumference of which was surrounded by a meter-wide ring of the same soft clay ground from outside.

"Wait," said Séverin gently.

"What's there to wait for, *mon cher*?" asked Hypnos, grinning widely. He flung out a hand, gesturing to the ziggurat. "We know exactly where to go! Merely climb the steps and *voila*! Eternal life, eternal joy . . . eternal Laila."

Laila shook her head, smiling.

"Yes . . . yes to all of that and more," said Séverin, looking at her. Enrique noticed something painful flash in his eyes. "But we can't risk recklessness . . . not yet. We need to understand our surroundings."

"My tools are gone," said Zofia. "I don't have anything except my Tezcat necklace and matches and this—" She lifted her arm.

Hypnos frowned. "The use of one's right arm?"

"No," she said. "It's a Forged sleeve that can act as a torch without harming the individual. Enrique has one too."

"I do?" he asked.

She nodded, pointing her chin at the bit of silver cloth he had tied around his arm. It was a remnant from the Carnevale costumes. He had kept it on his person as a talisman for good luck.

"That's all well and good, but we don't need any fire," said Séverin. "What we really need are knives and rope in case something obstructs us . . . Do we have that?"

Zofia shook her head.

"I have this?" said Hypnos, waving around his fan.

"Maybe there's something left in the rucksacks," said Laila. "Give them to me."

Séverin shrugged his off, handing it over.

"I lost mine," said Enrique, thinking of the skeletal sirens.

"This won't do much," said Zofia, tapping her necklace.

"Mine is on the other side of the cave . . ." said Hypnos.

"I suppose we'll have to rely on powers of observation instead," said Séverin. "What do you see? Enrique? What caught your eye?"

Enrique pointed to the towering automatons.

"I thought they were . . . kings," he said slowly. "But now I'm not so sure. I believe the art dates from the eleventh-century Pala period of South Asia. Note the serene, almost tantric expressions—heavy-lidded eyes, relaxed mouth—likely influenced by Buddhism."

"Are they guards?" asked Séverin.

"I don't think so . . . they hold no weapons," said Enrique. "If they're the automatons I think they are, then they should be in possession of . . . what's it called again, Laila?"

"*Bhuta vahana yanta*," said Laila, frowning as she pulled out a frayed length of rope. The gilded box that had once held the map to Poveglia caught the light. "Technically it means spirit movement machines, but it's thought to be powered by Forging."

"Exactly," said Enrique. "But I don't see any machines."

"Could they be in . . . whatever that is?" asked Hypnos, gesturing at the silvery fog that shrouded the temple.

"Maybe?" said Enrique. He didn't like the idea of something lurking in the mist. Watching them. "But the key is *not* to trigger their appearance."

"Fair enough, but how do we avoid them showing up?" asked Hypnos.

Séverin stared at the floor, frowning a little. "Did the room always look like this in the images the temple showed us?"

Enrique tried to think back to all the images that had flown through his head. He remembered sunlight haloing the ziggurat.

"The floor . . ." said Zofia. "It's . . . it's changing."

Enrique's eyes flew open. Sure enough, the glass floor before them slowly lightened. The stars faded. A tinge of blush seeped out from the base of the ziggurat. He turned to ask Séverin what he thought it might mean, when an unfamiliar sound tore through the air.

"What was that?" asked Hypnos, spinning around.

Behind them, the archway made by Hypnos's fan still glowed

brightly. Something flickered in its distance. Light off the water, perhaps?

"Séverin," said Laila sharply.

Enrique looked to her. Moments ago, she had been rifling through the contents of their sack. But now she was holding the gilded box in a white-knuckled grip.

"The box is Forged," she said.

Séverin's eyes widened. "What?"

"I think—"

Something boomed in the distance, shaking the ground. Enrique lost his balance, his arms pinwheeling. Another boom rattled through the temple. Past the archway, stalactites crashed into the lake.

A high-pitched moan swept through the temple, raising the hairs on Enrique's arms. Smoke and fog bloomed through the void surrounding the ziggurat. Above them, the lush forest ceiling trembled. Vines and branches clattered to the brightening floor. Enrique's wound throbbed suddenly, and he winced as he brought his hand to cover it.

"What's happening—" Hypnos started, but his words were swallowed up as the archway went up in roaring flames.

A blast threw Enrique on his back. The world spun. Noise bled into silence and back. Smoke burned his lungs, and he fought for breath, waving at the air before his face.

Just as quickly . . . the smoke cleared.

And when Enrique could finally open his eyes, he saw that he was staring at the sharp point of a golden dagger right between his eyes. Beyond it, standing in the torn mouth of the archway . . .

"Hello, friends," Ruslan said, smiling.

PART V

31

LAILA

Laila's heart had never beat so furiously. Moments ago, she had been savoring that very feeling. When they had entered the temple sanctum, Laila had felt as if her whole body had been rinsed in myths and honeyed light.

She had returned to her senses to find them sharp, honed as if by a jeweler's lathe so that every sensation felt like a polished jewel. Even her blood moved sleekly in her veins. And perhaps the temple had changed something within her because the moment she touched the Forged box, she *knew*.

Ruslan had laid a trap for them.

But however the temple might have enhanced her abilities, it had not done so fast enough. Laila looked down to see a hovering, golden dagger pressed against her heart.

And she was not alone.

Enrique, Zofia, and Hypnos were similarly trapped. Séverin alone was untouched.

Not three meters away, Ruslan came into view. He held out his golden hand, and she realized he was somehow *controlling* the daggers. Behind Ruslan stood six members of the Fallen House, and something was wrong with them. Their *volto* masks looked scorched and dented. When they moved, their gestures were too stiff. Flies buzzed around their heads.

"My, my," said Ruslan softly. "What a wonder to behold . . . I suppose I should thank you for doing all the difficult bits, but it was *very* rude of you to try and kill me like that, Séverin! I thought we truly were friends."

"Ruslan, I—" Séverin started to say.

"Shhh. Let me bask, first, in the threshold of my godhood. I want to remember this moment."

As the smoke cleared, Ruslan's face came into focus and Laila froze.

Now, half of his face shone unearthly and strange and . . . gold. Part of his skull was smashed in, and light glinted off the golden dent.

"Do you like my new look?" asked Ruslan, smiling.

His teeth were either chipped or missing. What remained appeared to be smeared red with blood.

"It is, admittedly, a touch gaudy," he said, sniffing. "But it *was* hard to reconstruct myself after you tried to blow me up."

"You should be dead," growled Enrique.

"I should, shouldn't I?" said Ruslan. "But you see . . . that's the thing about my inheritance. The 'Fallen House' is such an ugly name. Its true one is so much better. We are and have always been House Attis."

At the name, the gold knife in Ruslan's hand shone. Behind Ruslan, the *volto* masks on the members slipped sideways revealing something sunken. Something *stinking*. Something far from alive. Laila's stomach turned.

"You see, *we* alone had a hint of the power in the temple. *We* could not create new life, but we could always revive it . . . in some fashion." Ruslan grinned as he gestured at the dead Fallen House members behind.

Ruslan dragged his knife across his own throat, laughing as the line bled gold instead of red. "So you see, my friends, you cannot kill me. In many ways, I'm practically dead already and it hasn't stopped me yet."

A shiver ran down Laila's spine. She glanced to her right and saw Séverin staring at her, the lines around his mouth tight with worry. The moment she looked at him, the golden dagger at her breast dragged up slowly, with all the languor of a lover's touch. It tapped beneath her chin, forcing her head up.

"Now, now, don't be so distracted, Séverin!" Ruslan laughed.

Laila swallowed hard. The dagger did not move from its new position at her throat.

"Gold and alchemy, transformation and ichor," said Ruslan, gesturing with a flourish of his wrist. "The use of such treasures always comes at a cost, you know." He paused, tapping the side of his golden skull. "But I was willing to pay anything to save myself. I'm afraid the same could not be said for my men however."

Ruslan snapped his fingers. As one, the six members of the Fallen House lifted their *volto* masks. A sweet, rotten stench filled the air. Beneath their masks was a ruined mass of flesh, mouths pulled into rictus grins and covered in a thin layer of gold.

"Not quite enough to call them living, but certainly enough to be useful," said Ruslan, shrugging. "And perhaps when I am a god, I will use my infinite mercy and ability to restore them to full life . . . maybe. That is what you want too, is it not, lovely Laila?"

The dagger pushed a little harder at her throat. Laila forced her eyes to the ground. Now, the glassy floor looked like rose-colored clouds. She imagined the sun rising slowly, warming her back. She met Ruslan's gaze, lifting her chin. Acid flashed through her chest, and Laila welcomed her own fear.

"You will never be a god," she spat.

Ruslan laughed. He turned to Enrique. "How's your ear, little historian?"

"Gone," said Enrique furiously. "Along with my delusions."

"And the mute, little engineer . . ." said Ruslan, turning to Zofia. "Hello."

Laila glared at the cruel jab, but Zofia remained indifferent. She stood with her back ramrod straight, her blue eyes furious and burning.

"I see you've kept around the abandoned puppy," said Ruslan, lifting an eyebrow at Hypnos. "Strange . . . you were supposed to be dead. That will change, though. I'd hate to make liars out of the Order."

Hypnos scowled.

"How nice to see you all reunited," said Ruslan, clapping his hands. "You lived together . . . now you may die together! What a gift. Now, Séverin . . . enough of this. I'll make you a deal, yes? Get me to the top of the temple, I'll kill you simultaneously, and thus spare you the agony of watching one another die. In return, you take me to the top of that temple and play the lyre. *Now*."

Laila watched as Séverin held up his hands slowly. She could see a plan frantically churning behind his eyes. His eyes darted to the changing color of the floor. Even though Laila could not turn around to see it, she still felt the presence of the giant automatons flanking the ziggurat.

"Ruslan, surely we—"

"Ugh," said Ruslan.

He jerked his chin to the right, and Hypnos yelped, doubling over. Laila sucked in her breath. The dagger at her throat pressed a little deeper against her skin, keeping her still.

"Hypnos!" Séverin called out. He spun around to help, but Ruslan called out: "No, no, Monsieur Montagnet-Alarie . . . you will stay right where you are."

Hypnos moaned, lifting his head. There was a long cut down his cheek. The golden dagger now rotated around his head.

"If you defy me again, the next cut will be along his throat," said Ruslan. "Now *go*."

Laila wished she could wrench this dagger away from her and plunge it straight into the patriarch of the Fallen House.

"No!" called out Enrique. "It's rigged with a trap. I'm sure of it!"

Ruslan raised an eyebrow. "Is that so?"

Laila held her breath. It was a dangerous thing to get Ruslan's attention, and yet if he did not listen, all of the lyre's power would be wasted.

"Look at the floor, Ruslan," said Séverin evenly. "It is changing even now to reflect different times of the day. Trespass upon a temple too early, and it is a sign of disrespect to the gods. We should go at noon, at the zenith of the day to mark the occasion. And that's not to mention the statues themselves—"

"They're straight from the legends I've researched," said Enrique, gulping down air. Laila couldn't take her eyes off the golden dagger now tapping his remaining ear. "It's a . . . a legend about King Ajatasatru. He ruled until 460 BC, and he was said to possess *all* manner of military inventions. Catapults and mechanized war chariots and—"

Ruslan started to laugh. "A clever little ploy! You can delay this as long as you like, but it won't make a difference—"

"It's true!" said Enrique loudly. "I . . . I know it. Something will happen."

Out the corner of her eye, Laila stared at the curling mist. What lay on the other side? Or who?

"'Something,'" repeated Ruslan, bored. "How frightening. Come, Séverin—"

Laila felt his gaze sweep over her.

"If we go now, we will be killed," said Séverin. "And then no one can play the lyre and turn you into a god. Is that truly a risk you wish to take?"

Ruslan paused. At first, he sighed, and then a little smile rose to his lips. Laila felt as if a cold wind had blown against her neck.

"Quite right," said Ruslan. "I cannot risk you . . . but Laila? Well. Quite a different thing. My dear, how many days do you have left anyway?"

Laila stared down at him. "Plenty."

"Not scared of death, are you?"

"I consider it a dear friend," said Laila through her teeth. "Practically family."

Ruslan grinned. "Then you will not mind taking the first step."

"No!" cried out Séverin.

"Another word out of you, and someone else will pay for it," said Ruslan quietly.

Séverin's eyes looked wild and huge in his face. Laila wished she could tell him that she wasn't scared. She couldn't explain why she felt fearless in this moment. Maybe it was what she had glimpsed when the temple grasped hold of her mind . . . there was a vastness at work here, and she was not frightened by her smallness within it because she had *felt* that there was a place for her.

"Go ahead, my dear," said Ruslan. "Walk. Or do you need encouragement?"

He snapped his fingers, and two of the guards broke off to join her. Their rotting flesh stank. When one of them grabbed her arms,

Laila could feel the man's finger bones pressing into her skin as he spun her around.

The shining floor looked like a freshly scrubbed dawn. Laila hesitated when she felt the knife travel down her throat, moving between her breasts and encircling the line of her waist before settling at the small of her back. A fresh wave of nausea ran through her. She couldn't help but imagine that it was Ruslan's sickly, golden touch on her skin. Laila wanted to look at the others, but a dead Fallen House member blocked her view.

"*Go*," said Ruslan.

Laila swallowed hard, keeping her gaze straight ahead and fixed on the ziggurat in the distance. It was less than thirty meters away. She had to tilt her head back just to see where it disappeared in the strange, green sky. The automatons remained still and serene as she took one step onto the floor. The knife dug into her back, forcing her to take another step. As she did, Laila noticed two raised lines encircling the ziggurat and the automatons.

She hadn't noticed them before when the floor looked like a melted night sky. Perhaps they were too dark to pick out, but now, as the floor lightened, they became visible.

"There's something here," said Laila. "Two . . . raised lines . . . I don't know what it is."

Ruslan huffed, annoyed. "A demarcation, perhaps—"

"No," said Enrique slowly. "The *bhuta vahana*."

"And what's that?" asked Ruslan.

Boredom dripped from his voice, but Laila felt as if the air around her had grown taut. As if the temple was mad . . . as if they were trespassing.

"Spirit movement machines," said Enrique, the words tumbling out of him. "I thought it meant the automatons themselves, but I was wrong. It has to be an actual device—"

A low rumble moved through the temple. A growl of thunder rippled through the temple, and a tremor rattled through the floor, powerful enough that Ruslan's dagger at Laila's back wavered, clattering to the ground.

"What is that?" demanded Ruslan.

From the corner of her eye, Laila saw the silvery fog bubbling. A dark shape moved behind the mist.

"Laila!" screamed Enrique. "Move! It's a track!"

Laila had hardly taken two steps away from the others, but she felt the distance like a great chasm as two, massive chariots the size of elephants burst out of the mist and raced across the floor. Sharp, glossy spikes jutted out from their wheels, spinning so fast, they looked like pointed blurs. Laila stumbled backward, and Séverin caught her against him, pulling her away just as the chariot spun past them in a deafening roar. When it finally faded seconds later, Laila lifted her head, turning slowly . . .

On the glass floor, the bodies of the Fallen House members lay in clumps of meat. Zofia retched onto the ground. Even the dagger poised at her heart wavered.

"Hmm," said Ruslan thoughtfully. "Perhaps you were right about the whole 'go at noon' business."

Laila could feel the sharp rise and fall of Séverin's chest. He moved to shove her behind him, but Ruslan was faster. The air sang as the golden blade cut through it and found her neck once more.

Laila tilted her chin, assuming the haughty L'Enigme expression that had once earned her strands of pearls thrown at her feet. She already wore death on her hand, a dagger at her throat made no difference.

"It's a miracle you're still alive, my dear," said Ruslan.

Laila said nothing. Ruslan turned to Enrique, who was shaking where he stood. Hypnos swayed, his head turned resolutely from the mangled bodies on the floor.

"Well done, Enrique!" said Ruslan. "You might've lost your ear, but you've certainly gained mine! Well . . . for a little while at least. Noon does not look as though it's very far away, does it? I suppose I can stand to wait a little while longer."

Around them, the floor continued to brighten. Now it was high morning. The sky upon the glass was clear and blue, and though noon promised danger, Laila felt nothing but hope.

When she looked down at her garnet ring, the number read zero, and still, Laila felt no panic. It was not because of an encroaching blankness, but rather a delicious absence of fear.

That number on her ring spoke true. She should have no days left, and yet, in the space of an hour, she'd glimpsed a night strewn with stars, a rubied dawn, and now a blue morning. The day continued, and still she stood.

Perhaps Laila really was just grave dirt and borrowed blood, and yet . . . she lived.

And she felt, deep in her stolen bones, that miracles were not yet finished with her.

32

༒

ZOFIA

ofia tried to count the number of steps that lay ahead of them, but by two hundred and seventeen, a headache pulsed behind her eyes and she was forced to stop. She could feel her fear burning around the edges of her thoughts.

Their ammunition was lost.

Their tools were useless.

Their options were gone.

"Why do you stand so far from me, my lovelies?" crooned Ruslan.

The patriarch of the Fallen House stood at the very base of the ziggurat. Séverin and Enrique stood on either side, daggers pointed to their hearts. A corner of the divine lyre poked out from the front of Séverin's jacket.

"Come, come!" said Ruslan, clapping his shining hands.

Zofia recognized the gesture as a common one used for dogs. Her lip curled.

"It will be okay, Phoenix," whispered Laila.

Zofia tried to turn her head to Laila, but the dagger point at the base of her neck stopped her. Even so, she could feel Laila standing beside her. Hypnos was on her left. Behind her, Zofia knew the four dead Fallen House members stood close by because a fly buzzed around her nose. Twice, Zofia heard the wet *plop* of maggots falling to the glass floor. She bit back a gag, forcing her gaze straight ahead.

Ruslan growled. *"Now."*

A Fallen House member shoved her, and Zofia stumbled forward on the glass floor. By now, the colors on the glass floor had brightened from morning to noon.

Ruslan had forced Enrique to take the first step onto the glass. Zofia had nervously looked to the silvery fog and the giant automatons, but nothing moved. It was as Séverin had said: The temple would not grant them access until the right time, and now that time had come.

The closer Zofia got to the ziggurat, the more she saw that a golden aura hung about the temple. High above, the forested ceiling now bloomed with white flowers that Zofia did not recognize. A fragrance wafted down. Though there were no candles, it smelled of the Havdalah spices passed around on Shabbat.

"Look at the flowers, Phoenix. They're almost like newborn stars, don't you think?" asked Laila softly.

Zofia could not read her friend's expression, but she was familiar with this pattern. Hela used to do something similar—drawing her out of the tangle of her thoughts with an illogical statement she would be forced to refute. It was done, Zofia understood, to comfort her. But Zofia did not want comfort. She wanted a plan not just for herself, but for *all* of them. What would happen to them? All those unknowns cropped up like shadows in her path. The uncomfortable brightness of the temple sanctum made no difference.

"Time to witness my glorious apotheosis!" said Ruslan. "Shall we?"

Zofia looked up, catching Enrique's gaze. His mouth was a flat line.

"Oh, *do* tell me," said Ruslan, pleading. "I love knowing all the useless historical bits and bobs of things—"

The dagger pointed at Enrique's heart dug in a little, and he gasped. "Let us go."

"That's it? No spouting of information?" asked Ruslan. The brightness of the temple reflected off his golden face. "Perhaps I should loosen your tongue—"

"No!" cried out Enrique. "Did you . . . did you know the word 'ziggurat' comes from the Akkadian tongue? *Zaqaru*, I believe . . . 'to build high.' As for sacrifice, I'm not certain whether—"

Ruslan burst into laughter. "I should reward you for amusing me! Should I kill you now so you don't have to watch everyone die? Oh, but I so dearly wanted to sacrifice Laila first—"

"*No*," said Zofia.

The word ripped out of her so fast that it took a moment for her to realize that *she* was the one who had spoken.

Ruslan's golden face turned to her. Zofia could feel Laila stiffen beside her. Zofia expected the dagger to dig a little deeper on her neck, but instead, Ruslan just flicked his wrist.

Zofia knew that gesture. Classmates and professors and people in the city used to do that around her all the time.

It meant one thing: Zofia was not worth notice.

"The mute speaks!" Ruslan's gold mouth curved, and he turned sharply. "As if you have any power to change things."

Heat flared on Zofia's face. Ruslan was wrong, and yet . . . all her inventions lay on the other side of the lake. Zofia had little on her person except for her necklace, three matches, and her Forged sleeve. None of it would help Laila. None of it would make a difference.

Beside Ruslan, Enrique's eyes had narrowed. Séverin had set his jaw and right behind her, Hypnos was breathing hard.

"Come, Monsieur Montagnet-Alarie," said Ruslan, snapping his fingers. "It is time to give me that which I am owed."

Ruslan stepped onto the shining ziggurat. Zofia watched as Séverin took a deep breath. He looked up, at the giant automatons, and then at Hypnos and her . . . before his eyes rested on Laila. Finally, he stepped onto the temple. Enrique followed.

"Phoenix—" Laila whispered under her breath.

But Zofia did not hear what she said. The guard shoved her forward.

"No dallying!" called Ruslan, climbing the steps. He looked over his shoulder, grinning and waving his knife. "For every hesitation, I'll take a finger!"

Zofia stepped onto the temple. *Focus*, she told herself. *One step at a time.*

That was all she could do now.

Up close, the steps were even larger than she had imagined. They stretched at least fifteen meters wide on either side, and required a good four paces forward before she reached the ledge to climb the next step. She made her way slowly, her heartbeat loud in her ears as she tuned out the world around her.

Zofia had just counted her twentieth step when the air around them rippled. The warm glow off the mud-baked bricks disappeared. Cold invaded the space around her. A high-pitched hum echoed in her ears.

Zofia shook her head, as if she could manage to dislodge the sound. The dagger at her back nicked her skin and she winced. When she looked down, she froze.

"What is that?" asked Ruslan, whirling around.

Black liquid beaded on the stone steps. Zofia looked up, managing to turn her head and finally catch sight of Laila standing beside her before the world exploded into thick, choking shadows.

Zofia stumbled back, losing her footing. The frenzied humming had built into a screaming wind in her ears. Something sharp slashed against her thigh. Dimly, Zofia thought she heard Ruslan's dagger clattering to the stone. Zofia clawed to reach a step, but only air and shadows met her hands.

Zofia squeezed her eyes shut.

One. Two. Three.

She opened them, but the dark hadn't faded.

Four. Five. Six.

Zofia turned her head, but the shadows had become thick and impenetrable. She might as well have been all alone. Inky shadows swirled around her.

Zofia fought back a sob, forcing her mind to ordered, neat things like numbers. She raced through multiples of seventeen as she fumbled in the dark, stretching her hands out before her—

Seventeen, thirty-four, fifty-one . . .

She tried to take a step forward, tripped, and banged her knees against something hard and rough. A sob caught in her throat. Her hands shook as she felt her way around, only for something wet and sticky to hit her fingers. Zofia clutched her fingers to her chest, curling around herself and counting her breaths the way her parents had taught her to do when she was young and terrified.

But it wasn't working.

She couldn't scream or sob. She couldn't see a way out, and soon the darkness became more than something staring at her from the outside. She could feel it inside her too.

Zofia blinked and felt Hela's last letter slipping from her fingers and vanishing into the murky lagoons of Venice. She remembered her classmates locking her in the classroom, the shrieks that she was nothing more than a crazy Jew, the fear that there were too many unknowns in the world and she would never find her way in the dark.

Seconds or full minutes passed before Zofia realized that her thought was not accurate.

She had found her way out of the unknown before. She had found ideas and solutions when there were none. She had saved her friends in the past, and hardly a week ago, she had freed herself from a prison of ice.

All those things had been dark at one point, but she had found her way . . . on her own.

Zofia opened her mouth. "Hello?"

Again, her voice was snatched, churned to black.

Language dissolved into ink, and Zofia's tongue tasted as if she'd licked the end of a burnt match.

Match.

Shaking, Zofia felt around for her box of matches, working only by touch. The pad of her finger grazed the sulfur-roughened strip of the box. The wood felt damp from her sweaty fingers. She could not see, and when she went to strike the match, it snapped apart in her hand.

Panic flared in her chest, but she shoved it down and reached for another match.

This time, she clutched the box in one hand, and struck it, but again, the stick broke.

The third match was her last, and Zofia's hand trembled as she raised it. Her mother's voice curled around her thoughts.

Be a light in this world, Zosia, for it can be very dark.

Something inside Zofia steadied. If she let the unknown darkness win, then she would lose all sight of what could change . . .

Zofia held her breath. She pictured her parents' warmth, Hela and Laila's loving smiles. Ruslan was wrong. She was not a mute, little fool who could change nothing. Her friends called her Phoenix for a reason. Her mother had told her to be a light.

Zofia would not fail them.

She struck the match. The light was small, but it was enough. *She* was enough. Zofia brought the fire to the Forged silk sleeve of her dress, and it roared up in flames. Heat warmed her skin as she turned, casting the light around her.

With every swipe, she cleared a path in the shadows. Zofia swung her arm left and right, her lungs straining from the effort to shove all the dark away—

A hand shot out of the dark, grabbing hers. "Phoenix!"

Enrique.

He looked disheveled and wild-eyed at first, but then a wide smile split his face. He raised his arm, ripping off the Forged silver cloth that had once been part of the costume she had made him. The moment it touched her torch, it ignited and together, they cut through the dark.

Enrique and Zofia's flames left bright trails, burning the blackness into translucence. Slowly, the screams faded into silence. As her eyes adjusted to the light, Zofia now saw that she had only fallen two steps down from where she once stood.

Hypnos was on the step behind her, curled into a ball. Six meters away on the same step, Séverin and Laila huddled against the stone.

"Zofia!" called Laila, springing apart from Séverin.

Shakily, Séverin rose to his feet. He smiled. "Thanks for sharing the light, Phoenix."

The knot in Zofia's chest eased. Seconds later, the air whistled once more with the sound of a blade cutting through it. The golden dagger that had clattered to the stone found its way to her throat

once more. She swallowed hard, holding herself still, her chin angled up and away from its sharp point.

"It appears the temple has yet to trust us," said Ruslan loudly.

Zofia glanced up to see him standing five steps ahead.

"Monsieur Montagnet-Alarie, Monsieur Mercado-Lopez," said
Ruslan. "Join me if you please. I want you by my side in case there
are any more surprises."

When he snapped his fingers, the four rotting guards lurched
down. One went to Hypnos. The other caught hold of Zofia's arm,
pulling her toward the next step. Two surrounded Laila. As Zofia
took another step forward, Ruslan snorted.

"I suppose the little mute is good for something after all," he said.

Zofia said nothing. She would not waste words on someone like
Ruslan. Besides, she was busy. She was studying the stone joints of
the towering automatons, the pattern of light on the ziggurat steps.

For the first time since Ruslan had appeared, Zofia did not
need to count the objects around her to quiet her mind's panic.
The unknowns had not disappeared, but their size had diminished.
Or perhaps, her perspective had outgrown it. The unknown would
come and go, but Zofia could always be a light. She had found her
way out of the dark once.

And she could do it again.

33

SÉVERIN

Séverin was beginning to lose all sense of time.

His legs ached, and sweat poured down his back. He'd shrugged off his jacket long ago, but it made no difference. He could not remember the last time he'd sipped water, and when he licked his lips, he tasted the blood and cracked skin of his mouth. By his count, they should be midway up the ziggurat by now, and yet, when he turned to his left, he saw that he was still no farther than the place where the automatons' hands rested against their stone thighs.

Wrong, whispered a tired corner of his mind, but even that voice of caution felt thready and wispy. *Something is wrong.*

Séverin snuck a glance to his left where Enrique trudged upward, step after step. Sweat and blood had soaked through his bandages. His jacket was now tied around his waist. He didn't raise his head, but Séverin could see his lips moving silently.

As if he were uttering prayers with every step.

Séverin wished he could turn around and look at Hypnos, Laila, and Zofia . . . but the golden knife pointed at his chest kept his gaze fixed on the steps ahead.

One more step, he told himself. *One more step and we will reach the top, and I will play the lyre and become a god.*

Ruslan's wishes made no difference.

He could command Séverin to play the lyre, but its power was not for him. Séverin closed his eyes, summoning the memory of his mother's voice.

In your hands lie the gates of godhood . . . let none pass.

He had no intention of disobeying her.

Ruslan's only power was in his threats against the others, and the moment they reached the top, that threat would cease to exist. Séverin would play the lyre. He would claim that godhood for himself and be rid of Ruslan once and for all.

Séverin wished he could tell the others not to worry, but it would have to wait.

Forged rope bound his wrists, and yet he could still feel the hard strings of the divine lyre chafing against his shirt. Through the fabric, he felt the dull pulse of the instrument. With every step, a hum built steadily at the base of his skull.

All he had to do was keep moving, and yet with every step, the top of the ziggurat seemed farther and farther away. The beauty of the sanctum now struck him as a taunt ripped from a Greek myth. Above, the thick, tangle of inviting gardens. Around him, the phantom perfume of lost flowers haunting the air. All of it just out of grasping reach.

No, he told himself. *This is yours . . .*

That was the point of everything, was it not? All that he had lost was in service to this one glorious gain. He was meant for this. It was the only explanation that made sense.

Séverin blinked, and imagined Tristan's cool, gray eyes crinkling in a smile. He felt Tante FeeFee's warm hand cupping his chin.

Another step, just one more, he told himself, lifting his leg up a shining, stone stair.

The divine lyre strings pressed against his heart, and for the third time in ten days, Séverin heard his mother's voice reaching to him across the years. When he breathed, he caught the sharp, bright scent of orange rinds that Kahina used to perfume her hair.

Shall I tell you a tale, habibi? Shall I tell you the tale of the orange trees?

Séverin told himself that he was hallucinating, but that only made the fragrance of orange trees grow stronger.

It starts with a king on his deathbed . . . you know how that is, my love. Death must have his seat at the table of tales, and he always sits first. The king had a son, and with his last breath, he gifted his child a golden key that would open a golden door on the far side of a magnificent garden.

He made him promise not to use the key, no matter what.

Séverin swayed on the spot. He felt his mother's cool hand on his elbow, pulling him forward. Kahina used to lure him with stories, laying them out like treats. For a bath, he received half the tale. For brushed teeth, he received the end of the story. For a good night kiss, she traded in short fables.

Come, habibi, don't you want to know what happens?

Now, it seemed, for a step forward, she would give up a sentence.

He took a step.

The prince was overcome with curiosity. You know all about curiosity, don't you, my love? But there are some things you must not know . . .

He took another step.

He kept his promise to his father for over a year before, one day, he took the golden key to the golden door on the far side of the magnificent garden . . . and he opened it.

Séverin stumbled.

Dimly, he heard Ruslan call out behind him, but he ignored him.

And there he found a wondrous orange tree. The fruit gleamed, shining with dew, and the prince knew a terrible hunger. He took his little knife, and split the fruit open, and when the rind parted, a seed fell to the ground and sprouted into the most beautiful woman he had ever seen and—come now, my love, one more step.

"I can't," Séverin tried to say, but his legs moved anyway.

The prince begged the woman to marry him, and she agreed, but when he carried her over the golden threshold of the golden door, she fell dead at his feet, turning back into a seedling, which in time became an ordinary orange tree.

Again and again, the prince tried to go back the way he came—or perhaps he was thinking of other trees that might sprout equally beautiful companions—but alas, he had left the key on the other side, and the golden door never opened for him again.

Séverin stopped walking.

Always throw away golden keys to golden doors, habibi. Such knowledge is a hungry creature, and it will swallow you whole. It will dine on your hopes, slurp out your heart, tear away bits and pieces of your imagination until you are nothing but a tough, chewy hide of obsession.

Séverin frowned.

That was not how the story was supposed to end, but before he could argue with his hallucination, he felt a sweaty hand closing on his arm.

"Enough of this," growled Ruslan.

Séverin turned on the spot.

"We haven't moved in *hours*," said Ruslan.

Séverin gathered the last of his energy, trying to convert it into focus . . . into *words*. When he looked at Ruslan, he saw that the patriarch's eyes were ringed with white. The golden side of his face looked sunken. Ruslan's face cracked into a strange grin.

"Do you think I haven't noticed what you're doing?"

"I'm not doing anything except trying to get us to the top—"

"Then why haven't we moved?" shrieked Ruslan. "Look at the automatons! We should be past them by now."

Wearily, Séverin looked to his left where one of the huge automatons stood silently. They had climbed so far that he could no longer see its feet or the Forged floor that had once held the likeness of the night sky. They stood hip height to the statues. Their impassive faces glared down at them, their expressionless eyes and mouths unchanging.

"I've counted . . ." said Ruslan, strain tugging at his voice. "Five hundred steps and we have not moved . . . we have not crossed any distance. You're doing it on purpose, aren't you? Trying to tire me out? To fill my head with this nonsense about playing the lyre at the top of the ziggurat?"

Séverin wet his dry lips, summoning the effort to speak.

"It fits," he said slowly. "Imagine that you are on a pilgrimage . . . that's what all holy spots demand. It wants your desperation . . . your hopelessness. If you felt otherwise, there would be no need to commune with any higher power. I have every faith the steps will lead us somewhere soon. We just have to keep going—"

Ruslan's arm swung toward him, and Séverin heard his friends cry out at the same moment that Ruslan's fist cracked into his jaw. He stumbled back, the dagger point lightly swiping against his throat, drawing blood.

"What are you doing—" he tried to say only for Ruslan to slam his elbow into his neck, knocking him to the ground.

From the corner of his eye, Séverin watched Hypnos and Enrique lunge toward him, only for the dead Fallen House guards to lurch forward, tackling them to the stone ground.

Séverin rolled over. When he looked up, a wind rippled through the branches of the upside-down trees. The divine lyre thudded against his chest. Séverin's bindings slipped down his wrist, but the moment he could move his fingers, Ruslan's boot slammed down on his chest, knocking the air out of his lungs.

"Stop!" screamed Enrique. "He can't play it without risking destruction of everything Forged! Remember what we found in the Sleeping Palace?" He gasped, fighting for breath. *"To play at God's instrument will summon the unmaking.* Everything Forged will fall apart! We *have* to keep walking—"

"No," said Ruslan, shaking his head. "No, we don't."

Too late, Séverin realized what he would do. He curved his body over the lyre only for Ruslan's molten hand to snap out, catching him around the throat. Séverin kicked out, thrashing against him. He wheezed, gasping for air, but Ruslan's golden grip was not human.

"I thought we could do this together, Séverin," said Ruslan, "but I see now that my kindness has gotten the best of me. I don't need your touch."

He plucked the knife still hovering above his throat.

No, he thought fiercely.

Séverin tried to turn his head, to demand the sanctum of the lyre to rise up and defend him. Even now, he felt the rhythm of something vast and celestial coursing through his veins the moment he pressed his fingers into the lyre's strings.

This is mine, Séverin told himself as Ruslan pried the lyre from his jacket. *I own this wonder.*

Only Séverin knew how the lyre truly looked when it was played—the light catching on the filaments and revealing a prism of colors, the pulse of stars nestled in the shining strings.

Ruslan slashed the knife across Séverin's hand, smearing the blood on his own golden hand.

"Stop—" Séverin croaked.

Around them, the stones began to shake and quiver.

"It won't work—" Séverin tried to say, but the words lodged in his throat.

Surely, it wouldn't work.

Surely, it was something fundamentally about *him* and *his* will that made the lyre powerful.

Ruslan swiped his bloodied hand across the strings, and Séverin could do nothing but watch as one of those straight and shining strings bent beneath his stained, golden flesh.

At first, relief rushed through him.

Ruslan could not play the lyre . . . not even with his blood.

But the presence of Séverin's blood on the strings had done *something*.

A low humming filled his ears. It bloomed outwards like a ribbon of ink in a glass of water. The air shimmered.

Overhead, the trees trembled, and tiny leaves rained onto the golden steps. The golden daggers dropped to the ground. Beside him, the dead Fallen House soldiers exhaled and crumpled.

"Laila!" cried Zofia.

No, thought Séverin. He threw his head back, desperate to see her. He caught a glimpse of Laila slumping forward, her head thudding on the stones.

"It's working," said Ruslan feverishly. "I knew it."

Séverin threw off Ruslan's boot, scrambling to his knees only for Ruslan to catch hold of him again.

Séverin knew he had screamed, but he could not hear it through the rushing sound of blood in his ears. The fragrance of orange perfume was gone, replaced with the smell of tears. His whole world reduced to the sight before him.

Laila sprawled on the ground, stirring weakly. Blood ran from her nose and ears, pooling on the stone steps. Hypnos cradled her head. Enrique looked at Séverin with a bleak stare.

No. This is not what I was promised.

The lyre had not worked how he imagined, but it was still his. Still his power. He saw Zofia fall to her knees, grabbing at her necklace in disbelief.

Her Tezcat pendant shone.

"Wait," he heard himself saying. "There must be a portal on the staircase! I can play the lyre, I can fix this—"

A cold shadow fell across him. Ruslan released him with a shove, laughing hysterically. Sound rushed in, and Séverin heard the creaking sound of rocks displaced.

A metallic scream ripped through the air as the stone automatons twisted their necks. The dull, metallic spheres of their eyes glowed brightly. A voice in a language he did not speak, but nonetheless *knew* roared at them.

This is not the hand we answer to—thieves. THIEVES.

The automatons swung up their arms, their rocky fists uprooting a copse of trees—

Séverin lunged forward, grabbing the lyre from Ruslan, careful not to disturb the strings. Even so, the rush of air against the shining instrument sent a high-pitched quiver through the sanctum. The thunderous crackle of ancient branches collided with the metal as dirt and debris rained down from the sky.

"Grab Laila!" shouted Séverin. "There's a Tezcat up ahead! It will take us to the top of the temple, I know it! We just have to keep going!"

Hypnos scooped Laila up in his arms. Zofia and Enrique staggered forward. Séverin had only managed one step forward when the stairs began to crumble into the floor and a great tremor rocked the ziggurat.

Behind them, he could hear Ruslan's shouts for help, but Séverin's gaze was on the step ahead of them, and the next step after that. The trees broke overhead.

Enrique shoved him forward just as a branch the length of his body smashed onto the steps. The smell of bruised fruit filled the air. They were all too weak to move up the side of the temple; Séverin was forced to crawl on his hands and knees.

Is this not how one meets God, he wondered, almost laughing at the thought. *I must not walk . . . but crawl.*

On his right side, one of the automatons smashed its fist into the rock of the ziggurat. Stones crumbled away mere centimeters from Séverin's face. The world smelled like blood and oranges, and when he looked down at his hands, he saw they were stained red.

"Séverin!"

He looked up blearily to see Zofia with tears streaming down her face. Laila's head lolled against Hypnos's chest. He tried to raise one leg, but his body shook.

"I . . . I can't—" he said.

Séverin tapped into the last reserves of his strength, gathering Laila from Hypnos and pulling her against him. Even now . . . even with the world breaking around them . . . she still smelled of sugar and rose water. He hoisted her over his shoulder, one hand braced along her back.

In the back of his head, Séverin heard his mother's voice:

Come along, habibi, don't you want to see the end of the story?

Séverin crawled, forcing one hand in front of the other, his body dragging over the rough-hewn steps. Enrique cried out, sliding down the side of the temple. With one hand, Séverin grabbed Enrique by the wrist, hauling him up even as his shoulder screamed and something hot and wet flooded down his chest.

"I've got you," said Séverin.

I protect you, he thought.

Hypnos appeared on his other side, gripping Enrique's hand. Together they dragged him, and themselves, forward.

"The portal—" said Enrique. "Where is it? Those things will kill us—"

"It's glowing brighter; it's closer," said Zofia.

Séverin looked up. There, at least twenty paces away, the air above the top-most step looked wrinkled with light. Both automaton fists slammed down close to her. Zofia fell to her side. Now the automatons moved closer, raising their other hands. Séverin looked behind him. Blood covered the stone steps. Ruslan was nowhere to be seen.

Séverin gazed up at the automatons' shining arms, their heads bending toward them.

Zofia raised her bloodied face, her blue eyes wild as she looked to Séverin. "They're going to destroy the portal."

Séverin froze. For a brief moment, he imagined what would happen. He understood why the people who had built the temple had hidden its true heart. If the portal was destroyed, then the lyre would never be played. There was only one last option to stop the automatons . . .

And it lay in his hands.

He knew the truth of it in a way he could not explain.

The moment he played the lyre, all Forged things would break around him. The automatons would go silent.

And Laila would die.

Against him, Laila stirred. He lowered her to the ground, heedless of the trees crashing into the stone steps, the strange vapors surrounding the temple rolling in like a deadly fog, the slowly lowering arms of the automatons overhead. She looked up at him, a defiant shine creeping into her swan-black eyes. She licked her inky, blood-black lips, and smiled.

"You know what you have to do," she said.

"Laila, please don't make me do this—"

"*Majnun*," she said.

How many times had he wanted to hear her call him that once more? But not like this.

Laila reached for his hand. Her skin was far too cold. He looked down. The garnet ring was gone, lost in the debris of crashing rocks. Another tremor jolted through the steps. Laila's other hand went to his cheek, and his eyes fluttered shut.

"I am not done with this world yet," said Laila.

What happened next took place with such swiftness that he didn't realize what had occurred until it was too late.

One moment, Laila's hand was on his. The next, she had jerked it forward, bringing his palm to the strings of the divine lyre. Séverin startled, his fingertips catching on those gleaming cords—

The world went silent.

34

LAILA

Laila discovered that dying was not so difficult as one might imagine.

She remembered the pain from the last time Séverin's hand touched the instrument . . . the slow pluck of death on her rib cage as if it would peel back her bones and shake out her soul.

But this time, there was no pain.

Maybe she was beyond it.

"Laila, keep your eyes open, please. I just need to get us to the top and everything will change—"

Laila blinked.

Overhead, there were trees, and if Laila could ignore the sharp, jolting steps or the sight of a monstrous bronze hand, she might have imagined she was at a park, lying in the grass and looking up.

When had she stopped going to parks?

She remembered a picnic, Goliath smuggled into a basket, Enrique screaming, Tristan insisting that the tarantula liked brie cheese and only wanted a little. She remembered laughter.

She would have liked another picnic.

Laila felt herself being thrown over someone's shoulder. Hypnos, she realized. Hypnos was carrying her up the stairs.

"Keep playing!" called Enrique.

"If I do that, she'll die," said Séverin.

"If you don't, she won't *live*," shot back Zofia.

Laila closed her eyes. Light seamed through her. She felt her memories rising up, pulling free from her, so that with every note, a part of her was shorn off like a cliff falling bit by bit into the sea.

Here, the memory of tying the *gunghroo* bells around her ankles before her mother taught her to dance. The bells smelled like blood and looked like gold, and when they chimed in her heart, she heard her mother's voice: *I will show you to dance the story of the gods.*

Pressure on her face. A rough-padded thumb lifting her eyelids. Enrique's soot-streaked face slowly coming into focus.

"You must keep your eyes open! We're nearly there!"

Laila tried. At least, she thought she was trying. She could still see the outline of Séverin limping up the steps. He clutched the lyre in one bloodied hand, his mouth a grim and determined twist.

Hypnos pivoted her just as bronze fists shattered on the steps, bronze fingers twitching weakly. Zofia and Enrique darted forward, kicking away the rubble. The Tezcat pendant now looked like a miniature sun.

"One more step and we'll cross through to the other side—" said Zofia, lifting her foot.

Séverin called out: "Wait! We need to make sure there's no final trap—"

Hypnos let out a ragged sigh, spinning her once more, and Laila's vantage point was stolen. All she saw was the thin line of blue light on one of the shining steps, the promise of another place. Her consciousness slipped—

Here, the memory of standing in L'Eden's kitchen for the first time, pouring ingredients for a cake, her hands dusted with flour and sugar. The beautiful silence of objects with no memory: pale eggshells, a palmful of finely milled sugar, split vanilla beans in a glass measuring cup.

Laila remembered hunger. Not the belly-pinching ache for food, but something else: her mouth watering, a cake slowly rising, water boiling for tea, the sound of friends' voices just outside the door. The promise that this ache would be filled and then some. She missed that hunger.

"Laila!"

Her eyes opened to Ruslan wrestling Séverin to the ground. Blue light glowed at the back of her eyes, and voices flitted in and out through her thoughts.

"There's writing on the steps."

Hide—

—Your

Face—

—Before

God—

—This

Is—

—Not

For—

—You

To—

—See

Those words meant nothing to Laila. Her memories bled from her swiftly—

Séverin's lips on her spine, kissing his way down her scar; the metallic smell of snow; the wax on the dance floor of the Palais des

Rêves; the startling blue of Zofia's eyes; the Forged tinsel deco-
rations on the stair bannisters of L'Eden; Enrique leaning puppy-
like against her legs; the strange tenderness of her first loose tooth;
Hypnos's throaty laughter; her mother splitting a pomegranate
with her bare hands; the scratchy luxury of a raw silk gown against
her skin; the thick heat of India; Séverin's wolf grin; a straw doll
catching fire and burning, burning, burning.

Dimly, she heard the others calling out, but their voices melded
together until she could not distinguish the speaker.

"Turn around!"

"Don't look!"

"Step backwards!"

Laila tried to anchor her consciousness to one spot, to raise
the hand she knew she must still have, but she was fraying by the
second.

Ruslan grabbed Séverin by the back of his neck. "You won't go
without me! It's mine too! I want to know. I need to see—"

The last thing Laila saw was Séverin closing his eyes, throwing
his arms up to shield his face. Laila did not see the light behind her,
but she saw it fall across Ruslan's golden face.

Hide your face before God.

The metal of Ruslan's face sank at the contact of light. A scream
ripped from his throat as his face melted in, his skull slipping
through red flesh.

But the gold stayed on his bones.

Ruslan had shining bones, thought Laila. Like a god. Like the
skeleton they'd found on the shores.

And right before the metal melted, right before death stole him,
Laila watched his eyes widen. He fell to his knees, mouth wide—
why?

An uncanny brightness glimmered, reflecting off the golden

mirror where his face had once been. It looked like gathered star-light, and yet somehow fathomless, like the black skin between stars.

This is not for you to see.

IT WAS HER last thought before the light swallowed her.

35

ENRIQUE

E ven before Enrique saw the writing on the steps, he knew that this was an end.

An end to what, he was unsure. He had come here thinking he might break off a piece of greatness for himself. He thought that whatever lay in this stone could drag down his dreams so they were within grasping distance. He had even imagined that Séverin might be able to do the impossible . . .

In the seconds before he closed his eyes and the light seamed out from the portal, Enrique caught sight of his friends on the burnished steps of the ziggurat. He saw Hypnos and Zofia leaning against each other, their faces grimy and tear-streaked. He saw Laila laid down on the steps, ragged as a doll. And then there was Séverin, regal as ever, not in the way of gods, but of kings. When the light touched him, Enrique imagined his friend looked like the kings of old . . . the ones who had once walked up the steps of ziggurats, laid sacrifices and offerings at the feet of the gods, and knew that their greatness was not without price.

Enrique watched as Séverin plucked a string. If it made a sound, he never heard it . . . but he felt the temple recoiling. In that second, it was as if the world had shifted on its axis . . . as if the stars in the sky held still to see what would happen next.

Enrique imagined long, slender fingers made of music dragging up his rib cage, strumming his bones as if they were the strings of a lute, as if it could turn him into a note that was part of the song that moved the universe.

36

SÉVERIN

Séverin Montagnet-Alarie was no stranger to death.

Death treated him like a son. Death roused him from sleep, coaxed him to test his ambitions, and reassured him—the way a mother might push the hair from her son's brow and tuck a blanket up to his chin—that there was no ambition too great. After all, Death would always be there. And no fear compared to her.

But in the moments when Séverin reached down to strum the divine lyre, he experienced a death he was not prepared for.

Here, on the stone steps of the ancient temple, Séverin experienced the death of certainty.

It was the moment when conviction crumpled into confusion, and Séverin had no choice but to grasp hold of weak-winged hope.

Séverin knew he was meant for godhood, but doubt's cold fingers hung new words at the end of that knowledge:

Séverin knew he was meant for godhood . . . *wasn't he?*

Ever since he had discovered the truth of his lineage and taken possession of the lyre, Séverin had imagined this moment every hour of every day. Every morning, he had turned the instrument in his hand and stared at the lavender lines on the inside of his wrist, knowing the promise that pulsed through his blood: *In your hands lie the gates of godhood . . .*

Was that not destiny?

Was that not the glorious purpose he was always intended to fulfill? Was that not the reason why his parents had died, why the seven sins had raised him and trained his tongue to be accustomed to bitterness, why he had held Tristan in his arms and did not move even when the blood started to cool on his own skin, why the woman he loved had been unraveling from the day they met?

But then why did his imaginings not match up to the scene around him?

He had imagined he would ascend these steps, clean and shining, his heart light. He had imagined Enrique grinning, Hypnos winking, Zofia smiling, and Laila . . . *living.*

And now?

Séverin could not even turn his head, but he sensed their broken spirits around him. He heard Hypnos softly weeping, and Zofia's panicked quiet. He heard Enrique murmuring prayers, and above all of it, the silence of Laila's soul.

This was not how it was supposed to be.

"I can fix this," said Séverin, keeping his head bowed.

The temple crumbled around him. His throat ached. His ears pounded. He raised his hand, touching the gleaming strings of the lyre—

"I can fix everything," he whispered. ". . . Can't I?"

Those words no longer felt like knowledge to Séverin.

It felt like a belief.

And it was here, in this space between fact and faith, that Séverin found himself praying for the first time in more than a decade.

"Please," he begged as his fingers strummed the instrument.

Please show me I was right.

Please fix this.

Please—

Something engulfed him, and Séverin felt as though he had been temporarily unmoored from time itself. In a few moments he would learn that he had been wrong about many things, and right about one: The lyre could remake the world.

And it did.

Venice, 1890

Luca and his brother, Filippo, were hiding in the shadows of the Rialto Bridge when it happened.

Up until two days ago, they had not been hungry thanks to the man at the dock. The man had given them apples full of coins, but now they were down to their last two, and the man was gone. Luca wondered what had happened to him.

Two nights ago, there had been an explosion in the lagoons. According to the gossip on the docks, the *polizia* had made no arrests. Normally Luca didn't care, but the unsolved explosion had led to more patrolling of the marketplaces, which made it that much harder to steal.

Every time he got close to snatching an apple or loaf of bread from the stands, he'd catch sight of the *polizia* with their large, Forged batons, and he would be forced to retreat back to the shadows. There was nothing he could do. If he did not steal, his brother would not eat. And if he got caught stealing, his brother would be undefended.

Luca turned to Filippo. "Are you hungry?"

Filippo put on a brave face and shook his head, but his stomach growled loudly.

Luca clenched his jaw, trying to ignore the gnawing ache at the pit of his gut. Instead, he stared at the gondola crossing the waters. A boy leaned against his father, half-asleep, an unwrapped sweet lying in his lap. Saliva filled Luca's mouth. Why must they scrabble in the corners? Was this what every day would be like?

At that exact moment, Luca heard a song.

It came from nowhere and everywhere. It rippled the lagoon waters. It shook the jeweled lanterns hovering above the streets and sent the Forged platters of food and merchant wares crashing to the ground.

Filippo gasped, pointing to the Forged platters holding up loaves of bread now falling and shattering hardly three meters from where they hid. Luca lunged forward, taking advantage of the distracted *polizia* as he stuffed the bread loaves under his jacket and grabbed his brother.

They took off at a run . . . the strange song nipping at their heels, tugging at their hearts. Luca knew, deep in his bones, that the world was about to change, though he could not say why. Away from the loud, crashing sounds, the brothers tore into their stolen food.

Maybe, thought Luca, as he ripped the bread . . . maybe the world would change enough that he might finally take a bite of it.

New York, 1890

A group of collectors were lounging in a smoke-choked room at the weekly meeting of the New York Historical Society of Forged Artifacts when it happened.

One moment, the auctioneer held up a gold and lapis-lazuli box the size of a snuffcase. A hippopotamus of carved jade appeared to lift its head and then partially disappear into the blue surface, as if it were a true creature reclining in the waters of the Nile. Thousands of years ago, the shining object had been the beloved toy of a young prince, so dear that it had been placed beside his tomb so that he might continue to play even in the afterlife.

The auctioneer cleared his throat. "This particular piece is rumored to have been the favorite toy of Akhenaton's son and is a donation from our wonderful friends in the Order of Babel—"

"*Friends?*" One of the members laughed loudly. "Some friends if all they give us are some useless toys!"

A small knot of members seated at the man's table began to agree loudly.

"It's true!" said another. "Why should they have all the glorious treasure for themselves—"

"I say we try to take something else—"

But perhaps the object was done being taken.

For the next moment, it burst apart, showering the room in shards of blue and gold so that it seemed as if the morning sky had crashed around them.

Manila, Philippines, 1890

Esmerelda was hiding outside of her father's study when it happened. Clutched in her hands was a stolen copy of *La Correspondencia de Manila*. Her parents refused to let her read the newspaper, but Esmerelda hungered for proof that the world was larger than she imagined.

At fourteen years old, Esmerelda had become convinced that her parents would prefer it if she spent the rest of her days with her hair neatly pinned back, her hands neatly folded in her lap, and everything so neat and dainty and orderly that a stray wind would send her into hysterics.

"What's next?" she heard her father scoff in his study. "Did you see the petition from the women of Malolos?"

"They want to go to *night school*," said one of his friends, laughing.

"Have they forgotten their place so completely?" asked another.

From behind the closed door, Esmerelda scowled. She had read all about the women who had delivered a petition to allow them to study. They'd delivered it straight to Governor-General Valeriano Weyler himself. She wished she could have walked alongside them, inked her name, and watched it dry on the paper. She wished she could follow in the footsteps of her brothers and cousins and learn.

And that was when it came.

Years later, Esmerelda secretly imagined that the angels above had heard her that day. That perhaps the sound that ripped through her home was the celestial trumpeting of a thousand horns, the kinds that she saw painted on the inside of cathedrals . . . the kinds that signaled that God was on her side.

37

SÉVERIN

*I*t had happened.

SÉVERIN STANDS AT the top of the ziggurat.

A short distance away lies a jewel-encrusted platform draped in translucent silks. It is surrounded by the melting stubs of candles that flicker like so many caught stars. An attar of roses fill the air, and a hum of distant lutes and chiming bells adorns the evening sky like precious ornaments.

This, Séverin understands, is hallowed ground.

But why is he here?

In your hands lie the gates of godhood, let none pass.

He knows this is not godhood, but it is something sacred all the same. Séverin blinks, and feels the heady weight of responsibility filling his chest. Though he has played the divine lyre, this is the highest status he might attain.

He is here as an emissary to the heavens.

He is here to commune with something higher than himself.

He is here, fully mortal, to touch the eternal.

And nothing more.

"Sire," says a voice at his elbow.

Séverin looks to his right. A light-skinned man wearing a veil offers him a candle. Another person steps before him, holding a large polished circle of bronze that acts as a mirror. In it, Séverin can see an ancient city in the midst of revels behind him. He sees himself and realizes he has been dressed in the raiments of a king. An ivory tunic and a finely dyed scarlet mantle of worsted wool and silk covers his body. A ribbon of thinly hammered gold twists about his brow. Someone has rubbed kohl around his eyes.

"She is beyond," says the veiled man.

She.

As he moves to the platform, he sees a slender silhouette behind the candlelit drapes and realizes the platform is, in fact, a bed. There is a woman waiting for him there, and he understands that sometimes she is a priestess and sometimes she is a goddess . . . but always she is out of reach.

Slowly, he parts the silks and sees her reclining against rich cloths and pillows embroidered with silver thread. There are gold coins strung through her hair. She wears a shift of thinnest linen dyed a rich red. Her hands are adorned with henna, as if she were a bride, and he knows that tonight, she is one.

"*Majnun,*" she says.

Séverin remembers himself. All of his selves. He remembers staring down at Laila's lifeless body, their friends hollowed out by grief beside them.

"Laila," he says, and her name melts like a prayer on his tongue. "What's happened?"

A shadow crosses her face, but then it vanishes. Instead, she moves a little, patting the place beside her.

"Come to me," she says.

He does. He is almost afraid to touch her, terrified that she'll dissolve beneath his fingertips. But he is spared from decision when Laila reaches for his hand. Her skin is warm. When he looks into her face, she smiles and it is the smile he has dreamt of many times.

In this moment, Séverin knows peace.

"All will be well," says Laila. "They are safe, Séverin. No one will hurt them. No one can touch us here."

This certainty moves through him, and though Séverin had imagined any failure would sting, this time he feels it like a pressure easing off his chest. He is not resigned to mortality, but oddly relieved by it, for in this moment, he knows he has done all he could, and even in failing, he has succeeded in keeping the people he loves safe.

Séverin blinks and remembers his losses. He thinks of Tristan's gray eyes, the orange fragrance of his mother's hair, the hard set of Delphine Desrosiers's mouth. He once thought that all that pain must be in service of something greater, but now he knows that it was never for him to understand. And when he looks at the fathomless night sky, he feels a serene contentedness in not knowing.

He turns to Laila. "Are we dead?"

Laila bursts out laughing. "Why would you think that?"

"Maybe because this feels remarkably like heaven," he says, stroking her hands.

Laila entwines their fingers, and his rib cage feels as though it might burst from joy.

"And what makes you so certain that you would be granted admittance to heaven?" says Laila.

Séverin grins. "Merely the hope that you'd be so awfully lonely and bored without me that you'd find a way to sneak me in."

Laila laughs again. She faces him. He notices that there is a line of gold at her throat, and that when the breeze shifts, the candlelight snares on the lush curves of her body.

She tips up his chin with one finger. "And how would you cure such boredom, *Majnun*?"

Séverin reclines against his cushions. He has not felt so light in ages, so untethered from sorrow. "Are you asking for a demonstration?"

"Or two," says Laila, leaning over to kiss him fully. After a moment, her lips move to his ear. "Or three."

Séverin does not waste time. In the back of his head, he knows that this heaven cannot last. That, eventually, the reality he has left behind will assert itself once more, inevitable as the dawn. He thrusts his hands into her hair, holding her against him, savoring each quick gasp and each small sigh. He kisses the line of her neck and traces her every curve with wonder and frustration, as if she is holy calligraphy in a language he cannot speak but longs to decipher. Eventually, Laila pulls him down to her, slinging her leg over his hip, guiding him to her. The world falls away. They come together like a hymn, the sacred set to song, and though Séverin knows he is not a god, their brief possession over the eternal makes him feel infinite.

Later, much later, Laila curls against his chest. He reaches for her hand, kissing the henna on her wrist. The city below is silent. A seam of gold touches the sky, and Séverin cannot account for the slow dread working its way through his body.

"You know, don't you?" asks Laila softly.

There is a lump in his throat. Yes, he has guessed, but he cannot make himself say it.

"It was the only way, Séverin," she says. "Once the lyre was played, the world changed. The temple was both the beginning and end of Forging, and as I am both Forged and human, the temple asked me to stay and guard it. I will oversee its power as it removes Forging from our world. In return . . . I will heal. I will *live*."

Séverin has always been in awe of her, but in this moment, his awe borders on reverence. The temple can indeed grant powers of godhood, but it has not chosen him. It's chosen her. He reaches for her hands, kissing the pulse at her wrist, and they lie like this for a few moments longer until Laila speaks once more.

"You promised me miracles, *Majnun*," she says, stroking his chest. "Tell me of them now, so I have something to dream of."

For a moment, Séverin cannot speak through his pain, but dawn is swift, and time is finite, and he must make use of what has been given to him.

He curls her hand to his chest and thinks of miracles. Once, he had promised her glass slippers and apples of immortality. Now, he wishes to show her something else entirely.

"I'll . . . I'll learn how to make cake," he says.

Laila snorts. "Impossible."

"No!" he says. "I will. I'll make you a cake, Laila. And we'll . . . we'll have a picnic. We'll feed each other strawberries to the utter disgust and repulsion of our friends."

Laila is quietly shaking, and he hopes it is from laughter. Night fades quickly. A poisonous tinge of blue touches the sky.

"Do you promise?" she asks.

"I promise that and more, if it will make you come back," says Séverin. "I promise to take you and Hypnos to the ballet in winter. We can stand in line for smoked chestnuts and try to stop Zofia from recreating such a delicacy at home with an open fire in the library. We can spend a whole day by the fireside, reading books and ignoring Enrique reading over our shoulders—"

"*Majnun*," she says.

But he is not done. He grips her hand tightly.

"I promise that we can waste time as if we were gods with endless troves of it."

The light grows brighter, and Séverin turns to her. He kisses her fiercely. Her tears wet his face.

She splays her hand against his, and when the light touches their joined palms, it is as if they have been knit together by a thousand dawns.

"You and I will always be connected," she says. "As long as I live, so will you. I will always be with you."

Séverin can feel it—this new interweaving between their very souls—but he does not understand what it means.

"Laila . . . wait. Please."

He knows he will never forget her, but he memorizes her all the same: sugar and rose water, the bronze line of her throat, her ink hair, such that only poets may write in its shade. When he kisses her again, her teeth hit his, and the moment is so achingly human, it nearly moves him to tears.

"I will come back to you, *Majnun*," she says. "I love—"

Dawn arrives.

It steals the night and her last words in one breath, and then— as ceremoniously as it brought him to the floor of heaven—it unceremoniously releases him back to his reality.

38

HYPNOS

In the years that followed, Hypnos would never be certain what he glimpsed that day on the top of the ziggurat. He had imagined a sentient, celestial presence . . . an engulfing of gold light. But it was not that. It could not be ordered into something so straightforward as color.

If anything, it was like a living song, undulating and incomprehensible.

For one single moment in time, that song moved through Hypnos, so that he was like a secret pane of glass through which the sunlight shone and the moonlight moved, and he was not illuminated so much as he was enlightened. He saw all the people he had been. The boy who loved to sing, forced to keep his mouth shut. The boy who yearned for song and was surrounded by a thousand different kinds of silence—the silence of his mother's race, the silence of his own desires, the silence of the luxuriously appointed rooms he haunted like a ghost. All his life, Hypnos had felt like a wandering set of notes, desperate to be set into music, and he had found it in the friends who had become family. Even with them, he felt nervous, as if they might throw him out of their music at any moment . . . but this grand song assured him otherwise. The song told him he was enough as he was, that his soul held a symphony of its own, for that was how he had been made.

But then the song released him.

And he was left with the memory of vastness . . . and the barest hint of warmth.

PART VI

39

ZOFIA

Three days after they had escaped the crumbling ziggurat and left Poveglia behind, Zofia sat in a private train compartment en route to Paris. Already, the world had changed. According to every newspaper, ancient Forged objects all around the world had ceased to function.

No one knew why.

There were reports of protests outside churches as religious leaders shouted that this was a sign that God was displeased with them. Industrialists spoke of how modern invention erased the need for Forging altogether. For those with an affinity for mind or matter, their art remained intact, but Zofia suspected that one day . . . even that would change.

Amidst all the uncertainty, there was one thing Zofia knew without a doubt: She did not know what would happen next.

In the past, this would have discomfited her. She would have spent the entire train ride counting the tassels on the rug, the hanging crystal pendants on the light fixtures. Now, she found herself far less bothered by the unknown. Even if the world were dark, Zofia knew she could be a light.

Alone in the compartment, Zofia stared at her hand, where Laila's large, garnet ring now shone on her finger. Inside the jewel, the number read *zero*.

The thought of seeing that number had once paralyzed Zofia. But that moment had come and gone, and though it had not ended at all how she imagined, it had not devastated her.

Zofia flexed her fingers beneath the weight of the garnet ring. She had found it near the clay-lined shores of the lake in the cavern, toppled beside a broken lantern. It must have slipped off Laila's hand right before they entered the sanctum.

When Laila had asked Zofia to make the ring for her months ago, Zofia had not liked the idea of the red stone. It was the color of blood and reminded Zofia of the warning signs she had once seen placed around the university laboratories.

"I like red," Laila had insisted, smiling. "It's the color of life. In my village, brides never wore white because we consider it the color of death. Instead, we wear bright red." Laila had winked. "Plus, I think red looks rather well on me."

Zofia turned the ring on her finger. When she thought of Laila, an ache opened up inside her. She remembered her friend lying lifeless on the stone, the temple crumbling around them. She remembered the burning light and the portal opening. But after that, Zofia's recollections became muddled. She could no longer recall what she had glimpsed on the other side, but she remembered the feeling of extraordinary calm. When she opened her eyes, the temple was silent and Laila was gone.

Séverin had pressed his hands into the place where she had disappeared, his head bowed. "She said she will come back . . . when she can."

There were no answers beyond that, and there was no time to look around the temple as it continued to crumble and break. Despite not knowing or understanding where Laila had gone, Zofia was not worried about her friend.

"Phoenix?"

Zofia looked up to see the door to her compartment pulled back and Enrique standing at the entrance. He wore a dark blue suit, and the hat pulled over his head nearly hid the bandage covering his wounded ear.

"May I join you?" he asked.

Zofia nodded, and Enrique took a seat across from her. In the days since they had returned from Poveglia, there had been so much to do and discuss that bringing up her own feelings was hardly a priority. There was travel to arrange, L'Eden to contact, and the Order of Babel to deal with.

Hypnos had finally contacted them, thus ending the Order's chase and exonerating the crew from what happened at the Winter Conclave a week ago . . . but now the Order wished to interview them about the death of Ruslan and the Fallen House. They had agreed to come up with a cover story to avoid mentioning the temple beneath Poveglia and what took place there. But truthfully, Zofia wasn't even sure what she saw. When she tried to concentrate on those minutes, all she could recall was a feeling of calm.

Alone with Enrique for the first time in days, Zofia's feelings felt sharpened. More acute. She remembered their kiss . . . the way he had held her hand when the siren-skeletons tried to lure her into the lake . . . how they had fought the darkness with matching flames.

Zofia wanted to tell him something, but what? That she enjoyed being next to him? That she wanted to kiss him again? What would that even mean? When she looked up at Enrique, she saw that he was staring at the ring on her finger.

"Do you believe what Séverin said?" he asked quietly. "About Laila? That she's truly well and safe . . . wherever she is?"

"Yes," said Zofia without hesitation.

"Why?" he asked.

Zofia opened her mouth, then closed it. There was no science behind her answer. And yet she had dreamed of Laila often in the days since they'd left Poveglia. In her dreams, her friend sat beside her and told her all would be well, that there was nothing to be scared of. Zofia could neither quantify where her certainty came from nor locate its source beyond the flimsy substance of dreams. And so the only words that came to her were not her own, but Enrique's, the same words he'd so often used to taunt her.

"Call it a gut feeling," she said.

A wide smile broke across his face. He looked out the window and his smile faded a bit.

"I know it's ridiculous, but sometimes I . . . I dream of her. I hear her telling me that all will be well," he said.

Zofia's eyes widened. "You dream of her too?"

Enrique looked back at her. His eyebrows went up. Zofia recognized his expression as disbelief.

"That can't be coincidence," he said, shaking his head. "I don't think I'll ever understand . . ."

Zofia did not know what to say. Enrique was right. He would never understand, and neither would she.

"Now what do we do?" he asked, looking at her.

A pause stretched between them. The train rumbled along the tracks. Rain smeared the glass windows.

Zofia had imagined that the world would come to a complete halt inside the temple, and yet it continued, gathering speed and momentum despite the changes. Science quietly asserted itself into the chaos. An object in motion would stay in motion unless acted upon by a new force. Zofia wondered if that applied to her feelings for Enrique. Perhaps it would always stay like this—silent and the same—unless she acted upon it. In the past, she would have said nothing. She feared rejection. She feared believing that she was acting outside of what was conventional.

But now, she found she no longer cared.

Zofia took a deep breath. In her mind's eye, she pictured Laila smiling encouragingly, and it gave her the strength to speak.

"I like you, Enrique. A lot."

Zofia studied his face. The look of disbelief shifted. A corner of his mouth tugged up. His eyes crinkled.

It was joy.

"I like you too, Zofia," he said, before adding: "A lot."

"Oh," said Zofia. "Good."

She had not planned for what to say after that. Her face felt warm. Her hands felt tingly.

"May I . . . hold your hand?" he asked.

Zofia tugged her hands farther into her lap. "I don't like hand holding."

Enrique was quiet. He made a "hmm" sound, and Zofia wondered if she had upset him, if he would go or—

"Tell me what you do like," he said.

"I . . . I would like you to sit closer to me."

He moved and sat beside her. Their shoulders touched. His leg brushed against her skirt. Zofia looked at him. She wanted to kiss him again. She wondered if she should ask first, or simply press her face to his, but then she remembered that if he was taking the time to ask what she liked, she should reciprocate.

"Do you like this?" she asked.

He smiled. "Yes."

"Now what do we do?" asked Zofia.

Enrique laughed. "I imagine we'll figure it out day by day."

Zofia liked that.

They had just settled into a comfortable silence when the compartment door opened once more, and Hypnos poked his head inside.

"I'm lonely," he announced. "I am joining you."

Enrique rolled his eyes. "What if I told you that you were interrupting?"

"Please *mon cher*, I never interrupt. I only complement or enhance, and in any case, it is not *your* permission I seek, it is our Phoenix's."

"I like when you're here," said Zofia.

Hypnos made her laugh. When the three of them were together, Zofia felt as if she were on steadier ground.

"You see?" said Hypnos, sticking his tongue out at Enrique before flopping onto the seat opposite them. Like Enrique's, Zofia noticed that Hypnos's gaze caught on her garnet ring.

"You know," he said quietly. "I dream of her."

Enrique looked at Zofia and then Hypnos. "We do too."

Hypnos laughed a little, his eyes shining with tears. "I don't know what I'll do when I return . . . the Order is a mess. I have no desire to be part of it any longer."

"Then don't be," said Zofia.

It seemed simple enough to her, but Hypnos only smiled.

"And do what with my life, *ma chère*?" he asked. "My lifestyle would hardly be considered economical, and while I enjoy a good languish, I would get bored without an occupation."

"The Order of Babel still has their treasure . . . whether or not they're Forged, they're still powerful," said Enrique, before adding, "and they never belonged to the Order in the first place. I am sure there would be work in returning such objects to their rightful owners and countries."

Hypnos tilted his head. He looked pensive.

"Hm," said Hypnos, regarding Enrique. "You know you're far more than a pretty face. You're rather clever too."

"I'm glad you noticed," said Enrique in a flat tone.

"Oh, I notice plenty," said Hypnos, smiling as he looked from Enrique to Zofia.

The train lurched forward, and Hypnos turned to look at the partially opened compartment door. Zofia wondered where Séverin was.

He had barely spoken to them since they'd left Poveglia. In some ways, it reminded her of how he had acted after Tristan's death. But this time, even in his silence, Séverin had made arrangements for them instead of disappearing. He had even reassured Enrique and Zofia that no matter what awaited them in Paris, they would always have a home and work in L'Eden.

"Has anyone seen him since we boarded?" asked Hypnos.

Zofia shook her head. As far as she knew, Séverin had made sure they knew where their seats were and then taken off to walk the compartments alone.

Enrique sighed. "I think out of all of us, he must feel the worst . . . I mean, he . . ."

"Loved her?"

Zofia's head snapped up to see Séverin looking at them. His hands were in his pockets. His expression was inscrutable.

Beside her, Enrique blushed. "Séverin, I—"

"It's the truth," said Séverin. "It hurts, but, *c'est la vie.*"

Everyone stared at him in silence.

"You realize I purchased this entire cabin for us, and yet the three of you are cramped into one booth that hardly has room for two people," said Séverin.

"Even so . . . we could squeeze a fourth?" said Hypnos, scooting against the wall with the window. "If you wish to join?"

Séverin regarded the small seat. At first, Zofia thought he would turn and go, but he didn't. Slowly, he took a seat beside Hypnos.

"This was what she would have wanted, wasn't it?" asked Séverin.

They fell quiet for a moment before Enrique said: "You think Laila would wish to be squished in a train compartment with Hypnos's odious cologne? I doubt it."

Hypnos gasped. "How dare you? *Eau du Diable Doux* is a rare, coveted fragrance sold to a select few—"

"Perhaps because in large quantities it would singe the nose hairs off the general population."

Zofia laughed. A smile tugged even at Séverin's mouth. It was brief, but it was still there. The four of them watched the rain outside the window. Zofia could not say she was happy. Laila was gone, and Hela's fate still weighed heavily on her thoughts . . . but Zofia was hopeful for the future. That future was unclear, but it was, as Enrique had said, something to be figured out day by day.

THE DAY AFTER Zofia had settled once more into her suites at L'Eden, she found a note waiting for her in her laboratory.

URGENT ATTENTION REQUIRED
TELEGRAM WAITING FOR MME. ZOFIA BOGUSKA
FROM MR. AND MRS. IZAAK KOWALSKI

Kowalski?

Zofia did not recognize the name. She swayed a little on the spot, feeling that dark panic of the unknown fluttering at the edge of her thoughts.

No, she told herself.

She took a deep breath, opening her eyes and counting the familiar alembics and bottles all around her. Then, with her shoulders thrown back, Zofia left her laboratory for the main lobby.

In the past few days, L'Eden had transformed. Ever since the news about Forged objects failing around the world—some of which had exploded and even injured people—L'Eden had removed nearly all of its Forged decoration. Now, the grand lobby was austere, lit with dozens of candles. Black marble had replaced the polished wooden floors so that it almost seemed as though the guests stepped onto the night sky itself. Above, Séverin had removed the chandeliers, and an expanse of lush greenery carpeted the ceiling. Pale flowers grew upside down, and thick vines clambered around the pillars that supported the ornate staircase.

As Zofia crossed the lobby and moved past the finely dressed guests, her heart began to race. What was the telegram about? And who was it from?

Séverin's factotum greeted her with a small bow. "Mademoiselle Boguska, how may I assist?"

"There is a telegram for me," said Zofia.

"Ah yes," he said, reaching into his jacket. "Is that all I may assist you with?"

Zofia took the telegram with trembling hands. "Will you send Monsieur Mercado-Lopez to meet me here?"

"Of course."

The factotum left with a small nod, leaving Zofia with the telegram in her hand.

Zofia almost wished she could pretend she never saw the note on her laboratory desk, but that would be like losing Hela's letter all over again . . . and she was done hiding from the things she could not control.

Perhaps it was fitting that the night before, Zofia had dreamed of Laila. In her dream, they were sitting at the high stools in the L'Eden kitchen and dunking perfectly pale sugar cookies into hot milk.

Do you know what will happen next? Zofia had asked.

Laila shook her head. *It's as unknown to me as it is to you.*

You do not seem scared, Zofia had said.

All I can do is hope for unexpected joy . . . and if it turns out to be dark, well, nothing can keep the light away forever.

Zofia held her breath as she ripped the envelope open. Inside, was a little square of cream paper.

Did you receive my letter about our elopement? I have not heard from you. We are coming to visit in a month.

All my love,

Hela

Zofia exhaled loudly, her shoulders slumping forward. Behind her, she heard the sharp slap of footsteps.

"What happened?" asked Enrique, rushing toward her. He stopped only to kiss her cheek, a practice which Zofia had very much come to look forward to. "Is it bad news?"

"No," said Zofia, smiling and looking up at him. Laila's words from her dream flitted through her thoughts. "It's . . . unexpected joy."

40

ENRIQUE

Two months later

Enrique walked the long gallery halls of L'Eden, taking stock of the artifacts they had acquired: a bronze *kinnari* statue from the Kingdom of Siam, three canopic jars filled with the internal organs of an unnamed pharoah, and one jade carving of a horse from the Yuan dynasty. There were far more treasures in the halls, but these were the only objects that still needed to be packed off. The rest lay quietly in wooden crates filled with straw, waiting for the day when they would be sent back to the countries to which they belonged.

In a way, Enrique was right back where he had started.

Once more, they were stealing artifacts from the Order of Babel. Again, he was cataloguing make, material, history. Again, he was interviewing and corresponding with prospective native collectors who considered themselves cultural custodians and guardians of both history and heritage. They were different from the members of the Order who would have kept these treasures for themselves. Instead, these were people who promised to take care of the artifacts until the time of political and civic unrest passed, and they could once more be put on proud display for the benefit of all.

And yet for all the familiarity of his current tasks, it was the new quiet that made these halls feel alien to Enrique.

Once, these Forged objects would have been—in their own way— *alive*.

Now, they were perfectly still.

All over the world, the phenomenon of ancient, Forged objects losing their animation was now known as the Great Silence. Some people blamed God. Others, industrial pollutants. But no matter where the blame was placed, the consequence was the same: Forging would soon be a flourish of the past.

Even popular Forging artistry—floating chandeliers and illusions that muddled the senses—had become suspect. For the first time in all the years Enrique had worked at L'Eden, the lamp fixtures had been bolted into the walls instead of serenely floating through the foyers. It made the whole place feel oddly hollow.

"What are you doing? I'm not used to seeing you standing alone in the dark."

Enrique turned to see Séverin at the entrance of the hallway. He waved, and Séverin made his way over to him.

"I'm trying out new hobbies," said Enrique. "Pensive brooding, dramatic walking . . . I might even take up long, aggrieved exhales."

"Sounds like an excellent use of time," said Séverin. "I happen to excel in pensive brooding if you ever wish for instruction."

"How generous of you."

"Generosity is my new habit of late," said Séverin, eyeing the collected boxes. "Though I doubt the Order sees it that way. I believe they still think I'm after my old inheritance. They even offered it to me once more, which was . . . odd."

"What *are* you after?" asked Enrique.

Séverin's gaze turned distant, and he fell quiet. He had changed considerably in the past two months. Every day, he insisted that they all ate together. In the evenings, he would ask questions about their lives and sometimes he even laughed. True to his word, Séverin had not disappeared inside himself, and yet there were moments when it seemed that in his new lapses of quiet, he was somewhere else entirely.

"I think I'm after peace . . . whatever that might look like," he said, before gesturing at the assembled boxes. "My purpose feels clear enough."

There was a soft clarity to Séverin's voice. A sort of wistfulness that made him seem older. Séverin reached into his jacket, popping open his tin of cloves. Enrique wrinkled his nose.

"Must you?"

"I'm afraid I must," said Séverin. As he returned the tin of cloves, he tugged out an envelope. "Also, I thought you'd want to see this. I believe this would be, what, your *sixth* letter from them?"

Enrique recognized the script on the envelope. It was from the Ilustrados. Since the Great Silence, it seemed that some of the Ilustrados groups were finally interested in Enrique's treatises about the cultural power of objects.

"Something like that," said Enrique.

Séverin sighed. "I thought this was what you wanted."

It had been, thought Enrique. But no longer.

"At the risk of sounding exceptionally pompous, I must ask whether any perceived . . . weakness on my part is holding you back," said Séverin. "I will support you no matter where you go, Enrique."

"I know that," said Enrique, and he meant it.

"Do you no longer support their cause?"

"Of course I support it!" said Enrique, shoving his hands in his pockets. "I still believe in the sovereignty of colonized nations. I still want to see the Philippines treated as more than some vassal state to Spain. I just . . . I don't think I need to belong to them to make a difference. I'll write back, of course, and continue to pen things for *La Solidaridad* . . . but I think I must find my own way."

"I see," said Séverin quietly.

"I had a change of perspective," said Enrique.

In the silence, he knew they were both thinking of the ziggurat.

None of them could ever fully describe what they'd felt that moment when the light from the final Tezcat portal washed over them. With every passing day, the memory seemed softer. And yet, sometimes the feeling ghosted through him, and Enrique would remember that he had touched vastness and felt the pulse of the universe dance across his bones. He would remember what it felt like to comb his fingers through the infinite.

"How do you plan on finding your own way?" asked Séverin.

How strange, thought Enrique. He had asked Laila something similar last night in his dreams.

Sometimes, he dreamed of her. Sometimes, he and Laila merely walked peacefully along a shore that Enrique had once visited as a child. Enrique looked forward to those visits. Whether it was really her or not didn't seem to matter, for the feeling afterwards was always the same. It was a sense of peace.

Last night, they had spoken in a room that looked like the library of L'Eden.

Are you happy, my friend? she'd asked.

I am . . . happy, Enrique had confided. Which was true. He was spending more time with Zofia and Hypnos, and together the three of them seemed to have stumbled upon a unique happiness. *But sometimes I feel lost. I don't suppose you have any advice or heavenly insights.*

I don't think you're lost, said Laila. *You're just searching for the thing that fills you with light.*

Enrique had scowled. *Just because it's a dream doesn't mean you have to be so enigmatic, you know.*

Laila had sipped her dream tea and arched an eyebrow. *If I didn't sound odd and prophetic, then the dream wouldn't be memorable.*

Touché. He'd laughed and they'd clinked their teacups together.

"Enrique?" asked Séverin.

Enrique jolted out of the recollection.

"Perhaps I should leave you to your thoughts," said Séverin, warmly clapping him on the back. "Oh, and do be careful to lock up when you go. There are children in the hotel. Best not to let them run around in here."

Enrique's jaw dropped. *"Children?* Since when do you allow children to step foot in here?"

"Since I discovered how much more lucrative it is to allow families to visit," said Séverin. But there was a practiced distance to his voice.

There was something Séverin was not saying. Enrique opened his mouth to ask when Séverin cleared his throat abruptly:

"I'll see you at supper," he said. "Enjoy your brooding."

"I will," said Enrique, frowning as Séverin beat a hasty retreat down the hall.

For the next hour or so, Enrique tried to avoid brooding altogether by triple-checking the state of various artifacts, and yet the same question kept cropping up in his thoughts.

How *did* he plan to find his way?

Dream Laila had suggested searching for the thing that filled him with light, but what did that mean? Traveling out into the world? Taking up a new hobby?

It was around then that Enrique heard soft footfalls behind him. He turned to find that a young boy, about ten years old, had found his way into the hallway and was now poking the wings of the golden half-human, half-bird *kinnara* statue.

"Do *not* touch that!" said Enrique, striding over to him.

The boy, a rather serious-looking child with pale skin and a mop of icy-blond hair, stared defiantly back at Enrique. "Why not?"

Enrique opened his mouth, then closed it. For some reason, the boy reminded him of Zofia, golden and stubborn. And his curiosity reminded Enrique, oddly enough, of himself. He knew there were plenty of wonders to be found on L'Eden's premises. To venture into this particular gallery meant that the boy had first chosen to spend time in the library instead of outside on a bright, early spring day.

Enrique nearly winced to remember the trouble he had gotten into when he'd been this boy's age.

"You're lucky I don't have a *tsinela*," he muttered.

The boy frowned. "A what?"

"Never mind," said Enrique, sighing.

The boy scowled, and Enrique remembered making a similar expression whenever he anticipated that someone was about to yell at him. He had hated being scolded and much preferred when someone would explain something to him instead.

"Do you know how old this statue is?" Enrique asked, pointing at the gold *kinnari*.

The boy shook his head.

"At least seven thousand years old."

The boy's eyes widened. Why did children have such wide eyes?

Enrique could not explain why he continued. "Would you . . . like to hold it?"

The boy nodded enthusiastically.

"Very well," said Enrique. He drew a spare pair of gloves from his pocket. "It's *very* important when we handle such objects to treat them with the utmost respect. You are holding a piece of time, and you must be precious with it."

Solemnly, the boy drew on the gloves. He gasped a little when Enrique lowered the statue into his hands.

"This is called a *kinnari*," he said, "a half-human, half-bird creature. They were thought to be guardian spirits who watched over humans in times of danger. Rather like angels."

The boy's eyebrows shot up his forehead. "There's more than just angels?"

Enrique was rather stunned. He had braced himself to be refuted on the spot, or to be on the receiving end of a sneering response that angels could not possibly look like the golden statue in the boy's hands. But children were different. For all their small stature, they seemed far more willing to accept the expansiveness of the world, whereas adults seemed to lose that gift with age.

Enrique found himself wanting to show the boy other objects merely to experience his reaction to them. "Would you like to see canopic jars? They used to hold the organs of Egyptian royalty!"

The boy gave a small gasp.

Uh-oh.

"Wait, I—"

But it was too late. The boy had run down the hall, disappearing through the doorway. Enrique tried to ignore the sharp sting he felt as he turned away. He thought that would be the last he'd see of the boy, but a few minutes later, he heard a rush of approaching footsteps. He turned slowly to find at least a dozen children staring up at him. At the front, the blond-haired boy looked out of breath and excited.

"We want to see the canpopic jars!"

"It's *canopic*," corrected Enrique automatically.

He looked at the sea of shining, expectant faces. Even his best audience had never looked so enraptured.

"Heinrich says they used to hold the organs of Egyptian royalty, but that can't be right," said one girl, her arms crossed in front of her chest. She paused hopefully. ". . . Can it?"

Enrique walked slowly to the canopic jar, touching it lightly. "Heinrich is correct. Our tale begins about five thousand years ago . . ."

Children, Enrique soon discovered, were ravenous.

Once he had told them about the religious significance of canopic jars, they wished to know about gruesome underworlds and what monsters lived there. Then they wished to know about the gods and goddesses of different lands, whose names they had never heard. Every reveal was met with applause and wonder. There was never a point at which they seemed bored by his lecture. And with every new piece of history or new story, Enrique imagined he could actually see their imaginations flex in new directions.

Eventually, the children's curiosity even turned to him.

"What happened to your ear?" asked one of the children.

Enrique touched the light linen bandage over his wound. It no longer ached, and yet the absence of his ear was something that still caught him by surprise.

"I heard he fought a bear who was guarding the treasures and that's how he lost it . . ."

"That's a lie!" said another. "Bears don't guard treasures. *Dragons* do."

Enrique laughed. The children had dozens of questions, and he could scarcely get through them all one by one.

"Tell us another story!" said one.

"Are there mummies here? Have you seen one?"

"Can *I* see a mummy?"

Enrique had only just quieted them by beginning the tale of the Egyptian god Osiris—an abridged version of course, for it was not entirely suitable to children—when a tall, dark-skinned woman wearing a ruff of fur walked into the halls.

"I found them!"

A horde of adults followed after her, shouting out the names of their charges.

Oh dear, thought Enrique. If these parents were furious at him and asked for his name, Enrique resolved to introduce himself as Séverin Montagnet-Alarie.

One by one, the parents fetched their children.

"No, I want to stay!" said one girl. "We were learning about mummies!"

One boy refused to move and sat on the floor.

"Will you tell us more tomorrow?" asked another boy before his parent hauled him off.

The solemn, blond-haired child hung back, trying to hide behind one of the storage boxes. His mother, a tall woman with a shock of black hair, laughed and coaxed him out.

"The children seem to be quite taken with you," she said. "I hope they were not too much of a bother."

"They . . . they were not a bother at all," said Enrique.

On the contrary, it was the most fun he'd had in quite some time. The children's intense curiosity was like a furnace that his whole being might warm itself against, and their eagerness made him wish to return to his research and regard it with fresh eyes.

"What is your name?" asked the woman.

"Sév—I mean, Enrique," he said. "Enrique Mercado-Lopez."

"Well, I am indebted to you for your generous instruction. I have the feeling you've made quite the impression on him, and I won't hear the end of it for days," said the woman, smiling widely. "Heinrich? Tell the nice professor 'thank you.'"

"Oh, I'm not a professor—" said Enrique, but no one seemed to hear him.

"Thank you, Professor Mercado-Lopez," said the boy.

Enrique startled. He had not imagined how much he would love the sound of that title.

"Thank *you*," he said, feeling his heart strain against his ribs.

"I KNOW WHAT I want to do with my life," Enrique announced hours later.

He stood at the threshold of the library where he, Hypnos, and Zofia had agreed to meet before heading down to dinner. Zofia was poking at the fire, while Hypnos was curled up on an armchair, a glass of red wine in his hand.

Hypnos raised an eyebrow. "Make babies?"

"No!"

"You don't want children?" asked Zofia.

"Not at this particular moment, no," said Enrique.

Hypnos took a long sip of wine. "*Steal* babies."

"Gods no!" said Enrique. "This has nothing to do with babies! Well, perhaps a little to do with children, but—"

"Now I'm confused," said Zofia.

"I think I'd like to teach," said Enrique before either Hypnos or Zofia could misconstrue his words any further. His words came out in a rush: "I like that scholarship inspires others to think for themselves and look at the world differently. I don't want to simply try to change the world on my own by forcing my ideas on people . . . I'd much rather encourage them to think differently. I think that's where *lasting* change will come from and . . . and I think I'd be a rather good professor."

He waited for a moment, readying himself for their reactions.

"We knew that," said Zofia.

"What?" spluttered Enrique.

"Truly, I cannot see why it has taken you so long to come to a conclusion that Zofia and I have already agreed would be the best use of your talents," said Hypnos.

Enrique could not decide if he was more pleased or annoyed.

"Thank you for informing me," he said.

"Such things are best discovered on one's own," said Hypnos. "Though I am curious . . . what made you realize such a thing?"

Enrique found himself thinking of the dream conversation he'd had with Laila. He thought of her catlike smile and the horizon of some other world illuminating her.

"I suppose you could say it's because the idea filled me with light," said Enrique.

41

SÉVERIN

Six months later

Séverin Montagnet-Alarie was no god. As such, he could not change the past, but that didn't mean he could not break free of it.

Séverin stared out the window of his office, nervously turning a tin of cloves in his hands as he watched the winding, gravel path that led to the entrance of L'Eden. They would be here soon, and he wasn't sure what they would make of the place . . .

It was the beginning of winter, and the city seemed more fragile in the brittle sunshine. On the far side of the lawns, workers dug holes and erected trellises, while others lay down tarp to protect the flowers. Next year, the trellises would boast roses of every hue and fragrance. But amidst all that riot of beauty, there was only one star in the garden.

It had taken Séverin and a team of gardeners the better part of a month to find a single surviving rose cane from the variety

Tristan had once planted, and which Séverin had later ripped out of the ground and burned. Tristan had never named his roses, and so the duty fell to Séverin. Henceforth, that variety would forever be known as *L'Enigme*.

While some things had been rebuilt, others had been destroyed.

Gone was the Seven Sins Garden, and although some hotel guests might have mourned the loss of being able to say they had walked through hell and back in time for dinner, Séverin had found that he had enough of hell.

In its place, Séverin had constructed a rehabilitation menagerie for birds who, for a number of reasons, could no longer survive in the wild. There were songbirds who had fallen out of their nests too young, doves who had been mistreated by peddling magicians, sparrows who had once found themselves in the jaws of pouncing cats. There were other birds too, ones who had been kidnapped from their native homes and brought to Paris as objects of curiosity. Birds with plumage that rivaled sunsets, parrots with multihued beaks, golden-eyed falcons, and creatures sporting a crest of rainbows on their brows. All of them found a home in L'Eden and were now cared for by a resident veterinarian and zoologist and, surprisingly, Eva, who had retired her art and moved into L'Eden with her ailing father. To Séverin, each bird carried a piece of Tristan. When they healed, it was almost as if, bit by bit, his brother was healing too.

In the evenings, Séverin would walk through the aviary. Most of the time, he wasn't looking up at the birds, but staring down at the ground where his shadow sprawled unrecognizably beside him. In those moments, he could pretend that it wasn't his shadow at all, but Tristan's. He could pretend his brother walked beside him, Goliath balancing on his shoulder. In those moments, the chaotic murmur of Paris faded, replaced with the secret poetry of birdsong and the flutter of mending wings, and sometimes—*sometimes*—Séverin could almost hear Tristan sighing. The sound was like peace unclasping from pain and taking wing into the sky.

A knock at his office door released Séverin from his thoughts. "Come in."

Enrique appeared, a hopeful smile on his face and a sheaf of papers in his arms. "Are they here yet? Because I was thinking—ahh!"

A loud squawk erupted through the office, and Séverin turned to find Argos stalking toward Enrique.

Argos was . . . strange.

The one-year-old peacock had been kept in the cramped apartments of a brothel madame, who abandoned the creature on the street with his plumage plucked. When he had come to L'Eden, he had snapped at everyone who tried to care for him, except Séverin. A month later with good food and more space to roam, Argos had grown into a beautiful and illustrious creature. Argos had also, for reasons unknown to the staff and despite frequent attempts to shepherd him elsewhere, taken to following Séverin everywhere.

"Will you call off your demonic guard?" asked Enrique.

"Argos," said Séverin mildly.

The peacock huffed, settling himself by the fireplace. The bird did not take his eyes off Enrique, who inched around him.

"Honestly, that *thing* makes me actually prefer the company of Goliath."

"He's not so bad," said Séverin. "Perhaps a touch overprotective, but he means well."

Enrique fixed him with a look. "Argos nearly ran off the new chef."

"The chef overcooked the halibut. I can't say I disagree with Argos in his assessment of the man."

Enrique snorted, then handed over the papers. "These are the newest potential acquisitions."

Now that Forging was regarded with suspicion, the Order of Babel's power was gone and they had been forced to sell their considerable treasures to the highest bidders of the public. Wealthy industrialists and railroad magnates vied for the chance to display history in their sitting rooms, while Séverin and his family fought to return those artifacts either to their original owners or, barring that, museums in their native lands.

In the past, Séverin had stolen out of the hubris that he could take from the Order of Babel. Now, he was humbled by the thought of shepherding history into different homes. History might be shaped by the tongues of conquerors, but it was not a fixed shape or story, and with every object they repatriated, it was like adding or recasting a sentence in a book whose pages were as wide and infinite as a horizon.

Séverin leafed through the research. "Good work. I'll take a look, and we'll finalize a project for the fall."

Enrique nodded, his gaze darting to the window. "Are you ready for this?"

"Of course not."

"Well, at least you're honest," said Enrique with a small laugh. "Don't worry . . . you'll have help."

"I know."

"I think . . . I think she'd be happy . . . to know what you're doing," said Enrique quietly.

Séverin smiled. "I think so too."

He thought, but he didn't know for certain. He had gathered, in bits and pieces, that the others dreamt of Laila. In their dreams, she even spoke to them. But she never spoke to Séverin.

He waited for her every night, and though sometimes he *felt* her . . . he never saw her. In those moments when he missed her most, he would think on her promise. *I will always be with you.* In the wake of not knowing whether this was true, he had no choice but to believe.

"Well. I should go," said Enrique. "I have to prepare for tomorrow's lectures, and I'd like to do that before they get here."

"I'll let you know when they arrive," said Séverin. "*Please* make sure that Zofia has put away anything too flammable—"

"Already done," said Enrique. He frowned. "She was not enthused."

"And tell Hypnos not to drink in front of them."

"I've bought him a teacup in which he can put his wine. He was, also, not enthused."

"And try not to lecture them the moment they ask a question about anything on the premises," said Séverin.

Enrique looked highly affronted. "Would it really be a lecture?" He raised his hands and wiggled his fingers. "Or would it be an *unhinging* of their known world?"

Séverin stared at him. "Perhaps there is enough that is unhinged in this household."

"Hmpf," said Enrique. As he turned to the door, he cast a scathing glance at Argos, who was napping beside the fireplace. "You are an overpriced and overpainted chicken, and you are lucky you are not even *remotely* edible. I hope you know that."

Argos slept on.

Séverin laughed. When Enrique left, he stroked Argos's feathers and then returned to his desk. On the wooden surface lay a tarnished ouroboros that had once been pinned to his father's lapel. Séverin traced the shape slowly, remembering the sneer in Lucien Montagnet-Alarie's voice as he imparted what he considered the most precious piece of advice to his son:

We can never escape ourselves, my boy . . . we are our own end and begin-
ning, at the mercy of a past which cannot help but repeat itself.

"You're wrong," said Séverin under his breath.

But even as he said it, he didn't truly know whether he had
spoken the truth. There was much he could not claim to know.
He did not know what it meant when Laila had said they would
always be connected so long as she lived. He did not know whether
she would keep her promise and return to him. He didn't know
whether his efforts would make a difference, or whether the world
would turn on indifferently and leave his legacy in the dust.

Outside the window came the crunch of hoofbeats over gravel.
Séverin's heartbeat sped up as he looked through the glass and saw
them for the first time in months: Luca and Filippo, the orphan
brothers from Venice. It had taken ages to locate them, and a mere
month for the adoption papers to be drawn. Séverin had been
preparing for this moment for the better part of a year, but right
then, the sheer weight of what he was undertaking knocked the
wind out of his lungs.

He swallowed hard, his grip on the windowsill turning white-
knuckled as he held his breath and watched Luca and Filippo step
out of the carriage. It was not a large step, and yet Luca held out
his hand to the younger Filippo and did not let go even when they
both stood on the gravel. Though he had arranged for food and
shelter, they were still far too thin and rather small for their age. In
their too-big clothes and new haircuts, they looked like changelings
who had tumbled into the human world. When Luca wrapped his
arm around his brother, Séverin felt a sharp ache knifing behind
his ribs.

Slowly, he released his breath.

Slowly, he let go of the windowsill.

Behind him, Argos made an inquisitive screech.

"It's time," he said.

Séverin took one last glance at the ouroboros brooch. Maybe his father was right. Maybe he was fooling himself, and all he was doing was taking his place in an endless loop outside his control. Maybe his last kiss with Laila was nothing but a delusion brought on by the crumbling temple. Maybe she existed in the fringes of dreams and nothing more.

But faith was a stubborn thing, and the world's turning only acted as a lathe that made it that much sharper as it cut through the fog of all he did not know.

Could he live with this unknown?

Could he make peace with it?

Yes, he thought, although he often felt more certain on some days than others. Nevertheless, he would do what most mortals did.

He would try.

EPILOGUE

The first time Séverin made a cake, he used salt instead of sugar.

It was, as Enrique kindly put it, an absolute disaster.

Even so, Séverin was delighted. Laila had considered it impossible that he would ever make a cake. To do so, no matter how awful it was, made him think that perhaps other things that seemed impossible could come true.

And in some ways, they did.

Time treated Séverin with a light hand, and with each passing year, he began to understand what Laila had meant when she promised they would always be connected.

No gray touched his hair. No wrinkle marred his face. It had astonished Enrique and outright annoyed Hypnos, who believed that out of all of them, he was the most deserving of eternal youth.

Séverin himself didn't necessarily care for eternal youth. If anything, it only complicated his life in Paris and guardianship over Luca and Filippo, and yet it was a sign too. A sign he didn't understand until he spoke with Zofia.

"It means she's still alive," said Zofia. "She promised connection, and she kept it."

As long as I live, so will you.

Zofia smiled at him. For the first time, he noticed laugh lines around her eyes and mouth, and he was happy that life had marked her with joy. "Séverin . . . I think that means she will keep her other promise too."

Her other promise.

It was a thing none of them ever dared to speak aloud, as if the promise was so fragile that to utter it again would snap the possibility in half.

And yet he carried the hope of it inside him every day: *I will come back to you.*

As the years passed, he began to dream of Laila. Sometimes she visited his dreams every night for a week. Sometimes she disappeared for years at a time. And yet every time she returned, she would say the same thing: *I never got to finish what I began to say to you that night.*

He knew what she meant. She had said, "I love—" and then the world had dragged him away from her.

Tell me now, he would say, and each time she would shake her head.

No, Majnun. I need something to dream about too.

THE WORLD TURNED. Wars erupted, kingdoms fell, fashions changed. The years blurred past, and yet Séverin found moments that seemed to anchor him despite time's relentless momentum. There was the first time Luca threw his arms around him, and Filippo fell asleep with his head on his shoulder. Like him, it seemed as though the boys had many parents, and yet in this case, it was impossible to say which parent was more beloved.

Zofia conducted scientific experiences and taught Filippo numbers when he struggled in school. Hypnos snuck Luca his first drink at sixteen and spent the whole night by his side while he vomited and swore never to touch a bottle again. Enrique told them stories that kept them up at night, and Séverin did as his mother and Tante Feefee and Tristan had tried to do all those years: He tried to protect.

Even Argos grew to like the boys and did not seem to mind when they stuck his fallen tail feathers in the back of their pants and imitated the strange bird.

At first, Séverin could hide his continued youth with theatre makeup. But as every year passed, his youth became harder to disguise. After twenty years, he could hide no longer. On that day, he happily passed the reins of L'Eden to his adopted sons.

With Hypnos, he built museums and archives, funded visiting scholars, and loaned their pieces around the world. Enrique continued to teach and wrote books that found international acclaim. Zofia created and patented prominent inventions and was named an honorary alum of L'Ecole des Beaux Arts. Séverin was there when Luca married, and he was there when Filippo boarded a ship that would take him away from Europe and into the Americas. Séverin played with children and grandchildren, and spent countless evenings by the warm hearth where Zofia, Enrique, and Hypnos had made a home between the three of them.

Séverin was at their side for the rest of their lives, and he continued to be there for their descendants long after Enrique, Zofia, and Hypnos had passed from this world into the next.

In his work, he kept his friends' legacies alive, and all the while he waited for Laila to keep her promise.

IN OCTOBER OF 1990, Séverin got off the Paris Métro and headed for his home in Paris's eighth arrondissement. Frost whispered in the air. Artists sang on the streets, and schoolgirls walked past fighting over the use of a Walkman.

His apartment was the penthouse level of the now-renovated L'Eden Hotel. The government had named it a *monument historique* a few years ago for its past as a renowned nineteenth-century institution with exceptional architecture, and the birthplace of the *L'Enigme* rose which was one of the most popular flowers in Paris.

To Séverin, his home was L'Eden in name . . . and nothing else. The gardens were gone. The library had become a coveted wedding venue, and the hidden suites of his office had been converted into a swanky bar that was filled with supermodels and actors on the weekends. And yet, as he did every day, he paused outside the doors he had designed himself . . . and he hoped that today would be the day when she came back to him. He had been hoping for what felt like an eternity, and with every year, his hope only grew stronger. Hope led him by the hand as he continued his work in various museums. Hope tilted his chin to the sky. Hope coaxed him to wake up in the mornings and meet the day with his shoulders thrown back and his spine straight.

And so, as always, and with hope in his heart . . . Séverin pushed open the doors.

THE MOMENT HE stepped inside L'Eden, he felt the hairs on the back of his neck prickle. He stared warily around the lobby, but nothing was out of the ordinary. Even so, the light seemed to waver through the windows. Without knowing why, his heartbeat began to race as he entered his private elevator. Inside, he steadied himself. Perhaps he was light-headed with hunger, or else coming down with a fever . . . but then the elevator doors opened.

The first thing Séverin noticed when he stepped into his hallway was not a person but a perfume. The unmistakable lilt of rose water and sugar. He held his breath, unwilling to release it in case none of this was real. But then the door to his apartments opened. A slender shadow fell across the carpet. Séverin could not bring himself to lift his gaze. His hope was too heavy, too painful. When he was forced to breathe again, it felt as if it were the first breath of a new life.

FOR YEARS, HE has lived not as a god or as a man, but as a ghost, and in two words, he finds himself gloriously resurrected. Two words, which make him almost believe in magic, because time, so still to him for so long, now lifts its head eagerly at the sound and begins to move forward once more.

"Hello, *Majnun*."

ACKNOWLEDGMENTS

The end. . . .

I cannot believe the Gilded Wolves trilogy is officially finished. This story has lived in my heart for so long that I feel a bit hollow and extremely *weepy* to know that this story has concluded.

Even more overwhelming than this cathartic sadness is the debt of gratitude I owe to everyone who has helped bring this story to life. My biggest thanks go to my readers, who have shouted about this trilogy from every corner of the internet. Thank you for your art, your playlists, your memes, your messages, your bookstagrams, and your enthusiasm. My thanks, especially, to the members of the indomitable Gilded Wolves street team! I cannot tell you how much your support and gorgeous (and oftentimes hilarious) photo edits have picked me up and inspired me. A special thanks to Mana, one of the first readers and champions of this trilogy who has kindly lent her impeccable humor and creative flair to sharing this story with even more readers.

I am, as always, indebted to the various teams who oversaw

the sales, editorial aspects, audio recording, book production—
TRULY LITERALLY EVERY SINGLE HUMAN—at Wednesday Books. Eileen, thank you for always supporting me and for all the "romantic punching up." DJ, thank you for celebrating the magic in the story. Mary, thank you for giving it extra shiny publicity placement! Thank you to Christa Desir for the thoughtful copy edit and gently taming my Penchant To Capitalize Things For No Reason.

To my family at Sandra Dijkstra Literary Agency, thank you! To Thao, agent extraordinaire, who is the fiercest champion around. To Andrea, for all the book passports and careful documentation of elaborate Halloween setups. To my assistant, Sarah, who makes sure that I am alive and functioning.

The friends I have made in the writing community are my favorite coven of witches. Renee, JJ, Lemon, your friendship is a magic I deeply cherish. Lyra, thank you for turning your Dread Eye upon my drafts. Ryan, for the uplifting string of meep meeps. Jennifer, who lifts me up when I have been stampeded by bad writing days.

To the friends who remind me of the world outside my head, thank you. Niv, best of friends and best of dreamers. Bismah, enigmatic and wise as a cat. Marta, the warmest of human sweaters. Cali, for convos in Stitch character. Ali, for evenings as dancing potatoes. McKenzie, for tipsy graveyard walks. Cara-Joy, the most fashionable and intimidating of cheerleaders. The entirety of the Golden Hores (Kaitlin, MeiLin, Nico, Hailey, Katie, Natasha)—I'm indebted to your good humor, company, and your kindness in indulging my historical tangents. I must also thank the abundance of Erics in my life. Eric Lieu, who let me borrow his name, and Eric Lawson, for titling the end of this trilogy (sorry, McKenzie, I know what I've done).

I am blessed with a family who inspires and uplifts and, critically, keeps me fed. Momo, Dodo, Mocha, Puggy, Cookie, Poggle, and Rat—I love you. For Ba and Dadda, who told me stories and took me to bookstores at every hour of the day, thank you. For Lalani and Daddy Boon, I wish we'd had more time for stories, but your memory guides me nonetheless. To sweet Panda bear, who guarded the start of this trilogy, and for Teddy, who protected the end.

Last but never least, to Aman. Thank you for talking me off my many cliffs. There is no journey worth going on without you.